CATHY SHARP

An Orphan's Dream

HarperCollins*Publishers*

HarperCollins*Publishers*
The News Building,
1 London Bridge Street,
London SE1 9GF

www.harpercollins.co.uk

HarperCollins*Publishers*
1st Floor, Watermarque Building, Ringsend Road
Dublin 4, Ireland

A Paperback Original 2021
2

A catalogue record for this book
is available from the British Library

ISBN: 978-0-00-838767-9

Set in Sabon LT Std 11/14pt by
Palimpsest Book Production Limited, Falkirk, Stirlingshire

Printed and bound in the UK by CPI Group (UK) Ltd, Croydon CR0 4YY

MIX
Paper from
responsible sources
FSC™ C007454

CHAPTER 1

March, 1938

Sister Rose Harwell stopped and smiled as she saw Nurse Lily Brown walking towards her. They were often on different wards at the Rosie Infirmary of Button Street and sometimes alternate shifts, too, so didn't always meet at work. However, they were friends and she waited for Lily to reach her.

'How are you? It's lovely to see you,' she said, touching her arm with a warm gesture. 'I don't think I've seen you since just before last Christmas. I bump into Jenny most days, but for some reason *we* never seem to meet.' Lily's younger sister Jenny worked at the infirmary too and was often on the same shift as Rose.

A shaft of pale sun touched on the dark flame of Rose's hair, where it was visible beneath her nursing cap. Her eyes were soft green and lit just now with a look of friendship and affection, but sometimes they could become as cool and icy as the deep water of a mountain pool.

'I stopped on for an extra couple of hours today

because we were busy and one of our nurses didn't turn up,' Lily admitted, beaming at Rose. She was clearly pleased they'd met and eager for a chat. Her hair was as dark as her eyes and swept back in a tight knot that was less than becoming but sensible for work. 'Jenny tells me she has seen you sometimes but, to be honest, I hardly see my sister these days – she usually comes home when I'm about to leave for work.'

Rose smiled sympathetically. 'Yes, I know; it must be awful when you work different shifts to her, because then you only get a chance to talk at the weekends.'

Lily nodded, stifling a yawn. 'Sorry, it's just that it has been a long night. I'm on the chronic sickness ward at the moment and we've been non-stop – three of our elderly patients were very ill and we had to call the doctors in during the night.'

'Oh, I know how disrupting that can be,' Rose agreed. 'I'm on the children's ward now for a few months – and that is one of my favourite duties.' She gave a little laugh that was infectious and attractive, making Lily smile and nod in response. 'It doesn't seem to matter how unwell they are, children always do or say something funny. They just want a little love and attention – don't you find?'

'Yes, I've noticed it before,' Lily agreed wholeheartedly. 'I like that duty too – but someone has to care for the elderly.'

'Yes, of course, absolutely,' Rose said. 'And we came into nursing in the full knowledge that we would care for the sick whatever their age or illness, but the chronic ward is the most tiring – so much bed changing.' Incontinence was the bane of old age and something

2

that upset the patient far more than the carer in Rose's experience.

'Yes . . .' Lily smothered another yawn. 'Look, I have Sunday off this weekend so would you like to come to tea at ours? I know Jenny would love to have you, too, and we're both off this weekend.'

'Well, as a matter of fact I'm off duty too,' Rose replied, pleased. 'I'm helping out with a charity event at lunchtime – we're giving the old folk of the area a nice lunch in the Methodist Hall. Some of us are cooking and taking food in, others just serving, but it will all be over by three thirty and I could go home and change and be at yours by four thirty, if that would suit you?'

'Yes, sounds perfect,' Lily said. 'I would like to help out at an event like that – if ever you need more helpers?'

'How kind,' Rose said, responding with a smile. 'We can always find room for an extra pair of hands when we put on something of the sort – it's only every three months or so but the old folk do appreciate it.' She met her friend's inquiring gaze. 'We give them information about anything they can get help with or any free food that is being handed out by another charity, anything that may be of help to them.'

Lily frowned. 'Many of the old folk are too proud to ask for charity,' she said. 'There's a woman we know in the next street to us – Flo, her name is – and she just refuses to accept charity. Jenny takes her a cake or something as a gift sometimes, but Flo always gives her some flowers or a lettuce from her garden in exchange.'

'That's the problem with a lot of the older folk round here,' Rose replied, looking serious. 'Some of them are even afraid to come to the infirmary because they can't afford to pay and, although they know we treat them for nothing here, they still hesitate and will never call the doctor out if they can help it.'

'I know.' Lily shook her head regretfully. 'Matron does all she can, handing out leaflets at the church and all the clubs in the area but these East End women can be a prickly lot.'

Rose nodded, looking sad. 'I'll see you on Sunday, then – and now I'd better get to the ward or I'll be late and that does not set a good example to my nurses!'

'Yes, I'd better let you get on, but I'm glad we met, Rose,' Lily said. 'Oh, I understand you have a new nurse starting in your ward today?'

'Yes, we do – Nurse Margaret James,' Rose said. 'She's fully qualified but she's been working in a country hospital so I daresay it will be a bit strange here for her at the beginning because some of our patients are victims of poverty in a way she may not have seen before.'

'Yes, perhaps,' Lily agreed. 'Anyway, we'll look forward to seeing you on Sunday.'

They parted then and Rose hurried into the infirmary. The strong smell of carbolic met her as she made her way to the children's ward, where she was the Sister in charge for the next few weeks. When she arrived, Kathy, who worked in the kitchens and had married Bert, the Rosie's handyman, the previous year, was taking round hot drinks for the children. Rose noticed she looked a bit glum but had no time to ask if something was wrong.

Nurse Sarah Cartwright – now clearly pregnant with her first child – was already making a tour of the ward with a young nurse following her. Rose knew it must be the new girl. The younger woman was slim and of medium height with shiny dark hair tucked neatly under her cap and a pair of wide dark eyes. She had been assigned to the children's ward to make it easy for her to find her feet in the first few weeks of her duty at the Lady Rosalie Infirmary rather than being flung into the deep waters of the critical ward.

'Good morning, nurses,' Rose said going up to the young women. 'Did we have any new patients in overnight?'

Nurse Sarah turned, her pretty face lighting up in a warm smile. 'Sister Norton told me they had a quiet night last night. Oh,' she blushed and shook her head, 'sorry, I meant Sister Matthews. I should be able to remember that by now.' Sister Norton had been married some months.

'Yes, I doubt she would be too happy to hear staff using her maiden name, Nurse Sarah. However, we're not going to tell tales, are we, Nurse Margaret?'

'Oh no, Sister,' the new recruit said and blushed a delicate rose. 'I wouldn't tell on Sarah.' Rose noticed there was a faint sing-song quality to her voice and thought she sounded a little Welsh although the accent was not pronounced.

'Do you come from Wales, Nurse Margaret?' she inquired and the girl blushed again.

'I was born there, Sister,' she replied. 'My father was killed in a mining accident when I was ten so my mother moved to Hampshire, where she had an aunt living. I thought I'd lost my accent after twelve years in England!'

'You don't have a strong one,' Rose assured her. 'It's just a little lilt, that's all – it's really pretty and it won't make it difficult for the patients to understand you.'

'I'm glad.' Margaret was clearly very conscious that she was in a new job. 'I shouldn't want to do that.'

'What made you want to nurse in London?' Rose asked. 'This area isn't nearly as pleasant as the country-side in Hampshire.'

'I-I had an unhappy experience,' Margaret said and looked away as if the words were painful to say.

'Well, I'm sure you will be happy with us,' Rose told her. 'We are all friendly here at the Rosie – but I'm sure Sarah has already told you that.'

'Yes.' Margaret shot a grateful glance at Nurse Sarah. 'And she's asked me to tea at her mother's on Sunday.'

'Well, that is lovely. Mrs Cartwright is a really good cook and we all enjoy being invited to her home for tea.'

'We're having a little party,' Sarah said and now she blushed and placed her hands on her rounded stomach. 'Next week is my last week at the Rosie.'

Rose nodded. 'We shall all miss you, Sarah, but we'll all be visiting, and I hope that one day they'll change the rules about mothers working as nurses and perhaps you could come back part-time.'

'Yes, that would be lovely,' Sarah agreed. 'However, I certainly want to give my child and husband as much of my time as possible for a few years at least – but I'll be visiting you all and keeping in touch with my friends here.'

'Yes, you must,' Rose agreed and nodded. 'Good, well, I'll leave it to you to show Margaret the ropes. I want to read last night's reports and see if anything needs my attention.'

At her desk, Rose opened the night nurse's report

and started to read. She was feeling a little pang of envy over Sarah's happy event. She was in her mid-thirties and there was no sign of either a husband or a family for her. Nearly eight years had passed since her last serious relationship and sometimes she thought she would never find love again.

Perhaps that was just as well, though. Rose was dedicated to her patients and often lingered on the ward after her duty was finished. She had friends and a married brother, who lived with his wife and children in the country, her ageing mother, now unfortunately the victim of old age and a fading memory, was being looked after by a distant cousin who welcomed the small income that Rose paid for her care, and then there was Rose's own lovely landlady – surely that was enough for anyone? Rose really shouldn't envy a colleague just because she was having her first child.

Staff Nurse Lily Brown decided to take the bus home. She really was too tired to walk and the wind was cool. To be expected in March, of course, but they'd had a few days when it had been quite warm in the sunshine and it was always disappointing when it went back to being bitterly cold. She wore a silk head square over her hair, hiding the thick tresses that had somehow escaped from the tight knot she'd worn at the start of her duty. She'd removed her cap after leaving the Rosie and the wind had got in and played havoc with her luxuriantly long locks, strands of which now waved wildly about her face in the stiff breeze. Her hair was her best feature, or so Lily believed and she'd grown it longer lately, because Chris liked to tangle his face in it when they made love.

The thought made her smile and feel happy despite the fact that she was tired after a long shift on a busy ward and the biting wind. Whatever else was wrong in her world, the knowledge that she loved and was loved made her glow inside.

'Good night at work, nurse?' the conductor asked. He was a regular on her route and knew both her and Jenny well, so she nodded. Let him think what he would, she preferred to keep her secret tight inside her. Chris, and their love, was a wonderful secret she could not share with anyone just yet, because his work was a security risk and he was somewhere in Hitler's Germany working for the British Government as a double agent. Even Lily wasn't supposed to know that, but Chris had shared what he could with her without compromising himself or his mission. He was concerned, in this year of 1938, that war was looming and he was helping prepare for that eventuality.

Getting off the bus, Lily walked swiftly to the home she shared with her sister. Jenny had her uniform on ready to leave but the kitchen smelled enticingly of bacon frying.

'Oh, Jenny, that smells delicious.'

'I made myself a bacon sandwich and I'll do one for you before I go,' Jenny said with a look of affection. 'I've got tomorrow off as well as Sunday so I thought we might be able to have some time together.'

'Yes, lovely.' Lily smiled warmly at her sister. 'I've invited Rose for tea on Sunday – you don't mind?'

'No, of course not,' Jenny replied. She placed the hot bacon sandwich in front of her sister. 'I'll get off then – oh, there's a letter for you on the dresser.' She indicated the envelope, smiled at Lily and shrugged on her coat. 'Bye, then!'

Lily glanced at the dresser and her heart caught. She didn't often get a letter – could it be from Chris? She took a bite of her delicious sandwich as her sister waved goodbye and disappeared out of the kitchen door. Wiping grease from her chin with a napkin, Lily snatched up the letter and her heart did a little dance of pleasure. Chris's work meant he wasn't able to contact her often, his letters rare events, but here one was at long last and she hugged her treasure to her for a moment, savouring the pleasure to come of reading whatever he had to say.

Unable to wait any longer, she ripped the envelope open and devoured the short message:

In the mountains of a lovely ski resort. We should come here one day.

Hope to fly home for a visit shortly. Haven't time to write more but I wanted you to know I'm thinking of you, my darling Lily . . .

The letter was signed only with a kiss but she knew his writing and there was no one else it could possibly have come from. The postmark was Switzerland and Lily breathed a sigh of relief. If he was in Switzerland, he was safe and she would see him soon. When they'd parted some months ago, Lily hadn't expected that she would see her lover again for a long time, perhaps years.

It still seemed strange to think of Chris, who had once been Jenny's boyfriend, as her lover. When Jenny had first started seeing him, Lily had believed he was one of Mosley's Blackshirts and, as such, a bad influence on her younger sister. Once she'd understood that he'd infiltrated the dangerous political group to help bring it down, however, Lily had begun to like him more and more and, gradually, she'd fallen in love – but she would never have let him know if Jenny hadn't told him she no longer wanted to see him. He was her sister's boy-friend and for Lily that meant he was out of bounds. She'd fought her feelings, never letting anyone see that she was unhappy. Only after Jenny had told Chris she didn't want to go on dating him and they'd parted, did Lily find the courage to tell Chris that she wanted to be his friend. Chris had asked to meet and talk – and then they'd just fallen in love, in a way that took her breath. The flare of desire was something she'd never known or understood before and it was wonderful. Their passion had been consummated in a hotel bedroom just before Chris left England when he'd thought he might not return for years – but now it seemed he was coming home and Lily's heart sang for joy.

She didn't know how long his visit would be for, but she would take every precious moment and enjoy it. She smiled as she finished her sandwich and went upstairs to bed. Jenny must have known who the letter was from, but she'd left her to discover it for herself.

A little frown touched her brow. She hoped Jenny wasn't regretting her parting from Chris because Lily could never give him up now . . .

CHAPTER 2

The house in Little Lane was filthy; no one had cleaned it for months and it had never been a very pleasant place to live, although when Doris Bryant had been alive she'd waged a constant battle against the dirt and the vermin that crawled out of the walls. Since her death, however, the mould and the cockroaches had taken over and now progressed at their leisure with no one to stop them with a dose of carbolic or hot soapy water.

Danny shrank into the dark corner next to the old pine dresser that was dented and scarred with the years, hoping to avoid detection as his drunken father lurched through the kitchen door. Jim Bryant had always been a violent man but, with the death of his wife in childbed six months earlier, his temper had grown worse and worse. At first he'd got drunk just on Friday and Saturday nights, drinking most of his pay away, but after he'd lost his job in the cardboard factory, where he'd been a packer for the past three years, he'd spent most of his time in the pub, scrounging drinks from the mates who felt sorry for him for losing his missus.

11

And now that Doris Bryant was not there to demand the rent money and her housekeeping, Jim had ceased to bother paying his rent and there was no coal or food in the house. The house was freezing cold and there was nothing to eat in the cupboards and no money to buy any, although Jim had sold the brass candlesticks and the mantel clock his wife had been so proud of, along with her clothes and few bits of jewellery.

'Bloody landlord,' Danny heard his father mutter as he knocked into a chair and sent it crashing to the floor. 'Who the hell does he think he is, demanding his money? If he thinks he can toss me out, he can think again.'

Danny didn't answer. He never did when his father was this way, just held his breath and hoped that his angry parent would go to bed without noticing him. If his father saw him cowering in the corner, he would drag him out and beat him. Danny's school teacher – Miss Thomas – said that if Danny came to school with bruises all over him again, she was going to report his father to the welfare people. Danny wasn't sure how he felt about that, because he'd heard of other kids being taken away from their family – not that he had any to rely on. His mother was dead, his elder brother Kenny had gone in the Navy and hadn't been home for years, his grandparents were dead and his father was a vicious bully. He didn't know what had happened to his mother's only brother, because his father had driven him away with curses and blows when he'd come asking after his sister and nephew.

Danny had eaten the last scrap of stale bread when he got home from school and his stomach ached from hunger. If the teacher at school hadn't made sure he got a drink of milk and two of the sandwiches from her lunch packet every day, he thought he might have starved these past weeks. It was bad enough on school days, but at weekends he often had nothing to eat at all, unless one of the neighbours saw him kicking a stone in the street and brought him a bit of bread and dripping or, very occasionally, the woman from the corner shop gave him a bun that was going stale. He could hardly remember what it was like to have a hot meal and a proper cup of tea with milk and sugar.

'What are you doin' skulking there?' His father jerked towards him, staring at him through bloodshot eyes and breathing beery fumes over him. 'Come out here, you little rat.'

'Please don't!' Danny cried but his father's fist exploded in his face. Another blow caught his ear and a third felled him. He screamed as the heavy boot connected with his side over and over again, and then he passed out.

Time passed and he lay on the floor where he'd fallen, only ignored because the man had collapsed in a drunken stupor. When Danny came to his senses again it was just getting light. He sat up gingerly, holding himself as he felt the pain in his head and his side where he'd been kicked. His mouth was sore and swollen and he could hardly see out of one eye. He was fearful of another attack, but the sound of snoring told him that his father had fallen asleep on the kitchen couch. Getting carefully to his feet, Danny felt his way to the kitchen sink and filled a chipped mug with water, drinking thirstily for a few minutes, before tipping the rest of the water onto a kitchen rag that had once been spotless white and used for wiping up crockery; now it was filthy but the cold dampness of it against his split lip and swollen eye felt good.

Danny stared at his father as he snored and hated what he saw. But the beating he'd endured that night would be the last that bully would give him, he promised himself. He couldn't go to school as he was, so he would run away. Glancing around the kitchen, Danny saw an old overcoat that had belonged to his grandfather. He took it down from the hook together with the rucksack that hung underneath it. His father hadn't left much of value in the house, but Danny knew that his grandfather had left a silver watch and chain to his mother and, so far, his father hadn't discovered her hiding place. But Danny knew it and he would take the watch, haversack and coat and then he would leave this house for good.

He lifted the floorboard in the bedroom that hid the watch and a brass tin with some old coins in it and placed them in the haversack along with his spare jumper and his one extra pair of socks. It would be bitterly cold sleeping out under the arches, but that was the only place Danny could think of to go. He knew that vagrants slept under the arches every night, because he'd seen them there when he'd been on a bus with his mother. She'd told him he shouldn't look down on homeless people the way some did, because they were more to be pitied than scorned. His mother had been a lovely person; she'd loved Danny and his brother and even his father, who had always been a bit of a bully – but she'd stood up to him, protecting her children.

'We don't know what's brought them down, Danny

love,' she'd told him that day on the bus, when speaking of the vagrants. 'Some of them had homes once but ill fortune or the drink took them low. The demon drink is an evil thing, Danny. Your father used to drink too much but I won him from it and he promised me he would never get drunk again when we wed. He's fallen once or twice but mostly he's kept his word to me – I'd box his ears if he didn't and he knows it.'

Danny felt the sting of tears as he remembered. His mum had been a good 'un and she'd loved him. She'd stood up to his father and for some reason the big man had always backed down before the small woman. Danny could still remember the smell of the lavender water she sprinkled on her clothes and the sheets too, because she said it helped you to sleep.

Why did she have to die and leave him alone with his father? Danny knuckled his eyes to stop the tears as he walked away from the house. The gutters were choked with filth, paint peeling on windows and doors, and at this early hour no eyes peered from behind grey net curtains. His face hurt and his body ached all over, and he had a sick feeling inside. He wanted to get as far as he could away from his father and the misery of the past few months. He knew it was going to be cold and he might often be hungry, but he'd got his grand-father's trinkets and his coat, and he would manage somehow. Mum had said the tramps went to a soup kitchen at the Sally Army every day to be fed, and Danny's mouth watered as he thought of hot soup and thick bread, and a mug of strong tea. His belly ached with the need for food, because he hadn't eaten much for days and he wasn't sure when he would eat again. He wasn't even sure how far it was to the place he'd seen with his mother, where the tramps had been sitting around a fire in an old steel drum, drinking from bottles and huddling into their blankets. If he could find them, perhaps they might share their fire and tell him where the Sally Army handed out their soup and bread.

Danny knew the archway was down by the river so he reckoned he just had to head for the dockyards and keep walking until he found somewhere to sleep. Perhaps he might even find someone who would give him food for running an errand or carrying things. Danny was twelve, thirteen in August, but he was tall for his age and, though thin, well built; if he lied, he could get away with pretending to be fourteen and therefore old enough to work. He wouldn't mind working if he got the chance and would do anything that was asked of him. Danny wasn't going to be like his father and drink his life away!

Mum wouldn't have liked to think of her son living rough, but Danny didn't know what else to do. He couldn't stay with his father any longer, because one of these days Jim would kill him in a drunken fit. He'd rather take his chances with the tramps under the arches. One of them had seen him watching them that day with his mum, and he'd grinned at him. Danny had thought he looked approachable. If he could find someone like that to teach him how to go on, he would be all right – the only other alternative was to go to school and let his teacher report him to the welfare.

Why should he let them send him away to a home somewhere when he was nearly old enough to leave school? Danny wasn't sure what orphanages were but he knew his mum didn't approve of them, so they couldn't be good. He would be working in another year or so and he might as well find a job now if he could. Brushing the tears from his cheeks, Danny stuck his head in the air and strengthened his stride. His father wasn't going to break him and he didn't want to be packed off to Canada or Australia, like some unfortunate kids his mother had told him about.

'I've heard all sorts of stories over the years, Danny love,' she'd told him, scraping marge and jam on a thick slice of her freshly-baked bread for him. 'Terrible it is. They're taken from their family and sent all that way on a ship. Now I think that is a disgrace. We might be poor but I wouldn't let them send my boy to a home or a place I've never seen. Them folk think they can do what they like with you, Danny. Once they've got you, you've had it – it's what they say that goes.'

Danny's mother hadn't liked orphanages. She said people did things to the kids there, things they didn't ought to, so Danny would live rough and eat whatever he had to eat to get by, but he wouldn't go in one of those awful places. But he wasn't going to be a tramp all his life. He was going to find proper work and then he'd have a room of his own and he'd be just fine. His dream of having a warm comfortable home with a mother and father that loved him was just that, an impossible dream. There was only him now and he had to learn to look after himself.

CHAPTER 3

'Thank you, Kathy,' Mary Thurston, Matron of the Rosie, said to the young woman who had brought up a tray of tea. She'd remembered to use their best china in honour of their visitor and that was well done in Mary's opinion. 'That is most welcome, my dear.'

The girl blushed, smiled and left, closing the door behind her. Mary looked at her visitor as she poured tea for them both. 'Milk and one sugar I think?'

'Yes, thank you, Mary.'

Mary handed her one of the best cups reserved for important visitors. 'So, what can I do to help you, Rosalie?'

'I don't think there is anything much just now. I really came to update you, Mary.' Lady Rosalie sighed as she took a file from her large leather bag. 'Sometimes I think the list of homeless children is never-ending,' she said as she gave Mary Thurston a sheet of paper. 'This is my list of possible foster carers. There are twelve on the list and I think we may get eight or nine good families from it. We have to be so very careful, Mary. I don't want a repeat of what happened to young Charlie!'

'No, indeed,' Mary said. Charlie and his sister Maisie had been in her care at the Rosie and they'd found him a foster home when his sister was ill but he was badly treated and ran away and since then Lady Rosalie had been even more careful about vetting prospective foster parents. 'And how many homeless children have you at the moment?'

'Twenty-five,' Lady Rosalie replied and sighed. 'All of my children are older – the adoption societies take the babies and very tiny children for whom they can find adoptive parents easily, but the children of six years and older are more difficult to place, particularly when they come from broken homes and are inclined to be difficult.'

'Yes, I do understand how hard it must be,' Mary said. Being Matron of the Rosie infirmary seemed an easier task compared to the one her friend faced. Placing a child with a bad foster parent could lead to all sorts of problems, even death at times – and it was so difficult to find enough of the right people, because it wasn't just a matter of background or even how well off they were: character and kindness were far more important in a foster parent. 'I am still looking for candidates for your list of carers, but unfortunately, I seem to add to your list of children needing care more often than I do your kind and honest carers.'

'Yes, and I'm glad you do tell me about necessary cases,' Lady Rosalie said and smiled. 'Well, keep your ears open for suitable foster families, Mary – and ring me whenever you need to.'

'Yes, I shall.' Mary smiled at her. She glanced at her watch and tutted; how fast the time went when she had company! 'I must make a tour of the wards – and I dare say you have another meeting to attend?'

'No, for once I'm going out to lunch with a friend,' Lady Rosalie said and smiled. 'Geraint was a friend of my husband. He lost his wife eighteen months ago and had to come up to London for some business today and so we decided to have lunch together.'

'Well, that will be a nice change for you,' Mary nodded approvingly. 'I'm sure you deserve to be taken out for lunch – and I hope you have a lovely time.'

'Yes, of course I'm bound to,' Lady Rosalie replied. 'One sometimes forgets one is still young enough to enjoy life.'

Mary nodded. She would be here at the infirmary the rest of the day and the evening too. Her little apartment was in what would be termed an attic by some but was comfortable and had all she needed; it meant she was able to be the first in every morning and only left the building to go for a walk in the fresh air or to seek some sleep when she could no longer continue at her desk. Her life had little of interest outside the Rosie these days and she occasionally thought that she really ought to take a holiday but thus far she hadn't found the time.

Sister Rose smiled at her colleague, Staff Nurse Alice Burwell, as they prepared to swap over for the night. Alice was taking her turn on the late shift and had come in fresh and bright to check the records for the children's ward.

'Just three cases to watch at the moment, then,' she said. 'It looks like being a quiet night.'

'Yes, providing you don't get any sudden admissions,' Rose said and yawned. 'Oh dear. I'm tired. I'm going straight home to bed.' She smothered another yawn.

'Have a good rest. It is sometimes good to be single, isn't it, and not have a husband and children to look after?'

Rose nodded and left her, switching her thoughts from the busy day in the ward and for a moment allowed herself to think of the man she'd once loved – or thought she did, until she learned that he was already married and cheating both her and his long-suffering wife. The worst thing of all was that he'd had four young children and he'd vowed that he would leave them all for Rose!

'I think that is terrible, Mike,' she'd told him, outraged. 'It isn't just that you deceived me, it's your wife and children – how could you ever think of deserting them? I could never love a man who could do that!'

'I couldn't help falling in love with you, Rose. You're so wonderful.' He'd gone on and on, extolling her beauty and her character, trying to flatter her into taking him back.

Rose hadn't listened to his excuses. He'd begged and pleaded but she'd left him standing there in the street and hadn't looked back. Later, in her bedroom, the tears had come, her heart breaking because she had loved him desperately.

Were all men as shallow as Mike Hardy? If they were, then, she, Rose Harwell, wanted nothing more to do with them.

She would never have gone for that first drink with

22

him if she'd guessed he was married and had children and it was no wonder she hadn't trusted anyone enough to love again since. Yet she had no real desire to be single, and though she would miss nursing desperately, would much prefer to be at home with a husband and perhaps a couple of kids. Or was it too late for her to have that sort of life? Should she accept that she had nothing but her nursing and her friends?

A sharp tingle went down Rose's spine as she thought about the clever doctor she'd started to like – more than like, if she told the truth, but she was still wary, still unsure that she could trust Dr Peter Clark.

Most of the time, Rose was sure about what she wanted in her life. She liked Peter a lot and she wanted children of her own; she hadn't realised how important that was to her until she held her brother John's first daughter, Harriet, in her arms. The feeling it had given her made her melt inside and she'd realised that perhaps her job wasn't going to be enough for the rest of her life. Rose wanted marriage and children. Perhaps deep love wasn't necessary. She'd been hurt too much that first time and she didn't intend to let anyone hurt her again that way. Much better to marry because you liked someone and you got on well – much safer.

Just as she reached the bottom of the stairs, she saw someone entering the front door and stopped, catching her breath. It was as if she'd conjured him up by thinking of him! What was he doing here? None of the children were sick enough to warrant a doctor being called out. 'Sister Rose.' Dr Peter Clark looked at her anxiously. 'Matron asked me to call. One of her patients is very ill – a woman in her seventies I understand?'

'I'm on the children's ward at the moment.' Rose smiled at him, brushing a strand of her flame-red hair away from her face. 'I'm glad to say we don't have any children who need urgent attention from a doctor just now.'

He smiled and his face lit up, the serious look banished. 'I'm glad about that,' he murmured.' His eyes were very blue as he looked at her and she noticed that his dark blond hair was too long again and fell forward into his eyes; he brushed it back impatiently. 'I'd better go and see what Matron wants.'

Rose nodded and walked on quickly, her heart racing. If only Peter Clark would say something to give her a clue as to his feelings! She sensed that he liked her and she knew for a fact that he wasn't married – Rose had asked about that the first time he smiled at her in a way she thought was special. He was always pleasant to her and she felt that he went out of his way to speak to her each time he was called to the infirmary – and yet he hadn't asked her out and he'd given no indication that he wanted to be more than a colleague.

Perhaps that was why he'd caught her imagination. Had he been the same as most men she met, making flirtatious eyes at her and asking her out on every occasion, Rose would probably have labelled him a flirt and that would have been that; she wouldn't have given him a chance. It might be because he made no advances to her that she liked him and had begun to trust him, not just as a doctor – she knew he was brilliant at his work! – but also as a man.

Rose lifted her head as she emerged into the dark streets about the infirmary. Situated at the end of Button

Street, the Lady Rosalie Infirmary was right in the heart of the East End of London. Little alleys, mean narrow streets, crowded courts and the broader main streets were all known to her, because she'd grown up only a short distance away, down near the dockyards. Now she lived only a few streets away in a decent lodging house in Bell Lane, which ran off from Shilling Street in a tangent. To get there she had to pass through some rough areas and it made her acutely aware of the extreme poverty of many living in this part of London. It was no surprise to Sister Rose that children came into her ward half-starved and filthy dirty, with nits in their hair and suffering from all kinds of illnesses, including broken bones and bruises. Often their parents were so poor that a slice of bread and dripping was a luxury for the kids and they never saw an orange or even a boiled egg. Most of them thought it was heaven being in the Rosie, where they were fed with good nourishing food.

Shivering, she pulled her coat collar up, glad of the knitted beret pulled over her glossy hair and her warm scarf. She pinned her thick hair up in a French pleat at the back of her head to keep it neat for work. Mike, before she'd discovered he was married, had once told her that her hair had the red-gold flame of a field of ripe corn at harvest time . . .

Rose walked swiftly towards the end of Button Street. The street lamps weren't particularly bright and she glanced over her should once, half fearing she was being followed. She'd been followed by a thug once before, but even as he'd tried to steal her nurse's bag a young man had appeared out of the gloom and driven him away. He'd taken her attacker in an arm lock and escorted him away, calling out over his shoulder that he'd see it didn't happen again. Rose hadn't even had the chance to thank him properly, and she had no idea of her hero's name. Yet she knew that, despite the poverty and the rogues that lurked in these mean streets, there were many honest, brave young men like him who wanted no praise for helping one of the Rosie's nurses. Folk round here respected the staff of the infirmary, who did all they could to help when they were sick. In the dim light she hadn't even seen the face of her rescuer clearly, but she'd thanked him in her head many times.

There was no one behind her now and Rose turned into Shilling Street and crossed the road, heading for Mrs Robinson's house at the end of Bell Lane. It was icily cold tonight and she would be glad when she was inside in the warm. A sigh of relief touched her lips as she entered the kitchen and the homely face of her wonderful landlady greeted her with a bright smile.

'Well, there you are, Rose. Tired and hungry I'll be bound. I've got a lovely fish pie in the oven and there's carrots and leeks to go with it, my love – and a nice cup of tea.'

'Did I ever tell you I think my guardian angel was looking after me when I found you, Beattie?'

Beattie Robinson beamed at her. 'That you have, my love – and he was looking out for me too, because I needed a lodger and there are some awful folk about – but I got you and I couldn't be happier.' Rose had come to the lodging house after her mother could no longer look after herself or be left on her own. Rose paid for her to be cared for by a widowed cousin who was grateful for the extra income and had been a nurse herself, so knew how to care for the mother who hardly knew Rose these days. Rose had found the lodgings cheaper than having to run her own home and although she now earned more, was too comfortable here to think of moving into a house of her own.

She went to Beattie and put her arms about her ample waist. 'I can smell that pie and it makes me hungry. They feed us at the Rosie – but nothing like you cook!'

'Sit you down and I'll serve,' Beattie said, 'and then you can tell me all about your day.' Beattie always wanted to know everything. 'How is that Matron doing and all your patients then?'

'Thank you so much for coming to see me, doctor,' Matron said and rose to her feet as they shook hands. 'My patient is very unwell. Her fever keeps rising no matter what we do – and I can't put my finger on the problem.'

'I'll be glad to take a look at her. At seventy she should be able to pull through an operation for the removal of a gall bladder. I can't see why she has a continuing fever – unless there is an infection.'

'Yes, I think that may well be the case – but I don't know why. Her dressings have been changed regularly and the wound is healing nicely.'

'Outwardly,' Dr Peter Clark agreed. 'It may be an internal infection – and they are the worst because we can't do very much about them.'

It was true. A wound to the skin or a limb could be kept clean, swabbed with a disinfectant and healing balms, but there was nothing yet available that would

27

cure an internal infection. You could calm a fever with medicines but if the infection ran too deep it too often killed the patient.

Following Matron to the ward, Peter glanced at the neat rows of beds, each surrounded by curtains which were drawn back to allow the patients to see what was happening. Several of the patients knew him and smiled or waved a hand and he smiled back. He was known to many of these people because he gave much of his time to the East End poor free of charge. Some of his fellow doctors at the London Hospital said he was mad not to ask for payment but Peter didn't care. He was fortunate to have been left an inheritance which meant that, if he chose, he could sit at home all day or visit a gentleman's club and drink port wine. But Peter enjoyed being a doctor. There was, in his opinion, nothing better than seeing a sick patient recover and go home to their family.

The curtains around Mrs Edie Simpson's bed were closed and she was lying with her eyes closed, her face flushed – too flushed. He felt her forehead, finding she was clammy and damp with sweat. Clearly, she had a fever and it made him frown, because he knew her operation had gone well.

He pulled the covers back and then inched her night-dress up to reveal the dressing, which he deftly removed. It looked perfectly clean and when he bent to sniff it there was no smell of putrefaction, which hopefully meant it wasn't the surgery that had caused this fever.

Using his stethoscope, he listened to her chest and frowned. She seemed perfectly fine – but the fever was a cause for concern. Turning, he looked at Matron.

28

'Do we have a ward where she can be placed in isolation?'

'Yes, there is a small room at the end of this ward, Dr Clark, but—'

'I'm not suggesting she has anything nasty but I think we should take precautions. It is just possible that she was incubating some kind of infection before her operation and it has now come out.' Replacing the nightgown to its proper place and drawing up the bedcover, he frowned. 'I suggest isolation and sponging regularly to cool her down – and something to ease her; she's moaning a little and may be suffering pain.'

'Yes, doctor.' Matron looked relieved. 'You don't think it is due to the surgery then?'

'No, I believe she may have brought this in with her – and that's why I want her in isolation. Gloves, aprons and masks when the nurses look after her. We don't want whatever she has to spread, do we?'

'No, doctor.' Matron smiled at him. 'I'm so glad you came. I was really concerned that we'd mistreated her.'

'That she was being nursed well was never in doubt,' he said. 'I'll wash my hands and then leave you, Matron, but please don't hesitate to call me again if you need me. Either I or my assistant will come whenever we are needed.'

Matron nodded. His assistant was a nice young man but he knew she preferred his personal attendance because, she said, he was so certain and sure – and gentle with the patients. Some of the doctors could be rough and Matron was known to disapprove of that, because a sick person needed gentle kindness, not abrupt words or careless actions.

After washing his hands thoroughly in the basin at the end of the ward, Peter left the Rosie and went out into the night. He hoped the patient's fever would turn out to be something simple but there was always a chance it could be nasty.

Walking briskly in the night air, Peter's thoughts turned to the young woman he'd spoken to briefly on his arrival at the infirmary and he smiled. He'd been attracted to Sister Rose from the first moment he'd seen her but some of his colleagues had warned him to watch out.

'She hates men,' the senior clinician, Richard Harris, had told him. 'I asked her for a drink at Christmas about two years ago and she nearly bit my head off – told me she wasn't interested in no uncertain terms.'

Peter had heard similar stories from other doctors who had tried to interest Sister Rose in a date and failed. At first, she'd seemed a bit frosty with him but recently her smiles had been warmer and he'd been tempted to ask her if she wanted to go for a meal or something, but his natural caution held him back. Peter had loved a young nurse at his training hospital but Sheila had been a terrible flirt and although she'd gone out with Peter for some months, he'd discovered she was dating others behind his back, and sleeping with them too.

When he taxed her with it, Sheila had laughed and said she wanted a good time before she settled down to one man and boredom. Her scorn had hurt him for a while but he'd got over it. A woman who gave herself to anyone that easily wasn't worth breaking your heart over. So, he'd got on with his job – which he loved –

and dated other young women casually, often in a group with other young medical personnel. It was fine while he was young and not particularly looking for a steady relationship, but one day he wanted a loving wife and a family. Although he lived in a small, family-run hotel, which was situated close to the London Hospital where he worked two days a week, he could afford a nice house with a garden, and that was what he wanted. He might even set up as a GP one day, with his own surgery, but it would still be in the East End of London. A country practice wasn't for him. While there were many sick people everywhere, something about the spirit of the East End people appealed and he liked treating them and seeing them go back to their hard lives with new hope.

Smiling, Peter found his modest and ancient Ford car – still with all its wheels intact. The lads round here would pinch anything but they knew the car was his and any lad who tried to nick his wheels would have his ear clipped by one of the others and told to leave Doctor Peter's car be.

Next time he saw Sister Rose, he decided, he would ask her if she would like to have a meal with him on her day off; in the meantime, he'd promised to help out at a meal given for the old folk at the Methodist Hall on Sunday . . .

CHAPTER 4

Danny shivered in the cold wind. His home had never been warm since his mother's death, but here on the streets it was bitter and getting worse as the night drew on. He'd been wandering for three days, sleeping in the doorways of shops to keep out of the rain that had fallen steadily. As yet he hadn't found the place he was looking for, but he'd met a boy he'd known by sight from school and he'd told Danny that if he kept walking towards the river there was a mission hall that would give him some hot soup and bread. However, he must have taken a wrong turning because he hadn't come near the hall.

Shivering with cold, Danny wondered if he'd done the right thing by leaving his home. Perhaps it would have been better to stay there and take the beatings his father handed out when he was drunk. He looked about him as the street lights started to go on and darkness fell. During the day, Danny had walked inside the larger shops, wandering around for something to do and keep warm, but now they were all closing. He'd spent an hour or so in a library but then the lady in charge had asked him why he wasn't at school. Perhaps he should go to school and ask for help – but his father might fetch him back and then he would really belt him hard. His fear of another beating was worse than the trouble he'd get into for missing school so he'd just kept on walking.

Now he stood undecided, dreading another night alone on the dark streets. Hungry, cold and tired, Danny was close to tears. He didn't get easily frightened but there was a hollow feeling inside him as he realised he'd got completely lost, and had no idea where he was or where to go.

'Feeling lost, son?' a friendly voice asked, and Danny looked at the man who had spoken.

He was thin and wiry, perhaps thirty-odd, with short dark hair slicked back and smartly dressed. His smile was reassuring and Danny nodded his head.

'I was looking for the Methodist Hall,' he confided. 'Jimmy said I can get some hot soup there.'

'Cold and hungry, are you?' the man asked sympathetically. 'It's not very nice, is it? I know what it is like to go hungry when you're young – that's why I work for folk who help lost children.' He looked at Danny, an odd expression in his eyes. 'Have you heard of the Sally Army?'

'Yeah, Ma always used to say they were all right – she said they would help yer without interfering like the council lot.'

The man smiled again, more confidently this time. 'Yes, that's right, that's what we do, lad. Now, I can't tell you where this Methodist Hall is, but I can take you to our place and I can do better than some soup – how

34

would you like a nice packet of fish and chips with salt and vinegar?'

'Can we eat them out of the paper?' Danny asked eagerly. 'I ain't never had fish from a chipper, though.' But he loved chips and it was years since he'd had a packet, the last bought as a birthday treat by his mother for his birthday nearly a year before she died.

'We'll get them now,' his new friend said. 'And then we'll go to the Salvation Army Hall. My name is Jim, by the way – just like your friend.'

The man's voice, smile and tone were reassuring and Danny fell into step with him. His stomach rumbled as he eagerly anticipated the food. He wondered what the fish would be like.

At the shop, Jim told Danny to wait outside and he stood looking into the window that was misted up with steam, stamping his feet to keep out the cold. His grandfather's coat was too big for him, but without it he would have frozen the last couple of nights and he felt comforted by the knapsack on his back. His silver watch and the few pennies he possessed were tucked safely inside his shirt.

'Here you are, lad,' Jim said handing him the newspaper-wrapped packet of fish and chips salted and soaked in vinegar, just the way Danny liked chips. He took them eagerly and began to woof them down, enjoying his first taste of shop-cooked fish in batter, burning his mouth in his haste because they were so hot – so hot but so delicious!

'Eat them slowly,' his new friend said, laughing. 'You don't want to choke yourself!' He hesitated then said, 'Will you tell me your name?'

'Danny – Danny Bryant,' Danny mumbled between mouthfuls. The fish and chips were so wonderful that all he wanted to do was concentrate on eating and it wasn't until they'd left the lights of the busy streets behind that he began to notice his surroundings. It was darker now in these narrow lanes and Danny felt the first prickle of unease. 'Where are we going, mister?'

'To the Salvation Army Home,' he replied easily. 'They'll give you a bed for the night and tell you where you can get free food and shelter.'

Danny nodded and continued to eat. He had no reason to doubt what he was being told and yet his feeling of unease began to increase as he noticed the increasing drabness of the streets through which they were passing – he wouldn't have thought the Sally Army would be here. At the back of his mind was being taken to the Salvation Army Hall by his mother. She'd gone to ask for advice when her mother had been ill and taken to the infirmary – Granny had died that winter and his mother had been sad for a while, but she'd wiped Danny's tears and told him that Granny had gone to Heaven. When his mother died, Danny's father had told him to stop his bawling and stormed off to get drunk.

'Finished?' Jim asked him and took the greasy papers, throwing them into the gutter.

Mum wouldn't have approved, Danny thought. She'd always said you should put your rubbish in the bin at home if there wasn't one on the street. The prickling at his nape increased as they stopped outside a door. Danny knew instantly that this wasn't the Sally Army Hall – it was just a very shabby house and he hesitated, holding back as Jim knocked at the door.

'Where are we?' he asked, feeling suddenly frightened.

'We're going inside, Danny,' the man said and reached out as if he would take hold of Danny's arm.

'No! You tricked me – this isn't the Sally Army!' Danny backed away as the man lunged at him, trying to grab him. He turned and ran back down the lane but the man was on him at once and he felt a strong hand grab him. As he was grasped by the arm, he kicked out and struggled, yelling and screaming out, 'Get orf me!'

The man's hold didn't lessen as they struggled and then he heard another voice and there were two of them holding him. Danny had no chance of getting away from two grown men and he was snatched off his feet and carried by his shoulders and legs back down the narrow alley towards the house that had terrified him.

'Thanks, Jake,' the man he'd thought of as a friend muttered. 'The little blighter seemed content but then he suddenly bolted.'

'Got more sense than some of 'em, then.' Jake gave a harsh laugh. 'You usually manage to get them inside afore they catch on.'

Danny struggled against his captors. He didn't know why these men had tricked and then grabbed him, but he vaguely remembered his mother telling him to come straight home from school and not talk to strangers, because you couldn't always trust them.

He was carried, struggling and protesting, inside the dingy house, which smelled bad of something he thought might be drains. Mum had battled against drains, armed with disinfectant and a scrubbing brush. After her death, Danny's home had acquired an unpleasant tang but nothing like as bad as this – it was the old, foul smell of years of decay.

'Let me go! I'll tell me dad on yer,' Danny threatened and continued to struggle as he was taken through a dark hall and up narrow stairs. He was banged unceremoniously against the wall and bannister and yelled as he felt the scrape of something on his arm. 'Ouch, yer hurt me!'

'Serves yer right,' Jake said. 'Keep yer trap shut and yer won't get 'urt!'

'I want ter go 'ome.'

'Yer'll do what yer told.' He was suddenly put on his feet and a large hand connected with his ear. 'Give me any trouble and I'll make yer wish yer had never been born.'

Danny's panic started to subside. Threats of this kind were normal in his home and it was the fear of the unknown that had made him panic and start running.

'I'm thirsty,' he complained.

'Behave and mebbe I'll give yer a glass of water.'

Danny decided that it might be best to keep quiet the way he had when his father was drunk. He had no chance of getting away while there were two of them guarding him – but if he got a chance he would run and next time he would make sure he slipped away unseen.

'Put him in with the others,' the man who had called himself Jim said. 'I'm going out again, see what more I can find – we're shipping them out in a couple of days.'

'Supposing he plays up?'

'You know what to do – give him some of the laudanum.'

Danny's blood seemed to freeze. He knew that name – the doctor had given it to his mother for her pain. He'd seen her lying in a deep sleep, unable to focus or speak properly. It would be daft to risk that happening to him so he told himself to calm down and think. These men were bad, he knew that now, and he would do all he could to escape them – but he had to be clever.

One of them had unlocked a door and Danny was thrust inside; the door slammed behind him and he heard the sound of a key turning. His instincts were to fling himself at the wood and yell to be let out, but he controlled the urge. If he did that, they might give him that awful stuff that would make him go to sleep.

'How did he get *you* then?'

Danny turned at the sound of the boy's voice and saw that there were another three boys and a little girl in the bedroom, which had just a double bed and some blankets on the floor.

'He gave me fish and chips. I was hungry . . .'

'Yeah, I got a pork pie.' The boy who was about Danny's age grinned at him. 'I were cold and 'ungry and I trusted the bugger.'

'I did too, at first,' Danny said and wrinkled his brow. 'Why has he brought us 'ere?'

'They're gang masters,' the boy said. 'I'm Ron, by the way, and I've been on the streets for nine months since me ma copped it. They'll send us off around London working for their lot, robbing and stealing, sometimes worse things . . . but I always told 'em to get lost – I really thought Bob was from the Sally Army.'

'He told me his name was Jim . . .' Danny frowned. 'He's a liar, ain't he?'

'Oh, he's worse than that,' Ron told him. 'I feel sorry for them . . .' He jerked his head at two of the younger boys. 'They can't look after themselves so well . . .'

Danny wasn't sure what Ron meant, but he didn't like the sound of it.

'If they start on me,' Ron said angrily, 'I'll kick 'em where it hurts and you want ter do the same – if we can get a knife we'll stick 'em!'

Danny nodded. He'd liked Ron instantly and it made him feel better that he wasn't alone. 'We should stick together, all of us.'

'Yeah,' Ron said and looked grim. 'But if I get a chance, I'll hurt that bugger and I'll be orf.'

Danny nodded, but his eyes were drawn to the other children, all of them younger than him, and he felt sorry for them as he saw the fear in their eyes. He wanted to run the way Ron said – but what would the other boys and that little girl do? She was such a pretty, delicate little thing and Danny felt sorry for her because she was clearly frightened and miserable, her face stained with tears.

Ron told him to sit down on one of the blankets and he sat next to him so they could talk.

'Tell me how you left home,' Ron said, 'and I'll tell yer my story.'

Danny nodded. The other children were quiet, looking at him and Ron and the little girl had inched nearer to them. Danny held out his hand to her and she came quickly to his side. He smiled and she leaned her thin little body against his stronger one. He felt protective towards her and the two boys who had been hurt but they huddled together, their eyes dark and haunted, not looking anywhere.

He silently vowed he would try to protect them if he could, but how could he and Ron prevail against men like the ruthless devils who had captured him and imprisoned him in this room? All he could do was wait and see what happened next . . .

CHAPTER 5

Rose walked into the kitchen of the mission hall and greeted the other helpers. She was given a pile of vegetables to clean and cook and set to with a will. They were serving cottage pie with extra vegetables – carrots, cabbage and baked onions – which were a favourite with the elderly folk who came to these lunches.

Once the food was cooked and the tables had been set, the doors were opened to admit the people who had been invited. They came in in ones and twos and greeted each other, enjoying the chance to gossip and meet friends as much as the good food they would be offered.

Rose started to serve as soon as they were all seated, because there were more than sixty people sitting down to a meal and it took several of them to get around the tables quickly enough to keep the food hot. She served her five tables and then, hearing a burst of loud laughter, looked towards a table nearer the door. Her heart stopped as she saw a man sitting down with some of the elderly ladies and knew him.

What was Peter Clark doing here? He'd been served

with a portion of the cottage pie and was eating it, teasing and laughing with the old lady sitting next to him.

'He's lovely with them,' Dora Nokes whispered in Rose's ear. 'Particularly with Jessie. She can be a bit of a tartar but he knows how to make her laugh.'

'Yes, I can see that,' Rose said and smiled. 'Does he often come to these lunches?'

'It's the first time he's been to a lunch but he turns up at all sorts of things,' Dora said and smiled. 'Apparently, Jessie wouldn't come for the lunch unless he did so that is why he is here.'

Rose nodded, but she had no time to do more than send another glance at Doctor Peter's table, because the old folk she'd served first had finished the first course and were waiting for pudding. Laughing to herself, she went off to collect used plates and then serve the tinned fruit and custard that was the favourite of many, followed by a cup of tea.

After serving was finished there was a mound of washing-up. Rose was helping to dry when a man's voice spoke behind her.

'Well done, Sister Rose,' Peter Clark said, and she turned to look at him. 'That was an excellent meal, everyone – I thank you on behalf of all of us.' He clapped them and Rose saw the ladies blush and twitter amongst themselves, pleased and flattered that he'd come to the kitchen to thank them.

'He was one of the men that first asked if we could organise a meal for the elderly,' Dora told Rose in a whisper. 'Works at the free clinic sometimes, so my husband says. Stan reckons he's a good bloke – always helpin' out where he can.'

Rose finished her work and walked over to Peter, smiling at him. 'Your ladies seemed to enjoy themselves. They were laughing and looked so happy, especially the one sitting beside you.'

'That's Jessie,' he said. 'She says some strange things.'

Rose shook her head. 'I think they were laughing at what you had to say!'

'Perhaps I contributed a little,' he replied. 'Are you finished here now?'

'Yes, I'm about to leave,' Rose said and took her coat from the hook on the wall. She turned and waved, calling goodbye to those she'd worked with all morning. 'I'm going home to change – and then to tea with some friends.'

'Oh, that's a pity.' He looked disappointed. 'I was going to ask if you'd like to have tea out somewhere with me?'

'That's very kind of you,' Rose said, 'but I have to hurry.' She nodded to him and turned in the direction of her home. 'Thanks all the same . . .'

Peter stood looking after her and she knew he was thinking she'd just turned him down for no good reason, but she'd stayed late at the mission hall and would only just have time to get changed before she was expected at Lily's.

Peter stared after the woman he admired, feeling puzzled. She'd seemed warmer and more approachable today than when they worked together and so he'd mentioned going out to tea together but then she'd rushed off as if the devil was after her. Was it something he'd said or was she really in a hurry? He was never sure about Sister Rose.

Shaking his head, Peter started walking. He'd gone to the luncheon because Jessie had refused all invitations, even though she really needed a good meal. She lived on handouts from the Sally Army and the occasional couple of bob he gave her. Probably she got a shilling or a few coppers from other people who felt sorry for her, but the sort of food they'd been served that morning was what she needed. Asked to persuade her to accept what she denounced as 'bleedin' charity', she'd demanded that he go along too and eat the same food.

'If it's all right for me it's all right for you, doc,' she'd declared, so he'd taken her challenge and eaten every bit of the food put in front of him. It was quite as good as anything he ate in the hospital canteen and he'd smiled as he'd cleared his plate and seen her do the same.

'That was delicious,' he'd declared as he finished and saw she'd enjoyed every scrap of her meal too.

'It ain't bad,' Jessie admitted grudgingly. 'I've tasted better in me time.'

'Where was that, Jessie?'

'I used to dine at the Ritz with my admirers,' Jessie told him and winked. 'Queued up at the theatre backstage to take me out they did – one of the best actresses of my day . . .'

'I don't doubt it,' Peter replied and grinned. 'I've seen you put on many an act, Jessie!'

She'd given a cackle of laughter. 'Gawd, but you're a green one,' she said. 'Tell you anythin' and you'd believe me.'

'Of course, I would, Jessie – why shouldn't I?' He'd winked at her saucily and seen her chuckle.

Peter knew that she had connections with the theatre but no one knew for sure just what she'd been or what she'd done. She might have been an actress or perhaps a dresser backstage for all he knew but she could strike a pose and she was a good mimic. She could make people laugh and he liked her a lot. Whatever her history, she'd fallen on hard times and now her home was wherever she could find a place to park her shabby old pram and sleep on the cardboard and blankets she carted around with her. She'd been offered various places in old folk's homes but refused them all.

'I need me freedom, doc,' she'd told Peter once. 'I'd die inside one of them places. I'm a wanderer – always have been and always will be.'

Peter knew better than to try and force her. She was just one of many who needed help and others were glad of the places she'd turned down. Peter, like others, did what he could to help those in need, but you could only do what they would let you do.

Sister Rose . . . his mind returned to the woman who was so often in his thoughts these days. He couldn't have told anyone why he was so attracted to her. Certainly she was lovely to look at and he admired her work – and he liked it that she'd given up her Sunday morning to help the poor of the district – but it was more than that. It was as if there was an invisible string attached to her that had somehow got tangled up with *his* strings and wouldn't let go, something that reached out from inside him to her.

He shook his head, laughing at his fanciful thoughts.

Sister Rose had done nothing to encourage him to think of her as more than a colleague – so perhaps he should try looking at someone else for a change?

'I'm not late, am I?' Rose asked as she was admitted to Lily's home and took off her coat. 'There was a big crowd at the luncheon and it took longer to serve and wash up than I expected.'

'Well, you're here now,' Lily said and drew her in towards the fire. 'The wind is chilly out, isn't it?'

'Yes.' Rose held her hands to the fire and looked around at the little front parlour. 'This is nice, Lily. You and Jenny are so lucky to have your own home.'

'It was Gran's house originally,' Lily replied and nodded her agreement. 'She took us in when our parents died and kept what little money there was from my parents' estate for us to see us through nursing school and then she left the house to us both.'

'I've never had a home of my own,' Rose said and sighed. 'My parents always rented until they died and of course I moved into the accommodation at my first hospital while I trained. Beattie's house is lovely and I'd like something of the sort one day – but I'm not sure I'll ever be able to afford it.' A house like her landlady's was more expensive than she could ever afford on a nurse's pay, even without the money she was still paying to support her mother.

'We couldn't have bought a house ourselves,' Lily admitted. 'We earn enough to have a few treats and enjoy life, but nursing wages don't allow you to save much for a house, do they?'

They smiled at each other in perfect accord as Jenny

brought in a tea tray. 'Those scones look delicious, Jenny – did you make them?'

'Lily did,' Jenny said. 'I made the sandwiches. Lily is a better cook than I am – though I can do a nice roast.'

'Jenny is a good cook,' Lily said and gave her sister a teasing look. 'She is just too lazy to fiddle with anything that takes a bit longer.'

'You!' Jenny said and made a face. 'When you can buy delicious fancy things from Lavender and Lace, I don't see the point in spending hours baking a sponge cake.'

Rose smiled, enjoying the sisters' banter. It was so nice to be with friends off duty. 'My landlady, Beattie, adores cooking and spends hours making wonderful food. I was so lucky to find her.'

'Yes, you were,' Lily agreed. 'Most of the nurses do nothing but complain about the food their landladies serve.'

'I know,' Rose replied, then, changing the subject, said, 'Have either of you been to see Sarah yet? I wonder how she feels about being at home.'

CHAPTER 6

It seemed a bit strange to Sarah to be staying at home every day. Steve was a little preoccupied before he left that Monday morning and when she'd asked what was wrong, he'd shaken his head.

'It's just my work, love,' he'd told her. 'Nothing for you to worry about, Sarah. I should be home at the usual hour. Take care of yourself and don't do too much.'

Sarah had smiled and kissed him, waving as he set off down the street. Everyone he met smiled and nodded to him, because he was well known in the district as a fair and capable officer of the law who took an interest in young folk. In the evenings he helped to run a club for the youths who had nothing else to do other than stand on street corners. They gave boxing and self-defence lessons at the club and some of the members had won prizes at a regional level.

Sarah's nice little modern police house took very little time to clean and she was too restless to just sit down and knit for the coming baby. So, when she'd finished her work, she pulled on her warm coat and went out, locking the front door behind her, and went off to visit

51

her mother who had two foster children living with her at the moment – Charlie, who had recently left school and taken up an apprenticeship as a carpenter, and Ned, who had a delicate stomach and needed a special diet.

Gwen Cartwright loved being a foster mother. She'd said that she would be fine living alone but Sarah was much happier that her mother had company. She certainly helped the children but they saved her from being lonely in the long winter evenings and gave her something to occupy her time.

She was baking when Sarah arrived, her face lighting up as she saw her. 'Sarah, love,' Gwen said. 'I was just thinking I'd pop round to see you when I'd got this batch cooked. How are you?'

'It's odd not going to the infirmary every day,' Sarah told her with a smile. 'How are you, Mum? Are the boys all right?'

'Charlie is thrilled to bits to be working,' Gwen told her and laughed softly. 'He couldn't wait to give me half his wages on Friday – I don't really want to take his seven shillings, but he is determined to pay for his keep, bless him.'

'Let him pay, Mum,' Sarah told her with a smile. 'You can save some of it for him and then one day, if he needs it, you can give it to him – or spend it on whatever he needs.'

'Yes, that's what I'll do – I used to do the same with the money you gave me. It came in handy for your wedding.'

'Yes, I know.' Sarah went to put the kettle on as her mother took a batch of sweet-smelling coconut tarts and another of rock buns from the oven. Her mouth watered in anticipation because those tarts had hot strawberry jam beneath the layer of crisp coconut and were delicious. 'Oh, my favourites!'

'Yes, I know. I was going to bring some round,' Gwen nodded and looked pleased. 'Ned likes them too.'

'Is he able to eat them now?' Not too long ago the young boy had had to be very careful with what he ate and most treats were banned.

'Last time we visited the doctor he told me to start letting him try things in moderation, so that's what I've done – and he can eat one of these without getting tummy trouble.'

'How wonderful. I must tell Matron when I visit the infirmary.'

'Yes, I expect you'll go in now and then just to see your friends,' Gwen agreed. 'Are you feeling well in yourself, love?'

'Yes, I'm fine, Mum. I could've worked a bit longer really but Steve wanted me to look after myself and I couldn't argue, because he's so loving and good to me.'

'So he should be,' Gwen said but there was only warmth in her tone. Sarah knew her mother truly liked her husband and was glad she'd married him.

'Look at those drawings Ned did at school,' Gwen said, indicating some pictures on the sideboard. 'I think he's very talented.'

Sarah picked up the drawings, which were of a dog, a cat and a cottage surrounded by trees and flowers. She was surprised how well done they were, far more advanced than she would have expected of a boy of thirteen.

'This dog is wonderful,' she said. 'You should frame it and hang it on the wall, Mum.'

'Yes, I'd like to – but they belong to Ned. He might like to give it to his mother.'

'After the way she behaved towards him?' Sarah shook her head. 'As far as Ned is concerned *you* are his mother now. He loves you and he would hate it if he was made to go back to her.'

Gwen nodded. 'I'm just his foster carer but I would adopt him if they would let me.'

'Perhaps you should speak to Lady Rosalie about it,' Sarah suggested. She had made the tea and carried the tray to the table and could no longer resist the tantalising smell of the coconut tarts, biting into one with relish, then going on, 'I know she's always looking for more foster mothers – it is possible they might even ask you to take another child on if they get stuck, but I'm not sure if you could actually adopt Ned.'

'I think I'll pop round to her office tomorrow,' Gwen said and smiled as her daughter reached for another of her favourite treats. 'You can take some of those home, love, you don't have to eat them all at once!'

'I hope you didn't mind my ringing you this evening?' Matron Mary Thurston asked her friend Lady Rosalie. 'Only, there is a little girl in our ward, June, and I know she was beaten severely before she was found unconscious in the school playground and brought in to the Rosie. Sister Matthews questioned her very gently and she said it was some bullies outside the school – but I believe it was either June's mother or father. Sister Matthews noticed she flinched when her parents were mentioned.'

'Then we must get to the bottom of it – and if June

has been ill-treated, we must intervene,' Lady Rosalie said. 'I shall start inquiries immediately if you will give me the name of her parents and her address.'

'Yes, of course,' Mary said and passed on the details. That done, their conversation turned to other things.

'When is your son coming home again?'

'He is going to a friend's home for a week for the Easter holidays; Freddie Forsdyke comes from a good, kind family so he'll be all right with them,' Lady Rosalie said, 'and I shall have both the boys for part of the long summer holidays – I'm taking them down to our cottage in Cornwall for a month then. Freddie's father is being posted overseas and his mother wants to go out and see him settled – and so I said I'd have both boys while she's away.'

'You'll enjoy that,' Mary suggested and heard the smile in her friend's voice as she agreed.

'Yes, I shall. Children are so special, it's why I love my work for the orphans we help to place in foster homes,' Lady Rosalie told her sincerely. 'However, a long summer break will be wonderful. I only wish you could come with us, Mary.'

'Well, I might manage to come down for a week,' her friend said, 'if you would like to have me?'

'Yes, I would love it – and your nurses are well able to look after the infirmary for a week.'

'Yes, of course they are,' Mary agreed. 'I'm not foolish enough to imagine I am indispensable, Rosalie. If I died tomorrow, I could be replaced—'

'You're not ill I hope?' There was sudden alarm in her friend's voice and Mary laughed.

'No, not at all, I assure you! I normally don't bother

to take holidays because I have no one to share them with, but if I could spend a week with you and your son and his friend, well, I should enjoy that.'

'Come for as long as you like. There is plenty of room.'

'Thank you – but a week will be sufficient, at least this time,' Mary said. 'Well, that has cheered me up! I've been worrying about a patient we have in isolation – a woman in her seventies who isn't recovering as she should – but the idea of a holiday at the sea makes me feel much better.'

'Good, I'm glad of that . . .' Lady Rosalie paused and spoke to someone over her shoulder. 'Forgive me, Mary. Someone has called and I need to speak to him. I shall keep you in touch with what I discover about June's family.'

'Yes, of course. Thank you.'

Mary replaced the receiver and smiled. A holiday at the seaside. Well, wasn't that nice? It was years since she'd been away for a holiday – not since her dearest mother passed on. In her early years of nursing she'd lived at home with Mama and, when her health failed, cared for her, interrupting her nursing career to look after her until she died. While she'd been able, they'd taken a little holiday each year, either at the sea or in the countryside visiting places like Ely in Cambridge-shire. Mama had loved that small town with its beautiful cathedral and they'd spent many happy hours by the river eating either at the Lamb Hotel, where they'd stayed, or in little pubs and cafés. It had been such a happy time . . .

Sighing, Mary put the memories – good and sad – to

the back of her mind. It was time to make her rounds of the infirmary. First of all, she would go to the kitchens and have a chat with young Kathy who had been looking a little down in the mouth lately so she'd see if she could help, and then she would call in on Edie Simpson and see how she was getting on. At least she had a chance of avoiding the spread of an infection – and she'd alerted Rosalie to the plight of little June. She frowned at the thought of the little girl's injuries. So many children in the district were ill-treated and she couldn't possibly help them all, but those that came to her attention would be looked after and cared for. She just wished she could stop the cruelty but it was a huge task . . .

Kathy finished her work in the kitchens and got ready to go home. Her husband Bert was still working, but she had a half day and she was almost reluctant to leave. Here there were people to talk to and have a laugh with but at home her mother would be grumbling as usual. Nothing Kathy ever did was quite right, even though she tried hard to please.

Bert could do no wrong in his mother-in-law's eyes but Kathy had only to suggest that she did one of the jobs her mother normally did and it brought down a ton of complaints on her head.

Matron had asked Kathy if anything was wrong, but she couldn't tell her – it would be disloyal, for one thing, and for another it would sound as if she were the one complaining. It wasn't that she didn't love her mother, she did – but perhaps two women living in the same house would never quite agree.

Kathy wished now and then that they had decided to live in their own house when they married, but her mum had offered to take them in and, as Bert said, it made sense.

Sighing, Kathy decided to buy a nice cream cake for tea from Lavender and Lace, the lovely little teashop around the corner that all the nurses liked to buy special treats from. Kathy liked them too, but Mum thought it was a waste of money – well, it was her money and for once she was going to do as she liked and take a treat home that they would all enjoy.

She thought about what Matron had been telling her about Lady Rosalie's orphans and wondered how folk could be cruel to young children. Kathy loved going up to the children's ward; she liked talking and playing with the children but couldn't stop long because she always had work to do.

It would be nice to foster one of those unfortunate kids, Kathy thought – or to have a child of her own. A smile touched her mouth. If she was living in her own home, she would have had a little girl or boy to live with her and be glad to help with some of Matron's hard luck stories, but of course it wasn't her house and her mother would say she had too much to do already – but Kathy had a big heart and perhaps one day she would have a family to match . . .

CHAPTER 7

Danny opened his eyes and looked about him. It was dark in this place, darker than it had been in the house he'd first been taken to and he thought they were somewhere near the docks from the sounds coming from outside. He'd heard hooting from barges on the river earlier, when a little light had still shown through the high windows, and the noise of a crane working – at least, he thought it was a crane. Once he'd heard men's voices coming from outside and he'd tried to call out to alert them but Jake had been there and had hit him hard just above his ear and knocked him to the ground. Danny had lost consciousness then and it was dark now that he was awake again.

'Are you awake, Danny?' he heard the soft timid voice of the little girl he now knew was called Marjorie and felt the touch of her small hand on his. She'd clung to him after he'd arrived at the house and he'd tried to comfort her through that first night and the next day until they were all given something to drink that made them fall asleep. When he'd woken, he'd found they were all still together and he was one of the last to wake.

'They give yer more ter make sure you was knocked out,' Ron told him when Danny tried to stand and fell back, his head spinning. 'I heard that bugger Ron say as you were a troublemaker.'

Danny had felt sick and his head was pounding. He'd sat on the floor until the dizziness passed and Marjorie had sat next to him, her shoulder against his, seeking warmth.

'I'm cold, Danny,' she'd told him. 'I'm hungry . . .'

'Yes, so am I,' Danny had agreed. His stomach ached because he hadn't eaten since he'd been given those fish and chips. He thought the men were keeping them hungry to subdue them and he felt the anger ball inside him. If he had something sharp, he would stick it into Jake the next time he came near him.

'Are you all right?' Marjorie asked now and Danny looked at her. She was only eight and looked so small and vulnerable that he felt protective of her. Those wicked devils had stolen her from the street outside her front garden when her mother was hanging out the washing in the back garden. She'd screamed and kicked but they'd bundled her into a van and driven off with her and she was terrified and often cried for her mother. 'I was worried when you didn't move after that man hurt you.'

'I'm all right, Marjorie,' Danny told her and put his arm around her, trying to instil some warmth into her frail body. 'I'll try to protect you as much as I can.'

Tears filled her blue eyes. 'What will they do to us, Danny?' she asked. She sniffed and wiped her nose on the sleeve of her coat which was blue and looked better than most of what the others were wearing. Danny thought she must have been taken from a better area. Her parents were probably frantic with worry, and they were right to worry, because unless he and Ron could find a way for them all to escape the future looked frightening for all of them.

'I don't know – but it isn't nice and it's against the law to hold us here like this,' Danny said. 'We're going to try to get out of here when they open that door, so you stick close to me, Marjorie. Run when I tell you to . . . do you promise?'

Marjorie nodded vigorously and her hand held on to his. He knew she was frightened and he tried to be brave and strong for her, even though, underneath, he was nervous himself. He would do what he could to get away from here, but he wasn't going without Marjorie and the others could come if they were quick enough. He knew Ron had been telling the other boys what their plan was: to all attack the men they feared at the same time, kicking, scratching and biting at once so they were overwhelmed. It wasn't much against men armed with drugs that could knock them out, men who had far more strength than them, but since they had no weapons it was all they could do. They had to fight or they were lost!

'I shall be glad to get off duty,' Constable Steve Jones remarked to his fellow officer after they'd finished pounding the beat allotted to them that evening. He stamped his feet to instil a little warmth into them. 'I suppose we'd better check out the information that docker gave us and then we can get off to the station for a cuppa. It will probably be a waste of time, but we've got to show willing.'

'Too bleedin' right,' Constable Reed agreed and grinned at him. He was a tall, thin man, new to the station and eager to earn his place amongst his colleagues. 'Even he said it's probably nothing – a light flickering last night in the old abandoned Hudson warehouse was probably vagrants sheltering overnight, but then he thought he heard a child scream this morning when he went into work and it's been playing on his mind so he decided to report it. So we need to make sure – especially with that little girl being reported missing Thursday last week.'

Some of their colleagues had already searched the docks looking for little Marjorie Lacey but so far there was no sign of her. The search was still going on but hope had faded of finding her alive. It was thought she must have wandered away and they were considering dragging the river for her body.

'The place has been empty, for years,' Constable Steve Jones said. 'The import firm it belonged to went out of business and for a while a gang of thieves took it over to store their ill-gotten goods, but we put most of them away last winter.'

They were approaching the warehouse now and it was immediately clear that the derelict building was once again being used, because the bar and padlock had been taken off and the door was slightly open. Constable Jones sent a warning look at his colleague and received a nod of understanding in return. Both men grasped their truncheons, determined looks on their faces. If someone was up to no good it was their job to sort it out.

Pausing outside the door, they heard a cry of alarm

and then a child's scream, followed by more yells. Galvanised into action Constable Jones wrenched the door open and charged in, followed closely by his colleague. One young boy and a small girl were huddled together under the guard of one disreputable rogue, while two others were holding a second boy on the ground. Another two slightly bigger lads were attacking the abusers with feet and fists and yelling.

Constable Jones' truncheon crunched against the neck of the man attacking the lad and Constable Reed hit the second man in the face. The rogue went down with a grunt and stayed down as a third man came charging in like a bull but the young constable swung his truncheon, hitting him three times in the face until he went down on his knees, blood streaming from a cut over his eyebrow.

'Bloody pigs,' the first man muttered as he fought back with his fists, but he was no match for an infuriated Constable Jones and went down after the fourth blow on his shoulder. Constable Reed kicked the man at his feet in the side but was warned by his more experienced colleague.

'Reasonable force,' he barked. 'Put your cuffs on him, mate.'

Constable Jones cuffed his own prisoner, resisting the urge to beat the filthy beast to a pulp. He knew how his colleague felt, but he also knew their superiors would kick up a fine dust if they worked the offenders over. It was dinned into their heads all the time that their duty was to apprehend and leave the punishment to others, no matter how much they would love to give the bastards what they deserved.

The boy who had been on the floor was shaking and another one of them was holding the side of his head, but the one protecting the girl was pale and angry. His eyes smouldered with resentment as he looked at the men now being ordered to stand up by the police constables.

'Why don't yer kill the buggers?' he said bitterly. 'It's what they deserve. I'd 'ave done fer 'im if I could.'

'And what's your name, young 'un?' Constable Jones asked.

The boy hesitated for a moment, then, 'Danny. I thought 'e was all right 'cos he give me fish and chips, but 'e's the worst of the lot.'

'You've learned a useful lesson then, Danny,' Steve said. 'It's best not to trust strangers – unless they're police officers or men who have been introduced to you by someone you know well.' He paused, then said quietly, 'Have you been hurt?'

'Only cuts and bruises – but I'm not sure about the other two, or what they had in store for me and Marjorie. They brought us all 'ere last night because they were goin' ter sell us to some bloke but 'e didn't turn up so they got drunk.'

'Good lad,' Constable Jones nodded to his colleague. 'Go and get some help here, mate. We need an ambulance for the children.' He glanced down at the men lying battered and bruised on the ground and then at the one he'd forced to his knees and cuffed. 'I'll take this one to the station.' He saw that Danny looked nervous and took his helmet off. 'You're not in trouble, lad. You seem bright to me and you can likely give me some more information.'

'Look out, sir!'

Constable Jones moved sharply as the cuffed man lunged at him. This time he used his fists and felt a satisfactory crunch as the man's jaw cracked under his hammer blows and he fell to his knees with a groan. Steve Jones shot a look of triumph at his victim.

'I'm an amateur boxing champion, you bit of shit, and that was sweet. Try it again and I'll break your ribs. Just have another go. Please. I'd love an excuse to do for you once and for all. Think yourself lucky I stick within the law!'

The man spat at his boots but Constable Jones didn't rise to the provocation. He knew the police doctor would question him rigorously about the man's injuries. Glancing at the smaller boys, he felt shocked to his core that these men could take advantage of these vulnerable children in this way. They were cruel and heartless, using them for their own ends and ruining their young lives.

'Tell your friends I'm sorry,' he said to Danny. 'Tell them they will be going to the hospital, where they will be safe and cared for.'

'All right – what about me?' Danny asked, his jaw jutting defiantly.

Steve looked at him, smiled and nodded. 'I'm going to take you to the police station and get a statement. After that I'll give you a cup of tea and a bacon sandwich – and then we'll see.'

'Danny has been through a rotten time,' Constable Steve Jones said to the matron of the Rosie three hours later. 'I've left him with Sister Matthews. He'll be all right with her, I know – but I thought I'd better tell you Danny's history.'

'He was one of the children they hadn't physically abused,' Matron said and the look on her face spoke volumes. 'Why was that do you suppose?'

'He said he fought them off and I think you'll find he's got a few fresh bruises – and some old ones. Danny was badly beaten by his father which is why he went on the run a few days ago. He couldn't remember exactly how long, but he thinks it might be a week or a bit more.

'How did he get picked up?'

'He was hungry and a man offered him food – told him he would show him where the Sally Army Hall was and that they would give him a bed for the night. Danny trusted him because his mum had told him the Sally Army was all right, but they locked him in a house in a dingy alley with the others and then moved them to the warehouse to be taken away by someone on a ship.' He shook his head. 'They would have been sold overseas and that would have been the end of them.'

'My God! It sticks in your throat,' Matron declared, furious now.

Steve nodded. 'I wanted to kill them – but I'm trained to obey the law.'

She nodded her understanding. 'Could Danny tell you where the house was?'

Steve nodded and smiled in satisfaction. 'He's a bright boy and when he realised what was happening to him, he started taking notice. He said the name of the alley was Treacle Lane and it was the fifth house down on the left and the window has a crack in it.'

'Very bright boy,' Matron said and looked surprised. 'I don't think many lads would have noticed that sort of detail.'

'His mum told him always to take notice of things so he could tell her,' Steve said, nodding. 'I knew there was something special about him so that's why I chose him to give evidence. His friend's name is Ron and he's been taken to another hospital while the little girl has been restored to her parents after a health check.'

'I am very glad to hear it,' Matron said. 'At least we have one happy ending.'

'Her mother cried. She'd been blaming herself for not watching Marjorie and I think her husband half-blamed her too – but they have their daughter back and they're lucky. Had a conscientious docker not reported what he saw and heard, she might have disappeared forever.'

'Poor little thing,' Matron said and now she looked angry. 'If I had my way men like that would hang.'

'The law doesn't allow for that – unless we can prove a child has died because of what they've done, but I know they will be put away for a long time. We caught them red-handed and we'll make sure they don't breathe fresh air again for years.' His eyes took on a grim look.

Matron nodded. 'They deserve all they get. And you say the other children have been taken elsewhere?'

'To the London Hospital, because they were in a bad way. The older one isn't talking but I think he has been on the streets a while,' Steve said. 'We know there's a gang trading in children – these brutes were planning to sell the children on to them, but when the buyer didn't turn up, they took their anger out on the kids. I dread to think what might have happened if we hadn't got there when we did.'

Matron crossed herself. 'Dear God, what is the world coming to? Men do such evil things sometimes – may the Good Lord forgive them and protect our children.'

'It's a terrible world, Matron,' Constable Jones said. 'It makes me sick to my guts sometimes – and this is the tip of the iceberg, believe me, though we manage to find some of the missing kids before it's too late.'

'I thought we had put that kind of thing behind us in Victorian times . . . Well, we'll be glad to take Danny,' Matron said shaking her head in distress. 'It's the least we can do – and you can be certain he will be safe here with us until Lady Rosalie can find a foster home for him.'

Constable Jones put on his helmet and smiled at her. 'We know that, Matron. My Sarah always says she knows you and Lady Rosalie will always do what you can for the kids round here. It's the reason I brought Danny here. I'm not sure what will happen to the others, because some of them will need psychiatric treatment, but Danny has a good chance of getting over this so we thought this the best place for him.'

'I'm glad you did,' she said and nodded. 'I'll go and see how he's doing shortly – and thank you for bringing him to us.'

'No, Matron, it's us that thank God for you.'

'Well, it's kind of you to say so – and don't worry about young Danny. We will look after him.' She smiled at him. 'Give my good wishes to your wife. Tell Sarah we miss her at the Rosie but she is to look after herself and enjoy preparing for her baby.'

'Thank you, Matron. I'll be off duty shortly and I shan't forget your kind words.'

He was thoughtful as he went down the stairs. Danny's history was a familiar one; abuse at home from a drunken parent sent the kids running from comparatively safe homes to the dangers of the street and those that didn't perish often ended up as child prostitutes or thieves stealing for an abusive master, unless they were fortunate enough to be picked up by the law. The kids had no idea that the misery they endured at home could get a hell of a lot worse on the streets. Danny hadn't wanted to go into an orphanage, but his experience in that warehouse had changed his mind. He could only hope the lad settled down now he'd got a chance of a better life. Some of them ran away again the first chance they got, but he had a feeling Danny might knuckle down and make something of his life. He was certainly in the right place to make it happen if he tried.

'Well, you seem well enough to me apart from those bruises,' Nurse Margaret said after she'd examined Danny. 'I'm going to give you a nice warm bath and then we'll put you in the isolation ward for a few days to make certain you haven't got anything infectious – and we'll give you something to eat.'

'Constable Jones give me a bacon butty and it weren't 'alf good,' Danny said, 'but I wouldn't mind somethin' ter drink, miss.'

'I'm sure Nurse Anne will give you whatever you like; some orange squash and a piece of cake, perhaps?'

Danny nodded. 'Yeah, thanks. I ain't 'ad proper cake fer a while, not since me mum died.'

'Was your mum good to you, Danny?' Margaret smiled at him kindly.

'Yes, miss,' he said. 'We were all right until she died and then me dad took to the drink – you won't make me go back to him, will you?'

'No, Danny, I'm sure you will be allowed to stay here until a safe home is found for you. If your father asked for custody the magistrates would refuse because of what he did to you – but I don't think he'll ask, do you?'

'Nah, probably wouldn't want me if'n he knew where I was. Glad ter get rid, if yer knew the truth.'

Margaret laughed and shook her head. 'I'm going to give you that bath now.' She gave him an encouraging look as he hung back. 'The water is lovely and warm, Danny. Now, do you want me to wash your back, or do you want to do it yourself?'

'I can wash meself but I ain't sure what ter do wiv the water – ain't 'ad a bath in a tub like this afore,' Danny said as she led the way into the shining clean bathroom and he saw the gleaming white bath with its steaming water.

'You just pull the plug to let it go, but don't worry, I'll be here to help. I'll leave you for a minute or two; I'm going to bring you some clean clothes and then we'll take you to the isolation ward until the doctor takes a look at you. You'll be by yourself for a while.'

'All right, nurse,' Danny said. 'I itch all over. I reckon I got fleas – and Mum would go mad if she knew.'

'Your clothes are filthy and torn, so we'll throw them away and you'll have new ones and once we've washed your hair with our special shampoo you'll be rid of any creatures. Don't worry, Danny, we have lots of children who have worse things than you. Just give yourself a good wash and you'll feel a lot better.' Nurse Margaret smiled at him as she prepared to leave.

Danny wondered if he should tell this nice lady about the ache in his midriff. Some of the other bruises hurt more, but the ache was unpleasant and he'd had it for a while now – since a few hours after his father had kicked him, but it was gradually getting worse.

Yet they seemed to think there was nothing wrong and he didn't want to make a fuss in case they sent him off somewhere else. The other kids had gone to the big hospital and might end up anywhere, perhaps overseas for all Danny knew. He'd heard Mum complaining more than once about children being sent to Australia or Canada and he didn't want to go to either place. It didn't seem too bad here, and after his recent experience he wanted to stay where it was safe and warm for a bit, so he would keep quiet about the discomfort he was feeling and hope it would go away . . .

CHAPTER 8

'How are you feeling, my love?' Constable Steve Jones asked his wife as she turned to look at him. She was wearing a pretty floral apron over her maternity dress and to him she glowed, her beauty increasing with every day that passed. 'Matron sent you her love and said to take care of yourself.'

'You look tired – was it a rough night?' Sarah asked her husband. She went to put her arms around him and hold him, loving the strength and solidity of him and his smell. 'I love you, Constable Jones.'

'I love you, Mrs Jones.' Steve smiled and bent to kiss the top of her head. 'Something smells good.'

'Bacon, egg, and bubble and squeak,' Sarah said. 'I know that's your favourite – and a fried tomato, of course.'

'You spoil me . . .'

'I intend to,' Sarah assured him. 'You need something warming inside, Steve, after a long night on the beat.'

'It was particularly rough tonight,' he replied, frowning as he remembered. 'We took some boys to hospital and there are now some rogues in the cells who should never be allowed out!'

'Oh Steve!' Sarah looked distressed. She didn't need to be told what he meant in so many words. Having worked at the Rosie for years, she knew all about abused and damaged children. 'I'm glad you caught those evil men.'

'We had a tip-off from a docker,' Steve said with a slight frown, 'And I wonder if he's in danger. The rogues we took in were only a small part of the abuse and I don't think for one moment we've stopped it. We've cut off a few tentacles but of course they'll just grow more.'

'You do all you can,' Sarah soothed. 'That club you and your friends run does a lot of good, Steve – look at Jamie and his friends. He is doing so well in the police cadets and he can defend himself against the bullies these days.' The previous year, Steve had helped a young lad who had been bullied to stand firm against the perpetrators and to make friends, too.

He nodded, smothering his sigh. 'Yes, we do what we can, same as Matron does what she can – and your mum. She took Ned in and Charlie lives with her now he has his apprenticeship. Gwen is a blooming marvel if you ask me.'

'Mum is rather wonderful,' Sarah said fondly. 'Do you know, I think she's courting a man from the friendship club she attends? She hasn't said anything yet but there's a look in her eyes – she's having fun!'

'Well, good for her,' Steve said and grinned as his wife set the plate of hot food in front of him. 'She deserves all the happiness she can get, love.'

'She certainly does,' Sarah agreed. 'I just want her to be happy. She loved my dad but they weren't always happy towards the end. He wasn't well but he hid it from her and she thought he was skiving off work when he was in too much pain to do anything much.'

'He should've told her,' Steve agreed. 'Whatever it is, it should never be a secret between husband and wife – not if they want their love to stay bright.'

Sarah nodded, agreeing with him. 'I hope this friendship turns out well for her. She hasn't told me much yet – but that might be because she thinks I will criticise her for caring about someone else too soon after Dad's death.'

'You wouldn't mind?' Steve looked at her, a forkful of bubble and squeak halfway to his mouth. Sarah shook her head. 'No, of course you wouldn't – but perhaps she just isn't sure yet.'

His wife smiled. 'I think you're right. You know Mum well. She likes you so much, Steve. She would probably talk to you.'

'I'll pop round this evening on my way to work,' he promised and tucked into his meal with gusto. It was hard work being a bobby on the beat in London's East End and this would set him up a treat.

'Three cases of measles?' Sister Rose arched her delicate eyebrows when Margaret told her the news the next morning. 'That is really unfortunate. Matron must be worried, because we could easily have a lot more of the children going down with it.' Measles was a highly infectious disease that anyone could catch; it spread quickly between children and could be dangerous if the child was already ill from another underlying condition.

'She's imposed a strict quarantine on all wards,' Margaret said. 'She asked me to tell the kitchen girls to make sure to knock and leave the trolleys outside the door. Kathy came in and got sent off with a flea in her ear! All visitors are banned from the wards until the outbreak is over – and Nurse Anne's mother telephoned to say she won't be in this evening, because she's taken it.'

'Now that *is* serious; it means we'll be short staffed again. Poor Anne, she will feel it having to stay at home when she knows we need her.' Sister Rose sighed; it never rained but it poured. 'And you say some of the adults have it as well?'

'It seems that a gall bladder surgery case brought it into the infirmary,' Margaret told her. 'She was brought in as an emergency and operated on that same night but although her surgery went well, she was running a fever. Matron called Dr Clark out the other evening, because she was worried about her. He suspected some sort of prior sickness and advised Matron to move the patient – she's called Edie Simpson – into isolation. She wasn't showing any other symptoms then, but lo and behold, the spots have now come out.'

'Poor lady,' Rose said sympathetically. 'It's bad enough to have an operation on a gall bladder but then to have the measles on top! No wonder she wasn't making progress.'

'Yes, she was quite poorly but Matron was relieved when the cause showed itself. She'd wondered if the infection was internal – which might have meant there was not much chance for Edie then, but the measles will go and apparently the sponging and soothing drinks are now helping to take down that fever.'

Rose nodded. Measles could be an extremely nasty illness, causing many unpleasant consequences such as deafness or fits in vulnerable patients but could also be quite mild.

'Well, it's a good thing all the sufferers are now in isolation and we must all be very careful about hand-washing and clean aprons, Nurse Margaret.'

'Yes, Sister.'

'Now, tell me, have we had any new cases brought in to our ward?'

'Yes, Sister.' Nurse Margaret handed her the report Sister Matthews had written before she went off duty. 'There is a young boy – well, he says he's thirteen soon but although he's very skinny he looks quite big and strong for his age. Nurse Sarah's husband brought him in last night – he'd been snatched from the streets and beaten but he wasn't abused like some of the other lads.'

Rose frowned as the nurse recounted what Constable Jones had told her about the boys being abducted and abused and felt slightly sick. Disgust wouldn't cover what she felt about men who could do that sort of thing – well, in her opinion, they weren't men, they were evil monsters.

'Poor child,' she said now, feeling the sting of tears but blinking them back. 'I hope they throw the culprits in the deepest darkest cell and throw away the key!'

'That's what my mum always says about that sort,' Nurse Margaret agreed and then blushed. 'Sorry, Sister . . .'

Rose ignored her blushes. 'Danny's injuries – they are just bruises from the beatings?'

'Yes, so Sister Matthews said. He is down for a visit from Dr Clark today but he seems quite perky. I was told he ate his breakfast this morning and wants to get up.'

Rose nodded. Nurse Margaret had been on duty since six that morning while Rose's shift on duty hadn't started until half-past ten. She didn't like this late start, because it always felt as if she had to run to catch up.

'I'll go and see him now – hear what he has to say for himself.'

Danny Bryant was sitting up in bed reading an old comic and seemed absorbed when she approached him, but the moment she got close he glanced up and, briefly, she saw fear flicker in his eyes. It faded the moment he saw her smile and he grinned cheekily.

'Mornin', Sister,' he chirped. 'Yer a bit late in, ain't yer?'

'Yes, I didn't start until half-past ten,' Rose replied, feeling amused by his observation. He was a bright boy and she had no doubt he'd been subjected to long-standing abuse. That instant reaction to someone coming close wasn't due just to his abduction – and she could see old bruises along with the fresh ones. 'Do you mind if I sit on the edge of your bed and talk to you, Danny?'

'Nah, 'course not,' he said obligingly. 'What can I do fer yer, Sister Rose?'

'How do you know I'm Sister Rose?'

'Because yer looked after me mum on the women's ward when she was sick.' Danny looked at her consideringly. 'You was real kind to her and she got better that time.'

'What was wrong with her, Danny?'

'Me dad said she had a weak 'eart,' Danny said and his eyes brimmed with tears, which he swiped away with the back of his hand. 'I dunno – but she just got weaker and weaker and then one mornin' she didn't wake up. Dad tried to make her but he couldn't. I saw him cryin' – I ain't ever seen him like that, 'ceptin' that time.'

'I expect you cried too, didn't you, Danny?'

'Yeah – she was me mum. Best mum ever. Dad was all right when she was 'ere.'

'Did he change after your mother died, Danny?'

'Yeah, 'e started drinking and that.' Danny's gaze fell away. 'Dad would belt me fer tellin' tales, but it's the truth and Mum always said ter tell the truth and shame the devil.'

'Where is your father now, Danny?'

'Dunno,' he replied and frowned. 'He came home drunk about ten days ago and belted the life out of me. I blacked out and when I woke up, he was snoring on the couch so I made a run fer it while I could. I took a few bits of me grandad's but they got pinched. I daren't go back 'ome 'cos he'd kill me.'

'I don't think we could let you go back to someone who treats you like that,' Rose said. 'I think Matron will let you stay here until we can find a safe place for you – either an orphanage or a foster home.'

'What's a foster 'ome?'

'It's a safe place where people who like young people take children without parents in and look after them, so it's like having a new mum and dad, sort of.'

Danny digested that in silence. 'I suppose it would

79

be all right. I thought I could manage on the streets, find a few jobs ter buy food – but it ain't safe out there, Sister Rose.'

'You've learned a valuable lesson then, Danny.'

'Yeah, reckon I 'ave,' he said and grinned at her. 'Know what I'd like, Sister?'

'Why don't you tell me, Danny?' Rose invited with an encouraging smile.

'I reckon the best thing in the world is makin' good food what folk like to eat,' he said with a serious look. 'Mum used to cook like an angel – leastways, that's what Dad said. He was always happy when she fed him a lovely dinner or a piece of her angel cake; light and soft that was and tasted luverly.'

'Is that what you'd like to do when you leave school – cook food for others?'

'Yeah . . .' Danny looked thoughtful. 'Dad said it was only fer sissies when I helped me mum cook cakes, but I liked it and she said I was good at it.'

'Well, I think it is a lovely idea,' Rose said. 'And your dad is wrong – there are a lot of men who cook good food – a man who cooks is called a chef.'

'Yeah? Yer ain't kiddin me?' Danny looked intrigued, his eyes alight with wonder.

'No, I wouldn't do that.' Rose smiled at him. 'Perhaps if you work hard at school you will become a chef when you're older.'

'I'd like that and then I'd bake a special cake fer you, Sister.'

'I shall hold you to that,' Rose said and stood up. 'I have other patients to see, Danny. Doctor will come and visit you soon – and then you may get a visit from

Lady Rosalie. She's a nice lady who will try to find you a suitable home with decent people.'

'Thanks, Sister.' Danny went back to reading his comic and Rose began her tour of the ward.

Danny was a brave boy and she hoped a good home could be found for him. She would make sure that Matron and Lady Rosalie knew of his ambition to become a chef, though she doubted he would be lucky enough to be placed with a family of cooks. Danny would be put on a list with others until an available suitable family could take him.

CHAPTER 9

Lily rushed to open the front door as the bell rang. She felt the joy of seeing her lover rush through her when she found Chris standing there and, a moment later, she was in his arms being thoroughly kissed and hugged.

'My darling,' he murmured huskily against her hair. 'I missed you so much – and it was murder not being able to write or receive your letters!'

'Come in,' she whispered. 'Oh, Chris! When you left, I wondered if I would ever see you again. But why are you back? I didn't expect you to be for ages yet.'

'No, nor did I,' he admitted and then his head bent and he gazed down into her eyes, touching her cheek lightly with his forefinger. 'Oh, I adore you, Lily! All those months I wasted not knowing my own heart. I'm so sorry,' Chris said, remembering how he'd courted Lily's sister Jenny for months until she realised she wasn't in love with him and only then had Lily let her own feelings show. The white-hot passion between them had flared swiftly and they'd become lovers. 'I wasted so much time and now—'

'Hush . . .' She placed her fingers to his lips. 'It doesn't matter, Chris. We have each other now and that is all that matters.' Smiling up at him, she drew him into the warmth of the cosy kitchen. 'Jenny is on duty tonight – we have the house to ourselves . . .'

'Lucky me,' he said and drew her into a passionate embrace. 'But can you continue to love me and trust me if I come and go with no explanations, as I must, Lily?'

'Yes, I can and I do.' Her eyes were soft with love and the trust he asked for. 'You make me happy, Chris, and that's all I need.'

'I don't know why you should love me,' he murmured but the words were lost as she kissed him.

'Let's go to bed, darling,' Lily whispered against his mouth. 'We can talk later . . .'

Smiling, they held hands as they went up to Lily's room. Chris looked about him at the neat plain furnishings that had their own simple charm, then smiled. 'This looks so right for you, Lily. Now, when I lie awake at night, I'll be able to picture you here, my love.'

Lily turned to him, letting him take her into his arms. He kissed her so sweetly with such longing that the flame was soon burning fiercely between them and they undressed each other, fumbling with buttons and zips and laughing as they tossed unwanted garments away in their haste to make love, but not before Chris had put on the protection necessary to keep his beloved safe. Then they were lying on the spotless white sheets on Lily's bed, flesh to flesh, warm and sensual, aware of each tingling sensation as they made love with all the delight of true lovers starved of each other's presence for too long.

Afterwards, when they lay satiated with physical pleasure, desire quenched for the moment, Chris stroked the satin softness of her back and sighed with content.

'Only you, Lily,' he murmured throatily. 'Only you would take me so willingly to your bed with such love and trust after I'd been away for months with no word.'

'I had one letter to say you would come soon . . .'

He looked long and deep into her eyes. 'It's all I can give for a while, my darling – is it enough?'

'No, of course not,' she admitted and moved in closer. 'I want to sleep with you by my side every night, be your wife and have a family – but I know that isn't possible yet.'

'One day,' he promised. 'When this sordid business is over . . .'

'When will it end?' she asked and then shook her head. 'No, I shouldn't ask. You warned me that you couldn't give me those things until your work was done.'

'I was lonely and I wanted you so badly,' he said. 'I'm here for two days, Lily . . .' He hesitated then, 'We could marry secretly, my darling – I obtained a special licence the last time I was here, but you can't tell anyone – not even Jenny.'

Lily's sudden surge of excitement was stilled. 'We could marry but I can't tell anyone?'

'If it was discovered I'd been back to England and married I should be vulnerable. You know why . . .'

Of course, Lily knew why she couldn't have a proper wedding. His work as a spy in Hitler's Germany was dangerous and, if his true allegiance was discovered, he would be shot as a traitor. Even to be here like this could prove fatal if it were ever discovered; he ought not to have risked it but he had for her sake.

'Then we shouldn't marry,' she said. 'I should never have asked.'

Chris smiled and rolled her over so that she lay beneath him once more. 'Of course, you should; you have the right – and I want to be your husband, Lily.' He laughed down at her. 'All right, tell Jenny if you wish, but she must understand it is a secret.'

Lily reached up to kiss him. 'No, it will be just us two – and a witness you can trust, Chris. Jenny might say something without meaning to. I refuse to do anything that risks your life.'

'No wonder I adore you!'

Lily frowned. 'Are you supposed to be back here at all?'

'No. Officially I'm in Switzerland making friends for Herr Hitler – but I had the chance of a flight home unofficially. I'm not even in the country. I didn't go through passport control.'

'You took such a risk!' She looked at him in concern. 'If you should be missed . . .'

'I'm supposed to be on a trip to a mountain retreat,' he said and hushed her with a kiss. 'You were worth the risk, my love.'

Lily put her arms around him, holding him tightly, her eyes damp with tears. For Chris to take such a risk just to be with her made her feel humbled and loved.

She wanted to hold him forever but knew that his visit could be no more than the two days he'd promised. It had to be enough, though it never could be.

Lily was sitting eating her breakfast alone when Jenny got home at eight thirty the next morning. She looked happy and relaxed, a hint of excitement in her eyes that made Jenny wonder.

'Has something happened?' she asked. There was a different smell in the kitchen, but she couldn't be sure what it was. Mixed with the odour of toast was a faint scent of cedar . . . much like the lotion Chris had used as a shaving aid. 'Has Chris been here?'

Lily got up to put some bread in the toaster. 'Would you like two slices, Jenny?'

'Yes, thank you, that would be nice,' Jenny said. 'I'll eat it and then I'll go up to bed. You'd better hurry or you'll be late for work.'

'I've got two days off . . .'

'Really? You didn't say.' Jenny stared at her sister's back. 'You didn't answer me, Lily – Chris hasn't been here, has he?'

'No, of course not. Why do you ask?'

'I thought I could smell his cologne.'

'Oh . . .' Lily hesitated and then laughed. 'It's probably that new stuff I bought to clean the bath.'

Jenny nodded and accepted the toast her sister brought to the table, buttering it and spreading on thick-cut marmalade. She ate her toast feeling puzzled. No bath cleaner could ever smell as good as an expensive cologne: Lily wasn't telling her the truth. Yet why should she lie? Jenny had accepted that her sister was in love with Chris and Jenny couldn't complain. She'd given him up of her own free will and she didn't regret it – though sometimes she missed being taken to smart restaurants and dancing. Lily didn't do any of that and she didn't think she had many letters either. It was all a bit secret but Jenny never asked awkward questions and although she was burning to ask now she refrained, though she felt a bit hurt. If Lily had been seeing Chris here in their house, she might have told her. They were sisters, after all. Surely *they* didn't need to have secrets? And it just wasn't like Lily to lie.

'Well, I'm going to bed,' Jenny said and wiped her mouth on a napkin. 'What are you going to do with your days off?'

'Oh, this and that,' Lily said. 'I might go shopping or visit a cinema.'

'Well, enjoy yourself,' Jenny said and went upstairs to her room, feeling a bit irritated with her sister. The door to Lily's bedroom was open and Jenny went inside. The bed was made and the room was as neat as ever but the scent of cedar was even stronger here.

Chris *had* been here – here in Lily's room! Jenny was certain of it. They must be lovers and Lily just didn't want to tell her. It rankled a little but she couldn't blame Lily in a way – when she'd first met Chris, she'd wanted to keep him a secret from Lily, because it had all been too new.

Shaking her head, Jenny went into her own room and started to undress. It had been a long day on the critical ward and she was tired. The last thing she wanted was for Lily to think she was jealous of her relationship with Chris, because she wasn't. She hoped they would be happy together – but why was Lily lying to her? It left an unpleasant taste in her mouth and made her realise they were no longer as close as they had once been, and that made Jenny feel lonely. Lily was all she had, because she'd met no one she wanted to put in Chris's place.

Had she made a mistake giving him up because he couldn't spend as much time with her as she wanted? For a moment she considered and then shook her head. No, she hadn't truly been in love with Chris. She just missed someone to go out with and in time she would meet someone else.

Yawning, Jenny got into bed and closed her eyes. She was far too tired to worry about such things – and when Lily was ready, Jenny was sure she would tell her the truth.

'You look beautiful, my darling,' Chris said as they met outside the small church. 'Did you manage to get away without Jenny suspecting anything?'

'She was fast asleep,' Lily said and smiled sadly. 'I think she guessed you'd been to the house – your cologne gave it away.'

'Oh yes,' he said and frowned. 'Jenny might indeed recognise it.'

'Is it an English make?' Lily asked.

'Clever girl,' Chris said softly. 'No, it isn't – it's American and readily available in Germany. I made certain of that, that's why I continued to use it – I have to be so careful.'

A little shudder went through Lily, that such a small thing could betray him made her realise how difficult his life must be when he was in Germany.

'Oh, Chris . . .' she whispered and his arm tightened about her waist.

'Don't look so upset,' he said. 'The vicar is coming now. His wife will be our witness.'

Lily nodded and took his hand as they went to meet the friendly couple.

'Well now, Miss Lily Brown and Mr Chris Moore, I believe?' He smiled and nodded as he shook hands with them both. 'This isn't the first time my wife has stood in as a witness. I understand family problems can make things difficult for young people – and I don't ask questions. I shall ask only if you both wish to be married in the sight of God and have the necessary papers.'

'I do,' Chris said and patted his breast pocket. 'It is very good of you, sir, to arrange this for us at such short notice.'

'Say nothing of it – your donation to the church roof was much appreciated, Mr Moore.'

Lily couldn't bring herself to speak. Inside she felt tight with tension. It had made her feel uncomfortable when she'd had to lie to Jenny at breakfast and she was wishing her sister was here now. The vicar's wife was pleasant and friendly and she'd even brought Jenny some daffodils from her garden, but it wasn't the same. A wedding should be a bright, open day that you were happy to tell the world about and Lily couldn't help feeling a little sad – even though when Chris turned to smile at her, her heart jerked with love.

'One day we'll be able to tell her and the world,' Chris whispered to her as they walked from the church after the ring was on her finger. 'It's just until I can come home for good and we don't need to hide.'

'It's all right,' Lily said and smiled up at him. 'I love you and I'm happy to be your wife.' And she was, even if the shadow of missing her sister on this day still hovered at the back of her mind . . .

CHAPTER 10

'Margaret, can you come please?' Rose asked as she entered the small room at the end of the children's ward. 'Danny has been sick on the floor and collapsed. I can't wake him. I think he must be really ill.'

Margaret ran to help just as Rose wiped the child's face. His eyes flickered open then and he looked up at her. 'It hurts . . . it hurts bad, Sister . . .'

'Where does it hurt, Danny?' He gestured at his side and Rose lifted his pyjama jacket; she drew a sharp breath as she saw the dark bruise that had come out on his skin. 'How long have you had this?' she asked but he shook his head, obviously feeling too unwell to answer. 'We ought to have noticed it when you came in; this must have caused you pain for a while. Why didn't you tell us, Danny?'

Danny's eyes focused on her. 'It just ached there before, after me dad kicked me, then when those men beat me yesterday it got worse.' He looked at her fearfully. 'If the cops go after me dad, he'll 'alf kill me!'

'Yes, I see,' Rose said and felt angry with the people who had made him so fearful. 'Well, I'm going to put you to bed again, Danny. I'm going to call the doctor to you, but don't worry, I'll be with you all the time.'

She turned to Margaret, who had cleared up the mess on the floor. 'Give me a hand to lift him. I'm going to ask Dr Clark to come out to him as soon as he can, but I want to give him a little wash first.'

'Yes, Sister,' Margaret said and moved to help lift the child into a more comfortable position. Danny groaned, even though he was clearly trying not to.

Rose looked at him and gently touched his hand. 'I'm going to leave you for a few minutes, but the doctor will come soon and we'll give you something to make you feel a bit better.'

Rose felt a bit worried by the dark bruising but knew that she mustn't make snap judgements. It might just be a case of gastroenteritis or something similar. Yet she knew that the child had been beaten, by his father and then by the men who had kidnapped him.

The thought crossed her mind that he ought to have been under close supervision and would have been had it not been for the outbreak of measles. Fortunately, it had been contained and only five patients had gone down with it. Knowing that it could have been much worse, Rose thought they'd got away with it lightly, but now she wondered if it had been at the expense of another child's suffering. Of course, Danny should have told them he was in pain, but he was obviously used to putting up with his injuries and hadn't wanted to cause a fuss – she just hoped that he wouldn't suffer too badly because of it.

Half an hour later, Rose listened to the doctor's verdict and felt even more anxious.

'It might be just a severe attack of a stomach bug, though I don't like the look of that bruising,' Dr Clark told her. 'But you were right to call me out, and I am going to have you keep him under strict observation and I'll order various tests and an X-ray. There's something I don't like the look of . . . can't put my finger on it, but we'll find out.'

'I think we should have kept a more careful watch on him,' Rose said, feeling awful. 'I know we've been worrying about the patients going down with measles but still, it ought to have been noticed before this.'

'Yes, it might appear careless,' he agreed, 'but I know you do all you can here. You mustn't blame yourself, Sister Rose. He should have told us he was in pain.' Despite his words she sensed disapproval and felt that he was reprimanding her, though that might have been her own guilt.

'I talked to him, but he didn't show any sign of being in severe pain – but he must have been.' Rose felt upset. She looked at Danny as he lay with his eyes closed. Dr Clark had given him a sedative to ease the pain and he seemed to be breathing more easily. Once again, she felt drawn to Peter Clark in a way a nurse shouldn't. As for Danny, she knew it was foolish to become too attached to a patient, especially when he would be moving on to a new home when he was better – but he certainly couldn't be moved yet, that much was certain. And she would do her utmost to make sure that he was given all the care and attention he needed while he was in her care.

'I'm sorry, Matron,' Rose said when her superior came to visit Danny later that morning. 'He isn't really well enough for Lady Rosalie to take him yet – perhaps in a couple of weeks, depending on how bad his injuries are internally.'

'One of us ought to have noticed something,' Matron said frowning. 'It's unlike Sister Matthews not to notice something like this and she admitted him – but I would've expected you to notice it and summon a doctor sooner.'

'Yes, but Danny was old enough to wash and dress himself, and deliberately hid his pain in order to protect his father or prevent him attacking him again, so a small part of the blame is his own, but I do agree that we should all have taken better care of him.' Rose felt she deserved the reprimand and it stung that she'd failed in her duty of care.

'Poor little boy,' Matron said, shaking her head in distress. 'Well, I shall ring Lady Rosalie and tell her that the family visit she had arranged must be cancelled and if it means another child is fostered in his place, Danny goes back on the list.'

'I did tell you he is very interested in cooking?'

'Yes, but unfortunately the candidates for foster homes do not get to choose, Sister Rose. Much as I would like to place him with the owner of a restaurant, it is unlikely to happen.'

'We have to hope that he will be well enough to be placed with a family at all,' Rose said, biting her lip. 'I feel so responsible, Matron. If he should become worse . . .' Her usual calm, professional manner had deserted her and she was close to tears.

'None of that, Sister!' Matron said sharply. 'You have a ward to run. Your nurse has been looking after him and she should have picked up that something was wrong. Tell me, is Margaret James up to the job?'

'Oh yes, she seems very caring,' Rose said instantly, because she was the senior nurse and the blame was hers alone.

'I asked if she was capable, not caring.' Matron frowned. 'I am very disappointed this has happened, Sister Rose, but we must do what we can to see it doesn't affect his chances in life – and make certain he has the best treatment available.'

'Yes, Matron. I assure you he will not be neglected again.' Rose choked back her feelings. She ought to have seen Danny wasn't right sooner and she must carry the guilt if anything should happen to him due to her neglect . . .

'Good!' Matron nodded briskly and walked off, leaving Rose feeling flattened. Matron sighed. Rose was clearly blaming herself for Danny but, in the end, Matron knew she was ultimately responsible. And *she'd* visited him and noticed nothing amiss. However, Dr Clark had him in hand and he should be fine now . . .

CHAPTER 11

'Well, then, Jessie,' Peter Clark asked as the old lady entered his room at the free clinic. 'What is it this time – your feet or your back?' He smiled at her, watching her eyes spark with mischief. He knew the real reason she came every week was to see him and for the few bob he always slipped her for a cup of tea, only sometimes because she had a genuine complaint.

'It's me chest, doc,' she said and wheezed convincingly. 'Really bad it's been these past few days.'

Peter hadn't seen any sign of a bad chest when she'd tucked into her free lunch at the mission hall but didn't contradict her. Instead, he listened to her chest, which sounded fine, tapped her back, then had a look at her feet – the yellowed toenails had been clipped short only a week ago and she no blisters on her feet. He smiled and nodded – his diagnosis was right, she just needed a little chat, a cup of tea and a bottle of his tonic, which she believed cured all manner of things.

Twenty minutes later she went off with her tonic, some ointment for her feet, half a crown for a cup of tea and a smile on her face. Peter was smiling too. He enjoyed his little sessions with the brave old lady, who had lived a chequered life. The saucy quips she'd came out with had him chuckling again as he washed his hands and prepared for his next patient, this time a man with a genuine cough and wheezy chest.

Three hours and twenty-odd patients later, Peter chatted to the nurse that assisted him and then left the clinic. He smiled as he walked along the street, acknowledging people who waved or called out a cheery greeting to him. He was well known in these streets and enjoyed the feeling of being a part of the busy life here. Men and women of all ages and walks of life came and went and most of them seemed to know him. His little car was one of the few that could be safely parked hereabouts, even though he hadn't brought it today. The first taste of spring sunshine had tempted him out and he enjoyed the exercise and the fresh air. Somewhere he could smell flowers and he looked round for the source, seeing the stall at the end of the road.

The old woman there looked up from her seat. 'Hello, doc,' she said. 'Been busy as usual?'

'Yes, Molly. I've been to the clinic.'

'Want your buttonhole, do you?'

Peter smiled and took a shilling from his pocket. She gave him a small pink flower to pin to his jacket and he paid her and then looked at the array of gorgeous flowers in her baskets. She hadn't sold many that day . . .

'How much for a bunch of the narcissus?' he asked.

'One and sixpence to anyone else – a shilling to you.'

Peter produced another shilling. The flowers were lovely but by the look of her basket she needed to sell more. 'And those tulips?'

'The same again.' Molly cackled. 'Got a young lady, 'ave yer?'

'I might have,' Peter said and smiled. 'Give me two bunches of tulips as well.'

He paid her and she smiled as she watched Peter walk towards the Rosie infirmary. The flowers he carried smelled of springtime and he could only think of one thing to do with them.

At the infirmary, Peter walked straight up to the children's ward. He saw Sister Rose bending over a child's bed and walked towards her, the flowers held behind his back.

'Good afternoon, Sister Rose,' he said and she turned to look at him.

'Oh – it's you!' she said. 'Have you called to see Danny? He seems a little better today I think.'

Peter sensed the reserve in her and his resolve failed. He couldn't offer her flowers; she would think he was mad. Bringing the flowers out, he said, 'I brought these to cheer up the children, Sister Rose – and I'll take a look at Danny. I can see you're busy . . .'

Peter walked on to the next bed without looking at her again. He felt a bit of a fool for thinking he could just give her flowers. The look in her eyes had had the coolness of a mountain stream and he would be a fool to think she was the least bit interested in flowers or a date with him . . .

Rose watched as he stopped by Danny's bed and then bent to gently pull back the covers and examine the child's side. He replaced the covers and sat beside him, talking to him and laughing.

Rose turned away as tears stung her eyes. For a moment, when he'd produced these lovely flowers, she'd thought they were for her. The disappointment had been sharp – as sharp as her answer.

Why had she spoken to him harshly? Rose didn't know, except that she'd felt he'd criticised her unfairly when she'd asked him to look at Danny's bruising. Yes, she ought to have noticed Danny was in pain and she did blame herself – but she didn't like it that both Doctor Peter and Matron had seemed to blame her. She wasn't the only senior nurse on duty . . . and yet, she told herself, it was her job and she should have known. So, she was being defensive when she ought not and that was foolish.

Rose shook her head. She had no idea why she seemed so emotionally involved both with Danny and Dr Clark. For goodness sake! She was a professional nurse and she should be able to respond to all challenges with an even, calm manner.

Dr Clark was leaving the patient now and she went up to him, giving him a cool, professional smile. '*Is* he any better?'

'Yes, I believe we've been lucky; there was no serious internal damage, just deep-tissue bruising,' Dr Clark said and nodded, every bit as cool and professional as she. 'I'll keep an eye on him – but I don't think there is much to worry about. However, let me know at once if there is any sudden change.'

'Yes, Doctor, of course.' Rose smelled the flowers. She couldn't help herself as she said, 'These are beautiful. It was kind of you to think of us on this ward.'

'My pleasure, Sister Rose. I can't think of a better

place for them – and Molly needed to sell a few bunches anyway.'

'I buy flowers from her every Friday,' Rose said and smiled. 'That was doubly kind of you. I know sometimes she finds it hard to earn a living.'

Dr Clark hesitated and then nodded. 'We all do what we can, Sister Rose. Put those in water before they fade – and goodnight.'

Rose watched him walk from the ward and then went to put the flowers in water, placing the vases about the ward so that all the children could see them and enjoy them.

Peter Clark was really a very nice man. She liked him a lot but she wasn't sure that he saw her as anything more than a nurse, one who didn't always come up to his high standards . . .

Peter walked home, stopping off for a pint at his local before going back to the small family hotel where he lived. The rates were reasonable, the breakfast was adequate and the beds were comfortable. He preferred it to living alone and sometimes chatted to the landlord and his wife before retiring. That evening he'd had a pie and a pint in the pub and it was all he needed. Sometimes he ate at the hospital canteen but mostly he would have lunch at a pub and occasionally he took a lady friend out for a restaurant meal in the evening.

There were half a dozen young women he could telephone for company if he wished, and friends and married couples who asked him to dine now and then. He wasn't a loner, but a successful young man who might have married long since if he'd found the right woman – only the one he wanted seemed wedded to her job at the infirmary and he wasn't sure whether she liked him or not.

She'd been hostile when he arrived with those foolish flowers – and yet she'd thanked him for them before he left and for a moment his heart had started to beat rapidly because those green eyes had seemed to be warm with approval and her smile had made him want to kiss her – but he could just imagine her reaction if he tried.

Ruefully, Peter shook his head. It was stupid to feel like this when the woman he liked hardly knew he was around. He should concentrate on his work and ask one of his friends out for a meal or to a concert. There was one coming up that he rather fancied so perhaps he would buy a couple of tickets and then decide who to take.

CHAPTER 12

'As you know, I always have a full list, Mary,' Lady Rosalie said when she took Matron's call the next morning. 'If Danny still isn't well enough to be fostered then someone else gets this chance – a pity, as it is a good family. However, I shall find another home for him when the time comes.'

'Yes, of course, Rosalie,' Matron replied. 'And I would prefer to keep him in hospital until he has quite recovered.' She paused, then, 'Have you heard about any of the other children who were rescued from that warehouse?'

'The little girl went home to her parents as you know and I understand she is settling well. I am sure they will not let her out of their sight for a long time! The two boys are being looked after and seem to be recovering, young people are so resilient but these boys have had a rough time, kindness and patience is what they need now – the one called Ron absconded from hospital before anyone had a chance to do anything for him!'

'Oh dear, that's unfortunate.'

'I understand the sister in charge of the ward told

him that I would visit the next day to tell him about a prospective new family – and when she turned around, he'd gone. They searched the hospital and then one of the porters said he thought he'd seen a young boy go outside and run away. He thought he'd been up to mischief and shouted at him, but he just kept on running.'

'How very unfortunate,' Matron said and Rosalie nodded, sighing. 'He will have gone back to his former life on the streets, no doubt. You would think he would have learned his lesson after what happened.'

'I think perhaps he may have had a bad experience in an orphanage and didn't want to be sent back,' Lady Rosalie replied. 'However much we try to prevent it, some of these places have employees who should never be allowed near children – and if that has happened to Ron in the past, he wouldn't trust anyone.'

'Why do people do such evil things?' Matron asked and sounded upset. 'I'm used to it, Rosalie, but I still find it impossible to understand.'

'Yes, indeed,' Lady Rosalie replied. 'I can only say that we do our best to help those we can and there is no more we can do. It is for people in high places to make the kind of laws that prevent this happening.' Lady Rosalie sighed. 'I made inquiries about little June as you asked me and we've discovered that she is known to the welfare people. Following my report, they are going to arrange for her to be taken into care – and then it seems there is a grandmother who will have her. The mother wouldn't allow it, but she will have no choice now.'

'It is so sad,' Matron said. 'I hated to let her go home but I'm glad you've told me – once the law steps in I know she will be taken to a place of safety for her own sake.'

'Yes, that is one off the list.' Lady Rosalie paused, then, 'Well, I mustn't keep you as I know you're busy.'

'Oh, I have my rounds to do but we're fairly quiet at the moment – once the weather picks up a little the cases of chest infections ease off. I think *you* keep busy all the time.'

'Yes, I have several meetings with prospective foster parents this morning – and this afternoon I am doing a handover to a new family. Shirley has been waiting for a long time and she is very excited about getting a new mummy and daddy.'

Lady Rosalie said her goodbyes and replaced the receiver. She wondered briefly about the young boy who had absconded from the hospital. It was a pity he had run away, because she might have found him a home where he could be happy, perhaps for the first time in his life. In all the blackness of poverty and abuse that brought so many orphans and unfortunate children to her notice, the goodness of some of the men and women who took them in shone out like beacons in the night.

A smile came to her face as she thought about Gwen Cartwright, one of the best of her carers. Gwen had asked if she could adopt Ned, the young boy in her care who needed special diets and lots of understanding. She'd told her that she would help her to begin the procedure and it gave her a warm feeling inside. If only she had a lot more like Gwen Cartwright on her list, she would be able to place all her current orphans in no time.

*

Gwen left her house and walked to the market to shop. Ned was at school, his tummy so much better these days that she could pack his lunch and know he would be fine. She'd told the school he couldn't have school meals, because his diet needed to be balanced, and the headmistress had been understanding and allowed him to eat his own food in the dining room with the others. Ned had told her that some of the other boys were envious of what he ate and wanted to bring their own food in now. She smiled at the notion that she'd started a new trend of healthy eating amongst Ned's school friends.

The market was busy that morning and she enjoyed what was the first really warm day of spring, taking her time to wander from stall to stall, buying only the freshest fruit and the best of the vegetables. She had plenty of time and was in no hurry, stopping to chat whenever she saw a friend or neighbour. It was when she'd finished her shopping that the voice spoke from behind her.

'Good morning, Gwen. How are you this bright spring day?'

'Good morning, Mr Thompson,' Gwen said as she turned and smiled at the man she sometimes played cards with at the friendship club they both belonged to. 'It is a little warmer today, don't you think?'

'Yes, it begins to feel like spring now,' he said. 'Well, we're now in April so it should.' His eyes dwelled on her and she was glad she'd put on a good skirt and her best red jacket. 'Shall we see you at the club tomorrow evening?'

'Yes, I think so,' Gwen told him. 'Ned and Charlie

are going to their Boy Scouts meeting so I shall drop them off there and pick them up later – we usually get some chips as we walk home which we all enjoy, though Ned can only have them once a week. It's his special treat and the doctor said he must only have a half portion. Charlie says he'll have the same – they're such good friends so I buy a packet and let them share.'

'You're good to those boys, Gwen.' Theo looked at her appreciatively.

'Thank you, Theo.'

Just as he was about to say more, a young lad darted up and tried to grab her purse from her hand. Gwen was taken by surprise and the boy would have succeeded in snatching it if Theo hadn't put out a hand and caught his arm, jerking it back firmly but without hurting him.

'What do you think you're doing, lad?' he asked gruffly. 'If you steal purses, the coppers will put you in prison so it's a bit silly, isn't it?'

The boy struggled but Theo held him tightly. 'I'm 'ungry, mister!'

'Why didn't you ask for food?' Theo said sternly. 'Thieving isn't the right way. What's your name, lad?'

'Ron.' The young boy's eyes flashed defiantly. 'If yer one of them perverts I don't want nuthin'!'

'I'm not – and nor is this lady.' Theo took the purse from Ron's hand and returned it to Gwen, while still gripping his arm.

'Let me go sir,' Ron said. 'I ain't a thief – I was just hungry and no one would give me a job.'

'I'll give you half-a-crown,' Theo said. 'Open your hand.'

Ron did so and a half-crown was deposited on his

palm. Theo let go of his arm and the lad darted away. When he was far enough off, he turned and looked back, calling, 'Thanks, mister. I'm sorry I tried to pinch yer lady's purse!' Then he was gone, disappearing into the busy market where he would no doubt buy or steal food.

Gwen looked at Theo and smiled. 'I wouldn't have thought you would just let him go, but I'm glad you did. There are only a few shillings in this purse. I never bring much with me, just in case, and I've spent most of it, but Sarah gave me the purse and I shouldn't like to lose it – so thank you, Theo.'

'It was nothing,' he said and smiled. 'Just luck I spotted him loitering and guessed what he meant to try.'

She hesitated, then, 'I was wondering whether you would like to come to supper one evening. Meet my boys . . .'

Theo's face lit up. 'I should like that very much, Gwen,' he replied. 'It is very kind of you to ask me.'

'It will make a nice change for us all,' she said. 'I'll ask Sarah to pop round later if she can.' Gwen looked thoughtful. 'She's having her first baby, you know, so she doesn't often come out at night and I don't like her walking home in the dark.'

'I could always run her home in my car if that would help – any time . . .'

'You've got a car?' Gwen looked at him in surprise. It was the first she'd heard of it.

'It's just a small Morris – and a few years old, but I keep it nice and it's useful. It might come in handy if your daughter needs to get to the hospital quickly when the baby is due.' He took a white card from his breast pocket. 'That's my telephone number, Gwen. If you ever need help just ring me – I'm home a lot of the time since I retired from my office.'

'Thank you,' Gwen put the card into her coat pocket and smiled. 'I'm going to have a cup of tea and a bun when I get home – if you wanted to come back with me for a little chat now.'

He looked so pleased that Gwen nodded to herself. She'd been reluctant to take the friendship further because she wasn't sure whether she knew him well enough. After seeing the way he'd acted with the young boy who had tried to grab her purse, Gwen felt he was the kind of man she wanted to know better. Had he hit the boy or shouted and threatened, she would have been put off but he'd been fair, firm and kind, and that meant she could trust him.

'We'll go in my car,' Theo said. 'If you've finished your shopping?'

'Yes, I only wanted a couple of things,' Gwen confirmed. He nodded and took the heavy basket from her. 'You're a kind man, Theo, and I like that.'

'And you're a lovely lady, Gwen,' he replied. 'I hope I'll always be around when you need a little help.'

CHAPTER 13

Danny moaned a little as he woke but then realised that he didn't hurt as much as he had. Sister Rose came up to him as he struggled to a sitting position and asked him how he felt.

'I'm all right, Sister,' he told her and managed a grin. 'It's a bit sore still but lots better than it was.'

'Doctor did tests as you know, Danny,' Sister Rose told him. 'He says you were lucky – the bruising was bad but it hadn't done too much harm internally so you're not damaged permanently.'

'Thanks, fer lookin' after me so good,' Danny said. He hesitated, then, 'What will happen to me when I'm better? When me mum got better, she went 'ome but I ain't got no home ter go to.' He looked so anxious and vulnerable that her heart went out to him and she sat on the edge of his bed.

'Matron is arranging something with Lady Rosalie – perhaps a foster family, as I told you before. She will let you meet the family and if you like each other you will go to live with them.' She touched his hand. 'Is that all right, Danny?'

'Yes, if they're nice,' Danny said. 'I just wish I had a mum, Sister Rose – someone like you, someone kind and gentle who would love me . . .' His face was white and strained, filled with yearning, and she felt the pull on her heart strings. This young boy was special to her and she couldn't deny it.

'I would certainly love you,' Sister Rose said, 'and I promise I'll always be your friend, Danny. If you're ever in trouble, I'll help all I can.'

'Thanks, Sister Rose.' Danny grinned at her. 'If I don't like 'em I'll run away and come back here.'

She smiled. 'I'm just so glad you're feeling better, Danny. Can I get you a drink of squash or some cocoa and a biscuit?'

'Thanks, Sister.' Danny hesitated and then put out his hand to touch hers. 'Do you know what happened to the others?'

'Matron told me that two of the boys were in a special ward being cared for while their families are traced – if they have any. Marjorie is back with her parents and Ron . . . well, he ran away.'

'Yeah, he would,' Danny said and frowned. 'I'd only been on the streets fer a while but he ran away from an orphanage six months ago 'cos he was 'urt by someone there. They tried to interfere wiv him and beat him when he fought 'em orf.'

'Yes, Matron thought it might be something like that.' Sister Rose hesitated, then, 'You don't know where he could be, Danny? Only Lady Rosalie would make sure that he was sent to live with a good family who would look after him if he came here to us.'

'Nah, I didn't know 'im until that devil caught me,'

Danny said and frowned. 'I reckoned me dad were a devil until I met them others – but he's just a drunk. He was all right until Mum died. He used to get drunk now and then but she kept him in line.' A smile lit his face. 'I loved me mum, Sister – I dream sometimes that she comes back and everything is all right again.'

'Well, I can't promise to bring your real mother back, Danny,' Sister Rose said, 'but perhaps Lady Rosalie can find you a mother you can learn to love.'

'If she was like you, I should love her,' Danny said and grinned. 'Yer all right, Sister Rose. If I were ten years older, I'd marry yer!'

'Maybe I'd marry you,' Sister Rose said and winked at him. 'I'll go and fetch that cocoa and a biscuit for you!'

Danny lay back against the pillows after she'd gone. He was glad Marjorie was back with her parents but sorry that Ron had run off. He knew Ron didn't want to go in an orphanage and Danny didn't blame him – his mum had never thought much of them – but a foster mum might be lovely, especially if she was as nice as Sister Rose.

'Is something wrong, Marjorie?' Mrs Lacey asked, sitting down beside her daughter on the rug. 'You're not upset again, are you? I'm so sorry for what happened to you, my darling, but you're safe now. I'll make sure those horrid people don't come near you again!'

'Mummy . . .' Marjorie looked up at her. 'What happened to Danny?'

'Who is Danny?' Helen Lacey asked. 'Is he a friend of yours, Marjorie?'

'He was *there*.' Marjorie breathed deeply, because it still frightened her when she thought of being grabbed, thrown in the back of a van and driven to that house. She'd been terrified the whole time until Danny arrived and then he'd looked after her. 'He was kind to me – I should like to see him, to know if he is all right.'

'I'm not sure . . .' Marjorie's mother frowned. 'Perhaps it's better you just try to forget what happened, darling. The police took those poor boys away and someone will look after them.'

Marjorie nodded but was thoughtful. 'Danny doesn't have a mummy – and his daddy used to hit him. He ran away because he was frightened but he protected me.'

'You're all right, Marjorie. Nothing bad happened to you – the police told me they arrived in time.' Her mother looked uncomfortable, as if she was embarrassed to talk about what had happened to her daughter. 'Danny will be looked after, I promise.'

'Will you ask Daddy to find out please, Mummy?' Marjorie said looking up at her pleadingly. 'He was my friend and I'm worried about him.'

Her mother hesitated, then reached out to touch her cheek. 'What a funny little thing you are, Marjorie. Yes, if you want, I'll ask Daddy to find out what he can – but I shouldn't set your heart on seeing him again.'

'Just as long as I know he is all right . . .'

'All right, I promise,' Helen said and smiled. 'Shall I make you a glass of orange squash and fetch a nice piece of sponge cake?'

'Yes, please,' Marjorie said.

After her mother had gone, she sat thinking and a tear slipped down her cheek. She'd always wanted a brother and Danny had been just like a big brother, telling her not to be frightened and comforting her when those bad men came. Marjorie knew she would have been very frightened indeed had Danny not been with her and she wanted to see him again, to tell him she would like him to be her brother always.

The other big boy, Ron, had been all right, but he hadn't been as kind or protective as Danny. The younger boys had clung to each other and cried most of the time. Marjorie had felt sorry for them but she hadn't known how to comfort them and the things they said about what had happened to them made her frightened. She hadn't told anyone about that – not even Mummy. She'd asked Danny what they'd meant and he'd told her she should just forget it but the pictures came to her mind of those men hitting Danny and the other boys and it made her afraid to go out. She didn't want to play in the street anymore in case those men tried to snatch her again. Mummy said she was all right now but Marjorie was still nervous of being alone.

She looked up and smiled as her mother brought her cake and squash. She hoped her mother wouldn't forget to ask Daddy, because she really did need to know that Danny was all right.

CHAPTER 14

Sarah opened the door to her mother and smiled. She asked her to come in and led the way through to the kitchen, glancing over her shoulder.

'It's lovely to see you, Mum. I was coming over later . . .'

'I've come to invite you to supper,' her mother replied. 'You and Steve if he can manage it – but just you if not. Don't worry about getting home afterwards, Theo will bring you back in his car . . .'

'Theo?' Sarah's eyebrows rose as she looked at her, noticing that she was wearing her hair brushed back in a new style and a good skirt and jumper. 'Is that the rather good-looking man I saw you playing cards with at the social club?'

'Yes. He is quite attractive,' her mother replied smiling slightly, 'but he's nice and that is what matters more to me.'

'Yes, of course. I agree,' Sarah confirmed. 'So, you've invited him to supper then?'

'Yes.' Her mother hesitated, took a deep breath and told her what had happened in the market. 'So, he took me home afterwards and he stayed for coffee and cake.' She looked a little self-conscious as she finished her tale. 'He was firm but kind to that young boy and I liked that, Sarah.'

'Yes, I do too – it's what Steve would have done,' Sarah said, a smile in her eyes. 'He often deals with young tearaways at the club he runs.'

'I know.' Sarah's mother looked thoughtful. 'I don't think this lad was really bad. He tried to take my purse and it was the one you gave me so I should have hated to lose it, but Theo grabbed his arm and took the purse back. When he asked the boy his name, he said it was Ron and that he was just hungry.'

Sarah frowned. Something her mother had said sounded familiar. She thought Steve had talked about a young boy called Ron who had absconded from the hospital where he'd been taken. Could it possibly be the same one? She wasn't sure but she would certainly speak to her husband when he came home.

Smiling at her mother, she put the kettle on and they sat down to enjoy a cup of tea and one of the delicious rock cakes her mother had brought in her tin. Their conversation turned gradually to other things – baby clothes, Sarah's health and the amount of times the baby had kicked that morning.

'You're probably carrying a boy,' Sarah's mother said looking at her thoughtfully. 'Will Steve be pleased with a boy or does he want a girl?'

'He doesn't care as long as we're both well,' Sarah said, 'but I'd like a boy this time. A boy first and then a girl.'

Her mother laughed. 'Well, you'll get what you get,

sweetheart. I'm with Steve, I don't mind whether you have a boy or a girl as long as you and the baby are well.' They looked at each other fondly, content to be together and contemplating a happy future for them all.

'We'd love to meet your friend, Mum,' Sarah said, realising she hadn't given her mother an answer. 'I'm very pleased you've found someone you can be friendly with and he sounds really nice.'

After her mother had gone, Sarah finished her housework and then made herself a cheese and salad sandwich and poured a glass of orange juice, taking it into the sitting room. The sun was pouring in at the window and it was pleasant to look out at the garden. Steve didn't have much time to work in the garden but he'd cut the lawn on Sunday and the flowerbeds were neat. Sarah would enjoy being out there and keeping it tidy when her baby had been born, but at the moment Steve had forbidden her to do any gardening.

She ate her lunch and then washed her hands before starting her knitting. She was beginning to quite enjoy her quiet afternoons when she sat and relaxed and dreamed of the day when her baby was born.

Steve smiled when Sarah told him that her mother had asked them to supper to meet her new friend Theo but he looked serious when she explained about the incident in the market.

'It sounds as if it might be the same young lad that ran off from the hospital,' Steve told her. 'The name is certainly the same and if Gwen thought he was more in need of help than punishment, it could be him. Danny told me he'd learned a little about Ron's past. His mother and both grandparents died of diphtheria about eighteen months ago and he was put into an orphanage, but he was ill-treated and ran away. Danny thought he'd been living rough for months and he'd got caught the same way as happened to him.'

'Mum wanted to help him,' Sarah said. 'Perhaps, if you see him on your beat, you could bring him back to us? We could look after him for a while and I know Mum would give him a home.'

'She already has two young lads to look after,' Steve reminded her. 'She has a big heart, Sarah, but she can't help all the orphans in London.'

'I know.' Sarah smiled sadly. 'What he really needs is a foster family but there is always another young child needing a home.'

Steve went to hug her and hold her close. 'Don't be upset, love,' he whispered close to her ear. 'If Ron is in the area, I'm bound to come across him one of these days and I'll try to get him to the Rosie then Matron and Lady Rosalie will look after him.'

Sarah nodded, knowing that if Steve found the runaway, he would do his best to see he was taken in and found a good foster family. Yet the thought of a young boy alone on the streets sent shivers down her spine. Ron had escaped one set of villains but there were always others ready to prey on vulnerable youngsters.

Ron had found a spot under the bridges away from the down-and-outs that habitually gathered there at night. He'd been lucky enough to stumble across an old Army coat and haversack that had been abandoned on a piece of waste ground. The haversack looked as if it had been an old soldier's and he'd looked inside eagerly but it was empty. Any valuables or money that had been inside were long gone.

He wished there had been something he could sell to buy food. The half-a-crown that bloke had given him in the market was gone and although he'd managed to pinch a currant bun from one of the stallholders that morning, he'd scoffed that down in seconds. His stomach ached and he hugged himself to ward off the nagging hunger. Living on the streets was hard for a lad of fourteen, though he'd managed to find work a few times, but it was getting harder and harder. Folk looked at him in suspicion and he knew his appearance didn't help; his boots were worn down and scuffed and his clothes were dirty. The hospital had tried to give him clean ones but he'd been too suspicious to let them take his old things and the nurse had been too busy to fight him.

She was the reason Ron had managed to get away, because she'd been called to another patient and Ron had run while her back was turned. Sometimes, when hunger gnawed at his stomach, he wished he was back there, where it was warm and they'd fed him hot food and cups of creamy cocoa – and yet he knew what would happen. They would put him in an orphanage and he didn't trust those places, not after what he'd witnessed.

Ron had known he was next in line for that brute's attention and so he'd left after he'd seen one of his friends sobbing because he'd been hurt and beaten for fighting off the superintendent. There had been a woman he might have confided in but she'd been away on holiday. Ethel, the matron, was kind and she would have believed him but he knew the other care assistants would have called him a liar, preferring to stay in with their boss.

Ron hunched his shoulders under the old Army coat and sniffed, holding back the tears. He wished Danny was with him. It was because of Danny that they'd fought off those devils in the warehouse. Danny was strong and brave and he wished he was his brother. If only they could live somewhere safe together . . . but that was just a dream Ron knew would never come true. He didn't even know where Danny had gone.

'Hello, lad, on your own, then?'

Ron started, his senses alert as he heard the cultured voice. He didn't trust men who spoke like that – in fact, he didn't trust many people, except that police officer who had taken Danny away with him. He'd been a good 'un but he'd taken Danny not Ron.

'Go away,' Ron muttered. He was on his feet, hugging his coat to him, fear making him shake inside though he tried not to show it. 'I don't want yer money or yer food!'

'I don't have much of either,' the man said. 'I've got a fire, though, and I'm making a brew, if you want a mug of tea.' He hesitated, then, 'My name is Ted – and I mean you no harm.'

Ron looked at him suspiciously. He wasn't smartly dressed, clearly down on his luck like the other men who slept under the bridges.

'What do you want from me?' he asked harshly.

'Nothing, lad. I'm just a bloke who lost all he had because of the depression and I live on the streets just like you.'

Eyeing him up and down, Ron decided that he might be all right. 'It ain't much of a life is it, mister?'

'No, it isn't,' the man replied. 'I was very ill for a while and I drank – but the Sally Army helped me out—'

Ron flinched away from him. 'Go away! I ain't fallin' fer that one again!'

'Been let down, have you?' The man looked at him sadly. 'You can trust me, lad – I'm just over there if you want to sit by my fire.'

'I'm all right.' Ron sat down and hunched into his coat. He wanted desperately to share this man's fire and his tea, but he was afraid to trust him after the last time. 'Thanks, though.'

'That's all right. I'm here most nights. If you change your mind you can come over and sit by the fire.'

Ron shook his head. He was cold, hungry and miserable but he couldn't bring himself to trust just yet. In the morning he would try to find the Sally Army Hall himself. He knew that if he could discover the real one, they would give him hot food, but he'd been tricked once and he couldn't let that happen again, because next time there might not be another Danny to help him.

'I wish you were here,' he whispered to himself. 'I wish you were my brother, Danny . . .'

CHAPTER 15

Rose smiled at her landlady, lingering to talk for a moment before she left for work. She was lucky to have found Beattie, who was like an older sister to her. A widow who had no children, Beattie had taken Rose in and treated her like a sister. She'd been so kind to Rose so would she – or could she – show the same kindness to a motherless boy?

'Is there something on your mind, love?' Beattie asked.

'I was wondering . . .' Rose took the plunge. 'We've got a young boy on the ward, Beattie. He has been through a terrible time and – well, I've got fond of him. I know it's a lot to ask, but if I offered to foster him, would you have him here? We'd have to get the proper permission but . . .'

Beattie's homely face lit up with a smile that came from deep inside. 'Well bless you, my dove, I'd like that fine. I've been wondering if your Lady Rosalie would accept me as a foster mother . . .'

'Oh, Beattie, you darling,' Rose said and hugged her. 'If you don't think I'm imposing?'

'Never!' Beattie said warmly. 'I wanted children but

my Matt was killed in the trenches during the German gas attack in 1915, as you know, and I never married again. We'd only been married a few weeks before he was called up and I lost my hope of a family when he died.'

'I know, I'm so sorry, Beattie,' Rose replied looking at her with love and sympathy. 'It has been hard for you all these years.'

'It isn't now I've got you,' Beattie replied serenely. 'And a young boy we loved and cared for together would be a gift from God, my dove.'

'He's a lovely boy, Beattie. He was treated badly by his father, a drunk who beat him savagely – and then he was captured by some rogues bent on evil. I want to give him a secure home but I can't do it alone . . .'

'You tell your Matron and that Lady Rosalie that we'll have him here,' Beattie said. 'If she wants me to answer questions I will – gladly. I've never done wrong by anyone and I could love any child that you love, Rose.'

'Oh, I love you, Beattie!' Rose told her sincerely. 'I'm going to see Matron today and ask her if we can be put on Lady Rosalie's list, then we can look after Danny together, give him a secure home where he can be happy! And he wants to be a cook so you could teach him.'

Beattie's smile lit up the room as she nodded. Everyone said she was the best cook ever. It was why she could have taken as many lodgers as she wished, but she would only take young women she trusted and for the moment Rose was the only one. A small advert in Mr Forrest's corner shop would bring her more lodgers immediately, but she managed well enough and was content because she thought of Rose as family.

Rose gave her a kiss on the cheek and left for work with a new spring in her step. She'd been puzzling over what to do for the best about Danny. He was recovering and Lady Rosalie would soon be searching for a family for him, but Rose didn't want to say goodbye to him. Had she been married or had her own home, she would have asked before this but now, with Beattie's agreement, she could ask if it could be arranged.

'Well, that sounds ideal to me,' Matron said when Rose told her the idea that she'd had for fostering Danny Bryant. 'Your landlady sounds delightful, Sister Rose – I should like to meet her – and I'm sure Lady Rosalie will be happy to interview her. If she passes the checks that we have to make you will be given custody of Danny and Beattie will be given a small allowance, since she will be providing the home and food.'

'Yes,' Rose said, 'and I will pay more towards our food and heat, and the allowance will help with his clothes and anything else he needs.' She hesitated, then, 'Do you think I shall pass the tests, Matron?'

'I have no doubt of it,' Matron told her with a smile. 'I am so pleased you have come up with an arrangement that allows you to foster without giving up your job.'

'I couldn't have afforded to do it if Beattie hadn't agreed,' Rose told her. 'Had I been married I would have spoken sooner – but Beattie is like an older sister to me.'

'Yes. You are very lucky to have found such a landlady, Sister Rose – and she, you. Some of my nurses do not have such pleasant lodgings, I fear, and most will never have a home of their own, I fear.'

'No . . .' Rose's smile dimmed for a moment. She'd thought for a short time that she might have found a man she might come to love and make a home with, but Peter Clark had not asked her out and she'd decided the friendly looks he sometimes gave her meant nothing more than respect for a fellow medical worker.

After she left Matron's office, Rose went to the children's ward. She saw Danny's eager look and went straight to him as he sat up in bed, smiling down at him.

'How are you feeling this morning?' she asked and his smile warmed her heart.

'I'm much better, Sister Rose. I'm glad to see you . . .'

'Yes, and I you,' she said and sat on the edge of his bed. 'If it could be arranged, would you like to come and live with me, Danny?'

His eyes glowed and she felt the tears burn but refused to shed them. 'Could I really do that, Sister Rose?'

'I've asked Beattie, the lovely lady I live with, and she says yes. Now, we have to get Lady Rosalie's permission, but if she says yes – and I think she will – you can leave hospital and come home with me, then we'll get you into the local school and you will live with us all the time.'

Danny grinned at her. 'Do yer reckon I can learn to cook too?'

'Beattie is a really great cook, Danny. She can teach you all she knows – and then one day I'll pay for you to learn properly at college.'

'I reckon you're a smasher, Sister Rose!'

Rose laughed, feeling happier than she had been in a long, long time. 'Thank you, Danny. I like you too.'

Danny was silent for a moment. 'If they let me live wiv you and Beattie, will you help me find out how Marjorie is – and Ron too?'

'I will ask Constable Jones to take a letter from you to Marjorie,' Rose promised. 'Her mother may let her write back to you then – and I'll also ask if they've found Ron. I feel sure Constable Jones will know if he has been taken to hospital or an orphanage.'

'If they'd brought him 'ere, he wouldn't have run away,' Danny said wisely. 'I'd 'ave told him you were all right, Sister Rose.'

'Thank you.' She smiled at him lovingly, wondering why his father had ever treated him so badly. All Danny needed was someone to love and he responded with eagerness. 'Perhaps we can help Ron once they find him – and I'm sure Marjorie will come and see you if we tell her mother where you're living.'

Danny nodded and she bent to kiss his cheek. As far as Rose was concerned, he was her son now and she would give him all the love she had inside her. Danny needed love and she and Beattie had so much to give . . .

Danny watched as Sister Rose walked away to speak to other patients. He felt a warm glow of happiness inside, because of what she'd told him. For the first time in a long while he felt safe and cared for and he couldn't stop smiling. She was lovely, was Sister Rose, and he looked forward to calling her Mum and to living with her. He even wanted to go to school and to learn how to cook with Beattie and then one day to become a proper chef – Sister Rose had told him that was the proper word for men who cooked.

Suddenly he saw a new life ahead of him. It would have been even better if he could spend it with Ron and Marjorie as well, but he didn't think that was likely to happen. He wouldn't dare push his luck by asking if Ron could come and live with them and Marjorie had her own home and parents to love her. Danny wondered if she was all right, but the one he worried about was Ron. If his friend was on the streets still, he could die of cold or hunger or . . . His mind shied away from the other terrible things that could happen to a boy alone, so he would like to know that Ron was safe too, but perhaps Sister Rose's friend could find out what had happened to him. Settling back with the comics one of the nurses had given him to read, Danny wondered how long it would be before he was told that he could go to live with Sister Rose.

CHAPTER 16

'Good morning, Nurse Jenny.' Peter Clark smiled at the friendly young woman who met him as he entered the critical ward. 'I've come to see one of your patients – a Mrs Hilda Jenkins I believe?'

'Yes, doctor,' Nurse Jenny replied, a faint blush on her cheeks. 'She was very poorly during the night – her breathing was difficult and she had pain in her chest, also a slight fever I'm told.'

'Lead on,' he said and followed her to the end of the ward where an elderly woman lay back against the pillows with her eyes closed. She opened them as he approached her bed and gave him a brave smile. 'Good morning, Hilda – how are you feeling now?'

'A little under the weather, doctor,' she whispered and he heard the rasping noise in her chest. Consulting the night nurse's notes, he nodded. It was probably acute bronchitis made worse by the poor conditions she lived in like so many of the East End of London's poor. She might recover enough to live through the summer, but he doubted she would see another winter out. The best thing he could do for her was keep her here for a week or two with plenty of bed rest and good nourishing food.

'Nothing much to worry about then,' he told her cheerfully. 'We'll keep you in hospital for a week or two, let you have a rest and feed you up a bit.'

She smiled and nodded, clearly happy to be looked after for a while. 'I've had a big family to care for, doctor – ten there were, six boys and four girls. Me and my Alf managed to get them all up to school-leaving age and then they went their own ways. I've got two out in New Zealand and another in America – he's doing well. He sends me some pretty things now and Jack went to Australia, works on a sheep station. My daughters are all married with families of their own and Terry lives up the road. He's got seven of his own and we don't know what happened to Noah. He went off one night and we ain't seen him since . . .' She sighed and a tear slipped down her cheek. 'My Alf died two years back and I've been alone since. They come to visit, those that live close, but they've got their own lives, doctor.'

'Yes, I expect so.' Peter frowned. He would try to discover if any of Hilda's children knew how ill she was. She ought to be living with one of her daughters – or at least they should visit often, even if they did have lives of their own. 'We'll soon have you up and fighting fit, Hilda.'

The elderly woman laughed and he moved on, washing his hands before examining the next patient who complained of a tummy ache. He thought that was probably wind and recommended something to calm it before making a quick tour of the ward. The patients

134

all knew him and wanted a word and he lingered with each, finally making his way back to Nurse Jenny who had returned to her desk.

'I think it is the bronchitis again for Hilda, nurse,' he said. 'It is something she's had a long time – but if she gets worse send for me.'

'She hasn't got long, has she?'

'The summer, perhaps – but the winter's fogs and cold will probably be the finish, unless we could get her somewhere warmer . . .'

'What about her sons in New Zealand or Australia?'

'Do you know how to contact them?'

'I think she might tell me – though she doesn't want to be any trouble.'

'Find out and I'll send a telegram.'

'Yes, doctor. I'll do my best.' Her smile lit up her pretty face. 'You're so kind to them – all of them.'

Peter turned away and then something made him stop. 'I have two tickets for a musical this Saturday evening – would you care to accompany me?'

'Yes,' she agreed instantly. 'Thank you, I should like that.' She smiled with pleasure.

'It's a date, then. I'll pick you up from here at six forty-five,' he said and walked off.

It was only as he left the hospital that he wondered what had made him ask the young nurse to accompany him to the theatre. His intention had been to pluck up his courage and ask Sister Rose, but something had stopped him. Nurse Jenny, outgoing and cheerful, was much less intimidating, and his request had been an impulse, which he half regretted. He had no doubt he would enjoy Nurse Jenny's company, but it was Rose he was truly interested in – if only she would let him show her.

Lily was ironing a blouse when Jenny came home that evening. She noticed at once that her sister was excited and smiled, raising her eyebrows. Jenny laughed.

'I've been asked to the theatre on Saturday evening,' she said looking extraordinarily pleased. 'You'll never guess who asked me?'

'I haven't a clue,' Lily told her, smiling. 'Go on, tell me then.'

'Dr Peter Clark,' Jenny said and let out her breath in a rush. 'What do you think of that?'

Lily looked at her, astonished and not quite sure what to think. 'Well, he is good-looking – and everyone likes him but . . .' She shook her head, because it wasn't her place to say what she didn't really know. But Lily suspected that Sister Rose rather liked Dr Clark and she'd thought he might like her, because she'd seen them talking once or twice and it seemed as if there was something right about it – but if he'd asked her sister out, Lily must have got it wrong. Besides, it wasn't her business. 'Are you looking forward to it?'

'Yes, I am, very much. It's ages since I went anywhere nice,' Jenny said and sighed, because sometimes life seemed all work.

'Yes, I know,' Lily said and felt vaguely guilty because of the wonderful two days she'd spent with Chris that she'd had to keep secret. Their marriage ceremony had been brief, and it had hurt Lily that she couldn't tell her sister, but the time they'd spent together had been wonderful. After he'd gone, she'd felt that awful cloud of loneliness descend on her again, but work and her friendship with other nurses and patients had lifted it within a day or so. Now, she was living day to day, as she knew she would until Chris was able to be with her again. He'd kissed her passionately before he left, telling her that he would write when he could and gone, tearing himself from her arms – and the worst bit was that she couldn't share her secret with her much-loved sister.

'Well, I'm glad you're going out for an evening,' Lily said looking at Jenny affectionately. 'It will do you good.'

'Yes.' Jenny's eyes softened with love. 'I do know how you miss Chris. It's a shame you can't be with him more, Lily. Have you heard from him lately?'

'Just a couple of weeks ago,' Lily replied struggling to hold back the tears. 'Don't feel upset for me, Jenny. I knew what Chris did for a living and I'm prepared to wait.'

'You really do love him,' Jenny said. 'I'm glad I told him we were over, Lily, because otherwise I'd still have been feeling frustrated that I wasn't going out and you would have been in love with a man you daren't tell.'

'Yes, you liked Chris and enjoyed his company but I love him,' Lily said. 'I hope that you will find someone you love one day, Jenny.'

Jenny shrugged. 'I liked Chris – and I like Peter Clark but I don't think I'm likely to fall in love with him; he doesn't set my pulses racing! I said I'd like to go out with him because I enjoy the theatre – but you know, Lily, I'm not sure I know how to love, not in the way you love Chris.'

'One day you will,' Lily said. 'It's going to hit you just out of the blue and then you'll understand the joy and the pain of loving someone so much you're incomplete without them.'

Jenny nodded and smothered a sigh. 'I think I'd like to discover what love really is but for the moment I'm just happy to go out with anyone decent that asks me.' She yawned. 'I'm going to have a bath, wash my hair and then go to bed – what about you?'

'I've got tonight off and then I start on days so we'll both be on days for a while,' Lily said. 'I'll listen to the wireless, do a little bit of knitting and then go to bed with a book.'

'Gosh, we lead such exciting lives,' Jenny said wryly. 'Good thing we both love our jobs.'

'Yes, we do love our jobs,' Lily agreed. 'I'll bring some cocoa up later.'

Jenny nodded and went out. Lily put her ironing things away and switched on the wireless, making sure that it was a light music station so that she could relax to it and knit at the same time. It wasn't surprising that her sister got bored sometimes; their lives really weren't very exciting but Lily wouldn't have changed hers, except to have Chris home and safe. To live a normal married life would be heaven for her – and she knew that if Jenny fell in love then *her* life would be so much better. Lily wanted it to happen for her sister's sake, but she didn't feel that Dr Clark was the right man for Jenny – he was too serious, too dedicated to his work.

Perhaps when she and Jenny were both on days together, they could go to the pictures and the theatre more often. It would help break the monotony of their lives and cheer Jenny up. Lily smiled. Chris had spoiled her sister when they were together, taking her to special places and giving her extravagant gifts and she was missing that, even though she hadn't loved him. If Dr Clark took her out a bit it should brighten her life – and yet, without love, it wouldn't last long . . .

Lily couldn't help wondering how Sister Rose would react when she heard that Jenny was going out with the handsome young doctor. If she cared for him, it would hurt her . . .

Life was so complicated at times. Sighing, Lily got on with knitting the new cardigan she was making for one of her patients. Rene was elderly and her hands could no longer hold the needles but she'd paid for the wool and Lily had agreed to make it for her. She enjoyed the rhythm of her work and felt at peace as the soft music filled the kitchen. A feeling of optimism came over her – Chris would come home when he could, just as he'd promised, Jenny would discover a new love – and perhaps Rose would find happiness too . . .

CHAPTER 17

Lady Rosalie looked at the ticks all the way down the page and smiled. It was so pleasing when applicants for fostering came through with flying colours. Sister Rose and her motherly landlady Beattie had fitted her criteria exactly. Beattie was to be the official foster carer since it was her house and Rose was Beattie's support so her wage would guarantee the household. It was an unusual arrangement but Lady Rosalie thought it a good one. And it would be good for Sister Rose who had recently lost her mother. Naturally, the nurse had been upset but she'd stayed at her post, merely taking a few hours off for the funeral.

'I can't do anything for Mum now,' she'd told Matron when she'd been asked if she needed leave to arrange things. 'I feel sad but it was a happy release for her at the end.'

It was sad the way Nurse Rose's mother had gone, gradually losing all sense of what was happening around her. Even if you were a nurse and understood what was happening, it was still hard to see it in a loved one.

However, the young woman could direct some of that love she had inside her to this young orphan.

If only she could find a lot more homes as good as this was potentially. Yes, she decided, it would do for Danny Bryant very well. He was energetic and needed young people about him, so sister Rose and Beattie were perfect for him.

A slight frown creased her brow at the latest news from Constable Steve Jones. He'd visited her to update her on the situation as regards to Danny's father.

'We visited the home of Mr Bryant and found it deserted and in a filthy state,' the police officer had told her. 'After discussing it with the landlord, we discovered that the rent had not been paid in three months and that he intends to repossess it next week. His solicitor told him that he's entitled to recover back rent from the sale of anything left in the house, although there doesn't appear to be anything much but some very old, rickety furniture.'

'And the whereabouts of Mr Bryant?'

'We have no idea. Our officers have a description of him and will keep a look out anywhere the homeless congregate.'

Lady Rosalie had nodded. 'So, you think we can go ahead with the fostering and are unlikely to receive a visit from Danny's father demanding his son's return?'

'I don't think it likely that he will come looking for his son. He hasn't reported him missing and, as far as we know, has shown no interest in his welfare. We will now take steps to make Danny a ward of the council and in your care so that his father cannot just take the boy away.'

'Thank you.' She'd smiled at the earnest young officer. 'I believe I have found the ideal home for him and shall proceed accordingly.'

With all the proper paperwork in place, Lady Rosalie was now ready to give Sister Rose the good news – but she would let Matron do that. Smiling, she picked up the telephone and dialled the number for Mary Thurston's office.

Mary replaced the receiver and nodded in satisfaction. She was very pleased that her nurse had been approved as a foster parent in conjunction with her landlady. It would not interfere with her work but it would give Sister Rose something extra in her life.

As Matron of the Rosie, Mary noticed everything that went on in the infirmary and she'd noticed that one of her best nurses had seemed a little lonely perhaps, a little unhappy. Rose Harwell was devoted to her work but work was not always enough even for the most dedicated nurse – as Mary knew herself. If you had no family or loved ones to care for, it could be hard, particularly at holiday times and Christmas. She had all her nurses to think of and had made the Rosie her life after her own mother had died, but even she felt the lack of relationships sometimes and was looking forward to her little holiday in the summer with Lady Rosalie and her son. Sister Rose was younger and perhaps needed more – either a husband or a child – and now she would have a young boy to love and care for.

It was with lightness of heart and mind that Mary went in search of Sister Rose. She found her, as she'd known she would, in the children's ward, tending a little girl who had been sick and was crying.

'May I have a word please, Sister Rose?'

'Yes, of course, Matron.' Sister Rose smiled at her and beckoned to one of their newer nurses. 'Nurse Margaret, can you just make Jinny comfortable, please?'

'Yes, Sister, of course.' The junior nurse came over and took on the task Sister Rose had been doing previously.

Sister Rose washed her hands at the basin and then approached Matron. 'Is something wrong?'

Mary beamed at her. 'Completely the opposite, Sister Rose. I've just heard that you have been given custody of Danny – and you may take him home with you whenever you wish. You will, of course, receive the official papers in due course and Beattie will be given a small allowance for his food and clothes – but there is no need to wait to take him home.'

'That is wonderful!' Sister Rose's face lit up with pleasure. 'He will be so pleased. He was bored with being here and now he can start school as soon as the school holidays are over.'

'Yes, exactly – you have all that in place?'

'Yes. We changed his school in case his father went looking at his old one so he'll be going to our local school. I'll take him the first morning and Beattie will meet him afterwards if he wants her to – though he says he's old enough to walk home himself and it's only just around the corner from Beattie's house.'

Mary nodded her satisfaction.

'Good – and before you go on with your work you may wish to tell Danny the good news.'

'Thank you, Matron, I shall.'

Mary watched as the nurse went off to tell the boy she'd offered to foster and watched as his face lit up with joy. It gave her a warm feeling inside. They couldn't often place a child with someone they already knew and cared for, but this time it had worked out perfectly and she imagined they would have no more need to worry about Danny Bryant.

If only it was the same for all the abused and orphaned children in London. Mary shook her head as she went on a tour of the other wards. Life wasn't all flowers and sweetness and it was so good when something went right for once. She went in search of one of the patients concerning her the most at the moment. She would ask Nurse Alice if she thought Hilda was about ready to go home or if she needed a few days longer in the women's ward.

'It's the most marvellous thing, Matron,' Nurse Alice said. 'Dr Clark managed to trace Hilda's son Noah. She thought he'd gone abroad but he hasn't, he is living in Wiltshire on a farm and was too ashamed to get in touch with his parents after he ran away because he didn't want to stay on at school. Anyway, he's coming up to London on Saturday to see if he can persuade his mother to go and live with him and his wife.'

'Now, how on earth did Dr Clark manage that?' Mary said, certain that the doctor must have gone to a considerable amount of trouble. 'Well, she may not live any longer but she'll be looked after for what remains of her life so we'll keep Hilda here until Noah comes and make sure she is sensible enough to accept his offer.'

Mary smiled as she continued her rounds. If only all her problems could be solved so easily – but there was always another one to take its place. Still, it was good of Dr Clark to take such an interest and she must remember to thank him next time they met.

CHAPTER 18

Ron saw that the man who had once offered to share his fire was in his usual spot again that night. What had he called himself – Ted? He'd looked at Ron a few times since that night but hadn't approached him again. He was brewing something over his fire and it smelled good. Ron hadn't eaten anything all day but a half-rotten apple a stallholder had given him and his stomach ached; even a cup of tea would be welcome. He walked hesitantly up to the man and stood looking at him.

'That smells good,' he said at last.

'It's soup,' Ted said. 'I got work today and I've made soup with meat and vegetables – you can have some if you want, lad.'

'Please . . .' Ron sat down, but not too close. The man nodded, poured some soup into a tin cup and offered it to him. He took it and sipped it, relishing both the warmth it spread through him and the taste. He found a bit of meat and chewed the delicious morsel. 'It's really good!'

'I learned to cook in the Army when we were out

on exercises,' Ted told him. 'It was a good life until I got invalided out with my leg.'

'I'm Ron and you're Ted, ain't yer?'

'Yes, that's right.' Ted grinned and saluted him. 'Sergeant Ted Harris reporting for duty, sir!'

A reluctant smile came into Ron's eyes. 'I reckon I might like to be in the Army if they teach yer to cook like this!' He accepted a small piece of bread and soaked it in the soup. It tasted so good! 'I'm sorry I was rude the other night.'

'You had a right to be,' Ted said. 'There's plenty of blokes you need to avoid. I'm not one of them – but you'll only know that when you get to know me better.'

'Am I going to know you better?' Ron asked, still a little wary.

'If you want to,' Ted said and grinned in a way that Ron could relate to. 'In the morning I'm going to work on the docks – and they might have a job you can help with, lad. You'll get some money at the end of the day and there's a canteen nearby where you can get a free meal twice a week. They have too many to feed us every day but they give us tickets and we can eat there twice in the week.'

'Thanks,' Ron said quietly and finished his soup and bread. 'Shall I wash this?' There was a dripping tap at the end of the bridge that all the vagrants used. Someone had installed it there years ago and it was gratefully used by all the men who had the things needed to make tea or, as Ted had, soup.

'I'll do it later,' Ted said. 'You can sleep near my patch if you want – but it's up to you.'

Ron hesitated. He still wasn't completely sure he could

148

trust this man, but he wasn't safe on his own either. Some of the other vagrants had been staring at him the previous night, making it impossible for him to sleep.

'I'll stay just here,' he said and huddled with his back to the wall a few feet from Ted's fire. It didn't throw out much heat but it was better than where he'd been, and he'd noticed that most of the others kept to their own patch. He was probably as safe here as anywhere. 'Thanks – I'll do the same fer you one day, Ted.'

'It's all right by me,' Ted said and settled back, closing his eyes. 'If yer need anything just yell.'

Ron nodded and closed his eyes. He felt safer than he had for many nights, because before this he'd only rested anywhere for a short time before moving on. Most of the tramps were too sunk in their own misery to take any notice of a young lad on his own, but there was one who had kept looking at him the previous night. Frightened, Ron had moved off when the man closed his eyes and found another place to rest. Now, perhaps, perched close to Ted, he might actually be able to sleep. He closed his eyes and felt the drowsiness steal over him. The warm soup and the fire were making him relax . . .

Ron woke with a start sometime later as he heard the shouting. He was aware of two men struggling and in the faint light from some distant street lights, he saw the flash of steel. One of the men had a knife! Even as he watched, the other flicked his wrist and the knife went flying, landing near Ron. Quick as a flash, he picked it up and hid it under his greatcoat. Then he heard a loud crack and a scream and the man who had been holding the knife cried out.

'You bugger! You've broken my arm!'

'Serves you right,' Ted's voice said clearly. 'If you try to molest that boy again, I'll kill you. Now clear off and don't ever come here again – I'm warning you, you filthy devil, I'll break your neck not your arm if I see you again!'

'How was I to know he was your property?'

'He doesn't belong to me or anyone else, but I've warned you – now sling your hook or I'll make you really sorry!'

Ron was shivering as he watched the dark shadow run off, muttering and swearing. Ted stood watching for a moment and then came to him, looking down at him.

'It's all right, Ron. He didn't touch you. I saw to that!'

'Thanks,' Ron said and found his teeth were chattering. 'How did you manage to get the knife off him?' He took it out and handed it to Ted, who accepted it with a grin.

'It's a trick I learned in the Army,' he said. 'It comes in useful – I'll teach you if you like?'

'Thanks.' Ron smiled at him. 'You're all right, Ted. I was lucky I stayed near you tonight.'

'Yes.' Ted put some wood on his fire. 'Stay here while I fetch water and I'll make us a brew. I think that devil has gone but you need to stay close to me for a while, Ron.'

'I shall – and I'll come to work with you tomorrow and to the canteen.'

'You do that,' Ted told him with a nod. 'Some jobs need two of us so we'll find more work like that – and we might earn enough to get a bed at the Sally Army, if you want.'

Ron hesitated and then grinned. 'Yeah, why not?' he said. 'I reckon I can trust you – you're like my friend Danny.'

'Got a friend, have you?' Ted asked smiling slightly.

'Yeah, sort of – but I don't know where they took him . . .' Ron drew a deep breath. 'Him and me – these men caught us and were going to sell us but the police came. Me and Danny had been fighting 'em – the others were too scared. I was hurt so they took me to hospital and I don't know where they took Danny.'

'Do you know his second name?' Ted asked.

Ron shook his head. 'Nah, we didn't bother, but I liked him a lot.'

'Maybe we can find out where he went,' Ted said. 'I know a couple of coppers that are all right. They'll ask around for us and if we can find him, you could go and see him, especially if we can get enough work to find a settled place.'

'Do yer think we could?' Ron asked, his interest caught. 'I ain't never managed more than an hour or two – and I ain't had that recently.'

'Times have been very hard,' Ted said. 'After I left the Army I worked in a factory for a while but it closed due to the depression and since then I've only found work on the docks. I'm a carpenter by trade but there aren't many jobs going – if I could find one, I could teach you the skills you need to survive on the streets.'

'Would you?' Ron looked at him in wonder. It was hard to believe that Ted was genuine, because he'd been let down too many times, but something inside was telling him that, at last, he might have found someone he could trust. 'I'd like that if I was any good at it.'

'You would be my apprentice,' Ted said and smiled. 'A carpenter often needs an apprentice and it would suit us both, I reckon.'

'Yes,' Ron agreed and realised he'd been holding his breath. It seemed too good to be true and yet he knew he couldn't go on as he had been. He would either have to go to the police and let them put him in an orphanage or trust this man – and he thought he would rather do that than go back to the place he'd run away from. 'Thanks again, Ted. I'd do the best I could, I promise.'

'I know you would,' Ted said. 'You're a nice lad, Ron, and you deserve better from life than you've been given. We both do – and perhaps this will be the turning point for us both.'

'I hope so,' Ron said and grinned. 'I'll watch the fire while you fetch the water.'

He saw the quick smile in Ted's eyes and his heart sang. Something about this man reminded him of Danny. It was a look, particularly when he smiled, and it made him think he was all right now. He'd found someone to rely on and he would stick close by his new friend. Perhaps together they could find Danny . . .

CHAPTER 19

Danny woke in the soft bed and stretched luxuriously. Even the hospital beds were not as good as this – but then, he'd never been anywhere he felt so comfortable before. His home had been all right while his mum lived but after that it had become a cheerless place – but this, this was wonderful. The smell of baking as he'd entered Beattie's kitchen was so delicious it made his mouth water. Beattie had hugged him and kissed him and told him how glad she was he'd come to live with her and Sister Rose and then she'd given him a plate of the most delicious casserole he'd ever tasted. Mum's cooking had been good but nothing like Beattie's.

'This is smashing,' he'd told her as he tasted the first mouthful. 'The meat is so tender it melts in your mouth.'

'Bless you, Danny,' Beattie had replied and her face broke into smiles that made her beautiful to his eyes. 'I made it specially for you and Sister Rose – it's one of my favourites: chicken cooked in a little wine with baby onions and carrots. My mother taught me how to make it but I don't make it often, just now and then for a treat.'

'I've never tasted anything like it,' Danny had said truthfully. 'I should like to learn next time you cook it.'

'I'll teach you to cook lots of things.' Beattie had looked pleased. 'You'll be home from school before Sister Rose gets back from work and we can get our supper together and on the weekends I'll teach you to bake cakes.'

'I'd love to do that,' Danny had said, smiling at her. 'Best of all in the world I love cakes – everyone likes them.'

'Then me and you will get on fine,' Beattie had told him. 'If making cakes gives people happiness, I reckon that's the best thing we can do with our lives, don't you?'

Danny had nodded, too busy eating his food to answer. He'd eaten every scrap of the chicken casserole on his plate and then cleared the raspberry jam sponge pudding and custard, following it with a cup of tea. He'd rubbed his stomach to show his content and grinned at her.

'That's the best meal I've eaten since me mum's brother came to tea.'

Beattie had looked at him and then at Sister Rose. 'Do you have an uncle, Danny?'

'Yes – at least I think I do.' Danny had frowned, trying to recall. 'I remember he came once when I was small – about five or six I think, but he fell out wiv me dad and Mum cried over it. She said later that she was fond of her brother but me dad didn't like him and had told him not to come again.'

'You don't know where he lives?'

'No.' Danny had shaken his head. 'I don't remember

much of him – but he brought me a set of lead soldiers. They weren't new or anything, but they were good. Me dad took them and sold them – said they were sissy things and I didn't need them.'

'That was a shame.' Beattie had looked sad. 'Did you never see your uncle again?'

'I think he came to the house after Mum died. I heard Dad shouting at him in the kitchen when I was in bed, but I didn't dare go down.'

'And he never wrote to you or came to your school?' Sister Rose had asked, turning around from the sink where she'd been washing up.

'No, I never saw him again.'

'Well, I don't think he will come looking for you then,' Sister Rose had said and Danny had seen relief in her eyes. He knew then that she and Beattie really wanted him to stay with them and it warmed him inside.

'I shan't go with him if he does.' Danny had smiled at her. 'I want to be with you and Beattie.'

'That's all right then,' Beattie had said, looking pleased again.

Danny brought his mind back to the present as he smelled something delicious coming from the kitchen. He jumped out of bed and ran to the bathroom he'd been shown the previous evening, giving his hands and face a quick wash, because it was what Beattie had told him to do. Then he went back to the bedroom and took off his new pyjamas and put on the lovely long trousers, shirt, pullover and socks and shoes he'd been given. He'd never felt clothes this good against his skin and it was lovely, all clean and fresh and nice. His light brown hair – which was like his mum's – was standing up on the crown and he pressed it down with his hands, though it would stand up again, because it always did, and then pulled the brush Beattie had given him through it. Satisfied, he looked proper, as he ought, he went clattering down the stairs, announcing his arrival.

Sister Rose was sitting at the kitchen table eating something that looked like pancakes with something runny and golden on them. Danny had never seen anything like that eaten for breakfast but it made him hungry and he looked hopefully at Beattie. Her wonderful smile lit up her face as she nodded.

'Yes, there's some for you, Danny. We like a pancake sometimes for breakfast. It makes a change and they're delicious with a little syrup.'

Danny watched as Beattie put two perfectly cooked pancakes on his plate and poured a spoonful of the golden stuff from a green and gold tin on his.

'Try it and see,' Beattie invited so he did and beamed at her in surprise.

'It's delicious – and the pancakes,' Danny said with his mouth full. 'Will you teach me how to make them?'

'When you've finished those, we'll all have another and you can watch how I do it,' Beattie offered. 'It's Sister Rose's day off so we don't have to get her off to work.'

'I wanted to have your first day at home with you,' Sister Rose said. 'I'll show you where the school is and the corner shop so you will be able to find your way home then, but Beattie will meet you until you're quite sure.'

Danny nodded, swallowing the last of the delicious food. He was so excited he hardly knew how to contain himself. This was the answer to his dreams! He had two mothers; he was eating and was going to learn to cook the most delicious food – what more could anyone want?

He thought fleetingly of Ron and Marjorie. He would have liked to know if they were managing all right and could only hope that somehow their lives were as good as his was now . . .

Marjorie sat looking out of the window, watching her mother hang out the washing in their garden. She had a headache and her throat hurt so she hadn't been allowed to go out even though it was almost May and quite warm now.

'Sit there and don't move,' her mother had told her before she went out. Marjorie was no longer allowed into the front street and so seldom saw any other children unless she was at school and she hadn't been allowed to return there yet, because Mummy was frightened someone would snatch her again.

As her mother came back into the room, she looked at Marjorie and frowned. 'That's a long face – what's wrong?'

'I was thinking about Danny,' Marjorie said. 'Did Daddy ask where they took him?'

Her mother hesitated and then sighed. 'He was taken to the Rosie Infirmary until he could be found a foster home,' she said. 'Daddy didn't think it would be a good idea to see him again, in case it brought back bad memories and upset you.'

'But I *want* to see him,' Marjorie said and tears filled her eyes. 'He is my friend, Mummy. I want to know he is well and safe . . .'

Marjorie's mother came to sit next to her on the settee in front of the window. 'Is Danny very important to you, darling?' She put out a hand and stroked her head.

'He looked after me – and he fought those men when they tried to grab me, Mummy. I was afraid until he came but he helped me to be brave, he protected me. When I was shaking with fright, he held my hand and stood in front of me when they came!'

'And then you weren't afraid?' Her mother looked at her sadly. 'You're not very well at the moment but when you're better I'll ask the nurses at the Rosie Infirmary if you can visit Danny – would that be enough?'

'Yes, please,' Marjorie said and then, mournfully, 'I don't play with anyone, Mummy – why can't I play?'

'Because it isn't safe in the lane,' her mother said. 'I'll ask some of the other children to tea when you feel better – how is that?'

'Thank you.' Marjorie smiled at her. She preferred the old days when she could go out to play when she liked but she didn't want to be snatched again so she obeyed her mother and stayed in the house. 'I'll be better to-morrow.'

'We'll see,' her mother said. 'Would you like me to read you a story before I get our tea ready?'

'Yes please,' Marjorie said and placed her hand in her mother's trustingly. 'I like it when you read stories.'

Sucking her thumb, Marjorie settled against her mother and closed her eyes. She was content for the moment with the promises she'd been given but she did wish she had some friends to play with and she did want to see Danny and maybe Ron. He was all right, too, though he hadn't been as nice to her as Danny.

Ron paused in the task of fetching wood for Ted and looked up at the sky. Ted said it was warm for this time of year and they were lucky because the nights weren't as cold now.

'We'll need to find a room of some sort before the winter,' he'd told Ron as they sat in the canteen and tucked into a meal of shepherd's pie and greens followed by tapioca pudding with jam. It was good, filling food and they'd both eaten every scrap before going back to work in the woodyard on the docks. Ted's boss had given him a trial and, if he found their work satisfactory, he was going to take Ted on permanently this weekend when he got paid.

Ron hurried to Ted's side with the wood he'd chosen. Ted inspected it, looked pleased, and selected the piece he wanted next. He was making a door frame and then he would fit the door and the lock to the shed Ron had been helping him build. The sheds came in all sizes and were made to customers' orders and the one they were making now was just for show, to help the customers decide what they wanted. This one was a garden shed about ten feet by twelve feet, but they'd made a larger one for industrial use earlier in the week. It was interesting watching Ted work and Ron knew that he would like to do the same when he was older and more experienced; he was already learning bits and pieces and Ted was a good teacher.

Their boss summoned Ted and he left Ron to hold on to the half-built frame while he went to speak to him. He returned in a few minutes and they finished the job together.

'There, that should do it,' Ted told him standing back to nod with satisfaction. 'Catch hold of that, lad – and we'll put it in place.'

'This is a decent job, isn't it?' Ron said as he obliged. 'I love the smell of the fresh-cut wood.'

'Yes, I like that, too,' Ted told him with a smile. 'And the boss has just told me – he's taking us both on. The wage is small – five and sixpence a week for you and thirty shillings for me, but it's enough for us to get a place to sleep safe. We can afford to use a hostel every night and we'll start looking for lodgings. We can't afford two rooms yet but one with two single beds would do – if you can trust me to sleep in the same room, Ron?' His grey eyes were steady as they looked into Ron's brown ones. Ted wasn't a bad-looking man, in his late thirties, so he'd told him, never married, and a bit of a loner since his married sister had died after childbirth from a fever. Ron knew that fever killed a lot of folk in the lanes and streets of the East End, such as his mother and grandparents; he'd told Ted about that and being put in an orphanage where the other boys had been mistreated. They'd talked a lot when they weren't working and Ted had told him stories of his life in the Army – a life he had loved, which had taken him all over the world.

Ron looked at him and nodded as he watched Ted

screw the frame in place. 'You're like the dad I never had,' he told him. 'I know I didn't trust yer at first but now I do – and I like yer, Ted. I'd never have found work without you, or these clothes . . .'

The Sally Army had given Ron a pair of long trousers in hard-wearing cord, two shirts, a pullover and a jacket and cap, also a pair of stout boots. Without Ted's help and guidance, he would never have found them nor would he have had the courage to go in the building if he had – and the job that gave him a little money of his own was like a dream come true. Ron knew he owed it all to his new friend and he felt a respect and liking he'd never felt for any other human, other than his mother and Danny. His grandparents had always treated him as if he was a nuisance and his mother's shame, and though he'd loved her, Ron had felt she should have stood up for herself and him more.

Ron still thought of Danny a lot, even though many weeks had passed since they'd been imprisoned together. Ted had spoken to a police constable he knew, asking for news of Danny, but so far they hadn't heard anything of him.

He probably wouldn't see his friend again, Ron thought regretfully, but he'd found another and he had to be grateful for that. Had he not met Ted, he might have been dead or in an orphanage once more instead of enjoying a job he knew he was going to love and the companionship of others.

The men on the docks were, in the main, a friendly lot and they often gave Ron boiled sweets from packets they kept in their pockets. There was no menace or bribery associated with the act, just a friendly gesture that he'd learned to accept, able now to trust a little because of the man he just knew as Ted.

Whistling, he helped Ted to fix the door in place and then stood back to admire their work. It was a fine-looking shed, the first of many they would make together, and the boss was smiling as he came up to them.

'Good job, Ted. I've got a big order here for you and the lad – a manufacturing company on the East India Docks need a large store shed for their goods. I'm sending you and Ron to look at the site and I'm relying on you to give me an accurate estimate of how long it will take to build it on site – think you can do that?'

'Yes, Mr Reynolds,' Ted said. 'Shall we go now?'

'Yes – you can drive, can't you?'

'Learned in the Army.'

His boss nodded in satisfaction. 'You'll need to renew your licence if it is out of date – because you'll be driving to various sites when I can't get away and to do the work if we get the contract.'

'Thank you, sir,' Ted replied looking pleased. 'My licence is still in date. I've kept it up just in case.'

'Good man.' The boss took some keys from his pocket and handed them to him. 'That truck is yours to look after in future, put fuel and repairs on my account at the Eagle Garage in Shilling Street. I'm trusting you, Ted. Don't let me down.'

'We shan't do that, sir,' Ted said and smiled at Ron. 'We'll do a good job won't we?'

'Yes, Ted,' Ron replied and grinned. 'You can trust us, sir.'

'I believe I can,' the boss replied, handed Ted some papers and walked off.

Ted looked at Ron and winked. 'Well, that's a turn up for the books,' he said. 'I never expected that – and it makes things easier for us in future. We'll be able to look further afield for a room if we've got transport.'

Ron looked at him as his excitement mounted. The truck was old and had seen better days, but as Ted gave him a helping hand up into the passenger seat he felt a thrill of pleasure. Things were so much better since he'd met Ted!

CHAPTER 20

'It's lovely to see you,' Nurse Jenny said to Sarah when she visited the children's ward that sunny morning in mid-May. 'How are you feeling?'

'Clumsy and my back aches,' Sarah said with a grimace. 'Steve says I've never looked more beautiful, but I feel fat and ugly.'

'Steve is right, you're glowing,' Jenny told her with a little laugh. 'It can't be long now, Sarah – and then it will be all worthwhile. Just think of having your own baby to love and care for.'

'The doctor says the next couple of weeks or so should see it all over with,' Sarah said and sighed, pressing her hands to her back. 'I thought I would come out for a walk and a breath of air. Mum and Steve fuss over me all the time and I sometimes feel I want to run away and hide.'

'Oh, Sarah!' Jenny went into a peal of laughter, causing Sister Rose to look at her sharply. 'Oops, now, I've done it . . .'

'Sister Rose won't mind you having a word or me visiting,' Sarah said as she saw the anxious look in

165

the other nurse's eyes. 'She's always been lovely to everyone.'

'Well, something has changed,' Jenny said in a low voice. 'I can't seem to do anything right for her just lately and I don't know why.'

Sister Rose came up to them. She smiled at Sarah and then turned a distinctly cool gaze on Nurse Jenny. 'Please continue with your work, nurse. Sarah, come and have a cup of tea and tell me how you are . . .'

Sarah looked at Jenny's face as she walked away. It was clear she was in Sister Rose's bad books but she couldn't imagine why. Sarah had worked with Jenny in the past and knew her to be both hard working and conscientious. What could she have done to upset the sister?

Sister Rose was pleasant to Sarah as she made a cup of tea and gave it to her in the ward's best china, normally reserved for doctors. She asked Sarah how she was, if she was prepared for the birth and what she hoped for.

'Steve says he doesn't mind,' Sarah told her. 'I'm hoping for a boy this time but he only wants us both to be well.'

'And, of course, that is the most important thing—' Sister Rose was about to say more when she saw Peter Clark approaching. Sarah saw the change immediately: Rose's face went cold and her eyes wary. She watched him speak to Nurse Jenny, saw the smile that passed between them and the flash of pain in Sister Rose's eyes, and understood the change in the nurse she both liked and admired. She had expected Sister Rose and Peter Clark to get together one day, had thought it only a matter of time. Now it seemed he'd turned his attention to the younger nurse – and she wouldn't have thought it of him. He'd always seemed a decent person and it was cruel of him to give Sister Rose reason to hope and then flirt with the younger nurse.

'I must get on,' Sister Rose said, becoming her brisk professional self. 'Take care of yourself, Sarah, and be sure to bring the baby to see us when you can.'

'You must come to visit us for tea,' Sarah told her. 'You could bring that young boy I hear you've fostered – and your landlady. We'll have a little party. Mum would love to meet them.'

Sister Rose smiled at her warmly. 'What a lovely person you are, Sarah. Yes, we should enjoy that and Danny will make you a cake. Beattie is teaching him and he is getting quite good.'

Sarah saw Jenny shoot a quick glance at her as she went off to fetch something Sister Rose had asked for, leaving her to do the rounds with the doctor. There was nothing Sarah could say to the younger girl, because she couldn't tell her what was Sister Rose's private business – and it was only her intuition, after all, but Sarah knew in her heart that the sister had been badly hurt and was fighting her pain. It was sad if Peter Clark preferred the younger nurse but no one could tell him who to love – that was entirely his own affair.

After she left the children's ward, Sarah went to visit Matron, who had asked to see her. Matron gave her a small parcel and, opening it, she found a very pretty dress for a baby. It was white and so would suit either a boy or girl and Sarah thanked her sincerely. As she was about to leave the infirmary, Nurse Lily came up to her with a smile.

'Have you been visiting Matron?' she asked.

'Yes, and the children's ward. I spoke to Sister Rose and asked her to tea when the baby is born – you and Jenny might like to come too.'

'Would you mind if we came at a different time?' Lily asked with a frown. 'I can't explain why but at the moment being there with Sister Rose might be awkward.'

Sarah inclined her head. 'I think I understand, Lily,' she said. 'You and Jenny can come another time – love can be so hurtful, can't it?'

'Yes . . .' Lily hesitated, then, 'I can't say more at the moment, Sarah, but I blame Jenny; she's just having fun and doesn't realise.'

Sarah nodded. 'That's a pity. Do you imagine he knows?'

'Men are often too blinded by a pretty face to know what's best for them,' Lily said with feeling. 'I wish I knew what to do – Rose is a friend but Jenny is my sister so I'm torn.'

'Leave things for a while, Lily – it may sort itself out,' Sarah said thoughtfully.

'Yes,' Lily's expression cleared, 'that's what I keep thinking – Jenny gets bored easily. I believe she'll soon tire of him.'

'She wouldn't hurt Sister Rose if she knew.' Sarah stuck up for her friend but knew how Lily felt. Jenny really ought to have known that there was something between Dr Clark and Sister Rose – if she didn't, then she was the only nurse in the infirmary who hadn't guessed.

Leaving Lily to return to work, Sarah walked home in the sunshine. A little girl aged about nine was standing opposite the infirmary, looking at it indecisively, as if she wanted to go inside. Sarah hesitated but just as she was about to go and ask if she could help, the child ran off and disappeared around the corner.

Sarah was knitting when Steve got in that evening. She saw at once that he looked anxious and went to greet him with a kiss.

'Something wrong, love?'

'We had reports of a missing child today,' he replied with a frown. 'So far there's nothing to connect it with the gang that were snatching them off the streets and I know we got all those rogues at the warehouse and they're still in custody, but we always knew there might be more.'

'I thought one of the boys gave you a good description of the house they were taken to?' Sarah's eyebrows rose.

'He did and it was raided – but we found nothing.'

She nodded, rubbing his arm as she saw how anxious he was. Steve was a good policeman and the thing that upset him most was the kind of criminal who hurt children. He devoted much of his time to helping them stay off the streets and learn to defend themselves.

'I've got your favourite beef and mushroom pie in the oven,' she said, hoping to cheer him. 'Perhaps the child will turn up, Steve.' Then something occurred to her and she recalled the little girl she'd seen outside the infirmary. 'Was it a little girl who went missing?'

'No, it's a boy – why?'

'I saw a young girl outside the infirmary,' Sarah said. 'She seemed to be wondering whether she should go inside or not – but then she ran off and I came home.'

'She probably has a mother in one of the wards,' Steve said sensibly and she agreed. 'This little boy went to school as usual but after playtime he disappeared and they haven't seen him since.'

'His parents must be upset . . .'

'His mother certainly was when she reported it, but I think from things she said that he may be afraid of his father.' Steve frowned. 'You know what it's like, Sarah. The father gives a child a good hiding and they run off, so that could be it, and hopefully we'll find him safe and sound and take him home again. Unless he's in danger of being harmed at home, in which case I'll take him to the Rosie.'

'Let's hope it's just a little squabble,' she said. 'Now come and have your tea, Steve – you've got to be at the club by seven this evening.'

'Will you be all right on your own?'

'I shan't be alone,' Sarah told him with a smile. 'Mum and Theo are coming over to keep me company. We might have a game of cards or just sit and drink tea and eat cake.'

Steve nodded and kissed her softly. 'You know I would stay home if you asked me, love?'

'Of course, I do, you soft thing,' she said and tickled him round his neck. 'Those boys need you, Steve. I'll be fine.'

Steve was thoughtful as he walked to the boxing club that evening. Sarah seemed to be taking her pregnancy in her stride, though he knew her back ached and she felt ungainly. To him she just got more beautiful and his love for her filled his heart. His lovely wife meant the world to Steve and so would his child, whether it be a girl or a boy. He could not imagine what he would do if someone harmed his child; it made him shudder to think of it and though he knew there were many good men and women in the East End, there were far too many rogues. He and his colleagues battled against them but it was an uphill struggle and for every villain they put away, another popped up.

He thought briefly of the little girl Sarah had seen staring at the infirmary. Children alone on the streets were vulnerable no matter whether it be for a few minutes or hours . . .

CHAPTER 21

'Mummy,' Marjorie asked as her mother tucked her up in bed, 'did Daddy say it was the Rosie Infirmary that they took Danny to?'

'Yes, darling, I told you yesterday when we walked to school,' her mother told her and frowned. 'But Daddy also told us that Danny has been fostered out to a very good home and he is well and happy. We don't know where he is now.'

Marjorie nodded and smiled as her mother kissed her goodnight. 'I'm glad he's being looked after, Mummy, but I should still like to see him. Do you think they know where he is at the Rosie?'

'Perhaps – but Danny isn't really suitable for you to know, Marjorie darling. I understand that you were grateful to him but Daddy says you should forget all that nasty stuff. Seeing Danny again might bring back your bad dreams.'

Marjorie knew better than to argue with her mother. If Daddy decided something, Mummy wouldn't go against him – but perhaps she didn't have to know. Marjorie had asked a friend at school if she knew where the Rosie Infirmary was and she'd said her mother had been there once when she was sick and she thought she could remember how to get there. Shelly went home to lunch, unlike Marjorie, and in her lunch hour she'd found her way to the Rosie.

'I could go tomorrow and ask one of the nurses about your friend,' she'd told Marjorie when she returned to school. 'There's a nurse I really liked called Sister Rose – she was very kind to me when my mum was ill. She wouldn't get cross if I asked her if she knew where Danny was.'

'Would you take me with you in the lunch break?' Marjorie asked. 'We could find out where he is and then I might be able to go and visit him – but Mummy and Daddy won't let me so I'll have to sneak out of school . . .'

Marjorie had waited anxiously for her answer, because she was afraid to wander off alone, but if Shelly came with her, she wouldn't be as nervous. She'd been frightened on her first day back at school, but Shelly was bigger than her and confident and Marjorie felt better when she was with her – just as she had with Danny.

'Yeah, 'course,' Shelly said and grinned. 'Mum won't be at home tomorrow and she told me to get some chips – she's giving me threepence and I'll share with you. We'll eat them out of the bag with vinegar and salt, and then go to the Rosie.'

Marjorie hugged the secret inside as she settled down to sleep. She would have preferred to visit Danny with her mother, because she loved her and didn't want to make her cross, but her parents didn't understand how

174

much she wanted to see her special friend again. It wasn't really bad just to sneak off to see him, was it? And she would be quite safe with Shelly, because she could kick and fight nearly as good as the boys!

Danny looked with pride at the batch of rock buns he'd made the previous evening after school. Beattie said they were as good as hers and she'd told him he could take half of them to school and give them to his friends when they gathered in the playroom.

'You're gettin' to be a real good cook,' she'd told him with pride. 'Sister Rose told Nurse Sarah that you would bake a cake for her when we go to visit her after her baby is born.'

'I should like to make a cake for some of the other nurses, too,' Danny said. 'They were all kind to me when I was in the Rosie and it would be a good thing to do, wouldn't it?'

'Yes, Danny, it would,' Beattie said and smiled at him lovingly. Danny loved Beattie nearly as much as he'd loved his mum. He loved Sister Rose too, but she was different, a little bit above him and Beattie, but Beattie – she was like kin. If it was possible to have a second mum then Beattie was his and Danny sometimes had to pinch his own flesh to convince himself that it was real. How could he be so lucky?

Sometimes, he remembered the times at home after his mother died. He'd heard his father sobbing and then the drinking had started and the beatings. It made Danny feel sad, because there had been a time when they'd all been happy. He wondered what would happen if his father ever turned up and demanded he go home with him, but Sister Rose said he couldn't take Danny no matter what Jim Bryant said, because the police would lock him up. Danny just hoped it would never happen, because he couldn't bear to leave this home he'd been given.

He thought of Marjorie sometimes and Ron, too, but the memories were fading. He'd hoped he might get to see them but Sister Rose said the police couldn't find Ron and Marjorie's parents didn't want her to be reminded of a bad experience.

However, he could bake a cake for the nurses and perhaps for that nice police officer too. Constable Jones might know where to find Ron one of these days and Danny would ask him if he got the chance.

Rose saw the two little girls loitering as she went out to purchase a bag of sugar and some other ingredients so that Danny could make his cakes that evening. They were still there when she returned with her shopping bag loaded and, as she hesitated, one of them ran up to her, followed more slowly by the second.

'You're Sister Rose, aren't you? You looked after my mum when she was in the Rosie.'

'Did I?' Rose smiled at her. 'Is she better now?'

'Yes, thanks – but my friend wants to ask you something.' The girl pushed the second one forward.

She shifted from one foot to the other looking shy and Rose smiled. 'It's all right, you can ask whatever you like.'

'I want to know if you can tell me where Danny is!' the child blurted out breathlessly. 'I'm Marjorie and he saved me – and I never got a chance to tell him how much I like him.'

'Marjorie!' Rose smiled at her, delighted. 'I know where Danny is, because he lives with me. He asked me to find out if you were happy and safe but your parents didn't want to speak to me or Danny.'

Marjorie frowned. 'Daddy doesn't approve of boys like Danny – but he saved me,' she said and her eyes filled with tears. 'I want to see him, Sister Rose – will you let me come and talk to him?'

'Yes, I would let you come,' Rose said without hesitation, 'but you must ask your mother's permission.' She took her nursing notepad out and wrote down her address in capital letters to make it easy for the young girls to read. 'This is my address and, if your mother agrees, you can come to tea this Saturday or any Sunday. She can come too – and your father if he wants to make sure we're respectable.'

'Thank you!' Marjorie took the paper and peered at it, nodding as she read it very slowly. 'Number seven Bell Lane . . .'

'Yes, that's right, Marjorie,' Rose said. 'Remember that you have to ask your mummy and daddy first – but I shall tell Danny that I've seen you and you are well and happy.'

'Thank you!' Marjorie's eyes lit up. 'I've been thinking and thinking about him and I'll come and see him soon.'

Rose watched as the two little girls ran off and smiled. Danny would be thrilled that Marjorie had asked after him, but she wouldn't tell him to expect a visit because she didn't think Marjorie's parents would agree. Her father was an office manager and he seemed to imagine they were above Danny and look down on him, just because he'd come from a bad home.

Her smile was replaced with a frown. There was no good reason the children shouldn't be friends but if Marjorie's parents didn't wish for it that was the end of it.

'Now you can visit him,' Shelly said looking triumphantly at Marjorie as they hurried back to school. 'You know where he lives now.'

'I don't know where Bell Lane is,' Marjorie told her anxiously.

'You can ask people and they will direct you – I don't think it's far from here so if you go to school and then the Rosie and ask, you'll be all right.'

Marjorie nodded, but felt a trickle of unease at the nape of her neck. She didn't like to deceive her parents but she would have to think of a way, because she didn't think they would agree to her visiting Danny at his new home. So it would mean venturing out alone and she was still a bit frightened of doing that. Shelly noticed and said, 'I bet your mummy would let you come to tea with *me* one Sunday. I'll bring a note, shall I? Then you can come to me and then we'll visit Danny together – I should like to meet him.'

Marjorie's face lit up and she hugged her friend. 'You're so kind to me,' she said. 'I know you'll like my Danny and Mummy approves of you.' Shelly's mother ran a little cake shop and her father was a manager in an office.

She skipped happily by the side of her friend. Shelly was clever and brave and she thought of everything and now Marjorie could see Danny and that made her happy.

CHAPTER 22

Danny smiled broadly when Sister Rose told him about the little girl who had gone to the Rosie in search of him and that she'd said she was thinking of him and wanted to see him.

'I thought she would've forgotten all about me,' he said and grinned. 'I reckon that's all right, I do.'

'I told her she could come to tea with her parents any Sunday if she wished or this Saturday. You will have to make one of your special cakes, Danny.'

'Yeah, I'll ask Beattie what we should make,' Danny agreed. 'Thanks, Sister Rose, you're a good 'un, you are.'

'I'm just happy it pleases you,' Sister Rose said and brushed his hair with her hand. Danny was always trying to make the tuft on the crown lie down but it persisted in springing up like a little brush. Even after the hairdresser had cut it properly and smoothed it flat, the next morning it was back.

'You made me happy when you brought me here,' Danny said and was careful not to drop the 'h' off the words, because Sister Rose spoke properly and she said if you wanted to get on in the world it was a good idea. She didn't scold when he forgot and Beattie sometimes did it too so Danny didn't feel bad about it, but he was trying hard at school to learn as much as he could, because Sister Rose said if he wanted to bake his own cakes and sell them in a shop one day he would do well to learn how to write, read more than a few words and do sums.

Danny didn't have difficulty in learning now that he was trying. His new teacher had told him he was a bright boy and he'd made friends with several boys in his class, including one called Jamie. He liked Jamie because he'd told him about a club he went to some nights.

'They teach boxing and self-defence,' Jamie had told him. 'Constable Steve Jones runs it with a friend of his who used to be a boxer – they call him Mad Max but he's all right. If you joined you would learn to stand up to anyone who tried to harm you.'

Danny thought that was a good idea. He'd spoken to Beattie about it and she'd asked Sister Rose and it was agreed that he should join. When he'd talked to Jamie the next day he'd found they didn't live far apart so he arranged to meet him and walk to the club with him the first time; if he liked it, they would meet on the nights they were both going to the club and walk home together.

'My brother Arch often comes with me,' Jamie had told him. 'There used to be a gang of bullies hanging around but we don't get any trouble now. We look after some of the younger ones just until they're good at looking out fer themselves.'

Danny liked his new friend Jamie's elder brother. He made a seed cake for them and they'd said he could go to tea with them at the flat above Mr Forrest's shop where they lived. Sister Rose shopped there and she said Mr Forrest was lovely and Danny could go there whenever he wanted. He was enjoying learning about self-defence but he wasn't very good yet, not like Jamie who had recently won a prize at national level.

Once again, Danny thought how lucky he was these days. He was glad Marjorie was all right but he still wondered about Ron . . .

Ron enjoyed the woodwork needed for making the sheds and Ted had started to teach him to carve wood. They made figures of animals and special spoons Ted thought they might sell at a fair or to a shop one day, called love spoons. They worked on their carving in the evenings in the room they'd taken at a hostel.

'Shall we have a treat today?' Ted said. 'It's Saturday and the boss gave us a two-shilling bonus this week.'

Ron hesitated, then, 'Could we have fish and chips?'

'Yes, if you'd like,' Ted agreed. 'We'll take the truck back to Mr Reynolds and then we'll go and get them. And there's a fete on at the Methodist church this afternoon. We could go after we've eaten – we might even buy an ice cream.'

'Can we afford it?' Ron said, because they were saving to get a proper room, two if possible, and have their own beds and chairs and other things they would need.

'We shan't spend much but we deserve a treat. We've been working together for nearly two months now, Ron. We should celebrate a little.'

Ron smiled and climbed into his seat. Ted had promised he would teach him to drive as soon as he was sixteen but that was a long way off yet to a fourteen-year-old boy. At least, he thought that was his age. No one had ever bothered to tell him his birthday or who his father was and his only memories were of grumbling grandparents and an ailing mother. Ted said he could pick a day as his birthday and they would celebrate it on that day, which was a grand idea and made Ron smile. In the end he decided on the fifteenth of September, though he had no idea why – perhaps because it was a way off yet and he wanted to look forward to it.

When they got to the lumber yard, Mr Reynolds was about to leave. He shook his head as Ted offered the keys to the truck. 'You keep the vehicle this weekend, Ted. You have my permission to use it to look round for that new accommodation you're after and I'll give the landlord a reference if they need one. You and the lad are my best workers and I want you to be comfortable in a home of your own.'

'Thank you, sir.' Ted touched his cap and looked pleased. 'We'll take good care of it for you.'

'Have a good weekend, Ted – and you, Ron.'

Ted grinned as he drove off. 'This means we can have a real good search locally after the fete and tomorrow. I did hear of somewhere that might be all right but it was nearly twenty minutes further afield than the hostel, perhaps more if I couldn't find the short cut so I hadn't bothered.'

Ron grinned at him happily. Life was good now and he couldn't think of anything he wanted he didn't already have – apart from his mate Danny, the only person who had ever stood up for him before Ted.

Danny went with Beattie to the church fete. She and Danny had baked a tin of cakes for it, which she'd taken to the hall the previous evening. They planned to spend half an hour looking round the stalls and then they would go home just in case Marjorie and her mother turned up for tea.

'I think they would've let us know,' Beattie said, 'but we'll just have a little look round the fete and then go home, shall we?'

'Yes please, Beattie,' Danny said.

When they got there the church garden was thronged with people walking around the stalls and buying things. Danny had a go at guessing how many beans were in the jar and Beattie bought a pair of pretty gloves made of lace, some coconut ice for Danny and a pretty compact mirror for Sister Rose. It had blue enamel and they both thought Sister Rose would love it. Beattie wondered that anyone would give it to a church fete, because the enamel was perfect.

'I always find some bargains here,' Beattie said, pleased with her purchase.

'I'd like to get something nice for Jamie,' Danny said. 'Look at that little penknife – it's only sixpence and I can afford it from the pocket money Sister Rose gives me. Do you think he would like it?'

'I should say your friend would love it.' Beattie smiled. 'Right, I'm just going to talk to the Minister for a moment and then we'll go home.'

Danny nodded and picked the knife up. It was perfect

and had engraving on the side of the cover. Smiling in pleasure, he took his sixpence out and gave it to the stallholder then slipped the knife in his pocket and turned to walk away. As he did so, a hand gripped his shoulder and a voice he dreaded spoke in his ear.

'Got yer, yer little bastard!'

'Dad!' Danny looked up in terror as his father grasped his arm in a painful grip. 'Let me go – please!

Danny glanced around desperately, trying to attract Beattie's attention but she had her back turned and didn't see or hear as his father hustled him through the crowd, struggling and kicking and shouting Beattie's name. No one did anything to stop him being dragged off, just thinking he was an unruly boy, and his father was too big and strong and relentless as he hauled him from the church garden and into the street.

'Please let me go,' Danny begged again. 'I live with Beattie now and she's my legal foster mother.'

'Yer my son and yer'll do what I tell yer,' his father muttered and cuffed his ear. 'I'll make yer sorry yer ever run off and pinched me things.'

Danny cried out and begged a passing woman to help him. 'Tell Beattie me dad's got me!' he cried but she just looked frightened and walked off. Danny was filled with despair. He should have known that living with Beattie was too good to be true; his wonderful dream looked as if it had come to an end, and there was nothing he could do . . .

Ron glanced out of the truck window as Ted tried to find a place to park near the church. He caught sight of a man and a boy struggling and then, just as they turned the corner and disappeared, something struck a chord.

'That's Danny!' he said. 'And some bloke has got him.'

'What?' Ted asked, not truly listening as he parked but the minute he'd braked, Ron jumped out and ran down the road. He reached the corner and paused, because there was no sign of them. Ted came rushing up to him then. 'What's wrong? Why did you run off like that?'

'I saw Danny and someone had got him,' Ron said. 'He was struggling, trying to get away, but whoever it was had him firm and wouldn't let go. I saw them turn down here but they've disappeared.'

'Are you certain it was Danny?'

Ron hesitated. 'I think so, but I only caught a glimpse before they turned the corner.'

'Do you want to have a drive around and look for him?'

'Can we?' Ron asked. 'He helped me – and that boy was in trouble.'

'All right then, lad, we'll go and look for them.'

They ran back to the truck and Ted pulled safely out into the road. He followed the route the two had taken but at the end of the road there was a junction and they weren't sure which way to go.

'Right or left?' Ted asked.

Ron hesitated. There was no sign of the man or the boy. 'Let's go left and just drive around for a bit,' he said and so they did but then Ted turned left and up another road, which then led into another and back into the road in front of the church. He shook his head, frowning.

'I don't know where to go next, son.'

'We shan't find them,' Ron said. 'I think I should tell the police – that constable who took me to the hospital. He knows about Danny.'

'All right, we'll do that,' Ted said and started the engine.

'You wanted ter go to the fete . . .' Ron said. 'I'm sorry.'

'That was a treat for you,' Ted said. 'We'll go to the police station and report what you saw.'

Beattie turned looking for Danny and for a moment or two she didn't worry, thinking that he must have wandered off, but after a few minutes she began to get anxious. Where had he gone? Surely nothing bad could happen to him here? She rushed up to the stall where they'd seen the penknife and asked the man serving if he'd seen Danny and if he'd bought the knife.

'You mean the young lad whose father just took him off?' the stallholder said and laughed. 'I don't know what he'd been up to but by the looks of it he was in for a strapping when he got home.'

'Danny doesn't have a father – at least, he doesn't live with him, because he used to knock him about,' Beattie said. 'Did you see where they went?'

'He just dragged the lad off . . .' The stallholder frowned. 'He was struggling, trying to get away but he called him Dad – I didn't think anything to it.'

'The police have been trying to find Mr Bryant,' Beattie said. 'He used to beat Danny terribly – and he'll do so again.' She shook her head, tears welling in her eyes. 'Sister Rose will never forgive me if anything happens to him – and even if she does, I'll not forgive myself.'

Beattie walked away, her head spinning. She wanted to run and beg people to look for Danny – her precious boy.

'Is something the matter, Beattie?' the Minister asked as she moved past him distractedly.

'My Danny has gone missing – his father grabbed him.' Beattie gave a cry of despair. 'What do I do? He's a wicked bully and he'll hurt Danny, I know he will!'

'You must go to the police at once,' the Minister told her. 'Just a second and I'll take you in my car.'

Beattie looked at him and burst into tears. He was being so kind and it was all her fault. If she hadn't been so busy talking Danny would still be safe and sound.

CHAPTER 23

Rose looked at the clock. It was nearly four o'clock and Beattie wasn't home. She'd said that she would be back at three thirty so that they could all greet Marjorie together if she came with her parents. How strange, Rose thought, because Danny had made special butterfly cakes with creamy filling for Marjorie and been excited that she might come.

As the hand crept round to half-past four, Rose began to feel really worried. It was nearly a quarter to five when the kitchen door opened and Beattie entered, looking pale and distressed.

'What's wrong?' Rose asked, her heart catching. 'Where is Danny?'

'He was taken off by someone claiming to be his father,' Beattie said. 'It's my fault, Rose. He went to buy something and I was talking, laughing at what Mr Parkinson, the Minister, was saying, and my back was turned to Danny.' She caught her breath and sat down. 'I looked for him everywhere but he wasn't in the garden and then – then the stallholder told me he'd been taken off by his father and it looked like he was

189

in trouble.' A great sob escaped her. 'Mr Parkinson took me to the police station and I told them the story – but that nice Constable Jones wasn't there and the others didn't know anything about it. They said Danny wasn't missing until he'd been gone at least a week and that his father was entitled to custody. They wouldn't listen when I told them I was his foster mother.'

'I'll go and see Sarah,' Rose said. 'She'll make sure her husband knows and he will do whatever is necessary.'

'Oh, Rose, I'm so sorry!' Beattie sobbed. 'I know it's my fault but I never thought anything bad could happen on a lovely sunny afternoon at the church fete.'

'Why should you?' Rose replied. 'Make yourself a cup of tea and put a drop of brandy in it for the shock. We'll sort this out, Beattie – and until we do, we'll just have to pray Danny is all right.'

Sarah and her husband were having tea when Rose knocked at their front door. Sarah went to answer it because Steve had only just got in.

'I'm sorry to disturb you, Sarah, but it is urgent,' Rose said before Sarah could even say hello.

Sarah hurried her into the kitchen.

'Sister Rose is here, love, and I think something is wrong.'

'It's Danny,' Rose blurted out in distress, 'he was snatched at the church fete by his father!'

'Good grief!' Steve was immediately concerned. 'Come and sit down, Sister Rose. Tell me as much as you can, please.'

Rose sat down on the chair he'd vacated. Her hands

were shaking and she felt a little sick as she explained what had happened, ending, 'The stallholder believed it was just a normal father, angry with his son,' Rose said. 'People tend to turn a blind eye to things like that – they don't like to interfere . . .'

'No,' Steve backed her up. 'A few might if they see a fight but a young boy and a man claiming to be his father?' He shrugged expressively. 'People think they'll be in the wrong if they interfere.'

'Beattie wouldn't have let it happen had she seen it,' Rose said. 'She thought it was safe in a church garden. Everyone said Mr Bryant had disappeared.'

'We thought he might be dead,' Steve told her with a frown. 'Had we found him he would probably be in prison – and he knows that.'

'Then he must have a hiding place in the area,' Rose said.

'Mmm. There are hundreds of places he might hide,' Steve said. 'Derelict warehouses, slum houses that are waiting to come down, outhouses at the back of factories, under the bridges . . .'

Rose gave a little gulp of despair. 'So it's hopeless?'

'I didn't say that, Sister Rose.' Steve reached for his helmet. 'I'll have something to eat when I get home, Sarah – I'm going to the station and then I'll ring round a few more, see if anyone has heard anything.'

'I'll come with you,' Rose said but he shook his head.

'Go home to Beattie. She'll need you; and someone has to be at home all the time in case Danny manages to get away and comes home.'

'Do you think he might?' Rose felt a flicker of hope.

'He did before, but his father might keep a closer

watch on him. He'll probably get beaten, but hopefully nothing more. Danny said he wasn't too bad except when he was drunk.'

Rose looked at him sombrely. Danny would be frightened and perhaps in pain and there was nothing she could do to help him.

'Can you find him for us please?' she asked tearfully.

'I'm going to do my best – and so will the rest of us,' Steve promised as he left the kitchen.

Rose nodded. She looked at Sarah, who was sitting down and obviously tired. 'You should rest. I'm sorry to take your husband away from you like this.'

'It's what Steve does,' Sarah said with a smile. 'Would you pop round to my mum and tell her I'm on my own this evening, Sister Rose? I don't feel like walking that far.'

Rose looked at her and realised she might be very close to having her baby. 'Yes, of course I shall. You sit there and rest Sarah and I'll tell Gwen that you need her.'

'Did you hear that?' Gwen said as she came back from answering the door. 'Will you run me round there, Theo? I think Sarah might surprise us all and have her baby a little early.'

'Of course, I will, Gwen,' Theo said and smiled at her affectionately. He glanced at the two boys, who were bent over a jigsaw puzzle. 'If Mrs Cartwright is gone for a while you should lock up and go to bed, Charlie.'

Gwen looked at them. 'Are you two all right on your own for a while?'

'Of course, we are, Mum,' Charlie said. 'Ain't we Ned. You stop all night if you have to.'

'Yeah, we're all right,' Ned agreed.

'You can have cake for your supper and a glass of milk. Just don't light the gas to make cocoa if I'm not back.'

Theo winked at the boys. 'They won't set the place alight, will you, lads?'

'No, sir,' Charlie said. 'We're all right.'

'Be good then,' Gwen said and sighed as she went to kiss them both before leaving them. They were good sensible lads and she knew they would be fine but she didn't like to leave them alone for long. Perhaps Steve wouldn't be long and if not, she would send Theo back to make sure they were safe.

Gwen looked round the kitchen once more and saw everything was in its place. She gave them a smile of reassurance and left.

Charlie grinned at Ned. 'Mum don't half fuss – but I like it,' he said and gave a cry of triumph as he pounced on a missing piece of puzzle. 'She forgets I can make a cup of hot cocoa easy.'

'She just wants to look after us,' Ned said and smiled. 'She's the best is our mum!'

Sarah gasped as the pain hit her in the back. She'd been expecting her labour to start all day, because the pains had come and gone and she hadn't said anything because it was Steve's night at home and he would have fetched the midwife had he been there. However, it couldn't be helped. A missing child was important and her mother would be here soon. She took a deep breath, counting the seconds. The time between pains was getting shorter and she'd better get herself up to bed.

Clinging on to the handrail, she hauled herself up the stairs one by one, each seeming a mountain to climb. At the top she paused for breath then walked slowly to the bedroom and turned down the covers on her bed. In the bottom of her wardrobe she had a rubber sheet and some towels, which she placed on the bed to save the mattress if her waters broke once she was lying down. Biting her lip to stifle the scream that rose to her lips, Sarah eased herself on the bed and against the piled-up pillows. She'd been lying there for about twenty minutes when she heard the front door open and her mother's voice calling to her from downstairs.

'Are you up there, Sarah?'

'Yes. Mum, I need the midwife . . .'

'I'll sent Theo to get her,' her mother called up the stairs, 'and I'll put the kettle on!' A few minutes later Sarah heard her mum run lightly up the stairs. She was smiling and calm when she entered the bedroom. 'How are the pains?'

Sarah grimaced. 'My waters have broken, Mum. I think it won't be long now . . .'

'Well, don't worry, love, I'm here,' Gwen said. 'And just scream if you want to, Sarah, there's no one but me to hear!' She nodded. 'That water ought to be boiling now, I'll run down and get it.'

Sarah gave what resembled a growl rather than a scream, angry with herself for giving in, but then the pain came stronger and she screwed up her face and gritted her teeth. She let rip when her mother had gone, grabbing hold of a towel she'd tied to the bedhead. Panting as hard as she could, she counted up to ten before the pain struck again and made her moan. She arched upwards as her mother came back carrying a kettle of steaming water and a bowl.

'Those things on the towel on the dressing table – put them in hot water, Mum.' Gwen picked up the stainless-steel objects and put them into the enamel bowl, pouring hot water on. 'We'll need them!'

'Pant now,' Gwen instructed. 'I'm going to have a look . . .' She pulled up Sara's nightgown and looked. 'I'm no expert but I've seen a few babies born to my neighbours when the midwife was late – and I think you should push now if you need to.'

'I'm not sure I can . . .' Sarah grimaced but did as she knew she ought despite the agony, which felt as if she were being torn apart. 'Ahhh!' She screamed out loudly as she felt the worst pain of all. 'I think it's coming! Is it, Mum?'

Gwen looked again and nodded. 'Yes, love, the head is there; I can see it – you just need to do that again.'

'I can't!' Sarah flopped back against the pillows but then as the urge came she pushed once more, panting and groaning as the pain intensified to an agonising peak and then her mother gave a cry of triumph and bent over the bed to receive the tiny, slippery little body. She deftly wrapped towels around it and looked at Sarah, tears in her eyes.

'You've got a little boy, Sarah – but I'm not quite sure what to do now. I think I should tie a knot or something . . .?'

'The things you scalded in the hot water on the

dressing table, Mum. Clamps and special scissors. Bring them here and I'll tell you what to do . . .'

Gwen obeyed after laying the baby in a nest of towels at the foot of the bed and then, gritting her teeth against the contractions that had started to expel the afterbirth, Sarah explained how to clamp the umbilical cord then cut it. Gwen followed her instructions and then picked up the baby and gave him to Sarah. On his head was an amazing thatch of blond hair, still stained with Sarah's blood, but his eyes were open, staring at her and beautifully blue. Sarah smiled, feeling a flow of overwhelming love for the baby she'd just given birth to, comparatively easily compared to some births she'd seen during her nursing training.

'He's beautiful, Sarah, and you're so lucky – getting a boy the first time. Not that I would have swapped you for half a dozen boys, but I know you wanted a son . . .'

Sarah looked at her mother with eyes brimming with tears of love. It was right, somehow, that they'd brought this child into the world together; they'd always been so close and it gave them another bond they would always share. Sarah kissed her baby and smiled at her mother as she sat on the bed beside them. It was a special moment. She could hear the sound of the kitchen door opening. The midwife would be here any moment to take over and do all the necessary things but for just these few seconds, mother, daughter and grandson were together in perfect harmony.

Gwen turned as the midwife entered the bedroom. 'My clever daughter has managed most of it all by herself, but I'm sure you'll want to take a look at the baby and her.'

'Well, I can't say I didn't expect it,' the midwife said with a laugh. 'Sarah has a mind and a will of her own and I was prepared for this to happen – but since I knew she'd done the same training as me, I wasn't too worried.'

She moved round the bed and took a peek at the baby, approving what they'd done and then went to Sarah. 'I'll just have a look at you, too, love, to make sure you're all right.'

'Thank you.' Sarah smiled at her and then looked at her mother. 'I think Steve has just come in, Mum – take William and show him.'

'That was your dad's middle name,' Gwen said looking pleased. 'I'll show little Will to his father and then I'll put a kettle on again. I'm sure we could all do with a cup of tea!'

It was more than an hour later, when the midwife had gone and Gwen had returned home to the boys who waited for her, that Steve brought a cup of milky cocoa to Sarah and sat on the edge of the bed.

'I'm sorry I left you alone, love. If you'd told me I wouldn't have gone.'

'You had a job to do and Mum came,' Sarah told him smiling. 'I was all right with her and Theo fetched the midwife. He was very good, Steve. I'm glad she has him as her friend now – and if they get together, I'll be pleased for her.'

'He's certainly a decent chap,' Steve agreed, 'and I'd like to think that Gwen has someone in her life. I know she has the boys and you, but she needs someone to look after her too.'

'I know, and I think he will,' Sarah smiled. 'He spoils her, Steve, and I don't think she's ever had much of that. Dad was never able to do it but Theo can.'

Steve nodded and smiled as he kissed her cheek. 'Thank you for my beautiful son, Sarah. I'm so proud of you.'

'Thank you, darling,' Sarah replied. 'He is lovely, isn't he?'

'Beautiful!'

'We're so lucky – but tell me, please. Did you manage to do anything to help Sister Rose?'

'Yes, I've put the chaps on full alert – and I rang a friend of mine at Ale Lane Station to put the word out further and he told me they'd had a report of a man abducting a boy he claimed to be his son, whose name was Danny Bryant!'

'Danny! So, someone saw it and reported it?'

'Yes, a man and a boy of about fourteen. The man's name is Ted Phillips and the boy's called Ron.' Steve frowned. 'I can't help wondering if Ron is the lad that was with Danny when we found them in that warehouse – but as far as I know he didn't have any family.'

'Did your friend know where they were staying?'

'Yes, they gave their address as a hostel,' Steve said. 'Sergeant Bryan Marshall thought they were either brothers or perhaps uncle and nephew, something of the sort, because the younger one called the older man Ted.'

'You think it's the lad you've been looking for because he knew it was Danny and was concerned for him?' Sarah frowned as her husband nodded. 'Are you worried about Ron as well?'

'I'd like to make sure he's all right and hear what he saw,' Steve said. 'So, I'll go over to the hostel in the morning and see what I can find out.'

'Yes, that would be a good idea,' Sarah agreed. 'If it is Ron, he might be able to help – Danny may have told him places his father frequents.'

'You would make a good detective,' Steve said and leaned forward to kiss her. He took her empty cup from her. 'Go to sleep and rest now, my darling. Your mum will be here in the morning after the boys go to school and I'll be here until then. If you want anything just wake me.'

'I love you,' Sarah said sleepily and closed her eyes.

Steve smiled and went quietly from the room. He would sleep next door with both doors open for tonight to let Sarah get some proper rest, but if she woke and called out, he knew he would hear her, because his mind was too active to sleep much.

Was Ron with someone he could trust? And was Danny being ill-treated and in actual danger of his life?

CHAPTER 24

Danny shivered with cold as he lay on the ground, wrapping his arms about himself to try to keep some warmth in his body. He had no idea where they were, except that it was some kind of derelict building; he thought it was in a back alley not far from the docks, because during the night he'd heard the sound that the barges made when they were warning others to stay clear. However, now that his father's bit of candle had burned out, it was so dark in here that he couldn't see anything, even though a glimmer of light was coming between two boards blocking out what must have once been windows.

His father was drunk and sleeping. He'd brought Danny here the previous day and given him a hiding before settling down on some old sacking to start drinking. He was surrounded by empty bottles, food waste and rubbish and it was obvious that he'd been living here for a while. Danny could hear an occasional grunt and snore from him but hardly dared to move.

'Try running away again and I'll kill yer,' he'd warned Danny the previous day. 'You're me son and you'll do as yer told. I need ter find work ter get me drink and food – and yer can 'elp me.'

Danny hadn't answered him. There was no point, for Jim Bryant wouldn't have listened. Danny knew that he would be forced to do whatever his father told him until he found the opportunity to run away, but that might not come for days. If he'd known how to get out of wherever they were, he might have tried while his father slept, but he had no idea where the door was and he thought his father had some means of blocking it because he'd heard the sound of something heavy being dragged into place the night before and his father had muttered about keeping the buggers out. If someone was being kept out, then Danny was shut in and he had to wait until his father opened the door.

Lying there on the hard floor, cold, hungry and miserable, Danny thought about the wonderful life he'd had at Beattie's. It had been his dream of a home and a loving mother come true and he felt the tears on his cheeks, knowing it was lost to him forever. Beattie would think he had run away and perhaps she wouldn't want him back, even if he managed to escape.

Scuffing the tears from his cheeks, Danny knew he had to stay strong inside, just like Ron had told him.

'When they beat us and do things we hate, we just have to shut it out,' Ron had confided. 'Some men are bullies and beasts, Danny, but if we don't let them, they can't touch the real us inside – no matter what they do to our bodies.'

'I wish I was wiv you, Ron,' Danny whispered. Together they'd been strong. They'd managed to fight off the bullies who had tried to hurt them at that warehouse and then the police had come. Danny prayed that the police would come for him and take him somewhere safe, but he knew it was unlikely to happen again. No one knew where he was and his father said he had a right to do what he liked with his own son. Perhaps he was correct, but when a man beat and starved his son, that couldn't be legal, surely? If that nice Constable Jones knew what was happening, he would look for Danny.

The thought made Danny feel much better. Beattie and Sister Rose loved him. Perhaps they would go to Constable Jones . . .

Danny froze as he heard the sounds of his father stirring in the gloom. He coughed, farted and then spat. A few moments later a match flared and a candle was lit and held over Danny. He felt a drop of hot wax on his hand and flinched. Then his father's boot connected with Danny's side.

'Get up, you lazy little bugger. We've got ter go ter work if we want ter eat.'

'Where are we going?' Danny asked as he got to his feet and stood shivering.

'If yer want ter 'ave a piss do it over there in the bucket,' his father ordered, pointing with the candle.

Danny could now see enough to make out some broken crates lying around and some of them had been used as a table and a seat. He saw the bucket behind one of them and went to use it. The smell made him recoil because it had been used for excrement and not emptied for days. Taking a deep breath, he relieved himself and went back to his father.

Jim Bryant laughed. 'You'll get used to worse than

that,' he sneered. 'You wait until we finish cleaning the lorries from the boneyard – that's where the animal carcasses are brought when the meat's been stripped off. The stink makes yer sick ter yer guts – but it's the only work they'll give me. I can't do it fast enough to earn much, so you can help me and I'll earn plenty for my whisky.' He nodded. 'That's not all yer can do fer me either – I've got another job in mind but we'll do the cleaning first so it won't look strange when I don't turn up.'

'What do you mean?'

'Mind yer tongue or yer'll get me fist in yer mouth!'

'I'm hungry,' Danny said, 'and thirsty.'

'Drink this.' His father pushed a bottle at him. It was a whisky bottle and Danny shook his head. 'It's water in it, I wouldn't waste good whisky on you, runt.'

Danny took the bottle and wiped the top with his hand before lifting it to his lips and sipping. It was water and it tasted awful, but he swallowed just enough to help his throat and wet his mouth.

'Is there any food?'

'We'll get bread when yer've earned yer keep!' He aimed a blow at Danny's ear, but the boy jerked back. 'Little bugger – try to run and I'll kill yer next time!' He grunted. 'Yer can help me move this . . .'

By the light of the candle, Danny could see a large piece of wood had been pushed in front of the door to stop it coming open because the lock had been broken and there was nothing to stop it blowing back in the wind unless the wood was lodged behind it. Most men would have fixed up a lock if they'd wanted to use the derelict shed but his father hadn't done even that.

'How long have you been here?' he asked his father as they shifted the wood.

'Since yer went orf like that,' Jim grunted. 'The soft bugger landlord allowed us ter stay there when yer were wiv me 'cos he liked yer – and yer mother. Had a soft spot fer her I reckon. Well, the bitch died and left me ter look after yer – and now yer goin' ter earn yer keep.'

Danny kept his angry protest inside. He hated his father so much and couldn't bear to hear the mother he'd loved spoken of as a bitch. It was as if his father resented her for dying, as if it were her fault. Mum hadn't wanted to die and leave them. Tears were burning his eyes but Danny wouldn't let them fall. He had to stay strong the way Ron had told him and as soon as the opportunity came, he would take the chance to run.

'Ted Phillips? Yes, I know him and his apprentice well,' Mr Samson the hostel manager said and smiled. 'A decent man and I was sorry to lose them. They always kept their room clean and neat – and there was nothing funny going on. I'd swear to that, Constable. You can always tell *that* sort – no, they had separate beds and both were slept in. They couldn't afford two rooms but now they can and they've moved to new lodgings – two rooms in a private house.'

'Very informative,' Steve said writing it all into his little notebook. 'Can you give me their address, sir?'

'Unfortunately, I didn't ask. They never have letters so there was no forwarding address. I'm sorry . . .'

'That's a nuisance,' Steve said frowning. 'They may have important information that could be very helpful in tracing another young lad who has been abducted.'

'Mr Phillips wouldn't have anything to do with something like that!'

'No, I'm sure he wouldn't – but they were witnesses.'

'Ah, I see.' Mr Samson's eyes widened. 'Oh, well, in that case I can tell you where they work.'

'I should be very grateful, sir. I can assure you, they are not in any trouble.'

'Good, I shouldn't like to think that,' Mr Samson took a deep breath. 'They work for the Reynolds Woodyard at the East India Docks.'

'Good.' Steve nodded and wrote it down. 'You've been very helpful, sir. I can tell you that I am hoping that we can save a young lad from a life of brutality, and perhaps a violent death.'

Mr Samson tutted and shook his head. 'We live in terrible times, Constable.'

'I'm afraid this sort of thing never changes,' Steve said. 'We condemn the Victorians for turning a blind eye, but there's just as much evil goes on now, though much of it may be in the home and unseen.'

'Dear, dear me,' Mr Samson muttered and went inside.

Steve turned away. It was time for him to be at the station, but before he went home this evening, he would make time to call in at the Reynolds Woodyard and ask Ted Phillips and Ron to tell him what they knew.

'They weren't much help at the police station, were they?' Ron said to Ted as they worked on the new shed for Johnson's the Baker in Still Street. 'I know they took all the details down – and that Constable Howarth was all right, but they didn't seem to think there was much they could do unless they got more information.'

'Well, police work is twenty-five per cent deduction and seventy-five per cent luck.' Ted grinned at him and winked. 'If they get a tip-off it helps them catch the criminals and that is likely what will help them find Danny and the man they believe may be his father.'

Ron looked puzzled. 'Why do you think he snatched him and took him off like that?'

'I doubt it was for love or worry over his son – it must be something Danny can do he needs.'

'You mean help him with work, like I help you?'

'If it was something like that I wouldn't worry,' Ted replied and looked thoughtful. 'Is Danny a big lad like you?'

'Quite big,' Ron agreed, 'but thinner.'

'So, he'd be able to get in small windows and things?'

'Mebbe . . .' Ron's eyes widened. 'You think he wants Danny to help him steal things?'

'Perhaps – it just made me wonder, that's all.' He looked up at the sky. 'I reckon it might rain so we'll get this done, Ron, and then we can go for our break and have something to eat.'

Ron nodded but was thoughtful as he helped his friend and employer to finish the shed they were working on. He was hungry and it was just starting to rain as they packed up and ran for the shelter of the truck. Ron had been lucky when he met Ted, but Danny might be forced to do all sorts of things even if it was his father that had caught him. They couldn't be sure of that – it might have been one of the men who'd got them before . . . That thought made Ron shudder. If Danny had fallen into the clutches of men like that he would disappear, never to be seen again.

Ted was just about to move off when he saw the police constable coming towards him with an upstretched hand. He paused and wound down the window to hear what he had to say.

'Can I help you, Constable?'

'I think you may.' The officer smiled through the window. 'Hello, Ron – how are you?'

'Very well, sir. This is my friend Ted – we work together.'

The police constable nodded. 'And you think you saw Danny being dragged off by a man?'

'Yes, I'm sure I did.'

'Let the constable get in beside you out of the rain,' Ted instructed and Ron obligingly budged up to allow Steve the room to sit with them. 'You know Ron – so you must be Constable Jones.'

'Yes, I was able to help him and Danny,' Constable Jones replied. He reached across Ron to shake hands. 'I wondered if there was any more information you could give me?'

'We chased after them,' Ted said frowning, 'but by the time we turned the corner they had disappeared and there was a crossroads. We drove all the way round for a while but couldn't see them so we went to the nearest station and reported it.'

'You did exactly right,' Steve said and looked at Ron. 'I just wondered if Danny told you anything about his father – the places he went, what he did for a living . . . anything you could think of at all?'

Ron thought for a moment, then, 'I think he worked on the docks, last thing Danny knew, but he lost his job after his wife died and he started drinking.'

Ted frowned, his eyes narrowing in thought. 'What is Danny's second name? Do you know, Ron?'

Ron shook his head, but the constable said, 'It's Bryant – his father is Jim Bryant and they lived in Little Lane – why?'

'Good God!' Ted said and looked furious. 'Jim Bryant's my late sister's husband! I fell out with him before my sister died and he wouldn't let me in the house when I heard she'd died, so when Ron told me about his friend Danny, I had no idea. I haven't seen Daniel since he was about five.'

'So Danny might be your nephew?' Constable Jones wrote it all down in his book. 'That helps quite a bit, sir – you might know more than Ron, perhaps?'

'I know Bryant drinks a lot – that's why we fell out.' Ted looked thoughtful. 'He worked on the docks doing anything he could – unloading, labouring. He was never a skilled man as far as I know and I could never see what my sister loved about him. I thought he was a big brute, though I suppose he was better when she was alive.'

Constable Jones kept writing. 'So, we should look on the docks, then? We would have done so anyway but that certainly helps. Anything else?'

'Yes, there is,' Ted said remembering. His mouth tightened. 'He had a short sentence for housebreaking some years ago. I warned Doris to leave him then, but she forgave him for the sake of her son.'

'A mistake too many women make,' Constable Jones agreed. 'That may come in useful if he has decided to go back to his old ways.'

'Yes . . .' Ted frowned. 'Where was Danny living?'

'With his foster mother – a Mrs Beattie Robinson of Bell Lane,' Steve Jones said. 'Look, it might be a good idea if you went around to see her, sir. When we find Danny – and we shall – you may wish to be involved in his future?'

'Yes, I will indeed, and so will Ron,' Ted said. 'I was in the Army for years, Constable, but couldn't find work after I was invalided out and my pension didn't come through as it was supposed to and so I was reduced to living on the streets – which is where I met Ron. However, we're starting to earn a good living now and my hope is we shall have a home of our own one day.'

'I'm glad to hear that.' Constable Jones looked at Ron. 'Are you happy and safe living with your employer, Ron?'

'Yes, sir – the best I've ever been in my life.'

'Good.' Constable Jones smiled at him. 'I'm going to speak to Lady Rosalie and ask her if you can become Ron's legal guardian, Mr Phillips,' Constable Jones said. 'I know he's all right with you, but under the law you must be his foster parent – or adopt him. Lady Rosalie can, and will, I'm sure, help you do that with my recommendation. Will you give me your address so that she can arrange to meet you both?'

'Yes, of course,' Ted said and enunciated it clearly so that Steve could write it down. 'Once we get Danny back, I'd like to adopt the pair of them so that they can be together.'

'That sounds like a very good idea to me,' Constable Jones said. 'I know Danny has a good foster mother already but it might be better for him to live with a blood relation. I'll speak to Lady Rosalie and she'll be in touch.'

'That's good of you,' Ted said. 'We're going to get something to eat – can I drop you near the station?'

'Thank you, but I have other calls to make,' Constable Jones said. 'I'll wish you good day, sir – and I'll be in touch.'

'Please do,' Ted said. 'We'll keep a lookout on the docks and if we hear anything we'll come and let you know.' He looked at Ron when Steve got out and there was excitement in his voice. 'That is good news, lad – it means I'll be able to look after the pair of you.'

'And me and Danny can be brothers,' Ron said and grinned. 'It's all I wanted to make life perfect – as long as we find Danny safe and sound.'

'Yes . . .' A grim look came into Ted's eyes. 'If that devil harms Danny I'll kill him and that's no lie!'

CHAPTER 25

Peter Clark entered the children's ward with mixed feelings. He'd asked Nurse Jenny out on the spur of the moment the first time they'd gone out and he'd enjoyed his time with her on a few more occasions, but in his heart he realised that he'd made a mistake. The woman he wanted to get to know, had hoped he might perhaps spend his life with, was Sister Rose. He knew that Nurse Jenny was on night duty and so would not be working, but he saw Sister Rose immediately, ministering to one of her patients. Watching as she worked kindly and efficiently, he cursed himself for his idiocy in asking another nurse to the theatre when he'd planned to take the woman he loved.

Rose turned and saw him standing by her desk and for a moment he thought her eyes lit in the old way when she saw him, but then the light faded and her smile was no more than polite as she approached.

'Dr Clark,' she said in the cool voice she reserved for him these days. 'Thank you for coming. One of our patients is being sick a little too often and Matron thought we should ask you to look at her.'

'Of course,' he replied, his manner that of the interested doctor when underneath he wanted to beg her to forgive him – but of course he must speak to Nurse Jenny first. 'May I examine her, please?'

'Yes, of course,' Sister Rose told him. 'Her name is Laura and she came in with a tummy ache two days ago. We did an X-ray and could find no cause and then the pain disappeared and we were going to discharge her tomorrow.'

'And now she has started to be sick – how often?'

'Four times since breakfast.'

'It sounds like an infection,' he mused. 'Does she have a temperature at all?'

'Not when I took it an hour ago.' He frowned and she nodded, her manner softening as she forgot to be distant with him, her thoughts only of her patient. 'Yes, it is a little strange . . .'

They approached the bed where the little girl was lying up against her pillows. She looked anxious and nervous as he asked if he might examine her. She nodded but didn't speak as he lifted her nightgown and gently felt round her tummy, looking under her arms and lifting her gently forward to examine her back. Her breathing was fine when he used his stethoscope after blowing on it to warm it and he could find no sign of anything that might be causing the sickness. He was wondering if he should order another X-ray when the little girl touched Sister Rose's arm and looked at her in such a way that alarm bells rang in his head.

'If I'm sick you won't send me home, will you?' she asked tremulously.

214

Peter sat on the edge of her bed and reached for her hand, holding it gently. 'Would you rather stay here, Laura?' She nodded vigorously. 'Could you tell me why please?'

'I'll tell *her*,' Laura said staring desperately at Sister Rose.

Peter stood up. Children usually trusted and clung to him; if this little girl preferred to tell a nurse there was something very wrong.

He walked to the nurses' desk and stood there talking idly to Nurse Margaret, who was on duty that morning. Sister Rose was listening to Laura's tale and nodding. When it finished, she leaned forward and lightly kissed the little girl's cheek. He waited for her to return to him but had already made his own diagnosis.

'She is terrified of her stepmother,' Sister Rose told him. 'Her father was always kind to her but now he believes that she is naughty and smacks her when she's done nothing. Laura says her stepmother pinches her and hits her and tells her to go to her room. She claims to have been shut in the coalshed for a day and that her stepmother told her father she'd hidden there and he'd smacked her bottom and told her he was ashamed of her.'

'So, the sickness is either nerves or self-induced.' Peter nodded. It fitted with his own thoughts that there was nothing physically wrong with the child.

'In that case we must speak to Matron and Lady Rosalie at once,' Sister Rose said. 'If you could do that – p-please?' Her voice caught with emotion. 'I'm not sure I could do it without crying . . .' Even as she spoke a little sob left her and tears ran down her cheeks.

'What on earth's the matter, Rose?' Peter asked, forgetting to maintain his professional formality because she was upset.

'I can't . . . Forgive me, this is not professional. I should not bring my personal grief into the ward . . .'

Peter frowned, trying to think of what could have caused this emotional breakdown in the most efficient nurse he knew. 'Can't you tell me, Rose? I really would like to help you, personal reason or not.'

She shook her head, brushing the tears from her face impatiently. 'Speak to Matron, she will tell you – and now I really must not take up any more of your time . . .'

He watched as she walked away to one of the other children and fought the urge to go after her and make her speak to him. Giving his head a little shake, he left the ward and went along the corridor to Matron's office.

He spoke first of their patient, explained why he'd come to the conclusion that the child was suffering from anxiety rather than a physical complaint, and Matron agreed, thanking him for his time.

'I shall contact both Lady Rosalie and Constable Jones,' she said. 'He is very reliable, particularly in cases concerning children, and he will get to the bottom of this; if the child is telling the truth – which I personally do not doubt – the law will step in to remove her from their custody.'

'Yes, that sounds the best way to go ahead,' Peter agreed. 'And now, if I may – could I ask about Sister Rose? She seemed rather upset by the child's revelation – more than I would normally expect.'

Matron hesitated, then, 'Sister Rose and her landlady, Beattie Robinson, fostered that young lad who was abducted and was a patient here, Danny Bryant. Well, the poor boy has been snatched by his brutal father at a church fete and Rose and Beattie are both very worried and upset . . .'

'No, how terrible,' Peter said genuinely shocked. 'How could such a thing happen in full public view?'

'Apparently, Beattie turned her back for five minutes and the stallholder who witnessed it said he believed the man to be Danny's father and did not like to interfere.'

Peter muttered an oath, careful not to speak it out loud and offend Matron. He felt furiously angry and wished that he'd known sooner. It was a terrible thing to happen to anyone – but the fact that it had happened to the woman he cared for made it doubly wrong. Especially as he had no right to comfort her.

He was thoughtful as he made his way to the practice he now gave much of his time to these days. He was on call for the Rosie and also did two days a week at the much larger London Hospital, but the rest of his time was devoted to the poor of the East End.

Disturbed by the way he felt over Sister Rose's loss and her obvious distress, Peter knew that he must see Nurse Jenny later, before she began her next shift. He did not wish to hurt her but his instincts told him that she was not in love with him, any more than he was with her – they had just enjoyed a few outings to the theatre together.

He frowned as he realised that the mistake he'd made had quite possibly lost him any chance of winning the love of the woman he wanted more than any other, but that was his fault and he must accept it. For the moment his main concern was Rose and her distress over the missing boy. Was there something he could do to help trace Danny?

In his work at the clinic he often treated the vagrants that slept under the railway arches and other places. They came to him with coughs, wounds, weak chests and a hundred other ailments, and he treated them for nothing. Some of them made him smile – especially Jessie, who walked around with her bags in an old pram. She knew everybody and everything in her world and she might have heard something.

He would ask Jessie if she'd seen anything that could help them to trace young Danny, and if she had, he would go to Constable Steve Jones – because if Matron said he was very reliable, especially when it came to children, then that would be the right thing to do.

Jenny was just about to enter the Rosie later that afternoon when she heard Peter shout to her and saw him dash across the road. He was carrying a big box of chocolates and she smiled; he was a generous companion and she had enjoyed their theatre outings – it was nice to be taken somewhere expensive and be made a fuss of by a man as good-looking as Dr Clark.

'Jenny, have you got a minute?' he asked sounding hesitant. 'I have something important to say to you . . .'

'Well, I'm twenty minutes early for work,' Jenny said, 'So we could go across the road to the café for a coffee if you like?'

'Yes,' he said and looked uncomfortable. 'I think it would be good to be sitting down.'

Jenny looked at him then and she knew immediately, stopping in her tracks to face him. 'You can tell me straight out if it's over,' she said looking him in the eyes. 'I'm not a child, Peter, and I know it wasn't a big love affair for either of us.'

She saw the relieved expression in his eyes. 'I'm sorry, Jenny. I really am – I asked you out on impulse that first day and I shouldn't have done. There was someone else then and there still is . . .'

Jenny nodded, aware of feeling a bit disappointed but not miserable or brokenhearted. 'I think I always knew that – but I'm not going to pry. I did enjoy our outings but if there's someone you really care for you should tell her, Peter.'

'Thank you, Jenny. That's kind of you – and I am sorry for letting you down.'

'Don't worry,' Jenny said and smothered a sigh of regret for the outings she would miss, and indeed Peter, because she liked him and enjoyed his company but he wasn't the love of her life, not even close to it. Jenny knew full well she had yet to meet someone who could make her heart beat faster or bring her to tears.

Peter offered the huge box of chocolates. 'Please take these, Jenny. I know it doesn't make up for what I've just done – but I'd like you to have them.'

Jenny hesitated and then accepted them. 'Thank you, Dr Clark. I shall have to revert to that, shan't I? I have enjoyed our dates, but I'm not upset, truly, and thank you for giving me some lovely evenings.'

She walked away quickly, because, suddenly, ridiculously, she wanted to cry. Not because he'd broken her heart, but because she wished she could find someone who would love her and that she could love in return. Her sister Lily and most of her friends had boyfriends or men they loved, but she seemed to be cut off from that feeling, which everyone said was wonderful.

Was there something wrong with her? Or had she yet to find the right man?

When she got up to the children's ward, Sister Rose was just preparing to leave for the night. Her eyes went to the chocolates and there was a flash of something like hurt in them which made Jenny wonder. She'd thought once that Sister Rose and Peter Clark might get together but they hadn't – was she a part of the reason?

'I bought these for your friend Beattie,' she lied on impulse. 'I'm really sorry about what happened, Sister Rose – and if there is anything at all I can do to help please tell me.'

'That was kind of you, Nurse Jenny,' Sister Rose said, hesitated and then took the chocolates. 'I thought they must be a gift from your boyfriend?'

'Oh, no, I don't have a boyfriend,' Jenny said and smiled. 'I went out a few times with one of the doctors but he really wasn't keen on me, so that's over.'

'Oh, I see.' Sister Rose frowned. 'I'm sorry – perhaps you'll find someone soon . . .'

'One day,' Jenny said and nodded. 'I'd better read the notes. It's just Nurse Anne and me tonight – have we got any new cases?'

'No, no new admittances today,' Sister Rose said. 'We've found out what is wrong with Laura, as you'll see in the notes. Dr Clark attended her.'

'Yes, he's a good doctor,' Jenny said in an impersonal voice. 'Thank you, Sister Rose.'

'Goodnight, Nurse Jenny.'

Sister Rose sounded a little odd and Jenny thought she was on the verge of crying. Was it because she was so upset over the disappearance of the boy she'd helped to foster or because she'd realised that Peter's invitations to Jenny had meant nothing?

Rose blinked back her tears as she walked home that night. When she'd first seen the large box of Fry's chocolates, she'd thought they must have been a gift to Nurse Jenny from Peter Clark. She knew that he'd bought her chocolates and small gifts before that and assumed they were deep in a relationship, but Jenny's casual attitude to their break-up had convinced her that wasn't so.

Before Peter and Jenny had started going out together Rose had almost believed Peter Clark was interested in her and it had hurt her so badly when she'd heard that he was courting Jenny and she knew that when she and Nurse Jenny had worked together, she'd sometimes been unnecessarily brusque with her. It had not been professional of her and she'd struggled to contain it.

Jenny's generosity with the chocolates had brought her to the verge of tears – and the way she'd told her that her friendship with Peter Clark was nothing! – Rose had hardly got out of the infirmary before the tears started to trickle down her cheeks.

She was so anxious about Danny – and Beattie as well, because she was beside herself with worry, convinced it was her fault that Danny's father had managed to drag him off.

'I should've watched him all the time,' she'd said tearfully over and over again. 'I don't deserve to be his foster mum – it's all my fault he's gone.'

'No, it isn't,' Rose reassured her. 'Even if you'd stopped Danny's father that time – and I don't see how you could – he would have found another way some other time.'

It was the truth, but Rose couldn't convince Beattie and she'd cried for hours, her eyes red and puffy every morning since Danny's disappearance. Rose had cried too but she'd had to pull herself together, because her job was important. However, any small act of kindness or just a look could make her feel emotional and she knew she wouldn't feel truly better until they got Danny back.

She had to believe that they would one day, because otherwise she did not think she could carry on with her life . . .

CHAPTER 26

Danny's stomach ached because he was hungry. His father had bought pie and chips when they'd been paid, eaten what he wanted and then shoved the remains in Danny's hands. Left with three chips and a piece of unwanted dry crust, he'd swallowed them down to try to ease the hunger pangs but he still felt the cramps deep in his guts and the cold that came with it.

'Can I have something to eat?' he asked his father.

Jim Bryant's eyes gleamed with malice. 'Are yer ready ter do what I asked?' he demanded. 'I told yer, yer get a proper meal if yer go through that window.'

Danny stared at him in hatred, his anger burning fiercely inside. He hadn't believed his own father could be this evil but he was starving him into obedience. Not only did he have to work cleaning out the filthy bone lorries in the mornings, he was expected to help his father commit burglaries at night and he couldn't run for it because Jim Bryant had told him he'd hurt Beattie and Sister Rose if he did, even if he didn't go back to them.

Doris Bryant had been as honest as the day is long

and Danny had a horror of breaking the law. He could hear his mother's voice telling him that it would shame her if he ever did anything like that – and it was certain that Sister Rose and Beattie wouldn't want to know him if he became a thief.

'It ain't right,' Danny said defiantly. 'I did my share of the shovelling. I should get a packet of chips for that – and thievin' is wrong. Mum wouldn't have liked me to do that.' He gave a cry of pain as his father hit him on the side of the head, knocking him sideways. 'You're a bully and a monster but you can't make me steal for you!'

'Then yer'll starve,' his father grunted and thrust him into the dark place that he called home. 'I ain't goin' ter shovel muck fer the rest of me life. There's rich folk what have got more than their fair share from life and I intend to get some of it. You help me and you eat, don't and you starve.'

Danny stifled the bitter words that threatened to spill out of him. If he dared to say more his father would beat him senseless and he already hurt all over. He was going to have to make a run for it and go straight to the police so that they could protect Rose and Beattie or he would die of hunger. At work there was little opportunity and at night he was locked in with his father.

He could hear the noises his father made as he drank from his store of whisky. There was always money enough for that but never for food for Danny. He heard his father go to the bucket in the corner and then the sound of him emptying his guts. If Danny pretended to be sick when they were working – or to have the runs

. . . A plan began to form in his mind, because there was a toilet on site at their workplace. It was in his father's sightline and near enough for him to catch Danny if he tried to run, but there was a crack in the wood at the back of the old shed that housed the toilet. He wasn't sure if he could force it open and escape that way, but he knew he had to try while he still had the strength.

Before they left for work that morning, Danny made a show of having a stomach ache and then ran to the bucket in the corner, retching as he made himself sick.

'Don't think yer gettin' out of work,' his father muttered and glared at him as he emerged wiping his mouth with his sleeve.

Danny didn't answer and his father's expression was hard as he said, 'Ternight, yer'll help me rob that place I told yer about – if yer refuse I'll knock yer ter kingdom come!'

Danny hung his head and didn't answer. Let his father think he was subdued and ready to obey. Jim Bryant grunted and pushed him out of the door. Danny kept his eyes downcast as they walked to the docks. It was a warm day and the smell from the boneyard was horrendous. It wouldn't be hard to feign sickness here, because the stink turned his guts.

The gaffer gave them the usual job, glancing at Danny for a moment but saying nothing. Briefly, Danny thought of appealing to him for help but knew he wouldn't be interested. Jim Bryant was one of the few who would do this filthy job and it wasn't in the gaffer's interest to upset him.

Danny got on with his work but when he saw the pile of maggots heaving in the corner of the lorry that had been used to transport bones and old meat carcasses, his stomach turned and he scrambled down and ran for the shed that served them as a toilet.

'Hey!' his father called, then, realising where he was going, 'Don't be long, yer lazy little sod.'

Danny wrenched open the door and went in, bolting it after him. For a few moments he was safe. He went towards the board at the back that had shrunk, letting in a glimmer of light and tested it. There was a little give and if he'd had his spade, he might have been able to widen it to a gap big enough to force the plank out and escape, but it wouldn't budge with just him pushing. He would have to think of something else.

Danny relieved himself and then, just as he was unbolting the door, he heard shouting from outside. Opening the door slightly, he saw that there was an altercation going on. Three men were involved in a fight over money and Danny's father was one of them.

It was his chance! Danny knew he had to run and now. If he didn't go this minute his father would remember him and come looking for him when the fight was over. He slipped round the back of the toilet shed and started to run away from the docks and the sound of the shouting. He could still hear the yelling and his father's voice above the others.

'Bloody pigs! I'll see you in hell fer this!'

Danny ran for his life. He ran and ran until his chest was heaving and he couldn't breathe, and then he leaned against a wall to recover. Would his father come looking for him – and where should he go?

Danny wanted to get back to Beattie and Sister Rose but his father would come there and drag him off again. He knew that his father had seen him before that day at the church fete because he'd laughed about it and said he'd been waiting for the chance to grab him. So, if he went home to Beattie, his father would come after him again – and he might do as he'd threatened and harm Beattie and Sister Rose.

Danny found a park bench and sat down in the sun. A woman in a smart dress was sitting eating sandwiches and she glanced at him several times but didn't speak. When she got up and walked off, she left a packet with a whole sandwich in it on the bench. Danny fell on it and began to eat it. She turned and smiled and gave him a little finger wave and then walked off. She'd left it for him deliberately.

Danny was warmed by the small kindness. It reminded him that despite all the brutality he'd met with in his life there were other people who were kind and good. He decided that he would make his way to the Rosie and ask for help there. He would tell Sister Rose what had happened and explain why he couldn't live with her and Beattie for the moment – perhaps then the police would stop his father from catching him again.

He was a long way from his objective and it would take him a while to walk there. His clothes were filthy too and he knew he stank because he hadn't washed in days. Danny could only hope that they wouldn't turn him away in disgust.

It was only as he began his long walk that he thought of something – the men his father had been fighting had been wearing police uniforms. A smile touched Danny's face. Perhaps his problem was half-solved already. If the police had his father in custody, he would be safe with Beattie and Sister Rose again. He increased his pace, wanting now to find his friends as quickly as he could.

'Where is your son, Mr Bryant?' Constable Jones asked after they'd booked him at the station. He was hand-cuffed and silent, though still spitting defiance at them. 'Don't try to lie to us, sir, we know you snatched him at the church fete. We received information to that effect and now we want to know where he is.'

'How do I know where the little bleeder is?' Jim Bryant spat at Constable Jones, who wiped it away with his glove and continued to face him unflinchingly. 'He went to the toilet and scarpered when you lot nabbed me. There's no law says he can't work wiv me ter pay fer his keep.'

'He's not old enough to work,' Constable Jones replied calmly. 'And Danny was placed with a foster parent by the courts after you were found wanting as a father. He had injuries he claims were inflicted by you when he was found and you have a history of violence as well as a record for other offences. Therefore, the court has placed a restrictive order on you and you may not go within five miles of where he lives, goes to school or, in the future, works. If you touch him or in any way coerce him, you will be breaking the law and liable for a term of imprisonment.'

Jim Bryant spat at Steve Jones again.

'Filthy behaviour will not help your cause, Mr

Bryant,' Constable Jones said. 'Had you listened to us and not offered violence you would have been given a warning. Now you will spend a night in the cells and we'll have you up for assaulting a police officer in the morning. If I have my way, you'll be locked in a cell for years.'

'Pigs!' Jim Bryant sneered at him over his shoulder as he was led away. 'They'll give me a few months at most and then I'll be out – and I'll do fer yer, mate, and that little runt – you see if I don't!'

Steve looked at his sergeant as the man was taken below to the cells. 'That is one nasty piece of work, sir. I need to find as much evidence against him as I can or he's right – they'll give him a month or two at most and he'll be out again.'

'Find the boy,' Sergeant Morris advised. 'He might be able to give you more information. Do you believe he made a bolt for it?'

'Bryant's boss seemed to think so. Not that he was particularly helpful. Bryant is one of the few who will do the really dirty work and it wasn't him that tipped us off about Bryant.'

'A concerned member of the public, perhaps?'

'Someone who worked on the docks saw the way he treated the lad and reported it,' Constable Jones said. 'He named Bryant, so we were on it immediately – it's just a pity the lad ran for it.'

'Maybe he'll go to his foster home,' the sergeant said hopefully.

'I pray he will, but he may be too frightened to think straight.'

'Well, you'd best get back to the beat,' Sergeant

Morris told him. 'Good work, Jones – and you, Smith, that was a neat job.'

The two constables looked at each other and smiled. Both had a few bruises where the furious Jim Bryant had punched and kicked them but he must have some of his own and there was satisfaction in having put the man behind bars for the time being.

'We were lucky to get that tip-off,' Constable Smith said and they left the station together. 'Where did you say it came from?'

'An old lady named Jessie,' Steve said. 'I've given her a few cups of tea and some shillings now and then and we have a chat – if it's cold I find her a bed at one of the hostels. Jessie doesn't forget a kindness.' He looked thoughtful. 'She told me one of the doctors at the clinic asked her about the boy too, but she came to me, because she thought it was my job. She's a wise old bird.'

'One of the doctors?' Constable Smith lifted his eyebrows. 'How would he know we were looking for the boy?'

'I suppose it must have been through Sister Rose. She and her landlady are fostering the boy.'

'Ah, I see,' Constable Smith said, nodding. 'Small world, isn't it?'

'Sometimes,' Steve said. 'Right, you go down Bell Lane and round by the church and I'll go the other way and we'll meet up at the Rosie, all right?'

'Yeah – be seeing you!'

The two separated to walk their beat. Most of the time it was quiet and only needed one of them to be seen keeping an eye on things. It was surprising how much it disturbed the criminals to see a bobby on the beat. They turned tail and walked away most times and, if not, a loud summons from a police whistle would bring one constable running to the aid of another. However, a lot of their day was spent directing folk, helping elderly residents across busy roads, directing traffic if there was an accident, or helping a child separated from its frantic mother. Only a small portion of their time was taken up with actually catching criminals and it was rather nice when they achieved an arrest.

Steve's mother-in-law was standing at her front door as he went past. She smiled and offered him a cup of tea but he shook his head.

'Better not, Gwen, I've got to get on; we've a lot to do today.'

'I'm waiting for Theo,' she told him. 'We're going shopping and I'll be doing some for Sarah, too and then I'll be visiting with her for a couple of hours.'

'She'll be pleased,' Steve replied and smiled. 'The lad is growing fast, isn't he?'

'Just as he ought,' Gwen agreed. 'Ah, here comes Theo – have a good day, Steve, and stay safe.'

'I'll try to,' Steve waved his hand and set off down the street. At the bottom of the lane old Mrs Ransom was looking worried. He stopped and asked her what was wrong.

'It's my Tiddles,' she said. 'He's got stuck up the apple tree again, Constable Jones. I don't suppose you could get him down for me?'

Steve smiled, glanced at his watch and smothered his sigh. The cat was young, adventurous and could probably get down itself, but Mrs Ransom was old and easily upset. 'I'll see what I can do,' he promised. 'Let's have a look, shall we?'

CHAPTER 27

Rose was looking at her medicine chart when Nurse Margaret hurried up to her and caught hold of her arm. Startled, she was about to reprimand the young nurse when she saw the look of excitement in her eyes.

'What is it, Nurse?'

'Look, Sister Rose – it's Danny!'

Her heart gave a huge jump and she turned to look towards the door, tears of relief starting to her eyes as she saw him standing there, hovering uncertainly, his face dirty and his hair all messed up. She could see that his clothes were filthy and as she reached him, he put up his hands to ward her off.

'I'm dirty and I stink,' he said. 'I think the police have got me dad and so I ran off. I wouldn't have come if they hadn't 'cos he swore he'd hurt you and Beattie.'

'Oh, Danny, I'm so glad you came to me!' Rose said and threw her arms around him, despite the stink of his clothes and the fact that she would have to change her uniform. 'We've both been so upset!'

'I'm sorry, Sister Rose, but it weren't my fault.'

'I know it wasn't,' she said and smiled at him through

her tears. 'I'm going to take you home, Danny . . .' She turned to Nurse Margaret. 'Nurse – please go and tell Matron that Danny is here and I need to get him home and ask can she cover my duty for me, please?'

'Yes, Sister Rose.' The nurse went off looking delighted and Sister Rose looked at Danny.

'Are you all right, Danny?' she asked. 'You look thin – and are they bruises on your face or dirt?'

'Both I should think,' Danny said and grinned at her. She could see that a tooth was missing on the right side. 'Me dad hit me a few times but he didn't kill me 'cos he wanted me to work and steal for him. I worked on the stinkin' bone lorries down the factory, but I wouldn't steal so he starved me.'

'Beattie will get you something to eat as soon as we get back home,' Rose promised. She glanced around the ward. Fortunately, there were no urgent tasks waiting, most of the work had already been done that morning and they were waiting for Kathy to bring up the meals from the kitchen.

Nurse Margaret returned then with Nurse Anne in tow. 'Matron said she would keep an eye herself,' Nurse Margaret told her. 'She says to take as long as you need.'

'I'm going to get Danny home, then stop by and speak to the police.'

'Matron will telephone them,' Nurse Margaret said. 'She said you weren't to worry about anything and that she's really glad Danny is back and if you need help to go to her.'

'Thank you, nurse. I shall be back after lunch to finish my shift,' Rose said and smiled. 'But I do appreciate all your kindness – now carry on with your work.'

She had conquered the urge to cry as she led Danny through the hospital and outside into the sunshine. She had been imagining all kinds of things, convinced they would never see the young boy she loved alive again. Now, here he was and if his bully of a father was in prison then they were safe from him and their lives could get back to normal.

Beattie was standing at her parlour window, looking out. She gave a shriek of joy when she saw them coming and rushed out of the front door to greet them. Throwing her arms around Danny, she hugged him, making him wince.

'Did I hurt you?' she asked anxiously.

'It's just where me dad knocked me about,' Danny said and grinned at her. 'I'm not hurt bad, Beattie, just bruised, so don't cry. I'm happy to be home but I stink and me clothes are filthy.'

'I'll soon have you in the bath and get you some clean clothes,' Beattie said. 'Are you hungry, love? I'll just bet you are.'

'Starving,' Danny replied. 'A lady eating her lunch left me a sandwich on a bench – and that's what made me come to you.' He knew they didn't understand and laughed. 'I was frightened when I ran off and I didn't think who me dad was fighting 'till then, see, and because she was kind it made me remember the policeman that helped me before.'

'Ah, I see.' Rose smiled as the penny dropped. 'The police were fighting with your father so you ran off but then you thought it might be safe to come back to us if your father was in custody?'

'Yeah, that's it,' Danny agreed. Beattie still looked confused but it didn't matter. Danny was home safe and that was all that any of them cared about just now.

Later, after Danny was bathed, dressed and had eaten a huge meal of bacon, egg, mushroom, tomatoes and fried bread and declared it the most delicious food he'd ever tasted, he told them the story again, putting in all the details he'd left out.

Beattie looked enraged as she heard what his father had done to him and declared she would kill the devil before she let him touch Danny again.

'He mustn't be allowed to come near Danny ever again,' Rose agreed. 'I'm going to ask Constable Jones to come here this evening on his way home so you can tell him all of it, Danny. The more evidence we have, the longer we can put that evil man away for.'

'He should be shut away for ever,' Beattie said vengefully but Rose knew that wouldn't happen, even with the new evidence. Within a year or two at most Danny's father would be let out of prison and then he might come after him again. However, if he could be shut away for long enough, they could think about what they needed to do next . . .

Rose went back to work after Danny was settled. She discovered that Constable Jones had called at the infirmary to speak to Matron and left a message that he would come over that evening and take Danny's statement.

'He was ever so pleased Danny was back, Sister Rose,' Margaret told her in her slightly sing-song voice. 'Lovely man he is, Nurse Sarah is lucky to have him.'

'Yes, she is,' Rose agreed. 'But he's lucky to have her,

too. Thank you for holding the fort here, Nurse Margaret – was everything all right?'

'Yes, Sister.' The nurse hesitated, then, 'Dr Clark called in and asked to see you. I told him where you were and he smiled and said to tell you he was really glad Danny was back and he would come tomorrow.'

'Oh!' Rose's heart gave a foolish little skip of pleasure. 'Thank you, Nurse. Well, I think we had better do our rounds now and then prepare the medicines for this evening . . .'

Rose went off to check on all the children in the ward. She'd felt guilty abandoning them, even though she knew they were in good hands, but her first thought had been for Danny.

It was such a relief to have him back and not too badly hurt. She knew that he might have been dead or lying in a back alley somewhere, beaten unconscious, but, fortunately, his father had needed him to work for him and so he'd merely knocked him about a bit. She felt so proud of Danny for resisting his father's demands that he helped him steal from other people's homes, even though he'd suffered for it. And whatever happened in future, Jim Bryant couldn't be allowed to grab Danny again – because next time he might kill him.

CHAPTER 28

'I'm sorry I'm late home, love,' Steve said when he got in that evening. 'I had to call in at Sister Rose's place and take Danny's statement after work.'

'You found him then?' Sarah looked at him in surprise and pleasure.

'Yes, in a way – we arrested his father and Danny who saw it, made a bolt for it, turned up at the Rosie and was taken home to Beattie to be made a fuss of and cleaned up again. That was a pity in a way because some pictures of his condition might have helped to put his father away longer, but both Beattie and Sister Rose are willing to testify as to his condition and his bruises. He's covered in them again.'

'Poor little boy,' Sarah said. 'I know he's nearly thirteen now, Steve, but he's still only a child.'

'Yes, but next year he will be able to work – had he been fourteen we shouldn't have even as strong a case against Bryant as we have. We know he intended to use Danny to break into homes, because the lad told us, but it's only his word, so it's only forcing him away from his legal foster mother, forcing him to work illegally and resisting arrest. Not a great deal under the law. You'd think that his brutality towards the boy would get him put away for years, but if he gets two, I'll be surprised.'

'The law is so daft at times,' Sarah said as she put a cup of tea in front of her husband. 'There's you chasing all over trying to find him and Danny and when you do the judge will let the father out again in months, if that.'

'It all depends on the judge, of course,' Steve said. 'Some of them think prison does little good and want to encourage a community spirit and think if they are lenient the crooks of this world will be grateful and stop their wrongdoing.'

'Surely it's best to lock them away so they can't hurt people?'

'I'd throw away the key,' Steve said and sniffed the air. 'Something smells good love!'

'Mum got me some chicken pieces and I've made a lovely casserole with mashed potatoes, baby carrots and peas – all fresh not tinned.'

'Gwen told me she was going shopping,' Steve said. 'Theo was taking her in his car. She's quite the lady of leisure now, being chauffeured about.' He grinned at the idea and Sarah laughed.

'So she should be,' she said. 'It's about time she had someone to make a fuss of her. Dad loved her but he didn't show it much, perhaps because he wasn't well – or maybe there were other factors. I know there wasn't much money around.'

'I think it's the same for most families,' Steve said. 'In these streets, anyway. Work has been scarce since the twenties and we've been through a wicked depression, so many businesses gone to the wall and men thrown out of work. Even the shipyards have been empty for the past few years, but there's a bit more activity now. I daresay your father had given up trying to make more than a living – and if he wasn't well it would have been harder.'

'I wish I'd seen that he wasn't well.' Sarah sighed. 'I should've done, Steve. I'm a nurse; I should have known and made him stop work.'

'Don't blame yourself, love. Your father didn't tell you because he didn't want to worry his family and that was his choice, not yours or Gwen's.'

Sarah nodded. 'I know, Steve, but I wish I'd told him I loved him more.'

'That's something we all wish when someone dies too soon . . .' He stood up and put his arms around her. 'Your father would have wanted you to be happy, my darling, and he would've been proud of you, of your lovely son and the nursing. I'm sure, if there is a heaven, he's watching you now and applauding.'

Sarah smiled. 'How did I get so lucky as to have you?'

'I'll never know.' He grinned at her. 'Where is my supper, woman? I could eat a horse,' he teased and then kissed her.

'It was nice of Constable Jones to call rather than make us go down the station,' Beattie said as she and Rose sat drinking their bedtime cocoa. 'He is a lovely young man, Rose – you ought to have someone like that to look after you.'

'Oh Beattie!' Rose shook her head at her. 'You know I'm devoted to my work, and besides, we have each other and Danny.'

'Yes, I know,' Beattie looked serious, 'and he'll be safe for a while, Rose, but what happens when that monster is released? He'll come looking for Danny again, because that sort always does.'

'Yes, I know – and we'll have to talk about it, decide what to do for the best,' Rose said. 'We both like living here, Beattie, but we might have to consider moving for Danny's sake.'

'Yes, I thought of that.' Beattie frowned. 'I'd have to sell this house and use the money to buy another somewhere, but I'm not sure how to do it or whether I'd be able to afford anything as good as this elsewhere.'

'It isn't easy,' Sister Rose agreed and sighed. 'I've been thinking about the problem, Beattie. If there was a man about, he could protect us . . .'

'There you are then,' Beattie said and smiled. 'You'll have to find a nice young man and bring him home!'

'Easier said than done,' Rose replied shaking her head. 'We might be able to buy a house in the suburbs together – perhaps with a little loan from the bank.'

'The suburbs?' Beattie frowned. 'I've lived in the East End all my life and your work is here, Rose. Can we turn our lives upside down like that?'

'We have a little time to work it out,' Rose said, 'but I think we may have to consider it – after all, Danny comes first, doesn't he?'

'Yes, he does,' Beattie agreed. 'If it comes to it, I'd do anything rather than lose him.'

'Yes, I feel the—' Rose was interrupted by a knock

at the door. Startled, she looked at Beattie in alarm. 'That couldn't be . . .?'

'Danny's father? No,' Beattie said and got up to answer it. 'The police have him safe.'

Rose heard her speaking to someone at the door and Danny's name was mentioned. She got to her feet, feeling on the defensive. A man and a boy about a year or so older than Danny walked in and looked at her. The man was good-looking, in his early forties and dressed in cord trousers and a checked shirt, which was clean but far from new.

'Sister Rose – and Mrs Robinson. I'm sorry to disturb you at this hour but we work all day and we only just got the news. I'm Ted Phillips and this is my apprentice, Ron, who I'm in the process of applying to foster. Danny Bryant is his friend and so I'd like to take both the lads on. I can give them a home and teach them how to earn a living—'

'No!' Beattie blurted out in fear. '*We're* Danny's foster parents and we love him. He's happy with us!'

'Yes, so I understand,' Ted said, sad that he was hurting this woman who clearly loved his nephew, and looked at Rose. 'I know you gave Danny a home when he needed it and I'm sure he's as grateful as I am – but you see, he's my sister's child and I'd like to take care of him. Doris made me promise I would if anything ever happened to her and I did try once before but his father swore the lad was all right and I couldn't interfere then – but it is different now. I've got a good job and I've just discovered that money owing to me from an Army pension has mounted up to several hundred pounds, all sitting at a solicitor's office waiting for me.

243

With that money I can rent a decent house and the boys can live with me.'

'And Danny's like me brother,' Ron said. 'You ask him if he wants ter live wiv us.'

'Your sister's child?' Beattie looked at him doubtfully and yet she could see the likeness. There was definitely a resemblance.

'Yes, and the authorities think I stand a good chance of having him, because I am his uncle. I wanted to talk to you – and Sister Rose – about it and come to some amicable arrangement. I'd have no objection to his visiting or to you visiting him when I have my house set up – and, of course, I couldn't take him until then.'

'No!' Beattie shook her head. 'We won't give him up – we can't!'

'Can you protect him if Bryant comes after him again?' Ted asked looking at her steadily. 'I would kill Bryant rather than let him take Danny again. Ron and I have been searching for him every spare minute and I'm serious about this. I let his father turn me away once but I shan't let my nephew down again.'

'No, go away!' Beattie said, despite knowing instinctively that he was to be trusted. Under other circumstances she would have been happy to know him, but now she looked at Rose with desperate eyes. 'Make him go, please.'

'I think we ought to talk,' Rose said. 'Go up and tell Danny his friend Ron is here, Beattie, and I'll make some more cocoa. We need to think about this seriously and calmly.'

'Thank you,' Ted said. 'Miss – I'm not sure what to call you?'

'Just Rose,' she said and smiled at Ron. 'I'm sure Danny will be happy to see you, Ron. He has talked about you a lot . . .' Even as she said it, they heard a cry of joy from upstairs and then pounding feet as Danny came running down to the kitchen in his pyjamas.

'Ron!' he cried. 'Are you all right, mate? We tried to find you – didn't we, Sister Rose?'

'Yes, we did,' she agreed. 'Constable Jones told me this evening that he knew where you lived but I was waiting until things calmed down a bit – I didn't know you were living with Mr Phillips.'

'Please, call me Ted,' he said and sat down as the boys retreated to the far end of the room talking excitedly to each other. Beattie was glaring at Ted as if he were the devil and Rose knew her friend was very upset. 'I'm sorry to put all this on you, but I thought it best to come over straight away. We have to sort this out between us for Danny's sake.'

Beattie looked at the boys, who were clearly enjoying being together and her eyes filled with tears as she sat down, looking from Rose to Ted in hurt silence.

'You will have to give us time to come to terms with this new idea,' Rose told him. 'Beattie and I love Danny as if he were our own and I think you will find he cares for us too – and he is learning to cook, which is what he wants to do. I'm not sure what you do for a living . . .?'

'I'm a carpenter and Ron is learning the trade.'

'Danny wants to be a chef,' Rose told him and saw his quick frown. 'Beattie is a wonderful cook – and Danny will be too one day.'

245

'You could still teach him,' Ted said to Beattie. 'I'm not a hard man and I certainly don't want to break hearts, but I do think Danny will be safer with Ron and I. We work with good people and I'm ex-Army, well capable of protecting my nephew.'

'And the courts would probably give you custody,' Rose said, because she knew it was true. 'However, for the moment we are Danny's guardians, and I ask you to respect that.'

'I wouldn't dream of snatching him away,' Ted told them with a smile and Beattie could see that he was a pleasant, even charming man. He spoke directly to Beattie. 'I would prefer it if we could all become friends and help each other, but I do want official custody and I think I have the better right.'

'And what about Danny?' Beattie asked in a tremulous voice. 'Have you thought about that?'

'Look at them . . .' Rose said and Beattie's face paled as she saw the boys laughing together. 'I think we have to come to some arrangement, Beattie, much as I hate it . . .'

'Yes, well, we'll leave you to think it over,' Ted said and offered his hand. Beattie took it, conscious of its strength and firmness of grip. She flushed slightly. 'Please believe me when I say I want us all to be friends – and I don't want to take him away from you, Mrs Robinson, but I want to care for him and I think I can protect him best from his father.'

Rose saw Ted and Ron out and when she came back Beattie was sitting with her head in her hands with Danny looking at her unhappily.

'What's wrong, Sister Rose? Did I do something?'

'No, love. It's not your fault.' She hugged him. 'Go up to bed now and I'll bring you some more cocoa.'

He did as she told him, calling goodnight to Beattie. She looked up as Rose laid a hand on her shoulder.

'I can't lose him!' she said tearfully.

'I know how you feel, Beattie, I really do. But we have to think of Danny,' Rose said, her throat tight with emotion. 'We may have to agree for his sake . . .'

'I know,' Beattie said, 'and what hurts is that I know Mr Phillips is the right one to protect our Danny . . .'

CHAPTER 29

For the past three weeks Marjorie's mother had refused to let her play with Shelly on Saturday or Sunday. Instead, she'd taken her to tea with her friends and to church and then to visit her Nanna. Marjorie normally loved visiting Nanna but she so desperately wanted to go to Danny's house and have tea with the nice lady and him, but with her mother's eagle eye on her all the time she just couldn't slip away. Three Sundays had passed without her being able to get out of the house without her parents. So, it was one Thursday lunchtime when Marjorie decided to visit her friend's house. Instead of going to eat with the other children, she slipped out with Shelly and headed for the house in Bell Lane.

When she knocked at the kitchen door it was opened by a lady she hadn't seen before. She looked red around the eyes, as if she'd been crying, but she smiled when she saw the two little girls.

'Hello, I'm Beattie,' she said. 'What can I do for you?'

'I'm Marjorie and I wanted to see Danny,' she said

and pushed Shelly forward. 'This is my friend Shelly. She found the way here.'

'Marjorie – Danny's little friend!' Beattie smiled and Marjorie's fears evaporated. 'Come in both of you and have a cup of milk and some cake. Danny is at school, I'm afraid – but he will be pleased to know you came to see him.'

The two girls looked at each other and then trooped into the big warm kitchen that smelled so good. There was a scrubbed pine table set with plates of fresh-cooked buns and cakes and they sat down on the chairs Beattie indicated, tucking into the cakes she offered them with enjoyment.

'You're a smashing cook,' Shelly said, bolder than Marjorie. 'Better than my mum – or Marjorie's.'

'It's lovely cake,' Marjorie said shyly. 'I wanted to come to tea like Sister Rose told us but Mum took me to her friends and to Nanna's. My nanna is lovely but I do so want to see Danny.'

'Why didn't you ask your mummy to bring you?' Beattie asked her with a gentle smile that made her feel braver.

'Because Daddy doesn't think Danny comes from a good family but if Mummy saw your kitchen, she would let me come. Nanna told her she ought to let me see friends if I want.'

'What is your nanna's name?' Beattie asked smiling.

'Mrs Ethel Ross of 19 Rainbow Crescent,' Marjorie said, reciting it as she'd been taught with a look of triumph.

Beattie nodded. 'Supposing I went to see your nanna and told her about Danny and me and Sister Rose –

would your mummy listen to her if Nanna approved of me?'

Marjorie nodded vigorously. 'Mummy often listens to Nanna – it's Daddy who doesn't think I should remember what happened, but I do and it was Danny who looked after me.'

'Yes, I understand,' Beattie said. 'I'll go and visit your nanna, Marjorie – and I'll take her some cake. If we can talk, perhaps she will let you come to us another day, in the afternoon on Sunday when Danny is home – only it should be soon . . .' Beattie looked as if she would say more, then sighed and shook her head. She glanced at the clock. 'I think you two should get back to school – but you can come and see me another day if you like.'

The pair of them got up immediately, thanked her and left through the back door. They looked at each other, giggled, caught hands and ran back towards their school.

Beattie watched them turn at the end of the road. They didn't go to the same school as Danny – from their uniforms they went to the girls' school where parents were able to contribute to the schooling. That was why Marjorie's father considered that Danny wasn't good enough to be his daughter's friend. She frowned. Well, she would go to see Marjorie's nanna, Mrs Ethel Ross. Beattie wasn't sure where Rainbow Crescent was, but she had a tongue in her head and she could ask. She would go down the road and talk to Mr Forrest and see if he knew it. He had customers from all over and he did deliveries, too, these days, now that he had two strong lads living with him. If he didn't know, he could point her in the right direction.

Smiling, Beattie put her coat and hat on. She needed some more flour and some dried fruit so she would take her purse and basket with her. That little girl had looked so earnest and yearning when she asked for Danny and she knew he remembered her. It was something she could do for him while she still had him living under her roof.

She'd been crying before the little girls came, feeling sorry for herself because they were going to take Danny away from her. Now she realised that she wasn't the only one who would miss him and she was thinking sensibly again. Ted Phillips was a decent man and kind. He'd offered to bring the boys round so she wouldn't lose Danny entirely and that meant she would gain even more company. It didn't make up for having the lad she'd begun to think of as her son the whole time but it was better than nothing.

Life was so complicated. For a long time after her husband died, Beattie had felt as if her world was over, but then she'd started taking in lodgers and cooking for them. It gave her something to do and company – and then she'd met Sister Rose, who was more like a sister to her. All of a sudden life had been worth living again, and then Danny had come to her like a gift from God. It was unfair that she should have had a taste of happiness only to have it snatched away again, but she wasn't losing him forever.

Beattie felt her natural calm and feeling of wellbeing return. She wouldn't be alone and she would still see her Danny, still be able to teach him to cook, so she was luckier than most – and if Mrs Ethel Ross was a reason-able lady, perhaps she could fix up for Marjorie to visit with or without her mother.

'So, you're this Danny's foster mother?' Ethel Ross took Beattie into her neat kitchen. 'Well, I know you, in a way, for I've seen you at the church fetes and I know you're a marvellous cook because I've tasted the cakes you make for them.'

Beattie smiled at her. Now that she saw Marjorie's grandmother, she realised that she knew her by sight but not by name. It was a small world after all.

'Marjorie and her little friend Shelly came to see me. She seems quite upset because she can't see Danny and so I thought I would visit and ask if you could help arrange something?'

'Well, of course I'll do my best. My daughter's husband is a bit of a snob – thinks highly of himself just because he's something important in that office of his, but we're normal folk. I told my daughter, her father worked on the docks all his life as a foreman and if he was good enough for me, then I can't see why Marjorie can't see her friend – after all, if he hadn't been there, she might have been severely harmed or we might never have seen her again, so the police said.'

'What a relief,' Beattie said. 'Sister Rose told the chil-dren to ask permission to come but I think they just turned up at mine without asking anyone and I don't want to upset their parents, though it was lovely having them.'

'You leave it to me,' Ethel said. 'Now, why don't you sit down, Beattie, and I'll put the kettle on . . .'

CHAPTER 30

'I think it is wicked,' Lily said to Jenny when the sisters sat down to their Sunday lunch together. It wasn't often they had a whole day off at the same time and they had enjoyed each other's company, but Lily was upset because of what Sister Rose had told her the previous day when they chanced to meet at the change of duty. 'This man has turned up out of the blue and laid claim to Danny. Apparently he's Danny's uncle and he is already adopting Danny's best friend – and he wants to adopt Danny too.'

'But Beattie and Rose were made his foster parents,' Jenny said looking at her sister in distress. 'Surely they can't just take him away like that?'

'Yes, they can, if the welfare committee decides it would be best for him.' Lily frowned. 'It doesn't help that Danny was snatched from the church fete when he was in Beattie's care. She was talking with her back turned to him, probably for several minutes, so they could say she wasn't responsible enough. He'll be in school all day and the teachers will be warned about the father. In the evenings Mr Phillips and Ron will be home with him and as he's ex-Army and able to defend the boy it's likely that he would be considered better able to protect him from his violent father.'

'But Rose and Beattie adore that boy and he loves them,' Jenny protested.

'Yes, that's true – but Danny also likes this Ron and he likes his uncle. Mr Phillips is talking of sharing him, letting him visit them and go on with his cooking lessons, and Rose seems to think that's fair, though Beattie is still very upset about it.'

'Yes, well, she would be,' Jenny went on. 'It makes me feel even worse about what I did, Lily. When Dr Clark told me he couldn't take me out again, I tried to let Rose know that he'd never been in love with me – but I know she was hurt.'

'You mustn't blame yourself,' Lily told her and smiled her approval. 'It isn't your fault that you're very pretty and men ask you out, Jenny. There was no reason for you to say no – he was the one at fault, and perhaps Rose too. If she'd given him some encouragement, he might have asked her to the theatre that first time instead of you.'

'Yes . . .' Jenny gave her sister a quick hug as she got up to clear the table. 'Thank you for understanding that I never meant to harm Rose – I like her.'

'As do I – but you're my sister, Jenny, and I love you. You do know that, don't you?'

'Yes, I do, but I sometimes think you're hiding things from me . . .' Jenny hesitated, then, 'Chris was here a couple of months ago and something happened but you didn't tell me . . .'

'Because it was secret and it might have cost him his life. He wasn't supposed to be in the country.'

'Then don't tell me anything more,' Jenny said and smiled at her. 'I was upset at first and then I thought about what Chris does and I wondered if it was secret and I completely understand.' She took a deep breath, then, 'Are you two still all right together? I've noticed he hasn't written for weeks now.'

'No, because he can't and I knew he wouldn't be able to,' Lily said with a smile. 'We are very much all right – I've never loved anyone as I do him – except for you and that's different.'

'Of course, it is,' Jenny said and nodded. 'I'm so glad.' She thought for a moment, then, 'Have you seen Kathy recently? She doesn't look all that happy. I mean, she has only been married a few months and she was so confident it would all be wonderful but she seems a bit quiet to me.'

'I spoke to her yesterday morning,' Lily said thoughtfully. 'I think she's fine, Jenny. She said that Bert had taken her to see a good film at the Odeon the previous evening and she was talking of a holiday in Bournemouth in August.'

'Perhaps I'm wrong then,' Jenny said and dismissed the faint worry she'd had since talking to the young woman when she brought up the early morning drinks for the children. 'Let's get this washing-up done and then go for a walk in the park, Lily. It's such a lovely afternoon.'

'Yes, let's do that,' Lily said. 'We're so lucky to have each other and jobs we love, Jenny. One day we may both marry and have homes of our own but until then we've got each other's company.'

Kathy collected the lunch things from the children's ward and took them back to the kitchen. She'd volunteered to help out this morning, though she wasn't actually down for a Sunday duty but it was on Sundays that she found her life the most tedious, when she and her husband Bert were at home with her mother. Kathy's mother ran the house like clockwork and there was hardly anything left for Kathy to do. On Sunday she was allowed to peel vegetables and help with the washing-up, but the cooking was her mother's prerogative and Kathy didn't like to say that she would like to try her hand at cooking for her husband.

Bert worked in the garden on Sunday mornings and in the afternoons he was encouraged to sit in his armchair and go to sleep.

'Bert works hard all week, Kathy,' her mother had told her when she'd suggested to him that they go to one of the parks for a walk and perhaps out somewhere for tea. 'I've baked fresh cakes and you won't find anything better in a teashop, however much they charge you.'

Kathy had agreed because Bert seemed to like the arrangement. When she told him afterwards, he'd just smiled at her.

'Your mother likes having someone to make a fuss of on a Sunday, love. We go to work all week and we go out sometimes in the evenings – she spends a lot of time alone.'

Kathy couldn't disagree because it was true, but she

was young and sometimes she rebelled against settling into the ways of an old married couple. She wanted more fun and laughter, the space to tease Bert into doing what *she* wanted, which he would if he knew she really wanted it.

She wasn't dissatisfied with her marriage, because Bert was a kind and considerate lover and she enjoyed what happened in bed enough not to regret having married him. It wasn't earth shattering like she'd read about in some Ethel M. Dell novels, but it was nice enough now she'd got used to it. Her favourite outing was dancing and Bert took her on a Saturday night once a fortnight. He took her to the pictures twice a week and they usually saw the film she liked the look of and he bought her small gifts all the time.

Kathy knew that she had no real reason to complain but there was still a little doubt at the back of her mind, a feeling that things might be better if they didn't live with her mother.

She ought to have put her foot down at the beginning. Bert had had his own cottage, which was now let to someone else so that they could live with her mother, rather than leaving her to live alone. Kathy had thought it a kind notion and it had pleased her mother – but just now and then she wished they had a home of their own.

She sighed and put the niggling doubts to the back of her mind. She had a few more jobs to do and then she could go home for the afternoon. Bert would be waiting for her – but so would her mother. It would be so nice if she could just go home to her husband alone for once . . .

'Ah, Kathy,' Matron's voice spoke behind her and she turned. 'It was so good of you to give up your Sunday to help us out. I wanted to thank you personally.'

Kathy blushed. 'I was happy to come in, Matron. I don't have much to do on a Sunday morning. My mother cooks the dinner you see.'

'Ah yes, I dare say she is accustomed to it,' Matron agreed and looked thoughtful. 'Why don't you suggest making a change another week? If this lovely summery weather keeps up, you could all take a nice picnic to the park and enjoy a bit of sunshine – say you think she works too hard and you'd like to make a fuss of her for a change. You never know, she might enjoy that.'

'Yes, I might try that,' Kathy said thinking what a wonderfully understanding person Matron was. She hesitated, then, 'Is it fair that Sister Rose and her friend should have to give up their foster son to his uncle?'

Matron frowned and then sighed. 'No, Kathy. In my opinion it isn't fair, but in Danny's case it may be the best option. His father is a brute and not above threatening two women living alone. Mr Phillips is a strong man and the committee feel that he is better able to protect his nephew than Mrs Robinson was and therefore his request is likely to be approved. As soon as he has a decent home for them, and that will be soon, he will be given custody of Danny.'

Kathy felt sad. 'Sister Rose is being very brave about it but we all think it's a shame.'

'Yes, it is, but life isn't always fair, as I'm certain you know, Kathy.'

'Yes, I do, Matron.' Kathy smiled at her. It was strange but her own irritation at her mother's insensitive behaviour had faded into insignificance. Sister Rose had so much more to be sad about than Kathy.

'You get off home now, Kathy,' Matron told her kindly. 'And thank you for helping out.'

Kathy walked home at her usual pace, enjoying the sunshine. It was a lovely afternoon and she smiled as she approached the house and saw her husband come out and walk to meet her.

'Bert . . .' She smiled at him. 'What are you doing?'

'Meeting you, love,' he said. 'I didn't like to say anything in the house, because I don't want to upset your mum – but how about you get changed and we catch the bus up town and go for a walk round the shops? I know they're not open but we can window-shop and you can tell me if you see anything you'd like – and then we'll go somewhere nice to tea for a change. Your mum's cakes are good, but it's nice to go somewhere on our own sometimes, isn't it?'

'Oh, Bert,' Kathy said and hugged his arm. 'You're a lovely man! It's no wonder I married you.'

'You're not fed up or regretting it? I know I'm older – but if I get too set in my ways just give me a kick up the posterior, love. I've got a young and lovely wife and I want to make her happy.'

'I *am* happy, Bert,' Kathy said. 'I realised today how very lucky I am to have you – and Mum too. We ought to take her out one Sunday for a nice picnic lunch somewhere.'

'Why don't I suggest a trip to Southend on the bus?' Bert said and chuckled. 'She'll take it better from me, love.'

'Yes, she will – you're her golden boy,' Kathy said and giggled. Her doubts had dissolved and she knew once again why she'd married Bert. He was kind and generous and she enjoyed being with him, because he could make her laugh. 'I'll get changed quick while you tell her where we're going!'

CHAPTER 31

Constable Jones was waiting at the house when Danny got home from school the following Thursday. He looked serious and so did Beattie, her eyes a little red as if she was upset about something.

'What's wrong, Beattie?' Danny asked and felt scared. 'Have I done something bad?'

'Not at all, lad,' Constable Jones told him with a reassuring smile. 'It's just that your father was in court this morning – and he has been given three months in prison.'

'Three months?' Danny felt sick. 'I thought he would get three years at least!'

The police officer nodded. 'So did we all and he should have done but he got Judge Richards. He is one of the most lenient and your father pleaded poverty, told him that he'd taken you to help him earn a living and didn't know you had a foster mother. When he was accused of ill-treating you, he said that he'd never beaten you in your life and you must have fallen over in the place where you sleep because there is no proper light or sanitation.' Constable Jones shook his head. 'We brought all the evidence we had, including his past convictions – but the judge said we should help people like your father rather than send them to prison and gave him the minimum sentence.'

'He'll come after me again,' Danny said. 'He'd been watching me for a while before he grabbed me last time and he'll do it again.'

'Yes, we know,' Constable Jones looked at him sadly. 'That's why I'm here, Danny. Your uncle will have his new council house ready in two weeks' time. He's signed the contract and his furniture will be moved in over the next two weekends – and then he wants you to live with him. You will be thirteen in August and you can work with him and Ron on the docks during your holidays, though you will have to go back to school in term time. However, he says he'll take you to school and he and Beattie have had a talk and she will meet you, bring you back here, and he'll pick you up after work. She has agreed to go on doing that until you leave school.'

'But what about Beattie and Sister Rose's feelings?' Danny asked and looked at Beattie's red eyes. 'I love them – and Beattie teaches me to cook.'

'They've talked about that too,' Constable Jones told him. 'At holiday times and weekends you can come here and cook with Beattie – and Ron and your uncle can come to dinner on Sundays and tea on Saturdays. Besides that, you'll have time with Beattie after school each day before your uncle gets here.'

Danny nodded and looked at Beattie. That didn't sound too bad to him but she was close to tears even though she was trying to smile. 'I don't want to leave you!' he told her and ran to her side. She put her arms about him protectively. 'I love you – you're my second mum.'

'And you're the son I longed for and never had,' Beattie said. She brushed away her tears. 'That will never change, Danny – but what Constable Jones has told you about is better for you, love. If your father comes here, I can't protect you. I can't stop him taking you.'

'I'll stab him with my knife next time,' Danny said defiantly. 'He's a bully and a brute – he killed my mum and deserves to die!'

'Why do you say that?' Constable Jones asked him sharply. 'Did he do anything that caused her to die?'

'He made her ill,' Danny said. 'It was his fault she had the baby when he knew she shouldn't – and she told him so when she was dying.'

Constable Jones looked sad. 'Unfortunately, that isn't the kind of thing that we can arrest him for, unless he held a pillow to her face or hit her?'

'No – he just cried afterwards and got drunk,' Danny said and shrugged. 'He was all right once.'

'I think you have to accept that your father will try to take you again, Danny and so the best thing for you to do is live with your uncle.'

'Yes, it is,' Beattie told him, sadly, though having had time alone with Ted, discussing the situation, she was much more reconciled to it. And the more she saw of him, the more she liked and trusted him.

Danny nodded, looking from one to the other. 'As long as I can come back sometimes, Mum.'

'Yes, of course you can,' Beattie said and smiled at

him through her tears. 'We've got another two weeks before you have to go, Danny – so we'll make the most of it.'

Danny nodded. It was hard not to cry when he saw Beattie so upset. He didn't mind living with Uncle Ted and Ron – he liked them both – but he loved Beattie and he didn't want her to be unhappy.

'Yes, Mum. We'll come at the weekends and I'll go on with my cooking lessons, and I'll have an hour after school – I'll run all the way home,' he said and saw her smile. 'When I'm older I can choose what I want to do, can't I?'

'Yes, when you're twenty-one you can do whatever you like,' Constable Jones said. 'But your uncle cares about you and so does Ron, so you should be happy with them.'

'Yes, I will be,' Danny agreed. 'And I don't mind working on the docks with them as long as I can cook sometimes – and I want to see Beattie as much as possible, but otherwise it's all right.'

Beattie smiled at him; her tears gone. 'You're a lovely boy, Danny – and you're a good person, Constable Jones. Most would have let me find out through a letter but you took the trouble to call and see me.'

'I wanted you both to understand and I'm sorry I didn't manage to get your father put away for some years, Danny. Had you been eighteen when he came out, you might not have needed any help to deal with him.'

'One day I'll be big enough to clout him back if he hits me,' Danny said and jutted his chin. 'No one should use violence on others, sir – but he deserves it.'

'I couldn't agree more, Danny.' Steve smiled at him. 'And if you carry on coming to the club and studying hard, you might be able to do that sooner rather than later.'

'I think Ron would like to learn self-defence too,' Danny said. 'We both made up our minds no one was going to grab us again – but I didn't want to stick a knife in me dad, though I could've done when he was asleep.'

'That wouldn't have been a good idea, Danny,' Constable Jones agreed. 'Self-defence is another matter which will stand you in good stead all your life.'

Danny thanked him and then Steve left. Beattie started to get tea ready and Danny helped her. They didn't talk for a while, because it felt good just to be together, doing the things they enjoyed.

'I like just being with you, Mum,' Danny said. 'You're a lovely person, and I'll miss the times we're just on our own before Sister Rose came home and when you got a special breakfast just for me; I mean, I love her too, but not in the same way.'

'I know what you mean, Danny love.' Beattie smiled at him in her special way and he felt warm inside and loved. It was a good feeling and he knew it didn't have to stop just because he wouldn't be with her all the time.

'You don't stop loving someone just because they aren't there, do you, Mum?'

'No, Danny, you don't – you just miss them,' Beattie said and smiled. 'What a wise boy you are. There, I think that's all done – now we just have to wait for the food to cook while we sit down to a cup of tea and a little slice of cake – just a small one so we don't spoil our dinner . . .'

'I had to agree,' Beattie told Rose when Danny had gone to bed later that evening. 'It means that Ted – Mr Phillips – and Ron will be here most weekends so I hope you don't mind?'

'It's your home, Beattie,' Rose said. 'And I certainly don't mind, although I wish things could be as they were, but it is all for Danny's sake and that makes it fine with me.'

'Yes, and he understands that and that's why I had to agree, because if he is willing to accept the situation, then so must we, Rose.'

'Yes, I know.' Rose sighed. 'I almost wish I'd never suggested we foster Danny now – you wouldn't have got to love him then.'

'I don't regret a minute of it,' Beattie said. 'Never think that, Rose. Yes, I want him here all the time but if I can't have that, I'll take what I can and be grateful.'

'You're such a wise, loving person,' Rose said and smiled at her. 'Do you know how much I love you?'

'Yes, I do,' Beattie said and laughed. 'We've been like sisters or mother and daughter from the start, haven't we?'

'Sisters is right,' Rose said. 'I'm in my thirties and you're only forty-one so there isn't much difference.'

'I feel older,' Beattie sighed. 'I was sixteen when I married but my husband was lost almost as soon as we wed . . . Oh, that was a terrible war!' Her eyes glimmered with tears. 'Having Danny was like getting another chance at life – the child we never had a chance to have.'

'You're not too old to marry again.'

'I can't see it happening,' Beattie laughed. 'I never was a beauty, Rose.'

'Beauty is in the eye of the beholder,' Rose said. 'You're lovely to me – the loveliest person I know.'

'Now that,' Beattie said wisely, 'is another thing . . .'

CHAPTER 32

'Danny says Beattie is like a mum to him,' Ron told Ted as they were working together on a large shed for a manufacturer. It was to store the firm's raw materials and cheaper to build than a brick building, which was why Mr Reynolds was so busy at the yard. Times were better than they had been but there still wasn't much money about and timber buildings went up quicker and cheaper than conventional brick and mortar. 'He loves being with her.'

'Yes, she is a really lovely person,' Ted said and screwed a hinge into place, wiping the sweat from his brow. 'I don't mind telling you, Ron, I've had a few qualms about taking him away from her, and yet I feel my sister would want him to be safe with us. His father really could snatch him away from under her nose.'

Ron nodded and sighed. 'Yeah, I know.' He fetched some tools for Ted and watched as he smoothed out a knot in a doorpost. His employer was a perfectionist and wouldn't do less than a good job. 'It's a pity we can't *all* live together, isn't it?'

Ted turned to stare at him thoughtfully and then

nodded. 'You've taken the thought right out of my head, Ron – that just shows how well we understand each other these days. I wonder if Beattie would consider moving in with us?'

'We've only got two rooms,' Ron reminded him. Even the new home they were moving to had only two bedrooms, one for the boys to share and one for Ted. He scratched the back of his neck. 'She's got a bigger house than ours, though – perhaps we could move in with her?'

Ted frowned. 'I doubt Sister Rose would be happy about that. She needs peace and quiet when she's on nightshift and she often works weekends so it would mean being very, very quiet half the time, not easy with two great lads!'

'Perhaps Sister Rose would move out?' Ron suggested but Ted shook his head.

'We can't push her out of her home, lad,' he said, reddening slightly. 'There's only one way and I'm not sure Beattie would be willing to take it – after all, she hardly knows me . . .'

Ron stared at him, not knowing what he meant, but Ted was smiling to himself in a daft way so he didn't push it. He'd never seen his friend with such a look on his face and didn't know what to make of it so offered the only thing he could think of to say.

'Why don't you ask her?'

'Well, maybe I might,' Ted said, 'in a few weeks. We'll go over this Saturday and take something nice. She said we could go to tea so we will – and we'll see what happens . . .'

Ron didn't mind what they did, because his world

was so different and good that he was easy whatever Ted suggested. He sometimes thought that if his friend had asked, he would put his hand in the fire for him, but Ted wouldn't ask. It was because he had perfect trust in Ted that he whistled as he worked and looked forward to each day. Life couldn't get much better. He was looking forward to Danny living and working with them, but he'd be happy to live in Beattie's house, because Danny had told him what lovely food she cooked and he'd liked her house better than the one Ted had managed to rent for them. It was up to Ted . . .

'That will do for now,' Ted told him a little later. 'We'll take a break for a cuppa and a bite to eat. I want to finish this this afternoon, Ron, and we'll work all the better for a break now.'

It was as they were eating their bread and cheese that Mr Reynolds walked up to the shed and went all the way round it, looking at it carefully. He stood looking at them thoughtfully for a moment and then spoke to Ted.

'Would you come into the office a minute, Ted? I've got something to say to you . . .'

Ted looked anxious for a moment but got up and followed the boss into his office. He was gone several minutes and Ron waited, feeling worried. If they got the sack it might mean they would have to go back to living in hostels or even under the arches, but then he saw Ted coming back and he was grinning, looking a bit like the cat that got the cream.

'Is everything all right?' Ron asked, getting to his feet.

'Couldn't be better, lad,' Ted told him. 'Mr Reynolds

thinks I'm the best worker he's ever had and he's making me his head craftsman. If I can train you to take over from me then he's going to make me his foreman next year. He wants to semi-retire and spend more time with his family and he says I'm the man he can trust to run the business for him. He's also putting our wages up. It will be ten shillings for you and six for Danny when he helps out in the holidays, going up to ten when he can do what you do – and I'll be getting three pounds five shillings a week.'

Ron whistled because it was a huge rise for Ted and would make their lives so much better. 'That's great, Ted, but you deserve it.'

'For a long time, I had it hard when I was discharged and my pension didn't come through as it should but it seems my luck turned when I met you, Ron. It was knowing you needed my help that made me come after this job and then I discovered my pension had been paid for the last several years and I had a large sum owing to me. I could almost afford to set up for myself with that money, Ron. I was thinking of it until Mr Reynolds told me what he was planning. Now, I'll stop where I am and take over when he retires.'

'I reckon it was a lucky day for both of us when you stood up for me and I started to trust you, Ted.'

'I wouldn't have bothered to look for a regular job if you hadn't,' Ted said and grinned. 'Come on, lad, let's show Mr Reynolds he has made a wise choice and get that shed finished!'

Ron moved to obey eagerly. They worked steadily for the rest of the afternoon, despite the heat which had most of the other men in the yard groaning.

'Slow down, Ted,' one of them called to him. 'You make the rest of us look bad.'

'I want this done today,' Ted said. 'Do you want us to give you a hand to get yours finished?'

All he got in reply was a scowl, but Ron noticed the other men stopped moaning and got on with their work instead of standing about and complaining it was too hot. Ron smiled inwardly. Mr Reynolds knew what he was doing when he spoke of making Ted foreman; he would be good at the job and might even end up as the owner of the woodyard one day.

'I think we'll call on Beattie and Danny this evening,' Ted said when they finished work. 'We'll go home, have something to eat and a wash and then we'll take Danny a packet of sweets – and a little something for Beattie too . . .'

Ted had that daft look on his face again and Ron wondered about it.

When Ted came out of the newsagents with a packet of sweets for Ron, one for Danny and a small box of Cadbury's chocolates under his arm, something triggered in Ron's mind. Was Ted courting Beattie? Ron knew very little about family life or courting. He'd heard men talk crudely about things they did with women, but Danny had spoken of his mum fondly and Marjorie had cried for her mummy and daddy.

It might be nice to live as a family with Ted and Danny and Beattie. Ron had once seen a young woman and a young man sitting together in the park and kissing when they thought no one was looking. He'd also seen glamorous posters outside cinemas with men and women kissing – but he knew no more than that of love or marriage. Ron had never been to the cinema or read a book other than a school exercise book. He'd been forced to go to school for a while when he was in one of the orphanages he'd been sent to and he'd picked up enough learning to count money, measure lengths and scale things up, though Ted had taught him most of that, and write his name. He was wise in certain things, having lived on the streets and he'd picked up everything Ted had taught him easily, because he was bright – or so Ted said – but he knew nothing of a loving family, of affection between a man and woman . . .

When Beattie let them in that evening and Ted gave her the chocolates and thanked her for allowing them to visit, Ron noticed that she went pink. She smiled at Ron and told him to come and sit down and have a glass of the fizzy pop she'd bought for Danny and some cake.

Ron sat beside his friend and they exchanged news about their day while Ted was discussing something to do with a place called Germany with Beattie and Sister Rose. They mentioned an Anglo-French pact to defend the Czechs, whatever that meant. Ron knew, because Ted had told him, that in Germany there was a man called Hitler who was dangerous.

'Do you think there will be a war, Ted?' Sister Rose asked.

'Not if Mr Chamberlain can broker a peace with Hitler,' Ted said, looking grave. 'I'm not sure that I would trust anything that man says, but we have to hope for the best, Rose.'

'Yes, I suppose we do . . .'

'We've been making a chart for the world cup at school,' Danny told Ron and he turned to him, forgetting what the adults were talking about. Ron did know about the world cup because the papers were full of it and Ted bought a paper every Friday night. Besides, the other men on the docks talked of little else but football. He knew that it was all going to happen soon, but that Britain along with some other nations wasn't taking part.

'The chaps on the docks don't like it 'cos we ain't got a team,' Ron said and pulled a face. 'Ted took me to see a cricket match the other day and we'll all go to the footie when you live with us.'

Danny's face lit up. 'Beattie – Ron says I can go to football with them next season!'

Beattie turned to look at him and smiled. 'You'll enjoy that, love.' She turned to Ted, still smiling. 'That is very kind of you, Ted. We'll all enjoy that. Now, shall we expect you for tea on Saturday?'

'May we come to lunch on Sunday? I've got something planned for Saturday afternoon.' He looked at the boys. 'There's a cowboy film on at the Odeon and I thought I would take both of you, if you'd like to go?'

The cries of joy that met his suggestion answered that one and Beattie laughed. 'Have you come into a fortune, Mr Phillips?'

'No, but I've been given a rise and the promise of a better job next year – and I told you about my little windfall, didn't I?'

'Yes, your Army pension came through after all? What had happened?'

'It was paid into an old bank account and I didn't know. I hadn't tried to access it for three years or more, wasn't sure I still could, but the balance was nearly five hundred pounds. I could have started up my own business with that but Mr Reynolds is paying more than I'd probably earn at the start and in time I can take over from him. I intend to work hard and make sure these two have a good life.'

'I believe you will, Ted,' Beattie said and then looked almost shy.

'I can't tell you how grateful I feel for what you've done for Danny,' he said. 'I let things slip after I was invalided out of the Army and didn't try again to see him after Jim Bryant refused to let me see him, but meeting Ron and wanting to help him shook me out of my self-pity and it was the best thing that could have happened to me.' He smiled at her. 'I know you love Danny and he loves you – and I want him to feel he has more family now, not less. You're still a part of it, Beattie, and I hope you always will be . . .'

Ron saw the way they smiled at each other and wondered. Ted liked Beattie; he could tell that – but would he ask her if they could all live together?

Ted didn't ask that evening and he didn't say anything more to Ron about it, but he was whistling happily as they drove home in Mr Reynolds' old truck.

CHAPTER 33

Beattie was singing as she cooked porridge and made toast the next morning. She set the honey pot on the table in front of Rose and some lovely fresh butter.

Rose looked at her and smiled. 'That was interesting last night, Beattie – do you think Mr Phillips is courting you?'

'Never!' Beattie protested but her cheeks went pink. 'It was nice of him to bring those chocolates, though, and to say he wanted me to be a part of their lives always.'

'I think he *is* courting you,' Rose said and smiled. 'Do you like him?'

'Yes, I do like him – he's very pleasant and a sensible man,' Beattie replied. 'What do you think of him, Rose?'

'He seems intelligent, sensible and kind. I think he'll be good to the boys and no doubt he would be to his wife, if he had one. Have you noticed the slight limp? That must be why he was invalided out of the Army. I think he was a career soldier by the sound of it.'

'Yes, and he's served in several countries,' Beattie said.

'He talked about Germany and the state of things very well. Considering the way that he had to live for some time, I wouldn't have expected him to be interested or so well-informed.'

'Oh, once an Army man . . .' Rose said and drank her tea. 'I also think he was well-educated, as I think Danny's mother was because she encouraged him to take an interest in things, from what he tells me, and his speech is quite good – which just shows you should never judge a book by its cover. Ted admits he was on the streets for a while and works with his hands, but I imagine he might have done a white-collar job had he wished.'

'He speaks better than I do,' Beattie said. 'Another reason why he wouldn't be interested in me – not the way you said. I'm just an ordinary woman who left school at fourteen and married at sixteen.' She sighed. 'The Great War was just starting when my husband joined up – and he was just eighteen. I hardly knew what it was to be a wife . . .'

'Then if the chance comes you should think carefully,' Rose told her and stood up. 'That was a lovely breakfast, as always, Beattie. Have a good day and I'll see you this evening.'

Beattie watched as she left the house and then went to call Danny down for his breakfast. He didn't like porridge, even with honey to make it tasty, so Beattie boiled him an egg with bread-and-butter fingers. She was going to spoil him while she still had him.

The thought came to her that if she were to marry Ted Phillips, she could still have Danny every day, and Ron too. She liked Ron; he was a nice lad who just needed a bit of mothering to get rid of that lost, slightly wild look he had in his eyes at times. Beattie guessed that Ron had been ill-treated, ignored and unloved until Ted found him – and that was his lucky day. The way the boy looked at his saviour spoke volumes and if Beattie's instincts hadn't told her that Ted was a good man, the adoration in Ron's eyes would.

She could do a lot worse than marry him if he asked, she thought. Of course, he wouldn't ask – why would he? She wasn't ugly but there were many prettier women, Beattie knew that and chided herself for the fantasy. Certainly, she could look after them all, for she had a capacity to love and she was generous with her love, as she was with her cooking and anything else that she had. Her house was her own, because she'd bought it with a small legacy from an uncle and another from her parents. Running it as a boarding house for years had given her a reasonable day-to-day living, but she had only a few pounds' savings and not much else of value. So, she didn't have a lot to offer – unless a comfortable bed and a good meal were enough.

But Ted Phillips was a man on the rise and he didn't need Beattie because he could afford to rent his own home and care for the boys. Of course, if they wanted good home-cooked food . . . a little smile touched her lips. They said the way to a man's heart was through his stomach and Ted was coming to lunch on Sunday so she would give him a meal to remember – and if really that was enough, perhaps it might happen.

Beattie nodded and smiled. She was getting far too far ahead of herself, but she liked Ted a lot and she loved Danny. She thought marriage might be nice, because she'd enjoyed her first brief experience of the marriage bed and didn't see any reason to fear cuddling up to a good-looking man like Ted Phillips. No, if he asked her – and it was a very big if – she thought she would probably say yes and she would do her best to make it happen.

What did she have to lose?

Rose was thoughtful when she arrived at the hospital and left her dark blue nursing cloak in her locker. It had been pretty clear to her the previous evening that Ted Phillips had come courting. He'd been perfectly polite to her, including her in his talk of world affairs, and it was true he seemed to know quite a bit about the chances of war, but she'd seen the way he looked at Beattie and she thought he liked her rather more than he'd yet admitted to himself or allowed to show.

She'd been half-joking when she'd spoken to Beattie about it earlier but then she'd realised her friend *was* thinking seriously of a future that might include the ex-soldier. Obviously, a big part of that was Danny – but Beattie had been lonely when Rose first met her. Had Rose left her she might have been again.

Rose would do nothing to stand in her friend's way. She wouldn't push her into marrying but she wouldn't speak against it either. If Ted cared for Beattie, she would wish her happy – and then what?

She couldn't stay if Beattie married. Husband, wife and two growing boys would be a houseful and it wouldn't be the comfortable environment she'd known for the past few years either. Although she'd loved

Danny, two teenage boys together might make for a lot of noise and mess. Rose wasn't sure she would actually wish to stay on then.

Beattie was her friend and she wouldn't hurt her for the world so she would keep her thoughts to herself for the moment.

'A penny for them?'

The voice from behind her made Rose spin round. She found herself staring at Peter Clark and something about the way he was smiling at her made her smile too.

'I was wondering about a friend perhaps getting married,' Rose said. 'But it is still speculative.'

'Ah . . .' His smile caressed her. He hesitated and she thought he would walk on past, but then he stopped and planted himself so that she could not go past him. 'Rose – I like you very much. I've been wanting to tell you for a long time and now I've finally found the words to say: Will you come out with me one evening very soon – please?'

Rose laughed. She couldn't help herself. 'Was it so very hard to ask?' she asked. 'I'm sorry if I've been an ogress.'

'You haven't, of course you haven't. It's just that I'm a fool and you're wonderful!' he blurted out and looked so much like an eager little boy that she moved forward impulsively and he took her hand. 'Rose, please, please say yes?'

'Yes, I would like to come out with you,' she said. 'When?'

'This evening, to dinner. I think we should talk and that's the best way, over something delicious to eat.'

'All right,' Rose told him with a smile. 'I should like that very much, Dr Clark.'

'Peter, please – when we're off duty,' he said, his face alight with pleasure. 'I'm so happy, Rose. I promise you won't regret it . . .'

'No,' she said. 'I don't think I shall – will you pick me up from my home?'

'Yes, and I know where you live.' His smile was shy now. 'I walk past Mrs Robinson's house sometimes and I've seen you coming in and out. I visit my maternal grandmother who lives not far from there. She's very old and frail and is looked after by a retired nurse who lives in, but she enjoys me visiting her occasionally.'

Rose nodded, her heart singing. The church clock started to chime and she gave a start. 'I'd better go or I'll be late. I'll see you this evening at seven thirty.'

'I'll be there,' he promised and let her go.

Rose resisted the temptation to turn around, even though she knew he was watching her walk on and up the stairs to the wards.

Peter turned away when she'd disappeared from sight and got into his car. He was due on shift at the London Hospital in half an hour and would just make it. He was smiling at the thought of where he would take Rose that evening – somewhere special, somewhere he'd never taken any other girlfriend. Rose was different and he wanted it to be new, fresh – a new start for them both.

It was as he neared the hospital that he saw the queue of ambulances. He left the traffic, parked his car in his reserved place and ran, knowing that this was something out of the ordinary. They didn't have a queue like this every morning so it meant a bad accident must have happened somewhere in London – an accident, probably, in which a lot of people had been hurt and needed attention.

All thoughts of his personal life vanished as he saw the stretchers being carried into the hospital and he hurried up to one of the porters.

'What's happened, Ben?' he asked.

'Oh, Dr Clark,' the porter said, 'there's been a big gas explosion down the Commercial Road or just off it. A factory is on fire and at least forty people have been injured, many with serious burns.'

Peter nodded. The hospital was always busy and an accident of this size would keep them on their toes for the rest of the day. As well as the horrific burn cases there would be firemen overcome by inhalation of smoke and other small injuries . . .

CHAPTER 34

'Have you heard the terrible news?' Lady Rosalie asked Matron when she rang her at the Rosie later that morning. 'I know a couple of schoolchildren were hurt – caught in the blast walking past, I understand. Have they been brought to you, by any chance?'

'No,' Mary Thurston said. 'We haven't admitted anyone this morning – what has happened?'

'There was a gas explosion at a factory just off Commercial Road and it caught fire,' Lady Rosalie told her. 'I know most of the burn cases were taken to the London but some of the other cases have been taken to other hospitals – I think over a hundred have been hurt and there are more cases coming in. The smoke is toxic, apparently, and a lot of people in the area are complaining of feeling ill.'

'That's awful,' Mary said. 'Well, we may be called on yet so we should prepare, just in case.'

'That's why I rang,' Lady Rosalie said. 'And I have some news for you about the child you told me about last month. She was very unhappy in the temporary home she was placed in but I found her a new foster mother and she's really settled now.'

'Was that little Ginny?' Mary nodded her satisfaction. 'That was a clear case of neglect, Rosalie. I had no hesitation in reporting her case to the police and to you.'

'Yes, well, she is both healthy and happy now,' Lady Rosalie said. 'I shall hope to see you next week – but I'd better let you get on . . .'

Mary thanked her and replaced the receiver. She left her office and went first to the critical ward and then to the children's ward. Sister Rose was bandaging a little boy's knee. She'd just finished and she walked to greet Matron with a smile.

'What can I do for you, Matron?'

'I've just been told of a terrible accident,' Matron said. 'There are many casualties and the London Hospital has taken the brunt of it but we could well get our share before long. I believe there are some children involved and it may be that we get those.'

'They'll be working frantically at the London,' Sister Rose said and looked thoughtful. 'Was it an explosion of some kind?'

'Yes, yet another gas explosion. Some of these old factories are death traps, Sister Rose. The working conditions are crowded and poor and the equipment is old, so when something like this happens it results in a lot of injuries.'

'Yes, I can imagine,' Rose said. 'We don't often see that kind of thing here, Matron.'

'No, most of our patients are suffering from minor illnesses or simply old age,' Matron said. 'I'm not sure we could treat major burns so we shan't be asked to take those.'

Nurse Margaret came hurrying up to them. She'd just returned from a bathroom break and clearly had news for them.

'Matron, there are two ambulance men downstairs. They have two children with injuries to their hands, faces and legs, and there is a man suffering from smoke inhalation and a woman with a cut hand from flying glass.'

'Then I shall be needed. I'll leave you to prepare, Sister Rose, and I'll send one of my other junior nurses to help you.' She walked quickly from the ward.

'We have the bed at the end there and the two in the isolation ward,' Rose thought aloud, 'but we'll put them both in there, I think. If the children have serious injuries, it might perhaps be best not to let the other patients see them until they've healed a bit . . .'

Nurse Margaret went off to make sure the beds were turned down and ready for the children while Sister Rose stood at the door, ready to receive her new patients. They were brought in a couple of minutes later, a brother and sister aged ten and eleven.

'Both were knocked off their feet by the blast,' the ambulance man told her. 'The boy, Jack, was unconscious for about twenty minutes and he's feeling pretty groggy; he also has cuts to his leg and arm. Carol, the girl, has a few minor cuts to her leg and another to her face, but she's mainly suffering from shock and can't stop crying.'

'Thank you . . .' Rose took the notes she was offered

and looked at the brother and sister. Her practised eye noted the dirty faces and unkempt hair. 'At what time did this happen?'

'About six thirty this morning,' the porter replied. 'The children were taken to the London and the first assessment was done there but they are inundated, so we were asked to transfer them elsewhere – this was the nearest hospital that could take them.'

'We have two isolation beds that will be just right.' Rose bent over the young girl, who was crying. 'Hello, is your name Carol?' The child nodded, her eyes were wide with fear. 'It's all right, Carol. You've no need to be frightened. We shall look after you now, and your brother.'

'Is he dead?' Carol asked timidly. 'He wouldn't open his eyes.'

'Jack is feeling unwell for the moment,' Rose said, smiling at her gently, 'but we're going to make sure he's going to be all right. I know another nurse looked after you at the start, but I'm going to put you into bed and then I'll have a look at you, make sure you're comfortable. Does anything hurt badly?'

'My leg hurts and my face is sore,' Carol replied tearfully. 'But I'm 'ungry – we ain't 'ad anythin' ter eat since yesterday morning.'

'I'll get you something in a few minutes,' Sister Rose said and smiled inwardly. This patient wasn't too bad if she was more worried about being hungry. Apart from her worry about her brother, she would soon recover once she'd had a nice cup of milky cocoa and a ham sandwich.

*

Peter worked throughout the morning and the early afternoon and it was about three o'clock when a young policeman came up to him.

'Sorry to trouble you, Doctor, but we've got a problem and I've been told you're the one we need.'

'What is it?' Peter asked, his eyes moving round the busy ward. They had just finished dealing with every casualty brought in to them and he was about to take his break.

'I understand you know an old woman called Jessie – she walks about with a ramshackle pram?' the police officer said. 'She's a bit of a funny one but apparently she likes you.'

'Yes, I've treated Jessie at the clinic many times but, as you can see, we have an emergency . . .'

'Unfortunately, Jessie is a part of the emergency and she won't let anyone but you near her,' the officer went on with a frown. 'She's caught under heavy debris, Dr Clark, and we can't move her. She screams every time anyone tries to touch her and keeps asking for you.'

'In that case I'll come,' Peter said and signalled to one of the nurses. He explained to her where he was going and followed the police officer out of the ward and down through the hospital to the waiting car.

The scene of the accident was like a war zone, Peter thought as he approached it a short time later. Ambulances were still parked nearby and police cars, also people standing in groups watching, despite being asked to move on.

'I don't know why it fascinates them,' the police officer remarked. 'She's over there, sir . . .'

Peter approached a small group of doctors and policemen standing around what looked to be part of a collapsed building. As he approached, a police constable he recognised looked at him and smiled.

'Ah, Dr Clark – it's Jessie. She's trapped under there and we need to give her a sedative so we can pull her clear. It is going to cause her a lot of pain and we may have to amputate her leg to get her out.'

Peter frowned. 'Constable Jones, you can't do that – she couldn't live if she was stuck in an institution and that is what will happen if you take her leg.'

'Dr Raymond thinks it may be the only way.'

'Where is she?' Peter moved towards the pile of concrete and brick rubble that had trapped the old lady. He had to crouch down to look underneath to see her lying there, pinned by her leg and bleeding.

'Hello, Jessie,' he said in a calm voice. 'What did you go and do this for?'

'Wasn't my bleedin' fault,' Jessie snapped and then she recognised him and gave a cackle of laughter. 'Got you, did they, doc? Stupid lot – can't they just get on with it and pull me out?'

'I'm going to give you an injection so you don't feel the pain, Jessie – will that be all right?'

'Long as it's you, doc. Only bleedin' hurry up, I'm 'ungry.'

'Yes, I'm sure you are, Jessie,' Peter said. 'I'll be back in a moment.'

He went back to the other doctors and policemen. 'Once I've given her the morphine, what do you intend to do?'

'We'll have to cut her leg off to free her,' one of the

doctors said. 'That concrete is too heavy to shift and if we leave her any longer, she will die.'

'Take her leg and you condemn her to a lingering death,' Peter objected. 'I think once she's out for the count I can move her.'

'Not sure we can let you do that, sir,' Constable Jones told him. 'To get her out you've got to lift that heavy slab of concrete and it could bring the whole thing down on you.'

'I need something to prop it with,' Peter said and one of the firemen produced a handy-looking jack. 'Yes, that looks good, I'll use that.'

'Are you sure you want to take the risk?' Constable Jones asked while the others looked on and shook their heads.

'I'll give yer a hand,' the young fireman offered. 'I'm Mike and she reminds me of my gran – fiery old girl.'

'Thanks,' Peter said. 'I'll tell you when we can start.'

He went back to where Jessie was trapped and then crawled through the narrow aperture to her side. She opened her eyes and smiled at him.

'I knew yer would come,' she said just as the needle touched her skin.

Peter looked at the concrete trapping her as she drifted into sleep. He had to lever it up and secure it and then drag her out and get out before the released weight forced the whole thing to collapse.

Crawling back out, he spoke to the young fireman.

'We'll lift it easily with the two of us and that jack should hold it long enough to pull her out. As soon as we get her free, we go – understood? The weight won't hold long.'

'We know,' the young fireman said. 'I wanted to try earlier but they wouldn't let me – you seem to have more clout.'

'Let's get her . . .' Peter knew there was no time to waste. Jessie would die if she was left to bleed much longer and the whole lot could come down at any time.

There was just room for the two of them to stand, half bent over and apply the pressure to lever the concrete slab from Jessie's leg. Had she been awake the pain would have been too much for her to bear, but they had to work swiftly and having her limp and unconscious was the only way. Peter signalled for his helper to drag her out and then to keep going. He could feel the weight shifting and knew if he let go it would slowly collapse.

'We're out, sir – get out yourself.'

Peter heard the shout and let go. He heard the cracking from above his head and knew the debris was shifting. Head bent, he started to run in a crouch as fast as he could. He could see the light and knew he was nearly out, but the debris was falling on his shoulders and something hit his head, rendering him unconscious as the whole thing collapsed behind him.

CHAPTER 35

Rose hurried home from work that evening and changed into a pretty dress, fluffed out her hair and applied a little lip rouge and a touch of powder to her nose. She sprayed a few drops of her precious perfume on her wrists and looked at the clock. It was just twenty past seven and Peter would be here shortly.

Downstairs, Beattie and Danny were baking cakes. Beattie pointed to a box on the countertop. 'Those are for you to take into the ward tomorrow, Rose. Danny baked them and decorated them with butter icing and they're good.'

'Thank you, both of you,' Rose said with a smile. She opened the lid to peep inside. 'Gosh, they do look lovely – the children and the staff will enjoy these, Danny. You're so clever.'

'Well, Beattie showed me how and I do like cooking for people,' Danny told her and Rose nodded, then asked the question that had been hovering in her mind.

'Will you mind having to work with Mr Phillips in the woodyard, Danny?'

'No, I reckon I'll enjoy it,' Danny said and looked

thoughtful. 'I can still cook in the evenings and at the weekends and when I'm old enough to look after myself I can decide what I really want to do . . .'

Rose looked at him with approval. Danny was such a lovely and loving boy and she wondered how a brute like Jim Bryant could have fathered him. It was sad that he'd had such a hard life with his father but she was sure that he would be well looked after by Ted Phillips and Beattie would still be in his life.

The clock had crept round to seven thirty while they talked. Rose fetched her coat and put it over the back of a chair ready. She looked expectantly at the door, wondering where Peter was going to take her.

'Are you excited?' Beattie asked and she smiled a little nervously.

'Yes, excited and nervous,' Rose told her. 'I like Peter a lot, Beattie, but it took me ages to trust him and I still feel a bit apprehensive.'

'I'm sure he cares for you,' Beattie said. 'Anyone would.'

Rose saw her glance at the clock. The hands hadn't moved much even though each second seemed like a minute.

At a quarter to eight, Beattie put the kettle on. 'He must have been delayed,' she said. 'Perhaps it was to do with that big accident, Rose. The hospitals must have been overrun with emergencies.'

'Yes, they were, but I thought he would let me know if he couldn't get away . . .'

She sat down and drank the tea that Beattie offered and then a small piece of cake when the minutes kept ticking by and still Peter didn't come. At nine o'clock,

Rose ate a sandwich and put her coat back in the hall cupboard. Peter wouldn't come now. She felt upset but not angry because she was still willing to believe that he'd been detained by his work – and yet surely, he could've got a message to her somehow?

It was a quarter to ten and Rose was about to make a cup of cocoa to take up to bed when a knock came at the front door. She ran to answer it, staring in shock as she saw Matron standing there.

'Matron!' Rose cried. 'What is it – what has happened?'

'May I come in, Sister Rose?'

'Yes – yes, of course.' Rose led the way into the hall and then the kitchen where Beattie had taken over making their cocoa. She turned to face Matron and discovered that she was shaking. 'Please tell me what has brought you here?'

'It was lucky I was still at the Rosie, as I was about to leave for home to pack my things. As you know, I'm going away for a few days with Lady Rosalie and her son – however, there is another train I can catch later. I thought this more important, Rose . . .' She paused, then, 'I received a message from the London Hospital,' Matron said, looking upset. 'As you know there was a terrible explosion that hurt several people and killed one today . . .'

Rose went cold all over. 'Please, tell me . . .'

'I believe you may have had an arrangement to meet Dr Clark this evening?'

'Yes.' Rose sat down because her legs were suddenly weak. 'We were going to dinner.'

Matron nodded, looking serious. 'I'm told he was a

hero – went into a dangerous situation and propped up the debris so that an old lady could be rescued. Unfortunately, before he could get out it collapsed on him, trapping him and rendering him unconscious.'

Rose licked her lips. 'Is-is he still alive?'

Matron looked at her for a moment before replying. 'Yes, at the moment, although they are not certain whether he will last the night. And if he does . . .' She took a deep breath. 'It may be that his spine is crushed. It's early days and they can't be sure he'll walk again even if he lives.'

A cry of despair left Rose's lips even though she wasn't aware of it. Beattie came to stand by her, placing a hand on her shoulder to steady her.

'I am so very sorry to give you this news,' Matron said sadly. 'Of course, he is lucky to be alive. If it had not been for Constable Jones and a young fireman, who pulled him out, he might be dead already.'

'I must go to the hospital,' Rose said. 'Do you think they will let me see him?'

'Apparently, he had your name on something inside his jacket pocket and that's why they contacted me. I'm not sure if he has any close relatives left alive – so I imagine you will be considered his next of kin. So, yes, they will allow you to visit, Rose.'

'Thank you, I'll go now,' Rose said and looked at Beattie. 'I'll stop at the hospital all night if need be so don't sit up for me.'

'And I shall not expect you in tomorrow,' Matron said. 'You will let me know if you need more time off?'

'Yes – and thank you for coming, Matron.'

'It was the least I could do.'

Rose hurried to fetch her coat and came back with it and her handbag. Beattie embraced her. 'I'll be here for you, love, but don't worry about us.' She looked at Rose anxiously. 'How will you get to the hospital?'

'I'll get a taxi cab from the rank on the corner of Silver Street. They work until midnight.'

'You've got enough money?'

'Yes, I'm fine,' Rose said, gave her a quick hug and left.

It was still fairly light because it was a warm summer evening and Rose walked quickly to where she knew the taxis waited for business. Her heart was beating like a drum and Matron's words were burning in her head, but Rose wouldn't let them in. Peter couldn't die – not now, when they'd just found each other. If he lived, she could cope with the rest, she'd decided that instantly. Rose was a nurse and knew how to look after people. If he couldn't walk, they would get him a wheelchair and she would devote her life to caring for him.

Doctors made the worst patients, all the nurses said so, but Rose would do whatever it took to give him the best quality of life he could manage – it would take patience from both of them and she knew that a vigorous man like Peter Clark would resent it. No, she wouldn't let herself expect the worst. Sometimes miracles happened and perhaps Peter's injuries wouldn't be as bad as they feared. But first he had to survive the night – and if she was with him, perhaps she could somehow will him to live . . .

Sarah gave a little cry of relief when she saw Steve come in at last. He was late home and she'd guessed he was caught up in the terrible accident and had spent the afternoon trying not to worry too much. Then she saw the bruises to his face and the sling supporting his arm.

'Steve! What happened?'

'It's quite a long story, love,' he told her. 'Put the kettle on and I'll tell you.'

As Sarah made tea and a ham sandwich, Steve's story unfolded. He'd been called to the accident along with half of the police in London's East End. He described how they'd all stood about, wondering what to do, until Dr Clark had turned up and insisted on going in and dragging the old lady, Jessie, out to save her leg.

'And now he's in hospital fighting for his life,' he said as she put the tea in front of him. 'Mike Corrigan and I managed to pull the debris off him and get him into the ambulance but he looked to be in a bad way.'

'It was a brave but foolish thing to do,' Sarah said and Steve nodded.

'Yes, incredibly brave. The others were all for cutting her leg off to free her without disturbing what amounted to a ton or more of debris but he said that if they did that she might as well be dead because that was what would happen to her, stuck in an old people's home.'

'And now *he's* at death's door.'

'The medics who patched me up weren't hopeful. He had a concrete block fall on his spine and a smaller piece hit his head, so two serious injuries. It will be a miracle if he lives – and if he does, they're not sure he'll walk again . . .'

'Poor devil!' Sarah said and shuddered. 'Does he have a family?'

'He had Sister Rose's name on a piece of paper in

300

his pocket with her address so they've taken her as his next of kin, because no one knows.'

'I believe she's always liked him a lot,' Sarah said. 'Poor Sister Rose – she and Beattie are losing Danny and now this.'

'Yes, it doesn't seem right, but I think Ted Phillips will play fair with them over Danny.'

'Yes, but that doesn't help Sister Rose much if the man she loves is either dead or a cripple for the rest of his life.' Sarah looked at him sadly, distressed for the nurse she liked as a friend.

'No, it doesn't, Sarah. I wish I'd stopped him doing it now, but it seemed such a good thing to do.'

'Heroic but foolish in hindsight,' Sarah said as her husband demolished his ham sandwich. 'You wouldn't ever do anything so daft, would you?' She looked at him anxiously.

'I've got too much to lose,' Steve told her. 'I have a family to look after, Sarah and I think Dr Clark probably doesn't have much family these days. Not that I can claim to know him.'

'I don't think many of us do. Jenny Brown was seeing him for a while but she said he didn't talk about family and she didn't ask.'

Steve nodded. 'Well, he's going to need someone, so let's hope Sister Rose is willing to visit and help out a bit. I'll see what I can do when the time comes, naturally, but we don't know he'll survive the night yet . . .'

It was eleven thirty the next morning when Rose returned home. Beattie came to her at once, taking her coat and bag and looking at her anxiously.

301

'Are you all right, love?'

'I'm tired,' Rose admitted. She glanced at her friend, her face creasing in distress as she struggled against her tears. 'He made it through the night, Beattie, and about an hour ago he opened his eyes and knew me.' She choked back a sob. 'He apologised for standing me up!'

'So, he isn't damaged up here, then?' Beattie touched the side of her head. That had, of course, been one fear and it was a relief to know he wasn't brain damaged. 'Thank God for that.'

'Yes,' Rose said, and a glimmer of a smile showed. 'They think he will live now unless he has a relapse, which could still happen. But they also say he can't move his legs . . .'

'Oh, Rose! I'm so sorry!'

Rose shook her head, brushing away her tears. 'I'll take care of him, Beattie. I'll work shorter hours and look after him and we'll manage somehow.'

'You could bring him here,' Beattie offered instantly. 'He can have Danny's room and we'll share the nursing. I mean, I'm no nurse but I can help wash him and bring him drinks and food.'

'Oh, Beattie!' The relief showed in Rose's face. 'I couldn't ask such a sacrifice of you.'

'What sacrifice? Do you think I'd be happy if you had to move out and live in poverty to look after him? No, Rose, you're my family and I'll stand by you, love. If he lives long enough to leave hospital you will bring him here and we'll share the nursing. That way you can keep on earning a living, for how else would you live?'

'They threw away the mould when they made you,

Beattie,' Rose told her, eyes glistening. 'I can't tell you how much that means to me.'

Beattie hugged her. 'I was lonely before you came into my life, Rose, and then you brought me Danny. I know he won't be here all the time, but he'll visit and so will Ron and Ted – and Ted will give us a hand with whatever we need.'

Rose looked at her. Beattie seemed pretty sure of Ted Phillips' willingness to help. Their friendship must have got stronger without her realising it. She smiled at her friend and thanked her.

'I need to get some sleep and then I'll go back to the hospital. Thank you, Beattie, you've made things so much easier.'

Rose wasn't sure Peter Clark would accept their help and his grandmother, from what he'd told her, was too old and frail to get involved. He was bound to feel resentful and angry when he realised that he might never walk unaided again. A life confined to a wheel-chair wasn't much of a life for a man who had been fit and healthy until he risked everything to help an elderly woman. Tears stung her eyes but she brushed them away impatiently. She couldn't afford tears. She had to be strong, because Peter would only accept help if she convinced him it wouldn't bother her to look after him.

All she wanted to do was to put her arms about him, hold him and tell him she loved him, but if she did that he would probably decide he couldn't ruin her life and go off somewhere to convalesce alone – or he might turn his face to the wall and decide it wasn't worth the fight.

CHAPTER 36

Being a doctor made it all too easy to diagnose your own problem, Peter thought as he lay in bed and realised that he couldn't feel his toes and couldn't move his legs. He felt a wave of regret and self-pity as he understood that, even if he lived, he might be stuck in a wheelchair for the rest of his life.

'Sod it!' he muttered and the nurse tending the cuts on his legs looked at him anxiously. He shook his head. 'No, you didn't hurt me, nurse. I can't feel a damned thing . . .'

A look of pity flashed in her soft eyes and he felt a spurt of anger. He wasn't a poor, helpless creature to be pitied or cried over and, in that moment, he determined that he was going to live and, if it was humanly possible, he would regain some kind of mobility. Peter knew the odds: his spine had been damaged and if it was just bruising and minor damage, he might get some mobility back. However, if the cord had been cut or too badly squashed, then it would take a bloody miracle to get him on his feet again. But whatever, he wouldn't give up and he wasn't going to be pitied.

'Have I been X-rayed yet?' he asked the nurse and she gave him a scared-rabbit look and shook her head. 'I'm a doctor, nurse, so you can tell me the truth. I would much prefer you did.'

'I don't know, Dr Clark. I'm just a junior. I've been told to change these bandages, that's all.'

'Then fetch someone who *can* tell me!' he barked at her.

'Now then, doctor,' a voice he heard in his dreams said in a cool clinical tone that immediately quelled his anger, 'please do not bully the nurses.'

'Rose!' He looked at her and managed a smile even though his head ached like hell. 'I thought you were with me all last night . . .'

'I was most of the time,' she said and bent to take his pulse. Her calm, clinical manner made him laugh.

'You never change, do you?' he said, looking at her hard.

'Would you wish me to?' Rose smiled at him. 'I suppose I should forgive you for standing me up last night – though it was a rather silly thing to do to get out of our dinner.'

'I couldn't let her be crippled, Rose. She wouldn't have survived it,' Peter said. Rose's soft, sweet eyes looked into his and he knew what she was asking. 'Yes, I *will* survive, whatever. I may hate it – but I'll fight it every step of the way.' He strained to sit up but had to flop back against the pillows, exhausted. 'Sod it!'

Rose laughed and the sound of it was music to his ears. If he hadn't already adored her, he certainly would have then. 'Don't try too hard too soon, Peter. Let the nurses and doctors heal you as much as they can – and then we'll take it from there.'

'What do you mean?' Peter asked frowning.

'We'll see what can be done when you come home to Beattie and me,' Rose said. 'You live in lodgings, Peter, so it makes sense to let us help you. Beattie is losing Danny and she'll have time to help you while I'm at work; and when I'm not, I shall help you with the exercises. The stronger your upper body is, the better you'll manage to get in and out of the chair – should you need it.'

'I'll need it,' he said grimly. 'I can't feel my toes and I can't move my legs.'

'But you can move your arms and you're strong,' Rose said in the calm, practical manner he'd heard her use at the Rosie so many times. 'I had some experience with this sort of thing a few years ago and I'll research the latest thinking so that I know just what to do to help you.'

'And why should you and Beattie do this for me?' Peter demanded aggressively.

'I imagine you can pay rent,' Rose said in her unruffled manner. 'Beattie can do with a little extra help – and I happen to like you quite a lot.'

Peter looked at her for a long minute. 'I don't want sympathy. I could afford to pay for help in a special hospital if I need it.'

'Yes, of course you could, but why not be in a comfortable home with people who care for you?'

'Do you care, Rose?' he asked and waited, holding his breath.

'Yes, I do,' she said. 'I always have – but that doesn't

mean I'll cry all over you or let you have your own way!'

Peter let out his breath in a burst of laughter that made the other nurse look at him in astonishment. 'No, you won't, will you, Sister Rose? And I'll bet you won't let me slack or feel sorry for myself.'

'Why on earth should you feel sorry for yourself?' she asked. 'There are children who are born without the proper use of their bodies who never have the chance to live any other way. You're a strong man, strong enough to live independently in time, should you get tired of us – and if I have my way you will be able to do much of what you did before, even if from a chair. But I promise you, Peter Clark, we will do everything we can to get you back on your feet again.'

'No quarter given, eh?' His smile was amused as he relaxed. 'Well, Rose, I thank you and Beattie for the chance to live in your home – and if I make it out of this damned place, I'll probably take you up on your offer – just so that I can tell those kids at the Rosie that I know what it is like to be bossed about by Sister Rose.'

'Good.' Rose smiled at him. 'One of the things I like best is your sense of optimism, Dr Clark. I think we should say as soon as you get out of this damned place, don't you?'

'Oh yes, anything you say, Sister,' Peter said. He watched her straighten his bed automatically. Even here, where she had no sway, she was at her practical best. The nurse who had left his bed in a pickle would feel the edge of her tongue if she worked at the Rosie! 'That feels better, thank you.'

308

Rose sat down on the chair beside his bed. 'Just rest for a while now, please. I thought you might like to know that Jessie is doing very well. She is conscious and she knows you saved her and she sends you her love – and will visit you as soon as they "bleedin' let her".'

'It was good of you to visit her,' Peter said, his eyes never leaving her face. He wondered if she knew how beautiful she was and smiled inwardly. He would never have expected to woo the woman he wanted from a hospital bed, but if it was his only choice, he might as well start now. 'You look wonderful, Rose. That reddish-golden light in your hair is truly beautiful.'

'Strange,' she said, 'I've always wished for dark hair or deep auburn – this colour is neither one thing nor the other.'

'Oh no, I think it looks like the gold of ripe corn in the sunlight,' he said and she giggled, her eyes sparkling as she shook her head at him.

'I always knew you were a flirt,' she said. 'I didn't know you were a poet too!'

Peter closed his eyes, a smile on his face. His head ached and all he wanted to do was sleep but he tried to fight it because Rose was visiting and he so much wanted to be with her. He felt her breath on his face but couldn't manage to open his eyes as the exhaustion took over.

'Sleep, my darling,' she said. 'If I'm gone when you wake, know I'll come back as soon as I can and I'll never leave you . . .'

Peter gave up the struggle and slipped into the deep,

healing sleep his body craved. He dimly felt her hand touching his face and smelled her perfume and then he slept.

'His spine is badly bruised and crushed in one place,' the doctor told Rose when she asked. 'I can't rule out that it will heal eventually – the human body is a remarkable thing, Sister Rose, but it will be a long job and, if he does eventually recover movement, he will likely have quite a bit of pain to contend with for life. However, I don't have to tell you that, I know.'

'I didn't expect anything else,' Rose said. 'I am prepared for the worst, doctor, but I need to know if the damage is permanent?'

'I can't say for certain. There is damage to the vertebrae, but as far as I can tell the spinal cord is intact, though it is bruised and damaged. He will not walk or feel movement until that has healed, and it may never do so completely.'

'Yet there is hope.' Rose nodded. 'I want him to have hope, doctor. He will need it to begin the fight that lies ahead. In time he will grow accustomed to his limitations and we'll teach him how to adapt, but he needs a little hope.'

'He is a doctor. If I tried to sugar the pill, Sister, he would know immediately.'

She smiled. 'Of course. So the truth but don't damn him to the chair without hope. There is a small chance he can recover mobility and I want him to believe it.'

'You are a determined woman, Sister Rose.'

She smiled and inclined her head as if it were a

compliment. 'Yes, Doctor, I am – and if it is physically possible, I'll get him on his feet again.'

'With you to care for him it just may be,' he said. 'If ever I'm ill, remind me to send for you.'

Rose smiled. 'Dr Clark means a lot to me, sir, and I think he deserves whatever we can do to help him.'

'There's no doubt of that,' the spinal consultant replied. 'He's done a lot of work for charity – did you know that?'

'I'd guessed as much from what Jessie told me,' Rose said, 'but he'd never mentioned it to me. I dare say Matron knew but she doesn't break a confidence.'

'He has a private income,' the consultant told her. 'I've no idea what it is but it came from his paternal grandfather and that's why he gives so much of his time to the free clinics. We employed him two days a week but he devoted his life to the poor of London. He didn't deserve what happened – even if he was a reckless young fool.'

'Reckless and brave,' Rose said and lifted her head. 'Thank you for telling me about Peter's condition and his chances. I intend to make as much as possible of that chance and I expect we'll be seeing you for various appointments in the future, Mr Baker.'

'Yes, we'll certainly be keeping an eye out for him,' Ken Baker told her. 'I can only say good luck, Sister Rose, and I wish you well in your efforts.'

Rose nodded and left his office. Kenneth Baker was a busy man and she was grateful to him for seeing her. Now all she had to do was to prepare Beattie's front room for Peter. He would be using that as his bedroom for the foreseeable future, not Danny's room, but not just yet. The hospital consultants seemed to think that Peter was over the worst but now his long convalescence would begin and they would send him home to her when they judged he was ready for the move.

CHAPTER 37

'Thank you, Ted, these are lovely.' Beattie accepted the flowers and smelled them. Roses and freesias, gorgeous! 'They smell wonderful.' She glanced at the two boys, who were poring over a football magazine that Ted had given them. 'Will you have a cup of tea and a slice of my fruitcake? I know you're partial to fruitcake.'

'Yes, I like the way you make it with cherries and not dark like most,' Ted said. 'You can really taste the fruit like this and it's fresh and lovely.'

'I make a dark rich fruitcake at Christmas but I like this sort for everyday and so does Rose.'

Ted nodded and glanced at the boys. At that moment they got up and went racing up the stairs to Danny's room.

'Danny has some new football kit for school,' Beattie told him. She took a deep breath. 'I suppose you'll be taking him this weekend?'

'After Sunday lunch,' Ted agreed, hesitated, then, 'It doesn't have to be forever, though, Beattie. I wondered – if, when you get to know me better, you might consider being my wife?'

Beattie closed her eyes for a moment. It was what she'd wanted for weeks now, had dreamed of, but things were altered now. 'I might like that, Ted,' she said slowly, 'but it couldn't be while Rose needs me to help her.'

He looked at her and nodded. 'I thought you might say that.' He frowned and then said, 'It wouldn't be you if you let her down, Beattie, and I know I can't expect you to put me first because you hardly know me. And I first thought of it because of Ron and Danny, believing it would make things better for the four of us. But the truth is, Beattie, it's because of the way I feel about you. I-I'm very fond of you . . .'

'And I'm fond of you, Ted,' Beattie admitted. 'Very fond. If it hadn't been for Dr Clark's accident, I would have been happy to marry you right now. And I hope you understand that I can't let Rose down. She's like a sister to me, you see.' Her eyes glistened with tears. 'Oh Ted, you won't stop coming over, will you?'

'No, no I shan't do that, Beattie,' Ted said. 'I'm disappointed – because I'd hoped we could all be together sooner rather than later, but I shall still come over every Saturday and Sunday unless I take the boys out somewhere and, if I do, we'll come another night to make up for it.'

'Oh, you're a good man, Ted Phillips!' Beattie said and he got up and put his arms around her, kissing her softly on the lips. She blushed and gave him a little push away. 'Go on with you, we're not wed yet . . .'

'No, but that was for being the lovely woman you are,' Ted told her and kissed her again. 'Right, Ron and I had best be getting home . . .' He went to the foot of the stairs and called out and both boys came running down. 'Time to go, Ron. You'll be coming home with us on Sunday after tea, Danny, so get your things packed before then.'

'Yes, Uncle Ted.' Danny smiled as Ted ruffled his hair. 'Thanks.'

'Goodnight, then – say goodnight to Beattie, Ron. She's given us a tin of stuff to take home with us.'

'Thank you, Beattie,' Ron said. 'Your last cake was the best ever!'

'You like pear-upside-down cake, do you?' Beattie smiled. 'Then I'll make it on Sunday and you boys can take it home with you.'

After Ted and Ron had gone, Beattie made cocoa for herself and Danny and sent him off to bed. Rose was visiting Dr Clark and Beattie felt sadness descend for a moment. She would have liked to have given Ted her promise and she knew her home wouldn't be quite the same once Dr Clark was here, either. She thought the boys might have to be quieter if he was sleeping next door and wondered how it would work, yet she didn't regret giving her word to Rose.

'Beautiful flowers,' Rose remarked when she saw the roses and freesias in a vase on the hall table. 'Ted brought them, I suppose?'

'Yes, he did,' Beattie said. 'His house is ready now and he'll be taking Danny with him on Sunday after tea.'

'I see . . .' Rose looked at her with sympathy. 'I'm so sorry, Beattie. We knew it was coming but it is very hard, especially for you.'

'Yes, I shall miss him,' Beattie agreed, 'but I did know

315

it was coming – and I've learned to accept it. They will visit at weekends and Danny will come after school until he leaves, and that must be enough . . .' She nearly added 'for now' but checked herself in time. If Rose guessed what she'd turned down for her sake she wouldn't accept it. Beattie couldn't let her guess or notice anything or she would tell her she would make other arrangements and Beattie would never let her down.

'Yes, I suppose so,' Rose said but in a preoccupied way that told Beattie her thoughts were elsewhere. 'Peter was a bit depressed this evening . . . I think he'd been trying to exercise and found it harder than he imagined.'

'How soon do you think they will let him come home?'

'Perhaps in a month. It gives us time to fix the room up for him but it means some of your things will have to go in the dining room out of the way for now.' She looked apologetic. 'It means turning your home upside down, Beattie.'

'I know and I don't mind,' Beattie replied with a smile. 'I'll be glad to have him, so don't feel awkward, Rose. Whatever you need to do, do it.'

'Thank you – it is so, so kind. I'm not sure I could've managed without your help, Beattie. Peter has money and we could have hired a place for us and help, too, but it might not have worked and I wouldn't want to leave him with just anyone, whereas I know I can trust you.'

'Bless you for that, Rose.' Beattie embraced her lovingly. Her regrets over Ted and their immediate future vanished like morning mist. She loved Rose and Rose needed her, so Rose was going to get what she needed.

CHAPTER 38

Lily looked at the post. There were two cards; the first was a view of an English seaside resort and was from Mary Thurston. Matron had surprised everyone by actually going off for a week's holiday at Lady Rosalie's cottage in Devon but the message said she was having a lovely time. It would do her the world of good, Lily thought. They could all do with a little break from work in the sunshine. Smiling, Lily put the card on the mantle where Jenny would see it and then looked at the next card. It was a beautiful view of the Swiss mountains and carried a simple message, which made her heart race suddenly with excitement.

Enjoying a break in the sunshine. Wish you were here with me. Think of you always. One day, my love . . .

The card was not signed but Lily didn't need it to be. She was well aware it was from Chris and it made her ache with longing. The postmark was Switzerland and so clearly her husband was there again for some reason. She wondered if he might get home again for a surprise visit and lived in hope for ten days or so but then gave up expecting him. He'd taken the chance to send a postcard but that was all he could manage. She smiled and held it to her heart, as if somehow the hands that had written that message could touch her. If only he could come home and be with her! If only he did a nice safe sensible job in the civil service . . .

He wouldn't be Chris if he did, she supposed, and told herself to stop moping. Chris would come when he could, she knew that, so there was no point in wishing for the moon.

After their wedding and brief honeymoon, Lily had wondered if she might fall pregnant, but nothing had happened. She was in her early thirties and knew it was possible she might never have a child but she and Chris had discussed it and she'd said she didn't want to take precautions.

'If I have your baby, I'll be happy and proud,' she'd told him and he'd kissed her. Unfortunately, it hadn't happened. Perhaps it never would. Chris had told her all he wanted was her, though if she had a child, he would love it for her sake as well as its own.

'I don't mind, darling,' he'd told her. 'I love you, and as soon as I can I'll come back to you and we'll tell everyone we're married.'

Lily had smiled, secure in his love. She still felt that security but missed him. It was hard not having him close when she went to bed at night and her body ached for him.

Jenny was dating a young taxi driver at the moment. She'd met him when he'd fetched a patient from the infirmary and he'd come back later to ask her out. Jenny had agreed and he'd taken her dancing twice, to the pictures once, and to a lovely meal. He owned his own taxi and a nice car and earned a reasonable living, which meant he could take Jenny to nice places, which was what Jenny seemed to want from her boyfriends.

Lily worried about her sister sometimes. She wasn't sure how Jenny felt about Michael Grey. Was she attracted to the man or to the nice car he picked her up in, the places he could afford to take her to? But she seemed happier again and was often in a rush to meet her new friend. The sisters still went out to the pictures together every now and then but Lily spent more time at home alone than Jenny. She preferred to work nights and had volunteered for it when Sister Rose asked if she would take the night shifts and let Rose stay on days.

'That will make it easier for me when Peter gets out of hospital,' Rose explained. 'Beattie doesn't mind looking after him during the day while I'm at work, but I can't ask her to get up at night.'

'Of course, I don't mind being on nights,' Lily had told her easily. 'It's better for me at the moment.'

She slept for a while in the mornings, then got up and cleaned house or shopped but didn't bother with going anywhere much unless Jenny plagued her to go out with her. A good book was all the company she needed in her spare time and she chatted to their neighbours over the fence when she did a little tidying up in the garden. They had someone do the heavy digging once a year and then kept it tidy between them, though next door's teenage boy sometimes came over and did a bit of weeding for them. Lily had tried to pay him but he shook his head.

'You looked after me dad when he was in the infirmary,'

he'd told her with a cheeky grin. 'He says yer a smasher and I should 'elp yer if I can.'

'Your dad is very kind,' Lily had told him and smiled. It was good to have nice neighbours and when their tomato plants bore fruit, she took some of the surplus to his mother, who said she would bottle them.

'I make a lot of tomato chutney,' she'd said. 'I give it to the older ones.'

'Do a kindness and pass it on . . .' Lily said smiling.

It was still really warm even though the end of August could sometimes be chilly. The wireless was droning on in the background about the cricket scores and what Len Hutton had scored for England. About to switch it off and seek the garden, Lily heard the voice of the newscaster cut in:

'Sir Neville Henderson has been recalled from Berlin for consultations on the growing Sudetenland crisis,' his voice said gravely. 'The German threat to Czechoslovakia is now increasingly grave. The Government cannot guarantee that they would be able to go to the help of the people if they were attacked as it is likely that such action would lead eventually to war . . .'

Lily snapped the wireless off. She could do without dire news like that on her day off. The sunshine was calling to her and she wanted to make the most of it because any day now it could start to get chillier – and then the dark nights would gradually start to close in . . .

Shivering, Lily went outside into the warmth of the late August sun. She didn't want to think about what might happen if there was a war with Germany. Would Chris come home then – or would he be trapped for its duration? Rumours of war had persisted all summer long but the papers had seemed to say it wouldn't happen. The Prime Minister was set on keeping peace between the two nations, telling the people that he was sure Germany did not truly wish for war.

Dismissing the broadcast from her mind, Lily took her trug and cut a lettuce and pulled some fresh radishes for her tea. She had tomatoes in the house and some cheese and fresh bread. She would also pick some flowers to take in to brighten the critical ward. Few of the patients in the ward got many visitors and even fewer brought gifts, because they simply couldn't afford it, so Lily took in flowers from her garden when she could. She also took in a cake from Lavender and Lace once a week because the shop sold delicious cakes and was only just around the corner from Button Street. Those patients well enough to eat a slice were so appreciative of her efforts and she had little else to spend her money on other than her sister and herself.

Perhaps one day she would have a husband and even a child to spoil. Lily could only pray that Chris would turn up one day and say his secret work was finished and then they could live a normal life together.

Jenny saw that Michael's car was waiting at the end of Button Street when she left the infirmary that evening. She smiled, because his attentions were becoming more particular and she really liked it. At first, Jenny had just thought he was nice-looking and could afford to take her out and she'd been bored after Peter Clark had dropped her – poor Peter!

Jenny felt sorry for him and for Sister Rose. It was

hard luck when they'd just got together, too. She didn't think she could have done what Sister Rose was doing – but then, she hadn't been in love with him.

'Want a lift home?' Michael asked as she reached his car and leaned over to open the door for her.

'Yes, please,' Jenny said and slid onto the front seat beside him. It smelled of leather and lavender polish and made her feel special. Even Chris hadn't had a car like this one. 'You spoil me, Michael.'

'You're worth spoiling,' he said and turned his head to smile at her. 'Would you like to go dancing again this Saturday?'

'Yes, please,' Jenny said, 'but you must let me give something back – will you come to ours for tea on Sunday?'

'Yes,' he said without hesitation. 'I like your Lily – she's all right. Reminds me of my sister Dot. She's married to a businessman and got a house in the suburbs and a little car of her own, has Dot. We've done all right for ourselves, me and her. My dad was a dock worker all his life but Ma had some money left her by an aunt and she used it to set me up with my taxi and sent Dot to train as a secretary. She married her boss,' Michael said and grinned, 'and I bought this car which is a little goldmine because of him. I do private work with it that Dot's husband gets me a lot of the time and I've got me eye on a little house of me own.'

'You *are* doing well,' Jenny said and laughed. 'Are you trying to impress me, Michael?'

A laugh escaped him. 'Yeah – is it working?'

'A bit,' Jenny admitted and looked at him. 'I really like you – and I like being taken home in your car. I enjoy all the dancing and the treats . . .' She hesitated, then said honestly, 'I might more than like you but I'm not sure yet . . . do you mind?'

'A pretty girl like you is entitled to look around before she makes up her mind,' he said and grinned in a confident way she enjoyed. There was something cocky about him that appealed to her, made her feel he wasn't a pushover like so many other men who had asked her out. 'I enjoy taking you out and treating you, Jenny, and when I want more, I'll let you know.'

'Oh, will you?' She turned her head to one side. 'What makes you think I'll want to know then?'

'You'll want to know,' he said and grinned but didn't look at her as he turned into a busy road with traffic coming both ways.

Jenny couldn't help smiling. Michael didn't beg for favours. He said what he wanted and, so far, she'd been sufficiently intrigued to go along with him. She wasn't sure if she was in love – as yet she wasn't aware of feeling the way Lily did for Chris or Sister Rose for Peter Clark but she was enjoying the little game they played and for the moment it was enough.

CHAPTER 39

'Shall we have a day out at Southend this Sunday?' Bert asked his mother-in-law that evening after they'd had supper and the two women had washed up, refusing his offer of help. 'It may be the last good weather we get – someone on the wireless was saying it may break next week.'

'Oh, I don't think I want to go there again,' Kathy's mother replied but smiled at him. 'You two should go – I'll just stay quietly at home.'

'Are you sure, Mum?' Kathy asked, looking at her in surprise. 'You really enjoyed it last time we went.'

'Yes, I did but it was tiring,' her mother said and sighed. 'I'm not as young as I used to be, Kathy. I'll sit quietly at home and read, perhaps potter in the garden for a while. You can bring me back a nice box of fudge.'

'Yes, of course, we will,' Kathy assured her and then went to kiss her cheek. For all her annoying ways, she loved her mother and for the first time she noticed that she did look a little tired. 'Don't work, just sit.'

'Don't fuss, Kathy!' The sharp note told Kathy she'd

gone too far so she shut up and left it to Bert to say their goodbyes. He was better received, and when he told his mother-in-law to leave the work for a day, she smiled and said she would.

Kathy looked at her husband as they caught the bus to the train station. 'Do you think she's ill?'

'I think she's tired,' Bert said frowning slightly. 'Your mother hasn't had the easiest life, Kathy love. I know she's sharp with you and I wish she wouldn't be because underneath I know she loves you. It's just the way she is and she can't help it.'

'I know,' Kathy sighed. 'I do love her, Bert, even though she doesn't make it easy.'

'I'll try to get her to the doctor next week,' Bert said thoughtfully, 'so don't worry about her today, Kathy, just relax and have a good day out, love. You deserve it – we both do.'

'Yes, we do.' She smiled at him and reached for his arm but it wasn't until they were sitting on the train that she told him her news. 'I've been waiting for the right moment to tell you that Mum isn't the only one who will visit the doctor next week, Bert . . .'

'What do you mean? You're not ill, are you?'

Kathy laughed as she saw the sudden start of anxiety in his eyes. 'No, Bert, I'm not ill. And I can't be abso-lutely sure until I've talked to the doctor, but I think I'm having our baby!'

'Oh, Kathy, love, that's wonderful!' Bert's face lit up.

Kathy laughed and squeezed his hand. 'Are you pleased I might be pregnant?'

'I'll be delighted if you are,' he told her and lifted her hand to kiss it. The elderly couple sitting opposite were earwigging and smiled indulgently. 'What makes you think it, love?'

Suddenly conscious the couple opposite were listening, Kathy blushed. 'You know . . .' she said. 'A couple of things – I'll tell you later . . .'

'Oh, don't you mind us,' the woman opposite smiled at her. 'When I had my first, I wasn't sure but I missed my monthlies and then things that seemed a little odd started happening. I wasn't sure until I asked my doctor, though.'

'Jane,' her husband said and nudged her. 'Forgive us, but our children are grown up and they work abroad now. We haven't seen them or our grandchildren for two years so Jane likes to hear about other people, especially when it's good news like yours.'

Kathy laughed, because she was too happy to resent sharing her news with the friendly couple. 'Do your children send you photographs?'

'Yes, when they can,' Jane said and beamed at her. She delved into her bag and brought out some pictures which Kathy and Bert looked at and admired before handing them back. 'I should say you are definitely expecting – you have that look in your face,' Jane whispered to Kathy. 'Good luck, my dear. You and your husband look so happy.'

Kathy thanked her and then the train attendant came in and told them the restaurant car was open and the elderly couple got up and went off to have something to eat. Kathy looked at her husband and then burst into laughter.

'It just shows you're never alone,' Bert said and grinned. 'Nice couple, though, Kathy love. It must be hard for them with their children at the other side of the world.'

'Yes, I'm sure it is – at least Mum will have hers here where she can see him or her.'

Bert nodded. He couldn't stop grinning and she realised just how much having a child of his own meant to him. Her own doubt fled in the face of his pleasure and she hoped that the news from the doctor would be in the affirmative.

The day out in Southend was perfect. They walked along the front, went on the pier and then had fish and chips in a restaurant overlooking the beach. It was deliciously fresh and tasted completely different to the same meal in London. Followed by a pot of tea and an ice cream, it made a satisfying meal that sustained them throughout the afternoon and the journey back.

They had shopped after lunch, buying fudge for Kathy's mother, some sweets for Kathy to take in for the nurses and children at the infirmary, and Bert had bought her a pretty pair of earrings in the shape of roses. They were nine-carat gold and expensive and she scolded him for being extravagant, but he told her it wasn't every day he got told he was going to be a father and he wanted to spoil her to make it special.

Kathy thanked him with a kiss. It had been a lovely day and she bought a bag of buns to eat on the train going home. This time they had the carriage to themselves most of the way and so sat and munched in harmony.

Leaving the station, they were lucky enough to get a bus home almost immediately and were very soon standing outside the house. The street lights had started to come on but Kathy noticed at once that the house was in darkness.

'Mum?' She opened the back door and went in, snapping on the electric light. There was no sign of her mother but she could see signs that lunch had been half eaten and then left. A little spurt of panic went through her as she went into the hall. 'Mum?'

She looked in the sitting room. It was empty and her heart started to thump wildly.

'I'll go upstairs and look,' Bert said, holding her arm as she started forward. 'Put the kettle on, love. I shan't be long.'

Kathy filled the kettle and put it on the gas ring to boil. She was setting the tea tray when Bert came back down. Now he looked anxious.

'She isn't there, Kathy,' he said. He went to the kitchen dresser and took out his torch. 'I'm going to look in the garden.'

Kathy went to the back door with him and watched as he moved down the garden path, shining his torch over the darkness of the garden. Suddenly he moved forward quickly and then dropped to one knee.

'Have you found her?' Kathy called from the kitchen doorway.

'Yes. She's unconscious, but she is breathing. I'll bring her in and then go for the doctor.'

Bert carried his precious burden inside and took her straight upstairs. Kathy went quickly after him and pulled back the sheets. Bert laid the unconscious woman down and Kathy looked at her mother. She was so pale! She blinked hard as the tears threatened.

'Cover her and I'll fetch the doctor, Kathy,' Bert said. 'I think she may have had a stroke . . .'

Kathy nodded, holding back her tears. Crying wouldn't help her mother now. Realising she could smell something unpleasant she lifted her mother's dress, then removed her knickers and wiped her mother's bottom before taking them into the bathroom and fetching a flannel and towel. When her mother was dry and clean, she pulled the covers over her. Mum would have hated the doctor to know she'd messed herself and it so obviously wasn't her fault.

Kathy took her mother's knickers and stockings down to the scullery where she put them in water and soda crystals to soak. She would add them to the wash once they were rinsed and free of the mess.

Frowning, she washed her hands and went back to the kitchen to wait for Bert. The doctor wouldn't be best pleased about coming out on a Sunday night, but Bert would persuade him; he was very good at doing things like that and Kathy was glad he was her husband. Her life might not be the most exciting in the world, but Bert would stand by her and she knew that things might be difficult for a while now . . .

'How do you feel about nursing your mother at home after she has a couple of weeks or so in the infirmary?' Bert asked after the doctor had been, confirmed that Mrs Saunders had indeed had a stroke and arranged for an ambulance, and they were alone. 'He said the nurse would come in twice a day to help wash and medicate her – but it means a lot of work for you, Kathy.'

'If we don't have her back he said she could go to

an old people's place – and I couldn't do that to her,' Kathy said firmly. 'No, I'll look after her with the nurse's help, Bert. We'll miss my wage coming in but we shall have to manage.'

'When your mum asked us to live with her, I let my cottage out to tenants as you know,' Bert said, looking thoughtful. 'I haven't touched that rent money and I'll give it to you for the baby's things, love, so you won't need to worry about money. And I'll help with the lifting, because you won't be able to once the baby starts to make itself known.'

Kathy nodded and looked at him sadly. 'Is it my fault for not realising before that she was ill, Bert? I was always used to her being there, able to cope with everything, and she didn't seem different.'

'She never mentioned it until I asked her to come to Southend with us,' Bert said. 'You couldn't have known, Kathy love – and she should have told us if she was ill, but perhaps she didn't realise either.'

Kathy wiped a tear away from her cheek. 'Crying won't help her or me, but I feel awful. I just wish I'd done more to help her.'

'She wouldn't let you,' Bert said and Kathy knew he was speaking the truth. Her mother had insisted that they went out to work and she ran the house and did the cooking. Bert had been allowed to do the garden, but Kathy was allowed only menial tasks like washing-up and putting out the washing on the line. Even the ironing was considered too complicated for her to get it the way her mother liked it. 'Stop blaming yourself, love. It doesn't help anything. Your mum was a proud lady.'

'She still is,' Kathy said lifting her head. 'She's not dead yet, Bert – and the doctor says that with good nursing she might get better.'

'You'll do your best, love, and no one could do more,' Bert said and kissed her. 'Now, when she does come back to us, don't try lifting her alone, remember the baby. Mabel Griffiths next door says she'll help if you let her know – and so did Mrs Hodder, three doors down . . .'

Neighbours had come round, seeing the ambulance, to find out what was going on and to offer help.

'People are kind, but you know my mum.' Kathy smiled through her tears. Mrs Saunders would not be the easiest of patients to care for . . .

CHAPTER 40

'I shall be very sorry to lose Kathy,' Matron said when Bert told her what had happened that Monday. Back from her seaside holiday, she was brown and clear-eyed. 'Are you sure it wouldn't be better to place her in a home?'

'Kathy would never agree to that,' Bert said. 'Mrs Saunders would hate to end up in a place like that, Matron.'

'Yes, many people feel that way, but most have no alternative when it comes to it. Not many daughters will care for their mother forever – it is a big commitment, you know.'

'Yes, I do know,' Bert agreed and looked grim. 'Kathy thinks she is expecting her first child and it may be too much for her in the end. If we needed to move her for a while, just until my wife is better able to cope, could we bring her here? Just for a month or so?'

'Of course. I would keep her as long as I could to let Kathy get on her feet again.' Matron smiled. 'I applaud Kathy for what she is doing but I doubt she realises just what she has taken on – it is a good thing she has you, Bert.'

'I'll help her all I can and some of the neighbours have offered help with washing and cooking, things like that, but Mrs Saunders can be difficult and I don't want Kathy worn down.'

'It may well be that a home is the only answer in the end,' Matron said. 'Much as you will dislike doing it, it probably is for the best if things become too difficult and I will find out which is considered the best round here.'

Bert nodded. 'Thank you, Matron. It has helped me to talk to you and I'll keep an eye on things. Kathy wants to look after her mum for as long as she can but if I think it's too much for her, at least I have a halfway house until I can persuade her that she has to let her mum go to a home.'

'Yes, that is probably the best way to handle this.' Matron shook her head. 'I am so very sorry, Bert. Kathy was a good worker and I shall be sorry to lose her – but of course in a few months she would have left anyway to have your child. Congratulations on that and give Kathy my good wishes, please.'

'Thank you, I will.'

Matron sighed after he'd left. She was finding it hard to get good staff for the kitchen these days. Ruby had been the first to leave and she still missed her and wondered how she was getting on – and now young Kathy. Oh, well, she would have to place an advert in Mr Forrest's shop and hope for the best.

'I thought we would have a collection for Kathy,' Sister Rose said to Nurse Alice when they met at the top of the stairs. 'Buy her some flowers and whatever else we can afford.'

'Yes, that's a good idea,' Alice replied and smiled. 'And how is Doctor Peter? I think we should have a collection for him as well.'

'Dr Clark would not appreciate it,' Rose said with a wry smile. 'He doesn't want any fuss, Alice. It's kind of you to think of it but he would probably throw flowers from one end of the ward to the other, the mood he is in just now.'

Alice smiled and nodded. 'Reached the aggressive stage, has he? Well, that shows he is recovering his strength at least. I suppose you have no news on the situation with his spine?'

'At the moment the consultants are simply saying the spinal cord is still too swollen and sore to tell if there will be any recovery in his movement. It may take months or, with proper bed rest, it could suddenly start to recover, as I'm sure you're aware.'

'Well, miracles do happen,' Alice said with a little shrug. 'I shouldn't expect too much, Sister Rose.' She paused, then, 'I'll let you get on – I have to get home. My sister's husband has a birthday party this evening and I promised I would go even though I expect it will be all his friends and I don't much like them.'

Rose watched as the nurse hurried away. Alice was a bit of a gossip and not very reassuring when you needed it but she was a colleague and Rose couldn't bring herself to be rude. However, she didn't need to be told not to expect too much. She was trying to look on the bright side. Peter was recovering well in himself and the exercises he did with his upper body would make him able to lever himself in and out of bed with a pulley over the bed. It was better than having to be lifted everywhere but she knew that he would hate being reliant on others, even her.

His mood swung from loving and grateful to resentful and angry and she could never tell whether he would greet her with a smile or a scowl. Rose couldn't wait until she could bring him home to Beattie's and had already had a proper nursing bed installed and the pulley over it. She'd promised Beattie she would put everything right again when Peter was well and on his feet, but would he ever be?

Sometimes, Rose felt that she ought not to have taken over Beattie's home the way she had. Beattie had her own life to lead and although Ted and the boys came regularly each Saturday and Sunday to tea and lunch, nothing more had been said about him courting Beattie.

Had she ruined her friend's chances of a proper married life? Rose felt guilty that she might have done.

Beattie had visited Danny in his new home. It was a fairly modern house built by the council and it had a front room, a large kitchen and scullery, a bathroom and two large double bedrooms upstairs.

'It's a nice place,' she told Rose. 'There's a modern gas cooker and a lovely stainless-steel sink.'

'You sound as if you like it better than your own house?'

'In a way I do,' Beattie said. 'I bought this so that I'd have rooms to let out but it's old-fashioned and I could do with some of the things Ted has in his kitchen.'

'If he was your husband and lived here, he could put

those things in for you,' Rose suggested but Beattie shook her head.

'I think Ted and the boys are settled where they are, Rose. Danny says the oven is better for cake making than my range and . . .' She shook her head. 'It's all right, Rose love. It's better this way.'

Rose pondered over that remark. Beattie had given her word to help with caring for Peter but could she have married if she'd been free? Rose knew that she was going to have to ask her friend for the truth but she dreaded the answer, because she wasn't sure she could manage alone. She would have to give up work and she didn't truly wish to do that, though if it came to it, she would have no choice.

It was selfish of her to remain silent when the price was Beattie's happiness and she knew, as she finished her shift at the infirmary that afternoon, that she was going to have to speak to Beattie about the problem.

'That's daft, Rose,' Beattie said when Rose asked her if she'd given up her happiness for her sake. 'You know how much you mean to me – and what sort of a person would I be if I let you down now?'

'You would still be the person I love,' Rose told her. 'I shall be relying on your help, Beattie, and I've realised that might not be fair to you. So if Ted wants you to marry him, you should say yes. And I was thinking that perhaps you might let this place to me if you decided to live in his modern house – then I could get a retired nurse to come in when I worked.'

Beattie looked at her for a long moment. 'You could probably afford it if Peter paid the rent and the expense

337

of a nurse,' she said, 'but do you want a stranger looking after him – having the run of your home?'

'You know I would rather have you, Beattie,' Rose said truthfully. 'But I don't want you to lose your chance of happiness.'

'That won't happen,' Beattie said and smiled. 'Me and Ted – we have an understanding. He knows I can't leave you and wed him for the moment, but it doesn't stop us being comfortable together. He says it's giving us time to get to know each other better and he's right, Rose. I'm learning what a good bloke he is in all sorts of ways and he says I'm the woman for him and he'll wait until the end of time . . .' Beattie gave an earthy chuckle. 'He says he's waited all these years for the right woman so he can wait a bit longer!'

'S-suppose Peter never recovers?' Rose asked voicing the doubts that plagued her.

'Do you think he'll want to be pampered for the rest of his life?' Bettie asked. 'Isn't his temper these days because he can't quite do what he wants yet?'

'I always say you are the wisest lady I know,' Rose said and smiled. 'I also know that Peter will become almost independent if we give him time. He can already feed himself and he can have a wash with some help. He can swing himself out of bed with the aid of the pulley and into the chair . . .'

'So, he won't need too much help by the time he gets home,' Beattie said. 'We'll need to help him with bathroom stuff and steps, but that's about all, Rose.'

'If I gave up work, I could manage,' Rose said slowly.

'But it's your living and you shouldn't do that yet – give it a few months and see if you want to marry

338

him, Rose. If you do, then perhaps the two of you can manage with occasional help and then I could live with Ted and come in to cook and clean while you're working a shift.'

'Yes,' Rose looked relieved, 'that could work, Beattie. Are you sure you prefer Ted's house to this? I love your home and I would buy it if I had the money.'

'Then perhaps Peter will,' Beattie suggested. 'I'm in no hurry, Rose. Like I said, me and Ted have come to an arrangement, and we can wait to make it legal for a few months at least.'

'Beattie!' Rose looked at her, her eyes twinkling as she saw the naughty expression in Beattie's face. 'You haven't?'

'Well, I'm not one to tell tales,' Beattie said, 'but suffice it to say that he makes me happy in all departments!'

Rose giggled, her own problems vanishing like mist as she saw that Beattie truly was happy. 'When did all this happen?'

'About a week ago. The boys were playing football in the street and Ted showed me their room and then his own – and it just happened that we both felt in the mood for a kiss and cuddle . . .'

'You're a wicked woman, Beattie,' Rose said and laughed. 'I envy you and I'm glad you've found happiness at last.'

'Oh, I've been happy since you came into my life, Rose – Ted just put the sugar icing on the cake.'

Rose went into a fit of giggles and Beattie hugged her. They kissed and looked at each other, feeling the love flow between them.

'Do you know what I want now?'

Rose shook her head. 'A baby?'

'No, not a baby, at least not for me – but I'd like to see you with the kind of smile I had when the boys came in for their tea, Rose love. I want to see a gold band on your finger, a smile on your face – and then a baby in your arms.'

'Oh Beattie . . .' Rose said and her voice caught with emotion, 'so do I . . .'

CHAPTER 41

'Do you feel up to going home?' the consultant asked Peter that morning when he made his rounds. 'We consider you're over the threat to your life now, Dr Clark, and there isn't much more we can do for you here. If you were unprepared, we would see about getting you into a home for men like yourself, but as you have such a wonderful friend in Sister Rose, we believe you can be safely released into her care.

'Need the bed, do you?' Peter said gruffly to hide the sudden spurt of emotion. 'Well, I suppose it can be arranged if she's daft enough to take me on. So when can I go?'

'We're thinking tomorrow.'

'Good, the sooner the better. You'll be glad to see the back of me!'

The doctor smiled oddly. 'My nurses tell me you haven't been the best of patients, but I can't say I blame you, old chap. Being stuck on your back for weeks on end isn't much reward for what you did.'

'Serves me right for thinking I was God,' Peter said. 'They told me not to be a bloody fool.'

'So, red rag to a bull and you went ahead and did it.' The consultant nodded, 'You've made better progress than I expected at the start. Your last X-ray showed some improvement in the damage to your spine. I can't promise anything, but if you continue to do as you're asked and keep yourself fit you may recover partial movement of your legs. I doubt you'll run a mile, but it is possible now that you might walk with the aid of crutches or some sort of support – but that is only if the improvements continue.'

'Don't tell Rose,' Peter said. 'I wouldn't want to disappoint her if it doesn't happen.'

'What about you? Can you take the disappointment?'

'I have no choice,' Peter replied and frowned. 'But . . . can I be a full husband to the woman I love? I have feelings towards her but as yet no reaction down there – will it happen? Or did I damage something vital?'

'I imagine that side of things will improve as the feeling comes back in your legs,' the consultant said seriously. 'I understand you thought you felt something in your right foot when the nurse was exercising it for you the other day?'

'My little toe started twitching on its own.' Peter frowned. 'That might mean nothing – or it could be the start.'

'You're a doctor. I can't hide anything from you or give you false hope. You know the chances yourself. It may have been just a nerve reaction but it may be a sign of hope. If I were you, Dr Clark, I would pray very hard.'

Peter smiled wryly. 'A wing and a prayer . . . well, it can't hurt. Thank you.' He held out his hand and received a firm shake in return. 'You've been honest with me and you've done what you can – it is up to me now.'

'And God . . .'

'Yes,' Peter murmured. 'If he can be bothered with the likes of me.'

'I should imagine you would be high on his list. Not many would do what you did.'

The consultant rang his bell and a nurse appeared and wheeled Peter back to his small private ward. He'd been given all the care and attention he could wish for and he knew that it was truly in God's hands as well as his own. He had already achieved more than seemed possible at the start and his upper body strength helped him get from the chair to his bed with the aid of a pulley. He knew Rose had arranged something similar for him at home.

It was a long time since Peter had had a real home, not since he was a young boy, before his parents were killed in a terrible train accident and he'd gone to live with his paternal grandparents, who had been kind and loving but believed in children being seen and not heard. His maternal grandmother still lived locally and he'd visited her about once a month but she was frail and couldn't help him. Grandfather Clark's money had seen him through college before both he and his loving wife died of old age, only weeks apart, and the sale of the house and other money he'd been left had enabled him to live comfortably since then. He'd also been able to devote much of his time to helping the poor and the sick of London, something he felt worthwhile. If his grandparents hadn't cared for him and taken him in, Peter might have been stuck in an orphanage and he was grateful for the chances he'd had; a further legacy from his great-aunt meant he had no need to work.

So Peter could buy a house of his own when he was ready and he could afford to keep a wife and pay for the care he needed – but could he ask Rose to marry him when he was like this physically?

He was no longer in doubt of her feelings for him and he cursed himself for wasting so much time – time they might have had together. Sometimes, he thought he was a fool for what he'd done but knew he would do the same again. Jessie had recovered and was back walking the streets. She'd been in to see him once, much to the alarm of the nurses who held their noses as she walked past. Peter had laughed, because he was well aware of her pungent smell but he liked her and knew he'd done a good thing.

He'd just thought he could get away with it despite all the warnings. 'Letting me know I can't walk on water the way you did?' Peter murmured as he pictured a favourite scene from his grandfather's collection of religious paintings. Grandfather Robert had been a really good man, always helping the poor and Peter knew he would approve if no one else did.

'Talking to yourself again?' One of the nurses smiled as she placed a tray of fruit juice and some biscuits on his bedside table. 'I understand we're losing you tomorrow, sir.'

'Glad to get rid of me?' Peter responded with a grin.

'Oh yes,' she replied and laughed. 'I have much nicer patients than you!'

344

Peter laughed out loud. 'That's the right answer,' he said. 'I shan't miss being here – but you're not bad, Nurse Paula. You must have been listening to Sister Rose.'

'I have,' she replied. 'She told me you were grumpy and not to take any notice.'

Peter leaned back against the pillows and smiled. At least he wouldn't get smothered with pity when he got home. That was one thing he just couldn't take!

Rose smiled as she gave Matron the good news. 'So I won't come in tomorrow at all, because I'll need to fetch him and get him settled.'

'Of course, Sister Rose. And look, if you need a couple of days off you have some time owing to you . . .?'

'Thank you, but tomorrow is enough. Peter needs a routine and if I stay home to fuss over him, it will make him feel uncomfortable. We'll let him be as independent as he can manage. He will, of course, need a certain amount of help in the bathroom, but he manages quite well once he's there, so the nurses at the London told me.'

'Good,' Matron nodded briskly. 'And now I'd like to discuss what we're sending Kathy. I thought some flowers for her mother and some chocolates for her.'

'Yes, I think that's a good idea. We collected three pounds so that should cover a really nice bouquet, some lovely chocolates, and perhaps something for the baby as well.'

'My nurses are so generous.' Matron smiled approvingly. 'I shall let you get on with your work, Sister Rose. I have a meeting with Lady Rosalie in a few minutes.'

Rose watched as Matron walked away. She knew that Lady Rosalie was coming to collect one of the children. Little June had been found some foster parents and she would be taken to meet them this afternoon. If all went well, she would go to live with them in a few days.

Feeling a mixture of emotions, Rose started to make a round of her patients, stopping to talk with them all for a few moments, making sure they were feeling as well as they could be. Most were in the recovery stage and the ward was peaceful. She smiled, because these were the good days, when most of the children would be released to their parents very soon. Visiting for the afternoon would begin soon and she could see the children beginning to sit up and look eagerly towards the door.

Rose smiled. She would be visiting Peter in hospital for the last time that evening and in the morning, she could fetch him home in a taxi. She was looking forward to showing him the room she'd prepared for him and hoped he would be happy. Beattie's house wasn't posh but it was comfortable and it had nice big rooms, old-fashioned but with more charm than the modern houses the councils built these days. Rose had always liked living there and she hoped Peter would too.

'There you go, mate,' the cheery taxi driver said as he assisted Peter into his wheelchair. He looked at Rose. 'Can you manage, Sister, or shall I come in with you?'

'I think we can manage now,' Rose said, smiled and thanked him. Peter was able to wheel his chair himself but she positioned herself behind to give him a push if he needed it to get up the ramp to the front door. He managed it without help and wheeled himself into the hall, which was spacious, with a high ceiling. 'Your room is the door on the right but the kitchen is straight ahead, Peter.'

'I'd like to say hello to Beattie,' Peter said and propelled his chair to the kitchen door, which stood open in welcome. He negotiated the doorway with ease and continued into the room. It was large and welcoming, with an oak dresser at one end covered in Beattie's collection of blue and white china and a gleaming black range, above which hung a myriad of pots and pans. There was a smell of baking and herbs, which made him sniff appreciatively. 'That smells better than disinfectant and carbolic!' He held out his hand as Beattie looked at him shyly. 'Thank you for having me in your home, Mrs Robinson, and for letting Rose turn it upside down for my benefit.'

Beattie smiled at him, her homely face lighting up with pleasure and warmth. 'You're very welcome, Dr Clark – and please, call me Beattie, everyone does.'

'I'm Peter,' he said and took her hands in his own, his clasp strong. 'I am truly grateful and I shall try not to abuse your kindness.'

'Oh, you couldn't,' she said. 'I know you must be anxious and angry too – but I don't mind. What you did was a brave thing and I honour you for it.'

'Most folk think it damned foolish,' Peter said but smiled. He looked at Rose. 'I will go to my room now, if that's all right – I feel a bit tired. Stupid I know, I haven't done anything, but I am tired.'

'Of course. I'll show you,' Rose said. She led the way

back down the hall. There were three doors, one into what had been Beattie's lovely front parlour, one into a small cloakroom with toilet and the last to a dining room Beattie never used. Most of her parlour furniture was now stored in the dining room, but she'd left a comfortable chair, a bedside chest, a chest of drawers and a small table that Peter could use as a desk, as well as the special bed that Rose had bought. It was the type used in hospital and could be wound up to help the patient sit against his pillows. Fixed to the metal headrest was a pulley similar to the one he'd used at the hospital. 'I think you'll be able to manage here, but of course one of us will always be around to help with anything you need.'

'You really have thought of everything,' Peter said, looking about him. 'This is a lovely house, Rose. It reminds me of my grandparents' home – theirs was a bit larger but much the same. I shall be comfortable here.'

'I have always thought it lovely,' Rose replied. 'I'm so glad you think you will enjoy living here, Peter.'

'I would enjoy living anywhere with you,' he said, and the look he gave her made her blush with pleasure. 'The trouble with that bed is it is only big enough for one.'

Rose laughed. 'You haven't asked me to marry you yet – and I don't get into bed with just anyone.'

'I know . . .' Peter smiled up at her. He reached out and caught her hand. 'You know I want to marry you, Rose. But I'm not going to unless I can be a proper husband to you – and I'm not sure of that yet. When I can stagger down the aisle and make love to my wife then I'll ask.'

Rose bent to kiss him softly on the mouth. 'I wouldn't expect you to say anything else,' she told him. 'But one thing you should know is that I love you; I think I began to love you a long time ago but I couldn't trust you . . .'

'You'd been hurt and I made it worse by asking someone else out. I've no idea why I did it, Rose, except that you wouldn't smile at me and she did. But I regretted it immediately. Each time I took her out I wished it was you and, in the end, I had to tell her that it was over.'

'Poor Jenny,' Rose said and shook her head. 'We neither of us must make silly mistakes like that again, Peter. Life is too short – you could have died that day. I want to be with you for the rest of our lives but for now I am content to have you here and to help you where I can.'

'I don't need much nursing now,' Peter said with a wry smile. 'I might need help now and then but otherwise I'm fine.' He caught her hand and squeezed it. 'I'd love a cup of tea – and a bit of that cake I saw on the table. And, if I gave you the key, could you fetch some things from the hotel and cancel my room there, please? I have a car parked in their yard too, so maybe someone could fetch it for me?'

'Why didn't you ask before? You could have stored everything here.'

'I wasn't sure . . .' Peter looked at her. 'I know what you're taking on, Rose, and I want to be honest with you. I have money and I could buy a house similar to this and employ a housekeeper and a nurse, so if you ever wish for your freedom—'

'No, never,' she said firmly. 'Even if you won't marry me, I'd like to be your companion and care for you, but Beattie might marry and, if she does, we might need some help.'

'Does she want to bring her husband to live here?'

'No, she says I could rent this house from her. He has a more modern home and she likes that best.'

Peter nodded and smiled. 'One step at a time, Rose. I'm going to get myself into bed and then I'd love that cup of tea.'

CHAPTER 42

Jim Bryant scowled as the prison officer handed him his small bundle. He was told to check his valuables but he'd only had a few shillings in his pocket when he was admitted and the only things he had besides what he stood up in were the money for a train fare and his release papers, also a small penknife that had belonged to Danny.

He hawked and spat as the gate was unlocked and he was let out of prison. He'd been given two weeks' early release for good behaviour – more fool them. The only reason he hadn't got into a fight was because the other men stayed clear of him when he was muttering to himself and a fierce glare would send any that tried to speak to him walking off.

That bloody kid was going to pay for the past few weeks when he'd been humiliated and made to work for nothing. Prison wasn't just sitting in a cell doing nothing. He'd been made to break concrete for rubble that was used in some sort of construction and the warders hadn't given them much rest; the food was all right, because Jim wasn't used to better, but he hadn't had a drink and it had almost sent him crazy for the first couple of weeks. He was stone-cold sober now and burning with anger inside.

Locked up just for taking his own son away from that bloody woman! He was entitled to do what he liked with the little bastard and he would make him pay when he got him back. Someone had shopped him to the cops and he thought it might be the man he'd worked for – or one of the buggers who worked with him. If he knew who it was, he'd break their neck but he didn't know and he wasn't going back to that filthy job for pennies. He was going to get what he deserved out of life!

Jim had made up his mind he'd had enough of standing in line for miserable jobs that broke his back and paid hardly enough for the whisky he craved. He was going to steal what he wanted from the homes of those that had plenty, like that damned judge who'd sent him to prison.

A little smile touched Jim's face, because he happened to know where the judge lived. He'd seen a picture of the house in Hampstead in an old magazine in the prison library. Jim hadn't wanted anything from the trolley but the trustee had thrust the magazine at him and he'd come across the picture of the judge standing outside his posh house. That had made him smile. It was his chance to get even! He would break in that bugger's house and steal his things and then he'd live the life of a king. But to break in he'd need the help of his son. The boy could get through small windows and it was usually the little windows that people thought were safe; they didn't have locks or bars on like some of the others and were quite often left open a crack because the owners thought no one could get in – but a thin lad like Danny might; if not, he'd be of use as a look-out. Besides, he had it coming.

The vengeful thoughts kept Jim company as he trudged to the railway station. The prison had given him his fare back to London, telling him to go home and find work. He'd felt like spitting in their faces and telling them he didn't have a home to go to, even though he'd given his old address in court. But Jim knew the landlord had taken it over and put new locks on the doors. He had nowhere to go and only a few shillings between him and starvation. It wasn't enough to buy the whisky he craved.

Jim hunched up in a corner of the first carriage he came to. Several passengers walked by after taking one look at him and he muttered a curse. Who the hell did they think they were? Was he contaminating the air or something?

Then the door opened and three passengers entered – a youngish woman with a small boy and an elderly woman with white hair and kind eyes. The woman and child sat as far away as they could but the little old lady sat down near him.

She smiled vaguely at him. 'You don't mind if I sit here? The train is so full and there aren't many seats – we were lucky to find these.'

Jim grunted and turned his head away to look out of the window as the train pulled away from the station. He resented them entering the carriage but couldn't stop it.

'Well, I'm going to visit my daughter and grandchildren in London,' the elderly lady said to no one in particular. 'I come up every few weeks as my treat and they make a big fuss of me you know, but they're too busy to come down often so I come up.'

'That's nice for you,' the lady opposite said and reached forward to shake hands. 'Will and I are going to visit my auntie – she loves to see him and we visit several times a year, don't we, love?'

'Yes . . .' the boy was looking at Jim in the corner. He pulled a face as he saw Jim look at him and then stuck his tongue out. Jim glared at him. For two pins he would've given the lad a good hiding but the women would start screeching and all he wanted was to reach London without more trouble. He wanted to teach his bastard son a lesson.

After an hour or so the elderly lady took out a packet of sandwiches. The smell made Jim's nose twitch. He hadn't smelled anything that good in an age. His eyes slid towards the food as he saw her select a sandwich and begin to eat it. Wild thoughts of snatching them and running flitted through his head, but then, as though she read his thoughts, she took another and offered the packet to Jim.

'Please have these if you're hungry,' she said and he grabbed them. There were two left, ham and mustard by the smell and he devoured them both within minutes. 'You were hungry,' she murmured. 'I always pack more than I need.'

'Thanks,' Jim grunted. He eyed the basket. It was filled with bits and pieces but she didn't offer him anything else.

He wondered whether he could scrape enough

money together for a bottle of whisky when the train stopped. He'd ached for it the first few weeks of his withdrawal but now he just wanted it to put him on an even keel again.

The train announcer's voice said they would be arriving at London in five minutes and the elderly lady began to hunt through her basket. She took out a black leather purse and checked her ticket. Jim saw some pound notes and coins in the purse and his fingers itched to snatch it off her but the little boy was watching him like a hawk and he daren't try.

His best chance was to wait until they got off the train. As it began to slow, the elderly lady got to her feet and went into the corridor. Jim followed and stood behind, waiting his moment as the train scrunched to a halt. The door was opened and people started to get off; he followed close behind and then, just as the elderly lady got down, snatched at her basket. Surprising him, she fought back and Jim gave her a hard shove to the ground and took off, running through the crowd disgorging from the train. Behind him, he could hear shouting and a whistle.

He showed his ticket to the collector and was allowed through the barrier, though the next moment someone shouted and he heard someone start running after him. Going out into a rainswept street, Jim saw a bus halted at a nearby stop, ran to it and jumped on even as it drew away.

'That was a silly thing to do,' the conductor said but Jim just glared at him. He paid his fare and the man went away. Jim stayed on a few stops and then got off. He felt safe now and found a bench to sit on, out of the rain, delving in the straw basket to find what it contained. There was a tin containing a homemade cake, a silk scarf wrapped in paper and a pair of leather gloves, an ivory hair comb and a photograph of an old man and the woman, also the purse.

Extracting the money from the purse and the cake tin, Jim discarded the basket on the bench and walked off. The money would keep him in whisky for a couple of days and then he would go in search of that little bastard.

'So, how have you enjoyed working with wood every day?' Ted asked Danny as they stopped to buy fish and chips for their tea. Ron had gone running off with their order, but Ted told Danny to wait. It was the end of August now and Danny had worked with him and Ron for the last few weeks, during the holidays, but it was back to school on Monday. He'd worked well, running to fetch whatever was needed. Ron was growing in experience now and Ted could trust him to select the right wood for whatever he needed and lay it out ready for Ted to cut and assemble. Danny had taken over the fetch and carry jobs Ron had been doing until now. 'Do you think you might like working with us when you leave school next summer?'

'Yeah, it's all right,' Danny said and smiled at him. 'The gaffer is nice – he likes you, Ted. I think he couldn't manage this business without you.'

'He managed before I came,' Ted said. 'I do more than most of the others – but I've Ron to help me and you on Saturdays and holidays.' He looked at Danny seriously. 'I do want you to be happy, son. Ron loves the work so I know he's happy, but you like your cooking.'

'Yes, I do,' Danny agreed. 'I love cooking with Beattie, but I can do that at nights and weekends, especially if she moves in with us.'

'So, you don't resent me for setting you to this work, lad?'

'No, I like being with you and Ron,' Danny said. 'I've done a lot worse, Uncle Ted, and if I want to train as a chef when I'm older I can.'

'Yes, indeed.' Ted smiled because Danny was such an easy boy to love. 'And I'd never stand in your way then, but for now this means I can protect you all the time. Your father will be out soon and he may come after you.'

'Yes, I know, but Constable Jones showed me and Ron a bit of judo at the club so he won't find it as easy as before to grab me.'

'Well, that can't hurt,' Ted said smiling at him. 'But if I'm around I'll make sure he doesn't hurt either of you.' He ruffled Danny's hair. 'You know I'm fond of you – of both of you.'

Ron came back with their supper and Danny budged over to let him sit beside him in the front of the truck. 'Did you get some crispies?'

'Yeah,' Ron grinned. 'He gave me a bag fer free 'cos he likes me.'

'That's why we send you for the chips,' Ted said and chuckled. They didn't need to economise now all three of them were being paid something, but Ron couldn't resist asking and the fish and chip owner was a friendly man, who often gave what some others would charge for. Crispies were just little bits off the batter but children loved them and Ted didn't mind a few either.

'Are we goin' ter Beattie's fer tea tomorrow?' Ron asked as Ted drove them home in his employer's battered old truck. It rattled a bit but it got them around and the lads thought it was great.

Sometimes Beattie came to them and cooked, sometimes they went to hers. The previous week her new lodger had been settling in so they hadn't gone but this week she'd told them to come and meet him.

'She said it was all right for us to come,' Ted told the boys and smiled contentedly. He was happy with his relationship with Beattie, who was a warm, loving woman, who had been wasted for years and needed a husband as much as he needed a wife. He would be glad when they could marry but knew she wouldn't let her friend Rose down. 'She thinks it will be good for Dr Clark to have visitors – so what shall we take him?'

'Would he like some of our football magazines?' Ron asked. 'Or a packet of five Woodbines?'

'I'm not sure he smokes,' Ted said. 'We might buy him a quarter of that burnt toffee we all like – and get a quarter for ourselves too.'

'Yeah!' the boys chorused together and grinned at each other.

Ted wasn't exactly like a father to them, more like a favourite uncle or a big brother who gave them treats and looked after them, but he was also their employer who taught them a trade and while both respected and liked him, they adored Beattie and loved it when she came to their house or had them to hers.

'What about Mum?' Danny said. 'What shall we take her?'

'We have some of those little daisy things in the garden,' Ted said. 'She likes a little box of Dairy Milk chocolates too.'

Ron nodded wisely. 'Me and Danny will buy her those and you buy the toffee, Ted. We earn money too so we can pay a bit.'

'Danny only earned three shillings,' Ted reminded him. 'You got ten, Ron, so he can't pay as much as you.'

'No, I can pay half,' Danny contradicted. 'I don't want anything else this week, Ted. I'll save the money I've got left until next week.'

'Mmm,' Ted said, 'I think the chocs are one shilling and ninepence for a small box – so that is ten pennies and a halfpenny each.'

Ron nodded. 'Yer can get two ounces of Tom Thumb drops with yer change from the shillin', Danny.'

Danny grinned. 'I'll do that then, and I'll give them to Sister Rose. She deserves something too.'

Ted nodded thoughtfully. Ron had wanted his friend to have the sweets but Danny never bothered with them much; he hadn't been given anything like that for years and was content to share a piece or two of the burnt toffee they all liked as a weekly treat.

'I'm sure she'll enjoy them,' Ted said, smiling. 'I expect she has a lot to do these days.'

'She was lovely to me in the hospital,' Danny said. 'And I like doing stuff for folk, Uncle Ted.'

'You take after your mother,' Ted said fondly. 'She was always helping others too – it used to drive your father mad. He accused her of giving his hard-earned money away every time she baked a cake for someone.'

Danny looked at him. 'When does he get out?'

'I think in a couple of weeks,' Ted said. 'I'm sure the police will let us know.'

'Yes . . .' Danny smothered a sigh. 'Perhaps he's forgotten all about us.'

'Yes, perhaps,' Ted agreed, but in his heart, he knew they wouldn't get away with it that easily. Jim Bryant was a vengeful man and he would want to grab his son and get even for what he considered had been done to him.

CHAPTER 43

'Good grief,' Steve said when he listened to the officer on the station phone. 'Straight out of prison and he commits a far more serious crime – is the man a lunatic?'

A harsh laugh on the other end told Steve his colleague agreed with him. 'A woman and small boy were the witnesses. They say that Mrs Stokes gave him sandwiches on the train and he must have seen there was money in her purse, because he walked behind her, pushed her to the ground and stole her basket with the purse and other things she'd got.'

'Is she all right?'

'No, she's in hospital with concussion and has not yet recovered her senses – the poor lady is seventy-six and this could be the finish of her.'

'And then Bryant will be facing a murder charge.'

'That is about the size of it; at the moment it's theft with assault, so a two-or-three-year prison term – although some judges would give him at least seven years for it.'

'That would be a blessing,' Steve said and frowned.

'This is serious, Bob, thanks for letting me know. I'd better warn a few people that he's out and dangerous.'

'We'll be putting posters up throughout the East End, because that is where he'll head,' the officer went on. 'People need to be careful. If he has committed theft with serious assault once, he'll do it again.'

'Yes, I agree. The sooner he is back behind bars the better for all concerned.'

'Well, keep your eye out. He is probably coming your way because of the boy.'

'I'll pass the word on to my sergeant and he'll inform everyone.'

Steve replaced the receiver and wrote a report, putting it on the sergeant's desk. Sergeant Barlow was on duty and he'd taken a violent prisoner down to the cells with another young constable. Leaving the report for him to find, Steve put on his overcoat and headed out to continue his beat. He'd called in to report a traffic accident and grab a crafty cuppa and taken the call by accident, but he would certainly make sure he took the time to tell Ted Phillips at his home and then he'd go over to Beattie Robinson's on his way home later.

'Thanks for letting us know,' Ted said to Steve. 'You were lucky to find us here on Saturday afternoon – we're normally out somewhere but we just finished eating our fish and chips and we're going to the park when we've done our chores here.'

'Just be careful from now on,' Steve warned. 'I think he'll go looking for Danny at Mrs Robinson's first, but if he doesn't find him, he may find his way here eventually.'

'I'll be ready for him whenever he chooses,' Ted said grimly.

'A word of warning – protect yourself and the boys, but don't provoke him and don't do more damage than you have to, Mr Phillips. The courts may decide to punish you if he claims you attacked him.'

'Then the law is a fool,' Ted said. 'They can lock me up if need be – but he won't lay a finger on Danny.'

'I'd feel the same in your place,' Steve said, 'but I just want you to be aware.'

'Thanks,' Ted said. 'Why didn't they keep him inside when they had him?'

'Well, that was down to the judge – but next time he'll definitely be in for longer. And the lady he's hurt is in hospital and might die. If she does, he could hang.'

Ted shuddered. 'What a fool the man is – why do something like that for a few pounds?'

'I doubt he even thought about what he might do to a frail old lady. He's a mindless brute and to my mind he should be put away for good.'

'Are we still going to Beattie's?' Danny asked after Steve had gone. 'Because he'll go there looking for me, won't he?'

'Probably,' Ted agreed and put a hand on his shoulder. 'I promise I won't let him take you or hurt you, lad.'

'No, no – I was more thinking about Beattie and Sister Rose,' Danny said. 'I don't want him to hurt them.'

'Nor do I,' Ted said and frowned. 'Well, I think we'll go over there before we do anything else and warn them, Danny. They need to keep their doors and windows shut and not open them unless they know it is us or a friend.'

'Yes,' Danny frowned at him. 'Ma wouldn't have liked him hurting that old lady. She liked to help folk.'

'I'll never know why she married him,' Ted admitted. 'I always thought him a surly brute.'

'She told me she thought he'd had a rough deal after the last war and she thought she could change him, make him happy.'

'That was your mum,' Ted agreed and smiled oddly. 'I can't blame her for being kind and thoughtful – she was always good to me after our mum died and our father went off somewhere and we never heard from him again.'

'So you had a rough time too,' Danny said, 'but it didn't make you bad like my dad.'

'No,' Ted said, 'it didn't. But there's no explaining it, Danny. I'm just glad you're like your mother.'

'So am I,' Danny said and smiled at him.

'I've put the plates and cups in to soak,' Ron said, coming up to them. 'What do you want me to do next?'

'We're going over to Beattie's. Danny's father is out of prison and already in trouble and we need to warn her.' Ted shook his head and frowned. 'We'll all have to be on our guard now . . .'

'Constable Jones said he would call over this evening,' Ted told Sister Rose when she answered the back door, 'but I wanted to let you know at once, because Bryant is dangerous. He's already put one elderly lady in hospital and stolen all she had with her.'

'Thank you for telling me, Ted. Beattie is out

364

shopping and I'll tell her as soon as she gets in,' Rose said. 'Be assured we'll be careful not to leave the doors unlocked and to look before we open them.'

'We'll be back later, Rose, but the boys brought these for you and the chocolates for Beattie.' Ted ran his fingers through his thick dark hair. 'How is Dr Clark?'

'Very cheerful this morning,' Rose said. 'He was talking about going out in his chair for a little fresh air this afternoon.'

'Well, you should. It can get a lot cooler and wetter in September so best get out while you can.'

'Yes, we will,' Rose said. 'Thank you for letting us know about Danny's father – we'll be careful.'

'Good. We'll be over again for tea but I thought this couldn't wait.'

Rose frowned as she closed the door behind him and turned the key. Beattie would wonder what had happened when she got back with the shopping but Rose didn't want to run any risks. Jim Bryant was a dangerous man and, while she wasn't afraid for herself, she thought of her friends, particularly of Peter. Stuck in the wheelchair he was vulnerable to attack and the last thing he needed was to be fighting for his life from a knife wound or a blow to the head.

'What was all that about?' Peter looked up from the magazine he was reading. It was about motor racing and had pictures of expensive cars. He'd purchased it when Rose had accompanied him on a walk to the corner newsagents.

'Danny's father is out of prison early and already he is in trouble with the police,' Rose said. 'He seems to be even more violent than he was when he went into prison. He's put an elderly woman in hospital so Ted came to warn us . . . remember, he's the one that fetched your car for us from the hotel?'

'Yes, nice chap. It was decent of him to come and tell us.' Peter put his magazine down and held out his hand to her. 'It won't stop us going out, will it?'

'No, why should it? It's Danny Ted is worried about – and perhaps us if we tried to stop Bryant getting at Danny.'

Peter frowned. 'Why couldn't they keep the man locked up when they had him?'

'I wish I knew! Ah, I think that's Beattie trying to get in . . .'

Rose ran to the back door and let her friend in, explaining why the door was locked. Beattie looked upset.

'Does that mean Danny can't come here now?'

'Ted said they would be over as usual, but I suppose it might be safer if they didn't come for a while. You could always go to them, Beattie.'

'If I do, he might follow me there . . .' Beattie frowned. She didn't see a way out.

'No, I do see that.' Rose looked thoughtful. 'Don't worry, love. I'll speak to Peter and then we'll talk to Ted later.'

'Yes, all right. We'll talk this afternoon. I've bought some sausage meat for tea. I'm going to make balls of the meat with onions and we'll have them with chips and fresh cabbage chopped up with butter, salt and pepper.'

'Lovely. Peter really loves your sausage meat and

onion balls and so do the children. None of them had ever had anything like that before they came here and they all think it is a real treat.'

Beattie beamed at her. 'Peter seems a lot better, Rose – have you noticed that recently?

'Yes, he certainly seems happier,' she agreed. 'We're going out for a walk as far as Button Street later. We can go to the newsagents and the flower shop and there's a shop selling men's things he wanted to look in.'

'It is good he is taking an interest again,' Beattie said. 'I'll keep the door shut until you or Ted arrive and then let you in.'

'Yes, and don't forget to lock it after us!' Rose said and shook her head. 'Oh dear, why did that horrible man have to come back?'

Jim watched the house. He'd seen that Sister Rose come out, walking beside a man in a wheelchair. They'd gone off down the street and they hadn't seen him standing in a doorway halfway down the lane opposite.

He wondered who the man in the chair was and decided it must be one of Beattie Robinson's paying guests. She must be coining it in, he thought enviously. The council would be paying her to have Danny and she'd be earning big money from her lodgers, which she probably kept in cash in the house. Jim could do with a bit of that; he'd got through the money he'd stolen from the old lady in two days. Now he needed more for his whisky.

He'd come with the intention of nabbing Danny and taking him with him, back to the empty shed he'd used before. It was still empty, still as dirty and it stank just as bad, but it was dry and no one had bothered him there. Now, he thought, he might as well see what he could get from the house while he was about it – and if she had money stashed away, he'd take that as well as the boy.

He was hungry standing about in the shadows, and he craved alcohol so badly that it gnawed at his guts. He was about to go and try his luck at getting in Beattie's back door when he saw a builder's truck draw up outside and a man and two boys got out. They were all smiling and laughing and Jim's blood boiled as he saw who it was – bloody Doris's brother and he'd got Danny and another kid with him, the interfering bugger. He'd punched Ted a few times when he'd argued over the way he'd treated Doris and the boy and he'd soon give him what for if he tried to stop him taking what was his now, but he'd give it a while, see if they came out and he could grab Danny. He could always return for the woman's money another day.

'I think you should come home with me,' Ted told Beattie as she made tea and pushed the plates of cakes in front of him and the boys. 'Why don't you move in, love – just until they catch him. The police are looking for him so it can't be long.'

'Rose said she would talk to Dr Clark about it and I said I'd talk to you. I just don't like to leave her alone with Peter. I mean, if she was attacked, he couldn't help her, could he?'

'No,' Ted agreed. 'But Peter can afford to get paid help and I don't like you being here unprotected, Beattie. Bryant doesn't know where I live so we'll be safe. Even if he's watching the house now we'll be going off in the truck and he can't follow that on foot.'

'Yes, I know,' Beattie sighed. 'I know it's the sensible thing to do, so if Rose agrees and can get help, I'll come next weekend.'

'All right.' Ted smiled at her. 'I knew you wouldn't leave just like that – but I think it's time we got married, don't you?'

Beattie looked at him and then went to kiss him. 'Yes, I do – this has just made things clearer. Of course Rose can get the help she needs. Dr Clark doesn't need much and I can't stay here forever. In fact, he told me the other day that if I wanted to sell this house, he would buy it. And I wouldn't mind doing that, Ted. I could put the money by for us all if I was living with you, couldn't I?'

'Of course, you could, love. It's your money to do as you like with and if you want to keep some of it for Danny's future, that's fine with me.'

'That's what I'll do then. I know what it is worth. I'll tell Dr Clark – I just can't get used to calling him Peter – I'll sell it to him for them because I know Rose would marry him if he asked her.'

'Yes, of course she would – and that's more likely to happen if we marry first,' Ted said. 'Get him thinking straight.'

Beattie smiled happily and looked at the clock. 'They should be back soon. We'll tell them then.'

'Yes, we will.' Ted smiled at the boys. 'Right, the washing-up, you two – start as you mean to go on because Beattie is coming to live with us soon.'

'Great!' Ron said and started to clear the table.

'I'm glad, Mum,' Danny said. 'It's really good coming to see you but it will be better having you all the time.'

Ron looked out of the kitchen window. 'They're coming.'

'Oh good,' Beattie said. She went out into the garden and saw that Dr Clark had just turned into the back garden in his chair with Rose just behind him, carrying several parcels. Beattie went forward to help her with them, stepping onto the lawn to allow Dr Clark an easy access to the back door, and then she tutted and bent to pull out a weed. When she straightened up, she saw that Rose had stopped to speak to her and then she saw a dark shape launch itself at Rose and try to snatch her bag.

Rose dropped her parcels and turned to wrestle with the dirty creature who was attacking her.

'Rose!' Beattie cried. 'Stop it, you! Stop hurting her, you horrid man!'

She moved to go to Rose's assistance but something hurtled past her and straight into the man, whose back was now turned to the house as he and Rose struggled. Dr Clark's chair caught Rose's attacker in the back of his knees and sent him sprawling. His yells, together with Rose's screams and the man's curses, had brought Ted and the boys from the kitchen, and as the man got himself up and launched himself at the chair and started to wrestle with Peter Clark, swearing and cursing in a way Beattie had never heard, Ted ran towards them.

'You rotten devil!' Ted yelled as he hit Jim Bryant full in the face. 'That's about your mark – women and men in a wheelchair. I'll make you sorry you were ever born!'

'So, *you've* got the little bastard!' Bryant muttered furiously as he launched himself at Ted. Something glittered in his hand – the silver of a small penknife and Beattie screamed as he stabbed at Ted's chest.

'He has a knife . . .'

The words had hardly left her lips when, with a superhuman effort, Dr Peter pushed himself upright with his arms and launched himself at Bryant's back, his strong arms going around his face and his fingers digging right into his eyes. Bryant gave a scream of pain and thrust him off, then, deciding the odds were too great, took to his heels and ran.

Beattie, terrified, saw blood seeping through Ted's jacket and ran to him, sobbing. 'You're hurt!'

'It's just a scratch,' Ted said. 'I hadn't seen the knife but the doc saved me.'

Peter was lying on the garden path where he'd fallen after the effort that had taken all his strength. Rose knelt down by his side and touched his face.

'Peter, are you all right?' She felt all over him for a wound. 'Talk to me!'

Peter grinned at her, reached out and pulled her down to kiss her. 'I'm fine,' he said. 'Did you see what I did, Rose? I stood up before I launched at him – I actually stood upright for a moment!'

'Yes, my darling, I did,' she said and the tears ran down her cheeks. 'You saved me and you saved Ted – I'm so proud of you, so very, very proud.'

'But now I can't get up without help,' he said ruefully and laughed. 'I'm not miraculously cured, Rose, but I moved when I had to, so there's hope for us.'

'Yes,' she said softly. 'Yes, there is my darling.'

'He's gone,' Danny said, coming back from the garden gate where he'd gone to watch his father run off. 'He ran off down the streets as if the Devil was after him!'

'He knew he was outnumbered,' Ted said. 'Thanks for that, doc – I should've watched for the knife.'

'Get Rose to patch that up,' Peter advised, looking at the blood seeping from Ted's wound. He was back in his chair with a little help from Beattie and Rose. 'It is only a scratch but she'll give you something to stop infection.'

'Yes, thanks.' Ted frowned and looked at Beattie. 'You can't stop here – or we can't visit. You need to make up your mind.'

'Come inside everyone,' Rose said taking charge. 'I'll clean that wound, Ted, Beattie will make tea – and then we'll talk. I agree, Beattie can't stay here and perhaps we should go away for a while too . . .'

Peter looked at Rose after all the others had gone. He smiled and held out his hand to her. 'I'm glad that's all settled, Rose. Beattie didn't want to leave you but she isn't safe here.'

'I'm not sure you are either,' Rose replied. 'If he comes back for revenge . . .'

'Next time I'll have my pistol,' Peter said. 'It was in the things you got for me from my hotel. I think like all bullies he is a coward and if I point it at him, he'll run, as he did today.'

'Perhaps, but we could go away for a while, just to be safe.'

'On one condition,' Peter said. 'Marry me, Rose – and make it our honeymoon . . .'

372

She smiled and went to kiss him, all the love she felt inside in her eyes. 'I would have married you when you first came home, but you weren't ready.'

'I am now,' he said and kissed her back. 'Most of me is working again, Rose – I might not be Rudolph Valentino, but, as you saw earlier, I've got some movement in my legs back. I think I need to see a specialist I know whose advice will be honest and good, and see what happens.'

'Whatever you want, Peter,' Rose said and smiled tenderly. 'Are you really going to buy Beattie's house for us?'

'Yes. We both love it and I can have a few improvements done while we're staying elsewhere. Once Bryant is in custody again, Beattie will be near enough to visit often.'

'Yes, it sounds lovely, if that's what you want.' Rose knelt down by his side, looking into his face. 'I couldn't believe what you did, Peter – it was so brave.'

'He was hurting you,' Peter said. 'I just did what came into my head – and the same with Ted. I saw the knife flash and I couldn't let Beattie lose everything again, so I made myself do it.'

'And that shows your spine is healing,' Rose said. 'We always knew it could but until we get another X-ray we shan't know for certain.'

'The sooner the better,' Peter replied. 'I want to marry you and be with you, Rose. If today proves anything it's that life is too short and can end too suddenly to waste any time . . .'

CHAPTER 44

Steve saw Bryant across the street as he passed the Rosie Infirmary. He nudged his companion, making him aware that their quarry was in sight.

'I was told he might be somewhere here,' he said to Constable Smith. 'Let's get him before he does any more harm.'

'He's a real danger to the public,' Constable Smith agreed. 'He had a knife when he attacked Mr Phillips, so watch out for yourself.'

'You too,' Steve said and grasped his truncheon. He was grimly pleased that he was the one who had found Bryant. Most officers were out looking for him after the last incident at Beattie Robinson's house and Steve wanted the man behind bars as soon as possible, where he hoped he would stay for a long time.

Bryant had a bottle of whisky to his mouth, gulping it down as if it were water so he must have got money from somewhere – he'd almost certainly stolen it. His list of crimes was mounting by the day. As Steve and Constable Smith started to cross the road, Bryant saw them and dashed the empty whisky bottle to the ground, taking off up the road towards Shilling Street. Steve blew his whistle. There were other officers in the vicinity and they would answer his call: Bryant wasn't going to disappear into some back alley again if Steve could help it. He and Constable Smith gave chase, yelling at Bryant to stop, but he kept on running – and then it happened. A lorry came hurtling around the corner and Bryant ran straight into its path. It was going far too fast to stop immediately and caught him full on, throwing him high into the air, sending his body several feet to land with a thud at Steve's feet.

Steve bent over him. Bryant's eyes were closed and blood was running from the corner of his mouth. Constable Smith had caught up and stood at Steve's side, looking down at the villain. The lorry driver got out of his vehicle's cab and came towards them, white in the face.

'He came right at me – I never saw him!'

Steve gave him a hard look but didn't comment on his speed. He felt for a pulse. 'He's alive, just. I'll call for an ambulance – you give your details to my colleague. I can't say what the judge will decide, but this man is a criminal trying to escape justice.'

'What does that mean?' the driver asked Constable Smith. 'Am I in trouble – you saw what happened.'

'Yes, I did. He wasn't looking where he was going and you came around the corner and couldn't see him in time,' the young officer said. 'As far as I'm concerned this so-and-so deserves all he gets – he killed an old lady for the sake of two pounds and five shillings.'

'Bloody hell!' the driver said. 'I did yer a favour then.'

'I'd give you a medal,' Constable Smith said. 'I couldn't swear to your speed – and neither could me mate. You'll get off, don't worry.'

'Thank goodness for that,' the driver said. 'I don't know what to say . . .'

'Just keep your mouth shut and say as little as possible.'

'So, Danny's father is in hospital then?' Sarah said when Steve told her the story that evening. 'Would it be awful of me to say I'm glad?'

'There are quite a few would agree with you,' Steve said. 'He's a killer now, Sarah, and if he survives, he'll stand trial for murder, so it may be best if he dies.'

Sarah nodded. 'It must have been a horrid thing to see, Steve. I can see it's upset you.'

'Well, I was chasing him.' Steve frowned. 'My colleagues think it was a good thing that driver did and though I believe he was actually going too fast around a corner, Smith reckons he wasn't and I certainly don't feel like pressing charges. It's one of those situations that no one wins.'

'Do Rose and Beattie know?' Sarah asked.

'Yes. I went over to Rose's house and told her. She seemed relieved – but not triumphant. She's a nurse and her duty is always to save life. Her first thought was for Danny. After all, Bryant *is* his father.'

'Yes, I know and it's sad that his only memories of him will be of violence and brutality.'

'Yes, poor little lad, but he has his uncle and Beattie now. They're getting married in three weeks at the register office and she's asked us to go over to her old house for a bit of a reception. I said we would.'

'Yes, I should like that,' Sarah said and hugged him. 'Don't be sad and don't feel guilty even if Jim Bryant dies, Steve. That man was bad. There's no other word for him, no excuse for his behaviour whatever he himself believed.'

'I agree with you,' Steve said, then smiled. 'I think Rose and Dr Clark are going to marry too, but they didn't say when.'

'Oh, that would be lovely!' Sarah said and then turned as she heard baby Will cry. 'Oh, Mum wants us to go for dinner on Saturday night – I think she might have some news for us too.'

'We wanted you both together before we said anything,' Gwen announced and then looked at Theo. 'Shall you tell them – or should I?'

'Your mum has agreed to marry me,' Theo said looking like a dog with two tails. 'I'm going to move in here and sell my own home and we'll buy a caravan at the sea somewhere. It will be a holiday home for you, the boys and us – and you can all use it whenever you like at no cost. I'll rent it out when family don't want it and put the money aside for your little one, Sarah.'

'That is very generous of you, Theo,' Sarah said and kissed her mother. 'I know you'll make Mum happy, because you already have, and I'm glad you'll live here; the caravan is a bonus for everyone.'

'Thank you, Sarah. Gwen was a little nervous that you might not be able to accept me.'

'Of course I accept you,' Sarah said and gave him a

378

hug. 'If you ever hurt her, I'll have your guts for garters, but make her happy and I'll love you.'

'I can live with that,' Theo said and grinned as Steve shook hands with him and kissed Gwen.

'What do the boys think?' Steve asked.

'They like him,' Gwen said. 'Theo gave them the money to see a cowboy film and they've gone this evening together – Charlie looks after Ned for me and makes sure he doesn't eat anything he shouldn't.'

'So, when is the big day?'

'We thought as soon as possible,' Sarah's mother replied. 'Perhaps early next month.'

'It's all weddings,' Sarah said and smiled. 'Sister Rose is getting married too *and* her friend Beattie.'

'Must be something in the air,' Gwen said and laughed. 'I never thought it would happen to me again but it has and I'm delighted.'

'I'll drink to that,' Steve said and lifted his glass of shandy. 'To you and Theo, Gwen – and to everyone else who has found their happiness!'

Sarah saluted her mother with her glass of orange juice and then, just as she was about to say something, a cry came from the cot upstairs.

'I'd better go to him.' Sarah got up to attend to her baby.

'I'll come,' her mother said and they left the room together.

Upstairs in her mother's bedroom, Sarah changed her baby and put him back in his cot. She looked at her mother. 'You *are* certain and you *are* happy?'

'Yes, and yes,' Gwen replied smiling broadly. 'I really am, Sarah. When Theo first asked me, I had to ask for time, but now I know that it really is what I want – and he says if I want to foster more children that's all right with him.'

'You already have two,' Sarah objected with a smile.

'Yes, I do, but if another one or two need a home I'll be happy to offer it,' Gwen said. 'I've got so much, Sarah, and some of those kids have so very little.'

Sarah placed her baby back in his cot and moved to embrace her mother. 'No wonder Theo loves you – you're wonderful, Mum!'

CHAPTER 45

Lady Rosalie looked at the matron of the Rosie and smiled. 'I so enjoyed having you to stay with us at the cottage in the school holidays, Mary, and so I was wondering if you would like to come to us for Christmas? I shall have my son home and if you came on Christmas Eve and stayed for a couple of days, I would be delighted.'

'I should like that very much,' Matron said and smiled. 'I'll be near enough to return to the Rosie should a crisis occur, which is unlikely given that I have very good staff, and though Sister Rose is cutting down her hours now that she is to be married and I do regret that, Sister Matthews is very capable and I have a new nursing sister starting next month – a Helena Carew.'

Lady Rosalie nodded and looked pleased. 'Staff are bound to come and go, Mary. We must just find new people to take their place. Have you found someone to work in the kitchens instead of Kathy?'

'I have a new girl called Susie starting next week,' Mary said and sighed. 'The last one didn't suit us and I've taken my time finding her replacement. I'm not one for all these changes, but I suppose life moves on.'

'Yes, indeed it does and we must be grateful,' Lady Rosalie replied. 'I wanted to tell you that I have just added six new prospective sets of foster parents to my list, which is marvellous, because I am able to settle some of my long-term cases at last.'

'I did tell you that Gwen Cartwright is able to take on more children now that she is also getting married, didn't I? Her husband is comfortably off, which means they can afford to.'

'Yes, and she is adopting Ned. Her papers are in my bag and I'm going to deliver them myself when she returns from her honeymoon.'

'What a wonderful surprise for her,' Mary said. 'I suppose the boys are staying with Sarah while she is away?'

'Yes, they all get on so well, which is lovely.' Lady Rosalie smiled. 'Well, I have another meeting so I must go – but book a little time out to be with us at Christmas, Mary. I shall look forward to it.'

'Yes, so shall I,' Mary replied and felt pleased as her visitor left. She was always pleased to see Rosalie and had so enjoyed her seaside holiday. It would be lovely to spend part of Christmas with her friend and she could certainly arrange to have a couple of days – after all, she had worked throughout Christmas for the past fifteen years.

She thought about the letter she'd found on her desk that morning. Ruby Harding had written to tell her they were considering returning to London and asked if she would have a chance of her old job back? Apparently, the old lady she and her husband had been caring for had died and her nephew was going to sell the place where they'd lived since leaving London. They had two months to pack up and leave and, all in all, Mary thought she would rather like to have Ruby back at the infirmary – and if her husband needed a job there were always small tasks that needed doing here.

Smiling, she picked up her notepad and prepared to make her rounds of the hospital. It was time for her to make sure everything was running as it ought. She wondered how Sister Rose and Dr Clark were getting on with that specialist they'd gone to see and hoped that his recovery would be total.

'What's the verdict then, Simon?' Peter looked at the man he'd known since his medical student days. 'Am I going to be stuck in this damned chair for the rest of my life or not?'

'Only if you like it there, old chap,' his friend replied. 'Why didn't you come to me as soon as you were able to leave the London Hospital? I'm not blowing my own trumpet, but you might have known I could help if anyone could.'

'I had my reasons,' Peter said. 'Besides, I was told rest would do more good than treatment at first.'

'That is certainly true,' his friend agreed. 'But rest and time have played their part and now we have to work to get you on your feet again.'

'Will I be able to walk down the aisle with my bride?' Peter asked, trying not to sound anxious and not succeeding.

'In time yes,' Simon replied. 'Perhaps with crutches at first and there will be pain, but I can help with exercises and massage that should ease it – if you're prepared to work at it?'

'You don't need to ask!' Peter grinned at him. 'Just as long as I can be a man when I marry her, Simon.'

'I doubt if your wedding tackle was damaged,' his friend replied. 'And you'll manage to make her happy once I have you walking again, I don't doubt.' He smiled wickedly. 'Now, when do I get to meet the woman who made you want to put a ring on her finger? And what is she like?

'She's beautiful,' Peter said. 'And she's a nurse – and the reason I didn't come to you immediately. I wanted to get to know her better and I've been living in her home.'

'Crafty devil!' his friend accused, eyes sparkling. 'Well, I shall look forward to standing up with you, Peter – that is my right as your oldest friend.'

'Yes, and I wouldn't want anyone else,' Peter said. 'Thanks, Simon. I've been getting some feeling back in my legs and toes but I dared not hope until I spoke to you, the country's leading expert when it comes to dealing with spinal injuries.'

'Thank goodness I can give you good news,' his friend said. 'Well, I shall expect dinner at a very expensive restaurant so that I can meet your fiancée.'

'Of course, and Rose will look forward to it – but you can meet her now. She is in your waiting room.'

'Then what are we waiting for?'

CHAPTER 46

Beattie looked around the kitchen that Peter had asked Ted to do up for Rose while they were away. It looked sparkling new and yet fitted beautifully with the house, with the lovely oak dressers and the long table and matching chairs. The sink was a deep one and made of porcelain; Ted called it a butler's sink and Beattie thought it would be very useful.

'Everything looks wonderful,' she said to him as she finished tidying up in preparation for Rose and Peter's return from the country. 'I'm sure Rose will love it.'

'You're not regretting letting him buy it, are you?' Ted asked and she shook her head.

'No, our house is just right for us and the boys,' she said. 'This would be too big – and I could never have afforded to do all the things Peter has done for Rose. All the windows have been renewed and the bathroom is lovely and modern, just like ours now.'

'What time do you expect them to get home?' Ted asked.

'Rose thought about three this afternoon. Why do you ask?'

'That old lady he saved has been pestering the life out of me on the docks,' Ted said and laughed. 'She wants to see him and I have to give her a couple of bob for a cup of tea to get rid of her every time she comes and asks.'

'I suppose he has been very much missed at the free clinic.'

'Jessie says no one else looks after her the same.' Ted shook his head. 'I'm not sure if he will want to go back, though. After all, he has enough to do learning to walk again.'

'Well, I doubt he is the sort to sit about and do nothing,' Beattie replied with a smile. 'He can prescribe medicine sitting in a chair, can't he?'

'He could – but it wouldn't be easy to examine a patient.'

'Well, he'd need a nurse for that,' Beattie said and smiled. 'And that's easy enough – Rose is going in part-time to the infirmary now so she could help him.'

'Perhaps . . .' Ted put an arm about his wife as she locked the back door of her old home after them. 'We'd best get back and see what the boys have been up to, love. I know they're old enough to look after themselves for an hour or two but I still worry.'

'They'll be fine – and Danny is busy making cakes for when Marjorie comes to tea.'

Ted had been to see Marjorie's parents after they were married and explained that he and Beattie had adopted Danny. Combined with her grandmother Ethel's pleas for her daughter to let Marjorie visit her friend, they had at last given in and Mrs Lacey was bringing her daughter to tea that afternoon.

'Yes, no doubt he'll be busy, and Ron is making something he won't show me.' Ted frowned. 'I can't imagine why.'

'Because it's a special present for your Christmas gift,' Beattie said. 'Don't tell him I told you – but it's something you could do with.'

Ted frowned and then laughed. 'Not a tool box? Now I really do need a good strong tool box!'

'That would be telling,' Beattie said. 'Come on, Ted, let's get home and make a nice cup of tea.'

Rose opened the door and saw the vase of fresh flowers on the kitchen table and smiled. She knew exactly who they were from, because she knew that Beattie had intended going in to tidy up after the builders and Ted had finished the renovations.

'Oh, look at those,' she said. 'Aren't they lovely, Peter?' She looked about her and laughed with delight. 'This is just as I would have wanted it!'

'I thought you would like it,' he said and kissed her as she bent down to him. Progress was still slow but he'd made big strides at the clinic under the guidance of his friend Simon and could now stand for a few minutes unaided. To walk a couple of steps at a time, however, he needed help from Rose and a stout stick. He was practising with crutches and hoped to have mastered them in a couple of months. He glanced around the room, frowning. 'Will it do, Rose – will you live here with me as my wife and share my life?'

'You know I will, my darling,' she said and smiled at him lovingly. 'When do you want to be married?'

'I thought just before Christmas – just a small reception

with a few friends. Simon will come up and we'll ask Ted, Beattie and the boys – and anyone else you'd like from the Rosie – and of course your brother John and his family. We'll ask my grandmother, too, but I doubt she'll feel up to it; she's a little frail.'

'We'll keep it small,' Rose said, 'but I do want Sarah and Steve, her mum and Theo, Lily and Jenny – and I might ask Matron, too.'

Peter nodded his approval. 'I'll save a piece of cake for next time I see Jessie at the clinic – but I shan't ask her to the wedding!'

'Are you certain you're ready to return to the clinic?'

'Yes. I'll have to stick to the chair for now, but I'd like to be working again and with your help I can . . . and I'll be able to stand long enough to put the ring on your finger!' He looked at her triumphantly.

'I'm looking forward to it,' Rose said and smiled. She bent and kissed him. 'And now I think we could both do with a nice hot cup of tea and a slice of the cake I can see that Beattie has left for us.'

Lily was just making herself a cup of tea when the doorbell rang. She went to answer it, the teapot still in her hand – and it dropped to the floor with a resounding crash when she saw who was standing there. She stood perfectly still for a second and then she flung her arms around him.

'Chris – oh, Chris!' she cried, tears in her eyes. 'My darling, you're home at last! But for how long?'

'I'm home for good – or at least until they find me another job,' Chris told her with a smile of pleasure as he picked her off the floor in a bear hug and swung her round. 'My cover was finally blown and I had to get out fast – so here I am, back with my darling wife, and ready to tell the world our secret.'

'Oh Chris, Chris – I do love you so much!' Lily said, taking his hand and ignoring the shattered brown teapot as she led the way inside. 'We can tell Jenny at last and have a little party for our friends.'

'Yes,' he said and looked into her eyes, his hands on either side of her face, drinking her in like a drowning man might drink lifesaving water. 'Have I told you how much I love you, Lily? My darling, my wife . . .'

'Yes, just once, or twice,' she whispered and went happily into his arms. 'Do you want a cup of tea – if I can find the spare pot?'

'Later,' he said huskily. 'What I want right now, my darling Lily, is you!'

Laughing, Lily looked up at her husband, love and happiness filling her eyes as she led him upstairs to her bedroom. For Lily, the world had suddenly come right and she didn't want to think of anything else but a future with the man she loved. The Government might have passed a bill to build new air raid shelters in case of the war that seemed to loom ever closer and in Germany the violence and restrictions against Jewish people went on, but for Lily, at that moment, nothing mattered. Her sister, work, the rest of the world – well, they could wait!

Read more about Cathy Sharp's orphans whose compelling stories will tug at your heartstrings.

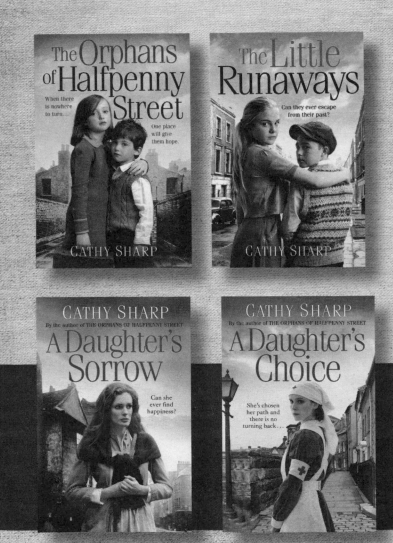